Dancing in the Moonlight

Rita Bradshaw was born in Northamptonshire, where she still lives today. At the age of sixteen she met her husband – whom she considers her soulmate – and they have two daughters and a son, and several grandchildren. Much to her delight, Rita's first novel was accepted for publication and she went on to write many more successful novels under a pseudonym before writing using her own name.

In any spare moments she loves walking her dogs, reading, eating-out and visiting the cinema and theatre, as well as being involved in her local church and animal welfare.

BY RITA BRADSHAW

RITA BRADSHAW

Dancing in the Moonlight

PAN BOOKS

First published 2013 by Macmillan

This edition published 2013 by Pan Books
an imprint of Pan Macmillan, a division of Macmillan Publishers Limited
Pan Macmillan, 20 New Wharf Road, London N1 9RR
Basingstoke and Oxford
Associated companies throughout the world
www.panmacmillan.com

ISBN 978-1-5098-1410-7

1 3 5 7 9 8 6 4 2

A CIP catalogue record for this book is available from the British Library.

Typeset by Ellipsis Digital Limited, Glasgow
Printed and bound by CPI Group (UK) Ltd, Croydon, CR0 4YY

Visit **www.panmacmillan.com** to read more about all our books
and to buy them. You will also find features, author interviews and
news of any author events, and you can sign up for e-newsletters
so that you're always first to hear about our new releases.

For my family.
Infinitely precious . . .

Contents

PART ONE

Two Families

1925

Chapter One

She wasn't ready to die. It was too soon. Death should come when you were resigned to it, when the pull of earthly ties had loosened their hold on the heart. That was the right order of things, the natural progression, but she grew weaker every day. Sometimes she'd swear the Grim Reaper himself was at her elbow.

Raising herself a little in the narrow iron bed in which she was lying, Agnes Fallow waited a moment for the dizziness in her head that the movement had caused to subside before she said, 'Put the kettle on, lass, and we'll have a cup of tea before they're back from school, shall we?'

Her daughter, who had just finished skimming the layer of froth from a scrag of mutton before adding the rice and mixed vegetables and putting the pan on the hob again, turned and smiled at her. 'All right, Mam.'

It was a beautiful smile. *Lucy* was beautiful. Agnes sank back against the lumpy flock-filled pillows, closing her tired eyes. Every day she thanked God for her Lucy.

It wasn't just that her oldest daughter was the only one of her brood to take after her, with her mass of golden-brown curls and deep-blue eyes, but Lucy was as kind as she was bonny. Look how the bairn had taken herself off across the bridge into Bishopwearmouth and bought that roll of material from the Old Market a couple of months ago. She'd got the lads to fix it up as a curtain, which could be pulled across the corner of the kitchen to hide her bed when she needed to use the chamber pot. None of the others had thought of that when she'd finally been unable to get outside to the privy, only her Lucy.

Once the tea was mashed Lucy brought a cup to her mother, but seeing that she appeared to have fallen asleep, she stood looking down at her.

Her mam was thinner; her body barely made a mound under the blankets. As always when the fear came, Lucy told herself her mother would turn the corner soon. That's what Dr Pearson had said the last time he'd called, and he should know. Rousing herself, she bent and gently touched her mother's shoulder, saying softly, 'Have a sup tea, Mam. It'll do you good.'

'What?' Agnes's eyes opened and stared for a moment before she blinked. 'Oh aye. I must have dozed off for a minute.'

Without being asked, Lucy helped her mother sit up and positioned the pillow behind her. The worn winceyette nightdress did little to conceal the way Agnes's bones protruded against the skin covering them, the emaciated

4

frame so frail that sick dread rose again. 'Can you eat something, Mam? A biscuit to dip in your tea?'

Agnes shook her head, the hair that had once been as rich and shiny as Lucy's now wispy and brittle. Pulling tighter the shawl Lucy had placed round her shoulders, she took the cup her daughter was proffering and shakily raised it to her blue-tinged lips. It felt too heavy to hold.

'I've put a spoonful of sugar in it. Sugar's good for you.' Lucy sat down on the edge of the bed with her own tea. Moments like this with her mam were rare and to be treasured. From six o'clock in the morning, when she dragged herself out of the bed she shared with her sisters – eight-year-old Ruby and the twins, Flora and Bess, who'd just turned two – she toiled without ceasing. After feeling her way downstairs in the dark she would light the oil lamp on the kitchen table and then persuade the fire in the range into a blaze, before setting the big pan of porridge, which she had left soaking overnight ready for breakfast, on the hob. It was always nice and warm in the kitchen, unlike the bedrooms, which were icy. After boiling the water in the heavy black kettle, she helped her mother wash her face and hands and tidy her hair. Then she made the first pot of tea of the day. Once it was mashed, she gave her mother a cup and took one through to her father, who slept in the big brass bed in the front room, which he'd shared with her mother until she had been taken sick eighteen months ago. Something to do with her heart, the doctor said. It had been then that they'd bought the narrow iron bed for the kitchen, where – in her mam's own words – her mother could keep an eye on things till she felt better. But she never had felt better.

By the time her two older brothers, Ernie, who was eighteen, and Donald, two years younger, came downstairs and joined their father at the kitchen table, their breakfast was ready and their bait tins full. The menfolk left for Thompson's shipyard at the end of the street as the buzzer started blowing at seven-thirty and were always through the gates before it stopped. It was something her father and the lads prided themselves on.

Then she would rouse five-year-old John from the bed he shared with his brothers and chivvy Ruby into helping her dress the twins. They wriggled like eels and more often than not earned themselves a slap or two from the impatient Ruby. Another round of breakfasts, followed by John and Ruby being packed off to school, and the day proper began; days of washing, ironing, cooking and cleaning like the ones before them, winter and summer the same.

And she didn't mind that, or the fact she often fell into bed too tired to undress, and had virtually had no schooling since her mam was took bad – she didn't mind any of it as long as her mam got well. On impulse, Lucy reached out her hand and touched her mother's, an unusual show of affection in a family that was not demonstrative.

Agnes smiled. For a moment the warmth in Lucy's deep-blue eyes banished the gnawing anxiety about how her family would cope once she was gone. If only there'd been grandparents or an aunt or uncle to lend a hand, but she and Walter had both been orphaned as babies. He'd been brought up in a workhouse Gateshead way, and she in the one near Bishopwearmouth Cemetery. It had been one of the things that had drawn them together when they'd met twenty-odd years ago one hot Sunday afternoon whilst taking a stroll in Mowbray Park, she with a girl friend and Walter with a group of lads he worked with. Sweet sixteen, she'd been.

Agnes turned her head and looked to the window as the bitter northeast wind drove icy chips of sleet rattling against the glass. It seemed so long ago now, another lifetime, but she had been bonny then and Walter had loved her. He still did love her, but a baby every year, only seven of whom had survived past their first birthday, had taken her looks and her health. She'd be thirty-seven years old in a few weeks, but she knew she looked double that. And now here was her beautiful Lucy already doing the work of a lass twice her age. She hadn't wanted that for her bairn, to bear the responsibility of caring for the family when she was nowt but a child herself. And Ruby was no help. Little madam half the time, Ruby was.

Agnes sighed, her eyes closing. The familiar lethargy was taking over. Even the effort of drinking the tea was too much for her worn-out body.

Thank the good Lord they had neighbours like the Crawfords, she thought drowsily. Aaron and Enid Crawford had moved next door into one of the two-up, two-down houses in Zetland Street a week after she and Walter had tied the knot. She and Enid had hit it off right away, and when Enid's Tom had been born seven months later, she'd stood by Enid and told any nosy parkers the baby had come early, although she'd known the truth. But it was funny, and whether it was the sins of the parents coming out in the children she didn't know, but she'd never been able to take to Tom Crawford. Enid's three other lads were nice enough, but her eldest had been different from the day he was born. Even as a little lad he'd had something about him which had made her flesh creep. She'd tried to discuss it once with Walter, but he'd looked at her as though she was barmy and she'd never mentioned it again. But she'd thought all the more. And now Tom was a man, a big, good-looking man, and he liked her Lucy. There'd been a day in the summer when the lass had been sitting on the back doorstep in the sun shelling peas, and Tom had stopped and talked to her over the wall. She had seen the look on his face, and her just a little bairn. But Lucy was growing up fast. Any day now she could start her monthlies.

A sense of urgency piercing the blanketing tiredness, Agnes sat up straighter. It was time to have the little chat she'd been putting off. She would have liked to have done it more gradually, a word here and there as the lass grew older, and then when Lucy got a steady lad she'd have given her an idea of what to expect on her wedding night, but she didn't have the luxury of time. She cleared her throat. 'Lucy, lass, I need to talk to you about – about the birds and the bees. You're a big girl now and – and soon things will change. Do you understand what I'm saying, hinny?'

Her daughter's blank stare was her answer.

There followed an exchange which was uncomfortable for both, but by the time the twins came hotching down the stairs on their bottoms, having woken from their afternoon nap, Lucy was better informed. And more than a little horrified at what went on after marriage. She'd known men and women were built differently of course, and she had changed John's nappy often enough before he went into short pants to have become acquainted with male genitalia, but on the occasions when her da and the lads had their weekly bath in front of the range after bringing the old tin bath in from the scullery, she and her sisters were not allowed in the kitchen. She still didn't quite understand how a lad's willy went into a lass – her mam had said that happened naturally after marriage when a lass's body became ready for it – but as it was the means of producing bairns, that must mean everyone did it. Even her own mam and da. And this monthly thing that was going to happen to her body, when she couldn't bathe or wash her hair in case she got a chill, sounded horrible. Following her mother's instructions she'd gone into the front room and delved into the trunk at the foot of the bed and found the wads of material that she had to pin into her drawers and wash through each day, but she'd felt like crying when she'd looked at them. Once it began, it would go on and on until she was old . . .

After changing the twins' damp nappies and settling the little girls on the clippy mat in front of the range with their pap bottles and a couple of the oatmeal biscuits she'd made that morning, she started on the stack of ironing. Her mother was sleeping again, but this wasn't out of the ordinary; she slept most of the time, and Dr Pearson said sleep was the best medicine. And gradually the everyday routine settled Lucy's agitation. The kitchen was cosy and warm and outside the sleet had turned to snow, a deep November twilight enhancing the glow from the range and bringing a charm to the battered kitchen table and chairs and her father's torn old leather armchair that they could never aspire to in the harsh light of day.

She had finished the ironing and was just adding dumplings to the mutton broth which had been slowly simmering on the hob when Ruby and John came bursting in, their cheeks and noses red. They were arguing, and as usual Ruby got in first with her side of things.

'Tell him, our Lucy.' Ruby stood, all melting snow and indignation, with her mittened hands on small, stocky hips. 'He swore in front of Mrs Travis up the street, he did.'

'Did not.' John stuck his tongue out at his sister for good measure.

'Ooh, you liar. Liar, liar, pants on fire.'

'Enough!' Lucy glanced over at the bed before drawing both children to her and sitting down on one of the kitchen chairs. 'What did you say to Mrs Travis, John?'

Her brother, a true Fallow male with his dark straight

hair and brown eyes, stared at her innocently. 'I asked her if her cat was better. It had half its ear bitten off last week.'

'You *said*' – Ruby was incensed – 'how was her *damn* cat.'

John's gaze moved to the sister he considered the bane of his life. 'Well, that's what Mrs Travis calls him. That damn cat.'

Lucy tried not to smile. John was right. She had never heard their elderly neighbour of a few doors away refer to the cat which she loved to distraction, but which caused her constant and vocal grief, as anything else but 'that damn cat'. The feline in question fought with every other moggy it came across, constantly vomited up the contents of its stomach in the house and was forever bringing half-dead mice and birds into the old woman's bed.

Keeping her face straight with some effort, Lucy shook her head. 'Ruby's right. You mustn't say "damn", John.'

'Why not?' John stuck out his chin. 'Mrs Travis does.'

'Mrs Travis is a grown-up. It's up to her what she says, but Mam and Da wouldn't like you using that word.'

'But I can when I'm grown-up?'

'You'll have to decide for yourself then.'

John considered this. 'How old is grown-up?'

Lucy tweaked his snub nose. 'You've got years and years to go yet, so don't worry about it. Now the pair of you know you should leave your wet things in the scullery. Go and take off your hats and coats and leave your boots on the mat, and come and get warm in front of the fire. You can play with Flora and Bess while I get you a drink and a shive of bread and dripping, to tide you over till dinner time.'

'I want to tell Mam I got a star in my writing book today.' Ruby darted over to her mother's bed before Lucy could stop her, only to turn and say, 'Lucy? Mam's bad.'

Lucy was at her mother's side in a moment and she could see what had alarmed Ruby. Her mother's eyes were open, but they seemed to have sunk into the back of her head and the deep pallor of her skin was frightening. A kind of a gurgle emerged from her throat, but when Lucy took her mother's hand, the bony fingers held onto hers with surprising strength.

Without letting go of her mother's hand, Lucy pushed her sister. 'Go and get Mrs Crawford. Tell her Mam's been took bad.'

Ruby didn't need to be told twice.

Mrs Crawford must have been doing some baking because her hands were floury and she had her big pinny on when she hurried into the kitchen a minute or two later. Lucy had never been so glad to see someone in all her life. Standing by the bed, Enid Crawford said softly, 'Oh, Agnes, lass. Now lie quiet and we'll send for the quack. Don't you fret none.'

'Shall I go for Dr Pearson?' whispered Lucy.

'No, hinny, you stay with your mam. I'll send our Jacob,' Enid replied in like tone. A big hefty woman with a voice on her that could drop a bullock at ten paces when she was in a temper, her face was uncharacteristically tender as she stood staring down at her longtime friend. If she wasn't mistaken, this was it, and in truth who would wish for Agnes to go on suffering? But she would miss her, and so would the little lass kneeling by the bed. The full weight of the family was going to fall on Lucy's shoulders, and her only twelve, but then it had been that way for the past eighteen months or so.

Enid's gaze rested on Lucy, taking in the gleaming golden-brown hair, tendrils of which had escaped the child's single thick plait to curl round the small heart-shaped face.

Bonny as a summer's day, this bairn was, and as bright as a button to boot. Lucy had always been top of her class and one night before the twins were born and Agnes had been took bad, her friend had come round bursting with pride because Lucy's school report had said something about the child training to be a teacher when she was older. Of course that had been knocked on the head, not that it could have come to anything anyway. Whoever heard of a bairn from round these parts – especially a lass – training for something like that? Where did these teachers imagine the money was going to come from? It was all folk could do to keep body and soul together, and with the slump worsening, there were plenty who couldn't even do that. Most of the shipyards were on short time now, and Thompson's would be next. Everyone was just waiting for the axe to fall.

Gathering herself, Enid bent down to Agnes. 'I'll send our Jacob for the quack, lass, and your Lucy'll stay with you. All right, pet? An' I'll take the others back with me an' give 'em their tea.' It was a stroke, by the look of it, and it had taken her left side; the corner of Agnes's mouth was dragging and her left arm and hand lay still on top of the blankets.

Enid couldn't bear to look at her friend's agonized face another moment. Turning, she glanced to where Ruby and John, each with a twin in their small arms, were watching her, tears seeping from their eyes. 'None of that,' she said briskly, although for two pins she'd join them. 'That won't help no one. We're going to leave your mam to have a little sleep till the doctor comes and you can help me make a round of singin' hinnies, would you like that? An' I've got a fresh pat of butter to go with 'em.'

Ruby and John's countenances changed. If there was one thing they loved it was the little currant cakes that made a singing sound while cooking on the griddle and were delicious eaten hot, with butter on.

Agnes lay looking at Lucy in the stillness that followed, the only sound her daughter's broken voice as she murmured words of reassurance. She was dying, she knew that, but she hadn't expected it to be like this, the pain in her head threatening to suffocate her and her throat closed up so that she couldn't swallow. Her chest was aching with a fiery ache and each breath was a conscious effort, but strangely the fear was fading as the light dimmed. She could hear Lucy saying, 'I'll look after the bairns and the house and everything, I promise, Mam, you just rest now and don't worry', but she couldn't see her daughter any longer through the blackness which had descended as the pain in her head became unbearable.

But then the pain stopped. Suddenly and completely. And at the same time an airy lightness came upon her worn-out body, filling it with pulsating energy, so that she was aware of every muscle and sinew, filling her mind too, with an overwhelming desire to move forward.

Through the darkness she could see a pinprick of something shining brightly in the distance and it was to this that she was drawn. She walked slowly at first, unused to the feeling of freedom, and then, finding she was as light as a feather, she gathered speed, carried along on a wave of happiness which consumed her to the exclusion of everything else.

The pinprick grew into a brilliant radiance, and now she was running forward with the joyful abandon of a child and smiling with every pore of her body; she was going home . . .

Chapter Two

The day of the funeral was dark and overcast, but the severe snow storms which had swept the Northeast for a week had let up to just the odd light flurry now and again. An hour ago the undertakers had come for Agnes's body. This had been lying on a trestle table in the front room since Enid and another neighbour had laid her out, the brass bed having been turned on its side against the wall. Walter had been adamant about this mark of respect for his wife and had slept in the bed in the kitchen since her passing. It was this same way of thinking that had prevented Lucy from attending her mother's funeral; her father didn't hold with women and children being present, and nothing she had said had been able to change his mind.

She looked across the kitchen now to where Enid was busy cutting up a fruit cake. Enid had brought this and several other items, including a large ham-and-egg pie, as her own contribution towards the wake. Lucy was grateful, although she knew her father wouldn't have liked what he'd have seen as charity. But Mrs Crawford understood her da and had waited until the menfolk had left, walking behind the horse-drawn hearse, before she'd appeared with her offerings. Once the men were back from the cemetery all the neighbours would come in and, although the table was groaning with food, it wouldn't go far.

Lucy bit down on her lower lip as she glanced at the table. On the same day her mother had died the shipyard had put their employees on short time and already they were feeling the pinch as a family, yet her da had gone out and bought beer and whisky for today with the rent money. She had felt like crying when she'd found out what he'd done.

'It's a fine spread you've put on, lass.' Enid smiled at her. 'You've done your mam proud and no mistake.'

Lucy smiled back, but said nothing. She knew Mrs Crawford wouldn't understand if she said what she was thinking. None of the neighbours would. A family could be starving and they'd still beg, borrow or steal to give someone what they called 'a good send-off'. And no doubt the neighbours had got up a collection for flowers for her mam, which would be placed on the coffin with some ceremony at the church before being left at the side of the grave later. Not only would most of the folk who would have contributed have been glad of the money for their own family, but she could have used however much it was for food or the rent money. And she hated the way these offerings were done, with a written list so that everyone could read what everyone else had put in. It was a form of blackmail, to her mind, and when she'd said that once to her mam she'd got the impression her mam agreed with her.

'Now, lass, with the bairns out of the way, how about you and me put the front room to rights for your da?'

Mrs Crawford's voice was brisk and Lucy had learned enough about her mother's friend over the past days to know the no-nonsense tone was the way Mrs Crawford hid her feelings about her mother's passing. That, and lending a hand when she could, like this morning when she had suggested Ruby take John and the twins round to her house so they weren't underfoot while the food was prepared.

Quietly Lucy said, 'Thank you, Mrs Crawford. I don't know what I'd have done without you over the last week.'

'Go on with you, lass.' Enid sniffed loudly, hiding the emotion that had brought tears to her eyes by flapping her hand vigorously as she stomped out of the kitchen. 'I've done nowt but what your mam would have done for me in the same circumstances.'

Once in the dismal front room, they worked in semi-darkness, the curtains remaining firmly closed as a mark of respect for the deceased. The small fabric bags filled with dried lavender flowers, which the undertakers had supplied when her father had called to see them to discuss the funeral, couldn't disguise the stench of death that lingered in the air. Lucy had always liked the scent of the fragrant shrub, but over the last days she'd come to hate it. She longed to open the windows wide to let the icy-cold breath of winter in, but such a scandal would never be lived down.

The bed restored to its rightful position and made up, and the room tidied, they returned to the kitchen. Lucy's eyes were drawn to the spot where her mother's bed had resided for the last eighteen months or so. It had been carried upstairs by her father and Ernie this morning, Donald following behind with the mattress, and had been squeezed in at the foot of the lads' bed. It had been decided John would sleep in it, as it was a small narrow single and the double bed was more suited to Ernie and Donald, who were both long and lanky. On hearing that John was to have a bed all to himself, Ruby had gone into a massive sulk, but Lucy hadn't had time to cajole her sister round, with the hundred and one things she had to do that morning. Consequently Ruby had left for Mrs Crawford's with a face like thunder, and Lucy didn't doubt the poor twins would feel the back of her sister's hand more than once.

'There, there, hinny. You're doing fine.' Enid had noticed the direction of Lucy's gaze and her family would have been amazed at the tender note in her voice, accustomed as they were to her sharp tongue. 'Likely you'll feel better once today is over and things get back to normal. I always say you're in a kind of limbo till the funeral's done. Look, they'll be back soon and then it'll be bedlam. I'll make a pot of tea, shall I?'

Lucy nodded, struggling not to cry. She wanted her mam, how she wanted her mam. She felt very young and helpless and frightened. She'd promised her mother she would look after the bairns and see to the house and her da and the lads, and she'd meant it. But could she? She didn't know how she was going to feed the family over the next few days, let alone the next months, now the menfolk were on short time. John had holes in his boots, so his feet were wet through and blue with cold, and Ruby couldn't fasten the buttons of her winter coat, it had grown so small. Mrs Crawford had said she'd feel better once things got back to normal, but they were never going to be normal again. That was the truth of it. Her mam was gone and she would never see her again.

Her breath caught in her throat in a great sob and the tears spurted from her eyes, rolling down her cheeks in an unstoppable flood. She felt Mrs Crawford put an arm round her and turned into the comforting bulk in a paroxysm of weeping, as the grief she'd been holding in demanded release.

It was a minute or two before she drew away and rubbed at her wet face with her pinny. Her eyes focused on Enid's face, which was also wet, and she murmured, 'I'm sorry, Mrs Crawford.'

'Don't be silly, lass.' Enid fetched out a none-too-clean handkerchief and blew her nose loudly. 'I think we both needed that. Now I'm going to make some tea and we'll have a quiet minute before they arrive. An', lass' – she cradled Lucy's flushed cheeks in her big rough hands – 'I'm only next door any time you want me, all right? You know where to come, hinny.'

Lucy nodded, smiling shakily and, satisfied she had done what she could, Enid turned towards the range.

Lucy watched her mother's friend making the tea, her thoughts clearer than they had been in days. Mrs Crawford was kind and she was grateful, but she wouldn't be running to her every two minutes with this and that. She had to stand on her own two feet and do what she'd promised. It was up to her to keep the family together and she would do it, no matter what. Her mother had taught her how to make a penny stretch to two; well, now it would have to stretch to three or four, it was as simple as that. They had a roof over their heads and she would see to it that she put food on the table. They'd manage.

Her small chin lifted and her shoulders straightened, and then, for an infinitesimal second, she thought she heard her mother whisper, 'That's it, hinny. That's my lass.'

It was so real that she turned quickly and looked about her, but of course there was no one there. Shaking her head at her foolishness, she told herself she was imagining things, but nevertheless the brief moment brought balm to her bruised soul and eased her grief, and the day she had been dreading no longer seemed such an ordeal.

Tom Crawford stood leaning against the far wall of the kitchen, a glass of whisky in his hand and a faintly contemptuous expression on his ruggedly handsome face. The kitchen was full to bursting with neighbours and friends and they were all eating their fill – like pigs at a trough, as he put it to himself. And the whisky and beer wouldn't last long, the way they were guzzling it down.

His father and two of his brothers were standing in front of him in a group that included Ernie and Donald Fallow, and he was half-listening to their conversation as his gaze wandered round the throng. Tom had the advantage of being a head taller than any other man present and broad with it. Anyone looking at him would have added a good six or seven years to his nineteen years. From a child he had been big and physically strong, and he had used the feeling of power this gave him to control and bully his peers, feeding on their fear.

His eyes rested on his father and Tom's lip curled. His da was rabbiting on like he always did when he'd had a drink. As usual the subject was the injustices doled out to the working class by their supposed betters as the slump worsened. Not that his father was wrong; any fool could see that with the strikes and threats of strikes in the docks, shipyards, railyards and mines, things were going from bad to worse, but that was all his da ever did – talk. Like the rest of his cronies. None of them had taken on board that the country was changing. There were no overseas markets for Britain's old industrial output, especially iron and steel and coal, and shipbuilding was dying on its feet. The Depression was going to get worse, not better, and no amount of strikes would change that. Not for the North. And the unions were worse than useless. It was every man for himself, that's the way he saw it.

He shifted his weight slowly and took another sip of whisky. It was poor stuff. Not like the fine old malt he'd acquired recently from one of his contacts down at the docks. Patrick McHaffie could get anything you wanted if you tipped him the wink along with a bob or two, but Pat's petty pilfering was the tip of the iceberg. Like so many, Pat was gormless and would forever be grubbing away and risking his neck for peanuts while the real money passed him by.

It was common knowledge among dock workers and the fishing community that the Kane brothers from Sunderland's squalid East End controlled the criminal fraternity on the south side of the river. The Kanes had built up a nice business for themselves and had their fingers in umpteen pies – smuggling, extortion, protection rackets and a wide web of brothels – and he wouldn't want to lock horns with them. Not unless he was prepared for a knife in the back one dark night.

Tom smiled grimly to himself.

But on the north side, stretching from Cornhill Dock and Wearmouth Drops round to Potato Garth and the North Dock near Roker, now that was a different story. There were lots of small rackets going on, but without any real leadership by one person or family. He intended to change that. Why else had he spent time inveigling himself into favour with the McHaffies of this world? He'd seen the way the wind was blowing, and the next step would be the shipyards laying men off permanently, he was sure of it. Others might be prepared to go cap in hand to the foremen begging for a shift here and there, but he was damned if he was. He wanted to get into the real money, the sort of money that came by being cannier than the herd.

Over the heads of the crowd he saw the door from the scullery open. Lucy and his youngest brother, Jacob, stepped into the kitchen, each holding one of the twins in their arms, with Ruby and John at their heels.

Tom's brown eyes narrowed. His brother had clearly gone next door with Lucy to fetch the bairns through for something to eat, but it wasn't that which set his jaw clenching. It was the way Jacob was shepherding them through the assembled company, his manner verging on proprietorial.

Tom watched his brother settle Lucy on a chair with a twin on each knee and John at her side, before he and Ruby pushed through to the kitchen table. They returned with heaped plates of food and, as Jacob reached Lucy, he bent down and said something that brought a brief smile to her sad face.

The little pipsqueak. Tom straightened away from the wall and swigged back the last of the whisky in his glass. After sniffing round Lucy, was he? He knew the two were friends, being the same age and all, but a blind man could see the way Jacob's mind was working. He'd have to have a little word in his brother's shell-like when the opportunity arose.

His brother bent down to Lucy again and it was enough to cause Tom to shoulder his way through the crowd to where they were. He kept his gaze on Lucy, ignoring Jacob, as he said softly, 'I'm sorry about your mam, lass, right sorry. You know you can call on us any time?'

'Aye, yes, your mam's already said.' Lucy nodded at him, but she didn't smile. This Crawford brother always made her heart pound, but not in a good way. There was something in his eyes when he looked at her – she couldn't describe it, even to herself, not having come up against unbridled lust before – something that made her flesh creep. And yet he was handsome, and she'd heard Mrs Crawford tell her mother more than once that the lasses were shameless in the way they threw themselves at Tom. Jacob wasn't half as good-looking and neither were Ralph and Frank, but she liked them much more, especially Jacob. Jacob was special.

This thought brought a flush to her cheeks and she quickly lowered her eyes, busying herself with feeding more rice cake to Flora and Bess, who were messy eaters at the best of times.

Tom saw the pink in Lucy's cheeks and smiled to himself. He was fully aware of the attraction he generated, even in girls as young as Lucy, and didn't doubt this was the cause of her confusion. He had been aware of his appeal since he was a lad of thirteen earning a few extra bob helping out with the hay-making at Garfield Farm. Farmer Garfield's buxom sixteen-year-old daughter had taken him into the hayloft and practically eaten him alive.

He'd emerged an hour later feeling on top of the world and with an appetite for more forbidden pleasures, and since then he'd indulged this appetite without restraint. He'd discovered he appealed to older women as much as the young lasses and he'd never had to pay for it, unlike half the men he worked with.

He liked two types of females: the earthy kind whose husbands weren't supplying their needs and who would allow any kind of liberties, and, at the other end of the spectrum, the young innocent lasses he had to cajole and persuade to give up their virginity. But the latter were always worth the effort; there was something about being first, about going where no one else had been, that excited him. Afterwards, when he wanted done with them, they were normally too frightened by what they'd permitted to cause him any trouble. There was the odd exception, like Amy Murray from Southport way who'd threatened to set her brothers on him if he didn't start walking out with her, but after he'd slapped her about a bit and told her what he'd do to her if she opened her mouth, she'd got the message.

He turned his gaze from Lucy's bent head to his brother and found Jacob was staring fixedly at him. For a strange moment Tom felt this young brother of his could read his mind, and this feeling was strengthened when Jacob ground out, 'Why don't you go and get yourself another drink?', his voice low, but weighted with a mixture of fury and dislike.

No, it was more than dislike, Tom corrected himself

in the next instant. Jacob, the little nowt, was looking at him as though he was muck under his boots. The rage that had won Tom many a fight in the school playground, and which had built him a reputation as being someone not to be messed with as he'd grown older, rose in a hot flood. Only the fact that he was at a wake prevented him driving his fist into Jacob's face. Glaring at his brother, he said, 'What's up with you?'

'Nothin'.' Jacob's tone and body language belied his words. Small but broad-shouldered, with curly brown hair that sprang in an unruly tangle from double crowns on his head, he gave the appearance of being top-heavy and had a very masculine shape. His skin was clear and ruddy, and his heavily lashed brown eyes seemed over-big for his face, a face that was always smiling. But not today. 'Just leave Lucy alone, all right? She's upset.'

Holding on to his temper with some effort, Tom lowered his voice. 'Aye, well that's to be expected, but she'll have to cope with folk giving their condolences, boy.'

Boy. Jacob's dark eyes became as hard as flint. Tom had said that to get him going, knowing how it annoyed him. 'Well, you've given yours, so you can push off.'

'Now look here, you little runt—'

'Please.' Lucy's voice was quiet, but of a quality that caused the brothers to become silent. 'It – it's my mam's funeral.'

'I'm sorry.' Jacob's hand reached out, only to drop away before it made contact with her shoulder. 'Lucy, I'm sorry.'

She said nothing, continuing to break up the rice cake and put small chunks into Flora and Bess's mouths, with Ruby and John stolidly working their way through a plate of food they had between them at the side of her.

Tom stood looking at the little tableau, his jaw working. As Jacob's gaze met his again, he muttered, 'I'll see you at home' and there was a threat in the words. Jacob did not answer, but stared at him, unblinking, and it was Tom who turned away with a growled curse.

'You've made him angry.'

Jacob had been staring after his brother, but now his eyes focused on Lucy's worried face. He smiled ruefully at her. 'It's not the first time and it won't be the last. We've never got on, as you know.'

She nodded. Jacob's other brothers – Frank, who was seventeen, and Ralph, who was fifteen – always kept on the right side of Tom, but Jacob didn't seem scared of him or intimidated. 'Be careful,' she said softly.

'Of Tom?' Jacob grinned. 'He's mostly wind and water.'

No, he wasn't. She didn't know how she'd come by the knowledge that Tom Crawford could be dangerous, but she was sure of it. As her mam would have put it, she felt it in her water. And maybe it was her mam who'd led her down that road, thinking about it. Her mam had never liked Tom; not that she'd said, but her face had changed when his name was mentioned. She'd always been stiff with him, different from how she'd behaved with Jacob and the others. Her voice scarcely above a whisper, Lucy said again, 'Be careful, Jacob. I mean it. I don't want him to hurt you and he would, you know.'

Oh aye, he knew all right. He'd had many a good hiding from Tom. But although he didn't want Lucy to worry about him, not with everything she had on her plate now her mam was gone, her concern gave him a warm feeling inside.

From the time he and Lucy had been two little bairns making mud pies in the back lane together, she'd been his world. They had begun school on the same day, faced the playground bullies side by side, and helped each other with their homework. Or rather Lucy had helped him, Jacob admitted silently. But he hadn't understood that the feeling he had for her was love, not until the last year or so. But with the changes in his body that puberty was bringing had come the knowledge that he wanted her for his lass, and no one else would do. He didn't want to mess around with this girl or that, like lots of lads did, he just wanted Lucy. For keeps. As soon as she was old enough he'd ask her da if they could begin courting – that's if she'd have him. But she would. She was his Lucy.

Becoming aware she was still staring at him, he bent his head and said quietly, 'Don't let on I've said, but me mam's got some bits for the bairns for Christmas that she's going to slip round nearer the time. She wanted it to be a surprise, but I thought it'd ease your mind, knowing that's taken care of, what with your da and the lads being on short time an' all.'

'Thank you.' Her voice was soft, her eyes were soft, and for a moment their gaze held, conveying what they were as yet unable to express in words. But for the present it was enough.

Chapter Three

The relentless snow and blizzards which the beleaguered North had endured for the first three months of the year had given way to an April of driving rain and icy winds. Lucy didn't know which was worse. The rain probably. She glanced at the kitchen window, where the force of the rain rattled the glass now and again. It made the back lanes seas of thick glutinous mud, which was tramped into the house no matter how often she told her father and brothers and Ruby to leave their mucky boots in the scullery. Wet clothes were draped all round the kitchen, and Flora and Bess hadn't been outside for weeks and were snotty-nosed and fractious. Worse, the menfolk's shifts had become increasingly few and far between. This not only meant she was at her wits' end trying to juggle putting food on the table while still paying the rent, but it was a continual battle to keep the twins occupied and out from under her da's feet. His temper was short these days.

But today was a Saturday. To Ruby and John's delight,

she'd allowed them to make a den with the clothes horse on the girls' double bed, with strict orders to her sister to keep the twins upstairs for a few hours. Her da was in a worse mood than usual, Ernie and Donald having picked up half a day at the shipyard while he'd been refused a shift.

She looked towards him now as she continued to knead dough for the bread to supplement the stew they were having for the evening meal, a stew consisting of scrag ends and the spotted vegetables she'd bought cheap the night before as the shops were closing.

Walter was aware of his daughter's gaze, but he didn't look up from his task of mending John's boots. It was the third time he'd done this since Christmas and in truth there was little of the original boots remaining, so patched were they. He was in no doubt they wouldn't last another month, but without boots John couldn't go to school. He kept his eyes fixed on the iron last between his knees as he hammered a quarter-inch nail into the boot he was working on, and with each blow of the hammer he was venting his fury at the foreman who'd turned him down.

Then, all at once, the rage he'd been stoking up to keep the despair at bay drained away and his hands became idle. It wasn't the foreman's fault, he knew that. Sid Chapman wasn't a bad bloke and he had his orders from on high to follow. If there wasn't the work, there wasn't the work. It was the same everywhere. The miners had come out with the slogan 'Not a penny off the pay, not a minute on the day' in answer to the call for less pay for longer hours, but it wouldn't get them anywhere. He'd worked at Thompson's since he was a lad and had thought he'd walked into hell his first morning, with the noise of the drillers, riveters and caulkers, and barely a day went by that some poor so-an'-so wasn't maimed or killed, but he knew where he was at the yard and he was damn good at his job. All this sitting about was driving him round the bend.

He ground his teeth before starting work on the boot again. At forty years old Walter was a thin, prematurely aged man who carried the evidence of his trade on his scarred hands – one of which had the tip of a finger missing – and the arthritis that racked his body, especially in the winter months. As a boy of twelve he'd had to get used to the fact he always seemed to be cold and wet, even on the hottest day, when working on the huge steel plates in the yard, but the discomforts he'd brushed off as a lad weren't so easy to dismiss as he'd grown older. But all his mates were the same, he told himself, stretching his aching back for a moment. Deaf as posts, welder's lung, vibration white finger, poor eyesight, crippling arthritis – they'd do well to make up one good body between the lot of them.

He smiled grimly. His Agnes had never wanted the shipyard for her boys when they were bairns, especially Thompson's, which was known as a 'blood yard' because of the number of accidents, along with Doxford's over the river. As the lads had grown she'd accepted the inevitability of it, though, bless her soul. She'd been a good wife and mother, none better.

Thoughts of his late wife brought Walter's gaze to Lucy. She was in the process of placing the bread tins, covered with clean muslin, on the hearth for the bread to rise. As always since Agnes's passing, Lucy's likeness to her mother was bittersweet. It reminded him of what he'd lost, but he took comfort in the fact that Agnes lived on in their daughter. He was glad at least one of their bairns had turned out like Agnes and was a beauty; not even their nearest and dearest could call the rest of them bonny. Mind, what good it would do her was questionable.

He heard the back door open and the sound of Ernie and Donald chaffing each other about taking their boots off. The next moment his two eldest sons came through from the scullery, wet through, but smiling. For a second he wanted to growl at them, 'What have you got to laugh about?', but he bit back the words. Nevertheless, he couldn't bring himself to greet them. When Ernie said, 'All right, Da?' he had to swallow deeply before he could say, 'Aye, as you see.'

Lucy signalled her two brothers by shaking her head, and quietly now they sat down at the kitchen table after taking off their sodden caps and coats and hanging them over the backs of their chairs. It was after Lucy had made a pot of tea and poured a cup for her father and brothers that Ernie spoke again. 'Saw Tom Crawford as we were coming in, Da. He said he might have a couple of days' work he could put our way, the three of us like.'

Walter raised his head slowly. 'Oh aye?'

'Loading and unloading at the docks, that sort of thing.'

'And how long has Tom Crawford been a gaffer at the docks?' said Walter flatly. 'It's only the gaffers that hire and fire.'

Ernie glanced quickly at his brother and then again at his father. 'He's not a gaffer, not exactly. This work'd be . . .' – Ernie cast another glance at Donald – 'on the quiet.'

'Oh aye, I know what the work'd be, if Tom's at the back of it.' Walter's voice was rising. 'I'm not daft. An' I've told you before, we're not going down that road. He's sailing close to the wind, is Tom, and likely he'll capsize before long and take everyone else in the boat down with him. And don't tell me he's trying to do us a favour, like he did when he offered us that butter and cheese and what-have-you last week, cos it won't wash. He's trying to suck you into his thieving, lad, and he knows if you do it once he's got you.'

Lucy's mouth had fallen open and she shut it with a little snap. Butter and cheese? Tom had offered them some butter and cheese and her da hadn't taken it? She thought of the scrapings of this and that she attempted to turn into meals these days. The stew simmering on the hob didn't have enough mutton in it to feed a sparrow, and the two handfuls of barley, and potatoes and turnips, couldn't hide the fact that it was watery and thin. The bread she was making to mop up the gravy would help fill their bellies of course, but butter and cheese . . .

'It's not like that, Da.'

'The hell it isn't!' Walter answered Ernie with a bawl and, when both boys stared at him in surprise, he took a deep breath. Then, his voice quieter but holding more authority than his bawl had done, he said, 'What the Crawfords do is up to them, but we're not soiling our hands by thieving – an' that's my last word on the matter. I know times are hard, but we'll get by if we pull together, all right? I've lived longer than the pair of you and sooner or later Tom Crawford will get his fingers burnt, you mark my words.'

Ernie shrugged. It was clear he wasn't in agreement, but his father's word was law and he didn't argue.

Lucy didn't either, but as she fetched out the bread and dripping which was their midday meal, before going to the foot of the stairs to call Ruby and John and the twins, she was thinking: Cheese and butter, *cheese and butter*; and her mouth was watering. Principles were all very well, but you couldn't eat them.

The next weeks were rife with talk of strikes, and when the coal owners' final offer of a return to the 1921 minimum wage structure – which would be equivalent to an average wage cut of about 13 per cent – was rejected by the miners, everyone knew the national coal stoppage had begun. Within five days, on May 4th, the first General Strike in British history was under way.

A formal state of emergency was declared, but as undergraduates, stockbrokers, barristers and other white-collar professionals up and down the country signed up to do the jobs of the workers on strike, a bitter class war split Britain.

By the time the TUC called off the General Strike, leaving the embattled miners to fight on alone, Lucy was sick of hearing about the whys and wherefores of the dispute. It might have only lasted nine days, but her father had talked of nothing else. He had been a force on the picket line and vitriolic in his condemnation of the owners and management. That he'd been as vocal outside the house as within its confines became apparent very quickly. Those shipyard workers who had held their tongues about their employers got any available shifts. Those who hadn't, didn't. The existence of a blacklist was strenuously denied, but then, as her father bitterly pointed out to anyone who'd listen, it would be, wouldn't it?

Lucy had been worried Ernie and Donald would be tarred with the same brush as their father, and this might well have been the case, but for the fact that Ernie's best friend was the foreman's son. Consequently Sid Chapman took the lads on for enough shifts for the family to survive, just. Lucy became adept at cooking the wild rabbits and wood pigeons her brothers trapped on the days when they walked umpteen miles into the surrounding countryside looking for anything the family could eat, and she made good use of the mushrooms, wild mint and thyme the summer produced. Her brothers bought flour direct from the mill, a sack of seconds, and took turns carrying it home on their backs, and again the lads walked miles to a farm that sold potatoes at a good price and often threw in any spotted or yellowing vegetables for free.

After a few fruitless weeks of sullen rage, Walter decided to try his hand at painting and decorating. He made himself known to the big houses and grand residences as far afield as Whitburn to the north of Monkwearmouth and Ryhope and Seaham to the south. His perseverance paid off in July when he got himself work for the landlady of a bed-and-breakfast establishment at Seaham. It meant a six-mile walk in the morning pushing the old handcart he'd mangled together, which held his tins of paint and brushes and other necessities, and the same come evening, and the pay was poor compared to what he'd earned as a skilled welder, but the change in her father when he began earning again transformed the atmosphere in the house and made things easier for Lucy.

She was worried how he would fare once the harsh winter months began, but put it to the back of her mind. For now it was summer and it was a hot one. The holes in John's and Ruby's boots didn't matter so much – once home from school, they went barefoot in the back lanes and streets like so many other children – and Flora and Bess's constant colds and coughs were a thing of the past. As a family they went searching for driftwood and pieces of washed-up coal and coke for the range on the beaches and round by the harbour mouth, Ernie and Donald carrying the twins on their shoulders there and back and making the exercise into a game. Lucy often delayed their departure home at the end of the day until the fishwives were selling the remainders in their baskets at next to nothing, wanting rid of the dregs after a long hot day. She could pick up a penn'orth of broken kippers or a couple of dozen herring in this way and eke out the fish for two or three dinners if she was careful. Jacob often accompanied them on these trips, helping Lucy with the little ones and making them laugh with his infectious brand of humour. The days when Jacob wasn't with them seemed harder and longer to Lucy, as though the sun had gone behind a cloud and everything was duller in consequence.

She glanced at him now through the kitchen window as she stood gutting and cleaning the herring they'd returned with that day. Jacob was helping Ernie and Donald construct a kind of lean-to next to the brick-built privy at the end of the yard. It would afford the driftwood and other bits and pieces they'd collected, to burn on the range, some protection in the winter. The lads had staggered back from the beach with half of a massive tree trunk earlier. Once dried out, it could be chopped up and used for weeks.

Lucy sighed happily. The kitchen smelt of the sea, the bairns were tired out after a day in the sunshine and were content to sit in a little row in the yard watching the lads' activities, and her father was finishing the job at the landlady's house in Seaham today, which had gone so well he already had another lined up a few doors down from her, which was also a bed-and-breakfast.

She began to dust the fish with flour and rolled them

carefully, before putting them in the oven dish where they lay, rank on rank, black and silver. After adding some boiling water and vinegar, she scattered a handful of the wild herbs the lads had collected a few days ago and popped the dish in the oven. They'd eat half tonight and the rest tomorrow, cold with baked potatoes cooked in the ashes of the fire. And all for a penny. The fishwife had wanted two, but Jacob had made her laugh as he'd chaffed and teased her and acted the goat, and in the end she'd emptied the contents of her basket into their bucket, pocketed the penny and told them to skedaddle.

Lucy's countenance changed as she looked through the window again as she began to clear the table. Tom Crawford had joined the others, a package tucked under his arm. His head was bent close to Ernie's and Donald's, his manner conspiratorial. She watched as Ernie shook his head, but whatever her brother had said, Tom wasn't taking no for an answer. What happened next occurred so swiftly it caused her to give a little scream of shock. One moment Jacob had taken his brother's arm and was saying something, and the next Tom had swung round and hit him, sending him sprawling backwards to land on his backside on the stone slabs.

Lucy stood frozen for a few seconds, her fingers pressing against her mouth, and then as she saw Tom aim a vicious kick at Jacob, which was only prevented from reaching its target by Ernie and Donald hauling him back, she flew out of the house. 'Leave him alone!' All fear of Tom was forgotten, she was so angry. 'He didn't do anything to you.' Turning to the children huddled together by the wall of the house, she said, 'Get inside and stay put.'

Jacob had scrambled to his feet as she'd been speaking, and now he launched himself at his brother. Donald sprang between them, holding Jacob off as Ernie hung onto Tom, although at Lucy's appearance Tom had become still. His eyes on her face, he said softly, 'Didn't do anything to me? Here I am, trying to do you a good turn, and he calls me every name under the sun.'

'I said you were thieving scum, because that's what you are,' Jacob panted, struggling to break free of Donald.

Lucy said nothing. From the moment Tom had spoken and her eyes had met his, she'd been filled with a sort of jerky panic that made her stomach jump.

As though Jacob hadn't spoken, Tom continued, 'I've brought you a side of bacon, lass, that's all. All right? I know you're hard pressed' – now he included Ernie and Donald in a sweeping glance – 'and I thought you could use it.'

'Like I said, man, we can't take it. Not that we're not grateful, mind.' Ernie's voice was apologetic. It didn't do to get on the wrong side of Tom Crawford if you could help it. 'But you know what our da's like, he'd go barmy. It's just the way he is.'

'Then maybe it's time he changed?' Tom's mouth twisted in a smile that wasn't a smile. 'The workhouses are full of folk like your da. Meself, I'd rather make sure my family's looked after, whatever it takes.'

'Cut the high-and-mighty claptrap.' Jacob had ceased

struggling, but the look on his face combined with the blood from his bleeding nose had turned him into someone Lucy barely recognized as her Jacob. 'You're feathering your own nest and everything comes second to that. You'd see our mam and da, Frank, Ralph, the whole lot of us sent down the line before you'd lift a finger.'

'Is that so?'

'Aye, and you know it, so don't come the Holy Joe about their da. He's worth a dozen of you.'

Curiously, Lucy noticed that the angrier Jacob became, the more Tom regained his composure. Now he straightened, shrugging off Ernie's hand on his arm before bending to pick up the package wrapped in brown paper and tied with string, which had fallen to the ground during the ruckus with his brother. 'You don't know what you're on about, boy, and I haven't noticed you refusing to eat the stuff I bring to the table. One law for your mouth and one for your belly, is it? And don't try it,' he added warningly as Jacob began struggling in Donald's grip once more, 'because this time I'll make sure you don't get up again.' Turning to Ernie, he added, 'So, I still can't persuade you to come in with me and tell Sid Chapman where to stick his paltry shifts, eh? You're daft, man, you know that, don't you? The yards have always been little more than slaughter houses, but they're worse now they've got the men fighting each other for work. Safety's gone out of the window. You heard about the accident at Pickersgill's yesterday? The gangway collapsed and there's fifty-odd injured and three dead.'

Ernie nodded. Pickersgill's was a Southwick yard, but bad news travelled fast and he'd heard lurid reports about men being hurled to the ground from a height of forty feet. Some of the workmen on the gangway had been painters carrying tins of red paint and the disaster had looked even worse than it was – the injured covered in paint, so that the whole scene had looked like one of the slaughter houses Tom had spoken about. But it was no good dwelling on what might happen when you were in the yards; you just had to get on with it. He said this now to Tom, who shook his head. 'You want to get out while you can, but it's up to you. Anyway, I'll take this in to Mam. She'll be glad of it, and I dare say baby brother'll eat his fill an' all, eh, boy?'

Ernie was helping Donald to hold Jacob as Tom sauntered out of the yard and into next door, whistling as he went. Once Tom was in the house, Jacob slumped, red-faced and looking close to angry tears. 'I hope he gets caught and they throw away the key,' he muttered bitterly. 'Him and his big ideas.'

Ernie glanced at Donald and then at Lucy, who was standing silently by, before saying awkwardly, 'Everyone does a bit of fiddling now and again, Jake.'

'Maybe, but it's more than a bit of fiddling, Ernie. Oh' – Jacob made a throwaway movement with his hand – 'to hell with it and him. He's always had me mam eating out of his hand and he rules the roost indoors, you've no idea. As soon as I can, I'm out of it.'

'You don't mean that.'

'Aye, I do.' Jacob's tone was flat now, weary-sounding, but as he glanced at Lucy, he added, 'I don't mean leave Monkwearmouth, just our mam's. Once I'm earning I'll get a room somewhere.'

'Aye, well, that won't be for a while yet, so if you take my advice you'll try and get along with him while you're under the same roof,' said Ernie stolidly, holding out a handkerchief for Jacob to wipe his bloody nose and mouth. 'Don't rile him, Jake. You can't win. And in his own way he was only trying to help.'

Jacob's face took on a blank look, but Lucy knew exactly what he was thinking and she agreed with him. Tom Crawford would never do anything out of the goodness of his heart. The bacon, like the previous offerings, was a means to an end. Her da had been right: Tom was trying to suck her brothers into his shady dealings and gain a foothold in this family, and the knowledge terrified her.

Chapter Four

Tom Crawford was whistling as he left the house later that same day, but his feeling of wellbeing didn't last long. The August evening was warm and sultry and the smell from the privies as he walked swiftly along the back lane made his nose wrinkle in distaste.

Filthy pigs, he thought savagely, as he passed one particularly ripe-smelling back yard. In spite of the late hour a woman was sitting on the back step nursing an infant at the breast, her skirts pulled up over her knees. A group of mat-haired, snotty-nosed children were playing around her, three of them naked and the fourth, a girl of about seven or eight, with a ragged dress covering her skinny body. The family was well known in the district, and when the woman called out to him as he passed and he didn't answer, a torrent of abuse followed him.

It wasn't until he had reached Milium Terrace and walked north past Potato Garth towards North Dock that he stopped to take some deep breaths. The air wasn't much sweeter, but anything was an improvement on the back lanes, he thought, his lip curling. He would say one thing for his mam: she kept the house and yard as clean as a new pin, and daily buckets of ash in the privy meant you could sit there without gagging, whereas some of them . . .

Tom turned and looked back the way he had come. Animals had cleaner habits and looked after their young better, too. As soon as he could he was getting himself a house on the outskirts, a place in its own grounds, where there was space between you and your neighbours. A grand house, fancy like. He could do it. He knew he could do it.

The light was all but gone now and the night was dark, a thin crescent moon doing little in the way of illumination, but this didn't bother him. He could look after himself, he thought grimly, and certain activities were best conducted under the cover of darkness. He began walking once more, massaging and flexing his aching right hand as he did so. But his bruised knuckles were worth it. That little runt of a brother had needed taking down a peg or two, talking to him like that in front of Lucy and her brothers.

He turned right at North Dock, past the lifeboat house and then the dock office and continuing to where the silent sawmills stood in pitch-blackness. The docks and wharves and warehouses were different places at night, the great cranes used to unload cargo standing like forbidding sentinels and only the sleek river rats and the odd cat or two scuttling about in the darkness. He had been fascinated by the river as a child, often escaping the back lanes to watch the dredgers and hoppers, cargo vessels, sailing ships, tugboats and huge turret ships, and small boats of every description as they'd gone about their business. The smell of industrial smoke and the sound of paddle-wheel blades beating the water had been almost romantic to a little lad, and when the small foy boats had carried hawsers to buoys in the river he'd watched for hours. In those days he'd dreamt of sailing the ferry or the water boat that took fresh water to the ships in the river and the docks when he grew up; funnily enough, he'd never wanted to be a sailor on the high seas. From listening to their talk it seemed too hard a life. He marched on, smiling to himself. He'd been canny even then.

It was as he reached the bulk of the mills, discernible as a dark mass against the night sky, that a number of shadows detached themselves from the blackness. Tom stopped abruptly, his eyes narrowing as he peered into the darkness. He'd only been meeting one man with whom he'd hoped to do some business, one of the dock foremen who had a large family to feed and who supplemented his wage by looking the other way when certain goods fell off the backs of lorries – or, in this case, ships. Had Archy Finnigan been playing a double game and got the dock police waiting for him?

He was poised ready to run, when a movement just behind him revealed another figure. This man was as broad as he was tall and built like a brick outhouse. He'd been standing out of sight behind a stack of crates. Tom must have walked straight past him. Realizing escape was impossible, he forced himself to stand still. He'd deny everything. They had no proof, they hadn't caught him in the act or with anything in his possession, although his mam's front room was packed with stuff. He'd been due to sell it on tomorrow, damn it. He began to sweat slightly.

'Mr Crawford, isn't it?'

The group in front of him moved closer, and now Tom found himself wishing it *had* been the police. Swallowing hard, he had to lick his lips before he could say, 'Aye, that's me.'

The Kane brothers had a man on either side of them, both of whom were great bruisers, and one of them had Archy Finnigan in tow. Even in the dim light Tom could see Archy was scared to death. He knew how Archy felt. The brothers themselves were slight, thin individuals with small hands and feet. When Tom had first had them pointed out to him some years ago, he'd thought their physical stature didn't match their reputation. It had been a little while later, after hearing about a particularly gruesome murder that the criminal fraternity had attributed to the brothers, that he'd come to realize brains combined with ruthlessness was more scary than brawn.

The brother who had spoken stepped right up to him, so close Tom could smell the tobacco on his breath when he said, 'And what brings you to this neck of the woods, Mr Crawford, and on such a grand night? I'd have thought you'd have been courting some lassie or other in a nice quiet spot, a handsome fella like you.'

Tom found his throat was dry and his tongue was sticking to the roof of his mouth. For the life of him he couldn't get any words out. He stared into the small rat-like face in front of him and now he fully understood how the brothers could inspire such terror.

After a moment or two Jed Kane smiled, his sharp yellow teeth adding to the impression of a human rodent. He could smell the fear coming off the man in front of him. 'But how remiss of me, Mr Crawford. I haven't introduced meself. The name's Kane, Jed Kane. And this is my brother, Leo. Mr Finnigan I think you already know.'

Tom, his wits returning, nodded. 'Aye, I know Archy.' Deciding he'd be telling the brothers nothing they didn't already know, he added, 'We'd got things to discuss the night.'

'Things to discuss . . .' Jed let his voice linger tenderly on the last word. He turned to his brother. 'Things to discuss,' he repeated softly. Swinging back to Tom, he said, 'What things exactly?'

'Jed, I swear you've got it wrong. I wouldn't pull a fast one—'

Archy's words were cut off as Jed made a movement with his hand and the man holding Archy punched him hard in the stomach.

Jed Kane smiled at Tom. 'Never knows when to keep quiet, our Archy. Have you noticed that?'

Tom smiled sickly back.

'So why are you here, Mr Crawford? Spot of business, was it?'

Tom looked into Archy's pleading eyes and then Jed Kane's merciless gaze. 'L-look, I know nowt about it being your stuff, Mr Kane. Archy said he had some extra left over from a deal he'd done recently and he'd let me have it for a good price, that's all I know. If I'd thought it was yours, I wouldn't have touched it with a bargepole, but—'

'But?'

'You – you don't normally have any truck with this side of the river, or that's what I'd heard.'

'Is that so?' Jed Kane tilted his head in a bird-like movement. 'Then you've been informed wrongly, Mr Crawford, but that's by the by. I repeat my question. What does this "stuff" you mentioned consist of?'

Tom thought about lying, but only for an instant. If Archy had tried to rip off the Kane brothers he deserved everything coming to him, and he wasn't about to risk his own neck by attempting to cover up for Archy. He was bang smack in the middle of this hornets' nest as it was. His only hope was to speak the truth; he had a feeling Jed Kane would know if he lied. There were rumours the Kanes' mam had been a Gypsy and they'd inherited her second sight, and he wasn't about to put it to the test. He looked from Jed to the other brother and then back again before answering, 'Rum, coffee and French brandy in the main.'

Jed nodded slowly. 'And you have clients lined up who are willing to buy from you?'

Hell's flames, this was getting worse. Tom hesitated;

he blinked and wetted his lips. 'Aye.' All he needed now was for his contacts to be ones the brothers used.

'An enterprising young man.' Jed had turned and was speaking to his brother, who had remained silent throughout. 'Wouldn't you say, Leo? Aye, an enterprising young man, sure enough, and intelligent too, I'll be bound. Is that right, Mr Crawford?'

Tom didn't know what Jed Kane wanted him to say and so he said nothing.

'Unlike our mutual friend here,' Jed continued, still in the same pleasant tone, 'who is stupid as well as being the worst type of ignorant scum. Because only stupid, ignorant scum would think they could do the dirty on us and get away with it. A man's word is his bond. Isn't that right? And if you can't trust someone . . .'

Tom felt his bowels coming loose at the implied threat. He could only imagine what Archy was feeling.

'But there's another thing at stake here. My brother and I run a business, and word soon gets about. If we're seen as mugs, what message does that send? You get my point?'

'Please . . .' Archy was crying now. 'Please, me wife and bairns. I'm sorry, Jed. I swear I'll never do it again. I must have been barmy.'

'Gag him.' Jed Kane didn't take his eyes from Tom's white face as he gave the order.

A cloth was stuffed into Archy's mouth and a scarf tied round his jaw, his terror-stricken eyes bulging above it.

'We're going for a little ride, Mr Crawford. Have you ridden in a motor car before? No? Then you're in for a treat. It's a very civilized and private way to travel. Keeps confidential business confidential, if you get my drift.'

'Look, this is n-nowt to do with m-me.' Tom couldn't prevent the stammering. 'I didn't know.'

'I believe you. Like I said, you're an intelligent man, I can see that.' Jed Kane's voice was soothing, but he nodded to the man standing behind Tom as he spoke.

Tom felt his arm held in a vice-like grip, which left no room for escape. Not that his legs could have carried him at more than a stumble anyway; they'd turned to jelly.

They left the shadow of the sawmills and walked along beside a row of locked and bolted warehouses. The Kane brothers led the way, with Tom and his captor behind and the remaining two thugs dragging Archy between them. In the distance, at the side of the road aptly named Harbour View, two Morris Cowley motor cars were waiting. Jed slid into the driver's seat of the first car and motioned for Tom's escort to join him. The remaining four men climbed into the other car.

The journey across the Wear Bridge into the Kanes' lair in the East End was conducted in silence. Tom could feel the sweat running down his face and his shirt was wringing, but he was too terrified to move a muscle; all the stories he'd ever heard about the brothers were running through his mind and causing a panic that had his heartbeat pounding in his ears.

The crowded dwellings, courts and alleys of the East End looked as squalid at night as in the day, the gin shops, brothels and gambling houses shamelessly flaunting themselves once darkness fell. It was hard to believe that the old river-mouth settlement of Sunderland was once a thriving and well-to-do area where much of the wealth of the town was generated; the fine buildings that had once housed rich merchant families were now decaying tenements where families lived ten to a room and the gutters ran with offal, dirt and human excrement. The wealthy shipbuilders and mine owners, gracious patrons of art and architecture, had long since moved from the commercial part of the town to the more fashionable and genteel elevated part of Sunderland, building grand houses in wide clean streets. The unimaginable depths of squalor and criminal strongholds in the East End they chose to ignore.

Tom, however, was unable to ignore that he had been transported to a place where the normal laws of civilized society didn't apply. He could vanish without a trace, or turn up as just one more bloated body floating in the murky waters of the docks.

The cars travelled along High Street East before turning into the labyrinth that was the East End proper. Once they finally came to a halt, Tom thought he was somewhere near Prospect Row, but he couldn't be sure. Not that it mattered. There was no possible chance of escape.

They were outside what appeared to be a warehouse of some kind, with a row of terraced two-up, two-down houses on the other side of the road and a public house on the corner, from which ribald singing could be heard. As they waited with the engines running, the large wooden doors in front of them swung open and two more big burly figures stood impassively holding them back as the cars drove slowly into the building, one behind the other.

Jed Kane switched off the engine. 'Here we are, Mr Crawford. Be it ever so humble, there's no place like home.'

When he exited the car Tom realized that if the building had been used as a warehouse once, it was no longer. He was standing in a large space, it was true, but apart from the two cars and shelves with various tins of oil and car tools, it was empty. The occupants of the other car having alighted, they proceeded to the end of the building and through a door which opened into a clean, high-walled yard.

The Kane brothers to the fore, they all climbed an outside staircase made of iron, which led to a small square landing. When Tom stepped through another door and into the second storey of the building he stopped dead, so great was his surprise, before the hard hand at his elbow urged him forward.

Instead of the great open expanse he'd expected he was in a thickly carpeted corridor lit by several gas jets along one wall. Various doors opened off it, but he was propelled along after Jed and Leo Kane so fast that he had no idea how many they passed before reaching the door at the end of the passageway.

To Tom's amazement he found himself in a large and well-furnished kitchen, complete with a huge black-leaded range, which had something simmering on it. A large table of the better kind, with a fancy leather-covered top, stood in the middle of the room with eight chairs tucked underneath it, and two enormous dressers packed full with dishes and crockery and kitchen equipment took up one wall. Under a long narrow window stood two more smaller tables, presumably used for cooking. On the wooden floor, along the length of the gleaming steel fender in front of the range, an expensive-looking mat had two fine upholstered rocking chairs at either end of it and one of these was gently moving, as though the occupant had just left it. Altogether it was the kind of kitchen that wouldn't have been out of place in a grand house, and this impression was further heightened by the two women, dressed in black dresses and lacy white aprons and mop caps, who were staring at them.

Jed Kane addressed himself to the older of the females, a fat, red-faced woman of about forty. 'We won't be needing you again tonight, Jessie. You and Polly get yourselves off to bed.'

The woman nodded, her eyes flicking back to Tom and the two heavies holding Archy as she said, 'Yes, Mr Kane. There's plenty of bread to go with the soup, fresh and still warm, the way you like it.' She pushed the younger woman in front of her and they left the room.

'My cook and maid.' Jed Kane indicated for Tom to sit down as he and his brother pulled out a chair from the table, although his men remained standing. Archy was standing quiet and motionless now, the gag still in place, and Tom couldn't bring himself to glance at him. 'Does it surprise you, this place?'

Again, Tom didn't lie. 'Aye, a bit.'

Leo Kane smiled, revealing teeth as sharp and discoloured as his brother's, and spoke for the first time. 'A bit, he says,' he said to his brother. 'Aye, an' more than a bit, I'll be bound.' His hard black eyes turning to Tom, he said softly, 'We was born in Blue Anchor Yard in the quayside near to the Death House. Bodies found in the river were kept there and there were plenty of 'em, so you could say we were well acquainted with what life dished out at an early age. Caged animals live in more cleanliness and comfort than what me an' me brother did. Ten bairns me mam had afore she died, an' only me and Jed to show for it, but them filthy tenements did one thing for us. They made us strong, an' folk know it.'

He turned to his brother.

'An' if anyone forgets that, we remind 'em, eh, Jed? An' now we don't live in one room, with our coal in a cupboard and the rain coming through the roof onto a stinking mattress and the walls crawling with lice.' He smiled slowly. 'We live like gentlemen, as you can see.'

'Mr Kane, I swear I didn't—'

'Shut your mouth.'

Leo Kane didn't shout – he didn't have to. His soft voice was more menacing than any bellow. And Tom shut up. It had come to him that, for all Leo's quietness, he was more to be feared than his brother. It was the deadness of his eyes.

Leo turned to the two men holding Archy. 'Mr Finnigan thought he could short-change us. A foolish notion. And dangerous. Dangerous for him, an' dangerous for us because we cannot allow such a notion to take root in our organization. And so a message needs sendin' out to others who might have similar foolish ideas – a very visible message.' He stood up, walking over to the range. 'Bring him.'

When Archy had been marched over, Leo looked into the grey terrified face. 'You thought you could short-change us an' make a bit more on the side, didn't you, lad? Do you know what the Arabs do to thieves like you? They cut their hands off. An' it works, cos that man never again puts his fingers where they didn't oughta go.'

He laughed at his macabre joke and the two men holding Archy sniggered obediently.

'But we're not Arabs, are we?' Leo continued. 'Besides which, that'd be a messy job.' He reached out and grasped the handle of the big pan of soup with a thick drying-up cloth. 'He who dabbles with fire gets burnt fingers, lad.' He nodded at the two henchmen, who each took one of Archy's arms at the elbow before plunging his hands into the bubbling liquid. Archy's high-pitched screams were muffled by the gag, and his struggles made not an iota of difference to the two burly men holding him. Leo continued to steady the pan, and now the sounds coming from inside the gag were inhuman.

Tom had risen to his feet, but at Jed's quiet 'Sit' he sank down again, swallowing at the nausea that had curdled into his throat, hardly able to believe what was happening in front of his eyes.

'He's passed out, Boss.' One of the men holding Archy spoke impassively.

Leo inclined his head and they lifted Archy's arms, bringing what remained of his hands out of the pan and letting the unconscious body fall on the floor. Now Jed didn't stop Tom when he rose and staggered over to the deep white sink in a corner of the kitchen. He vomited until there was nothing left in his stomach, the cold sweat that had taken him over making him pray he wouldn't faint in front of them all. He was vaguely aware of the two men dragging Archy out of the room and then of the clink of glasses, but it wasn't until he finally raised his head and turned round that he realized he was alone with the brothers.

Jed held out a glass containing a good measure of brandy. 'Drink it.' There was a trace of sympathy in his tone.

Tom crossed the kitchen on wobbly legs and took the glass, knocking back the brandy in two deep swallows. The liquid burned a path into his stomach, but it helped steady his voice when he said, 'What are you going to do with him?' as he obeyed the nod of Jed's head, which indicated for him to sit down.

'He'll be taken back to the place he came from.' Jed poured more brandy into Tom's glass and refilled his own.

'You could say he's lucky. Aye, he's lucky he's of more use to us alive, and serving as a reminder to other scum not to get any ideas.'

Tom pictured the two red lumps of meat he had glimpsed and gave an involuntary shudder. Licking his lips, he said, 'What about me, Mr Kane? I didn't know it was your stuff, I swear it.'

'Aye, you've said.' Leo spoke, his raspy voice impatient. 'Luckily for you, my brother believes you. He knows when folk are lying, does Jed.'

The Gypsy mother. Hell, he just wanted to get out of here. Tom gulped at his brandy.

'Funnily enough, we don't like this night's happenings any more than you do. They're bad for business.' Leo leaned back in his chair, reaching into his pocket and extracting a packet of Woodbines. He offered one to his brother and then to Tom. 'It's far better when everythin' ticks on like clockwork. We've enough trouble with the customs an' harbour police, we don't need more.'

The smell of the soup on the range was turning Tom's stomach. He finished his brandy and drew the smoke of his cigarette deep into his lungs.

'We'd heard your name mentioned afore.' Leo held up his hand as Tom went to speak. 'Nowt bad. Like me brother said earlier, the word is you're bright an' you want to get on. About right?'

Warily, wondering if this was a trick, Tom nodded.

'An' you're a North Dock lad, born an' bred. That means you're trusted over the river, aye?'

Tom nodded again. The divide between the East End and Monkwearmouth by the River Wear was more than geography. It was well over a hundred years since the bridge had been completed, joining Monkwearmouth on the north of the river to Bishopwearmouth on the south side, but he was fully aware of the 'us and them' instinct that existed. It wasn't talked about, but it was there, right enough.

'We need someone over the river we can rely on. Call it a manager, if you like. A local lad.' It was Jed who was speaking now and he replenished Tom's glass. 'Not just for the dock business, although that's the bread-and-butter, but further afield. You think you can handle that?'

'Me?' The vomiting and the cause for it, along with the brandy and cigarette and not least the sickly odour of the soup on the range, was making Tom light-headed.

'Aye, you.' Piercing eyes held his. 'Don't tell me I've made a mistake an' you're not up to it, Tom.'

It was the use of his Christian name that did it. Suddenly Tom knew he wanted this. It was his chance. The break he'd prayed for. And he sensed an ally in Jed Kane, impossible though such a concept would have appeared just an hour ago. He straightened in his chair. 'I'm up to it, all right. An' I won't let you down, Mr Kane.'

'I know that.' The black gaze held his for a moment more, before Jed turned to his brother. 'See?' he said softly. 'All taken care of.'

PART TWO

Along Came a Spider

1928

Chapter Five

Lucy opened her eyes slowly, her swollen lids a reminder that she had cried herself to sleep the previous night, which, in spite of the last two years being hard ones for the North in general and her family in particular, was unusual. Her mother had always said it was no good crying over spilt milk, and although the state of the country was more serious than spilt milk, the principle was the same and one Lucy agreed with. Crying got you nowhere.

Even her da now admitted the General Strike had been a disaster; how much of a disaster had come to light as time had gone on. The ignominious defeat of the trade unions had given the employers the whip hand, and the aftermath of rebellion had taken its toll on working-class men, women and children in the North. While the south of the country prospered from the new 'clean' industries that were springing up – cars, vans and trucks being built, electrical goods assembled, and printing and packaging going on in modern factories using streamlined production methods – many northerners were sinking in a bog of grim poverty and starvation.

The beginning of the year had seen nearly 500,000 people over the age of sixty-five receive their first state pension of ten shillings a week, but that was no benefit to her da and the lads, Lucy reflected. The bad winter, which had continued into March with blizzards sweeping the North in the middle of the month, had meant her da hadn't worked since well before Christmas, and the lads' shifts at the shipyard had dried up too. Their combined dole money barely paid the rent and bought food for the table, and now, in the middle of a cold, wet April, she'd pawned everything that hadn't already been sold.

For weeks she'd cooked oatmeal gruel and broth from boiled-up marrow bones and pearl barley for their main meal; the rest of the time it was bread with a scraping of dripping, unless the lads managed to snare a rabbit or hare in the fields, but with so many folk in the same boat the pickings from the countryside and the beaches had dwindled. Likewise any driftwood or washed-up coal or coke for the range; even the hedgerows had been stripped bare of twigs and blown-down branches and rotting logs.

All winter she'd comforted herself with the thought that things would be better once the warmer weather arrived. The lads could fish; there were cockles, mussels and shrimps to be had then too, along with crabs. Her mother had shown her how to clean and cook crabs and to be wary of their gills, which, being toxic, could kill. She'd refused to dwell on the inescapable truth that the rest of the unemployed in the town would have the same idea. She had needed to keep her spirits up for her da. He'd been in a deep depression for months. On dole days when he had to stand in line with his hand out – as he put it – everyone in the house had learned to tread on eggshells. Ernie and Donald often visited the refuge in Villiers Street Institute, where the unemployed gathered to play cards or dominoes, but as the institute also served as a distribution centre for charity for the men, her da refused to go near it.

Lucy sighed softly. It was her birthday today, but all she felt was despondency and crushing guilt. The evening before, for the first time in her life, she'd argued with her da, and over the bread knife of all things. The knife was a good one with a fine carved handle, her parents had bought it when they were first wed, and she'd pawned it for a few pence. There'd been nothing in the house to eat besides a little flour and yeast and half a cup of dripping, and with the money she had bought four penn'orth of fatty bacon pieces, along with two big onions and a few carrots and turnips and some spotted potatoes that the grocer had thrown in for a 'scrappy pudding', as her mam had always called it, using some of the flour and most of the dripping for the crust. With the rest of the flour, a little dripping and the yeast she'd baked two loaves of bread. It was two days till dole day, but the food would have to be eked out till then.

She had given Ruby and John and the twins a mug of the hot water the pudding had been cooked in before they'd all sat down for the evening meal together, hoping it would fill the children's empty bellies a little. It had held the flavour of the pudding and it had wrenched her heart to see the way they had gulped it down, relishing every mouthful. All four looked pale and wan and had had constant coughs and colds during the winter. She didn't have to worry about keeping the twins quiet when her father was home any more; they rarely had the energy to play for more than an hour or two and were content to sit close to the warmth of the range. When Ruby and John were home from school they did their chores without complaint and then joined Flora and Bess by the fire. Lucy was often aware of four pairs of eyes in too-thin faces watching her as she worked.

She had torn one of the loaves into eatable chunks and spread each with the merest scraping of dripping and placed this in the middle of the table, before dividing half of the pudding onto eight plates and calling the family to dinner. Her father had no sooner seated himself at the head of the table when he'd pointed to the plate of bread. 'What's that?'

She'd stared at him, genuinely puzzled. 'Bread and dripping.'

He'd made an irritable sound in his throat. 'I know that, I'm not stupid. I'm askin' why it looks as though an animal's bin at it.'

Her nerves had been stretched to breaking point for weeks. She was always hungry; she often went without so that Ruby and John and the twins could eat, and the daily struggle to feed a family of eight out of nothing and find fuel for the range, which was their only source of warmth and means of cooking, had taken its toll. Ruby's coat had been hers, which she'd cut down to fit her sister, and she'd made do with her shawl when she had to leave the house all winter. She was at her wits' end; she couldn't sleep for worrying about what would become of them all, and her da was complaining about the *appearance* of the bread? Something snapped. 'I did the best I could without the bread knife,' she said, her tone one she had not used before. 'What does it matter how it looks, if it tastes all right?'

'Don't talk to me like that, m'girl.' Angry colour had flooded Walter's face. 'And where's the bread knife? It was here this mornin'.'

'I've pawned it.'

'*You what?*'

For once she wasn't intimidated or anxious to placate him. 'We needed to eat and the bread knife was the only thing of any value to pawn. I'll retrieve it as soon as I can.'

'You dared to do that without asking me?'

'When have you been interested in what I've pawned, or what I've had to do to provide food for us?' Lucy had now risen from her chair, her face as white as her father's was red. 'You don't say a word to me or anyone else for days. It's like the slump has only affected you, but it hasn't. We're all feeling the same, except we get on with it, whereas you—' She stopped, aware she had said far too much.

For a moment silence reigned, deep and heavy. She watched her father's eyes leave her and move over the rest of his family. They lingered longest on the twins. Flora and Bess had long since lost the plumpness of babyhood, their dark eyes too big for their small pinched faces, but he stared at them as though seeing them for the first time. Then he stood up and walked over to the food cupboard, opening it and gazing at the empty shelves for what seemed like a lifetime to Lucy, who was now awash with guilt. Then he turned, stony-faced, and reached for his cap. Stuffing it on his head, he left the house, ignoring her agonized 'Da, wait.'

And now it was morning and she was fifteen years old. Lucy stared up at the discoloured ceiling, which didn't look so bad in the dim dawn light filtering through the old, thin curtains. Flora was snuggled into her side, and next to her in the double bed Ruby was fast asleep with her arm round Bess.

Gently, so as not to disturb her sisters, Lucy carefully slid out of bed and pulled her petticoat and dress over her shift, shivering in the freezing air. Flora had instinctively burrowed into Ruby's body under the blankets, seeking the source of warmth like a tiny animal. One advantage of being crammed into the bed like sardines in a can was that they were rarely cold.

Pulling on her thick woollen stockings, which had been darned so many times she'd lost count, Lucy tiptoed out of the bedroom holding her boots in one hand. She had waited up for her father until gone two in the morning the night before, but he still hadn't returned home before she'd gone to bed. Ernie and Donald had kept her company until midnight, trying to reassure her that their da wouldn't do anything silly such as jumping off the Wear Bridge. More than one desperate Wearsider had taken this way out. Nevertheless, she was overwhelmed with relief when she saw him sitting staring into the glow of the fire as she entered the kitchen.

'Oh, Da, I'm sorry.' She flew to him and he stood up and drew her into his arms. 'I didn't mean it, I shouldn't have said what I did. It was stupid and—'

He stopped her gabble by putting a finger on her lips. 'Don't, lass,' he said quietly, 'Everything's goin' to be all right, I promise. Mebbe it needed somethin' like last night to open me eyes. These are different times we're living in, an' different laws apply. You either sink or you swim, that's the truth of it, an' no beggar's goin' to help you unless you help yourself. Right and wrong don't come into it no more.'

Lucy stepped back slightly and looked up into her father's tired face. This didn't sound like him. These were not his words.

'Here, lass.' He reached into his pocket and drew out some notes, stuffing them into her hand. 'Go an' buy the bairns some grub, good grub, all right? An' coal for the range and lamp oil. We're nearly out, did you know? There's nowt but a few drops left.'

'I know,' said Lucy dazedly, looking down at the money. Raising her eyes to his, she murmured, 'Where's this come from, Da? What have you done?' He looked so much older this morning and it frightened her.

'Done?' He gave a strange bark of a laugh. 'I've done nothin' yet. This is on account, as you might say. There's a little job me an' the lads'll do tonight, lass, but I'll say no more about it. For now' – he flexed his shoulders – 'I'm goin' to get some kip.'

'Da, please take this back to wherever you got it.' She caught his sleeve. Whatever this job was, it wasn't legal if it had to be done at night and he wouldn't tell her any details. 'We'll manage, we will. I'm sorry for what I said, but I was tired, that's all. I shouldn't have taken the bread knife to the pawn without telling you.'

Walter put his rough callused hand over hers, but he was staring into the red coals of the fire again when he murmured, 'It was a bonny day when we bought that knife. We'd gone to the Michaelmas Fair on the old town moor, we'd only bin wed but a week or two. Your mam spotted it an' she said' – he shook his head, his eyes rheumy – 'she said it'd make the house a home, a fine bread knife. So I bought it for her, although it took every penny we had an' we couldn't go on any of the rides or buy a bag of chestnuts like we'd planned. But your mam didn't mind. I can see her now, walkin' round that fair clutchin' the knife wrapped in brown paper an' lookin' so beautiful she fair took my breath away.'

Lucy felt worse than ever. 'Oh, Da, I shouldn't have taken it.'

'No, hinny, no.' Walter came back to the present and

smiled gently at her. 'You did what you had to do, lass, that's all. An' it's time I started doin' the same, high time.'

'Da, this job—'

'No, lass.' He patted her hand resting under his. 'Ask no questions an' you'll be told no lies, cos it's better you don't know. That way, if owt should go wrong – not that it will, mind, but if it did – you can say hand on heart you knew nothin', all right? I'm off to me bed, but I wouldn't say no to a nice bit of cod when you go shoppin'.'

Lucy stood staring at the notes in her hand for a few minutes after her father had left the kitchen. She wasn't cold and yet she was shivering inside and it had caused a sickly feeling. Her da had been nice to her, the nicest he'd been in a long time, and yet she would have given the world to go back to yesterday before she had pawned her mother's bread knife. There was something about him this morning – she didn't know how to explain it to herself, except that he seemed smaller somehow, kind of defeated. She walked over to the deep stone sink set under the kitchen window and stared out into the back yard. The sky was low and grey and even as she watched, it began to rain, a solid icy sheet that came straight down and bounced on the stone slabs. She bent her head and began to cry soundless tears.

An hour or two later, when Ernie and Donald roused themselves, Lucy heard her father call them into the front room. When they eventually made an appearance in the kitchen they were as noncommittal as her father had been about the impending job and she could get nothing out of them. It remained the same for the rest of the day. She did the shopping and got the bread knife out of pawn, along with two or three other things, returning home to begin her housewifely duties, but with a heavy heart.

At six o'clock they all sat down to dinner – cod, as her father had requested, with plenty of mashed potatoes and vegetables and rice pudding to follow. The youngsters' eyes had nearly popped out of their heads when they'd seen this feast, and her father and Ernie and Donald had eaten with every appearance of enjoyment. Lucy had finished her food, but it had tasted like sawdust in her mouth. At seven o'clock she'd sent Ruby and John and the twins to bed, and at eight her father and the lads had left the house.

She was sitting with her head in her hands at the kitchen table when Jacob's knock came at the window. He came round most nights, ostensibly to play cards with Ernie and Donald, but she knew this wasn't the real reason, although nothing had been said. Lucy's heart leapt as it always did when she heard his rat-a-tat-tat.

On leaving school, Jacob had gone to work for the blacksmith in Southwick, with whom he'd had a Saturday job since he was a young lad, and although the pay was poor and the hours were long and hard he knew he was lucky in the present climate. Abe Williamson and his wife were childless and had always had a soft spot for him; furthermore Jacob always worked diligently and quickly, and stayed on when necessary until the job was done.

But tonight he had made sure he got away on time; it was Lucy's birthday.

She stood up when he entered the kitchen and he glanced round, saying, 'All alone?'

Lucy nodded, and he tried to keep the elation from showing on his face. It wasn't often he had her to himself; in fact he couldn't remember the last time. 'Happy birthday, Lucy,' he said softly, reaching into his jacket pocket and bringing out a small velvet box.

She stared at him, utterly taken aback. Everyone had forgotten it was her birthday, everyone except Jacob. 'You remembered.'

'Of course I remembered. Open it then.'

It wasn't so much what he said, but the look in his deep-brown eyes that made her blush. Shyly she took the little box and opened it. 'Oh,' she breathed. 'It's beautiful, Jacob. Really beautiful.' The thin silver chain with a tiny heart hanging from it was not of the best quality, but to Lucy it was the most exquisite necklace in the world.

'It's not much,' he said gruffly. 'By the time I've paid my board to Mam and what-have-you there's not much left and—'

'Jacob' – she put her hand on his arm – 'it's beautiful and I love it. Will you help me put it on?'

She turned after handing him the box, lifting up her thick plait so he could fasten the necklace in place.

Jacob gazed at the pure slender line of her neck, white against the burnished brown of her hair, and his heart began to hammer in his chest. He felt all fingers and thumbs as he struggled with the tiny clasp of the chain. Her soft skin was warm and silky as his fingers brushed it, and his mouth was dry by the time he'd mastered the delicate little catch.

The heart lay snugly in the hollow of her throat and she put her hand to it as she turned, saying, 'Thank you, Jacob. I'll wear it always, but you shouldn't have spent your hard-earned money on me.'

He wanted to say he would buy her the moon if he could, that nothing was too good for her, that she was the most beautiful girl in the world, but her eyes playing over his face made him drunk with feeling and no words came. Instead he drew her to him, gently, worshipfully, and did what he'd ached to do for a long time. The kiss was sweet and as he felt her lips, tightly closed, beneath his, he began to tremble inside. For a mad moment he wanted to crush her to him, but not wanting to frighten her he controlled himself. Raising his head, he said softly, 'I love you, Lucy. I always have.'

When she made no reply, but blinked her eyelids rapidly, he kissed her again; the reward for his forbearance in the fact that her lips were not as tight as before.

She smiled as his lips left hers and he stood looking down at her, her voice breathless when she said, 'I – I love you too.' It was the first time she had been kissed on the mouth by anyone. They rarely kissed as a family and, if they did, it was always on the cheek. She had liked it and she'd liked being in Jacob's arms. In the last two years he had shot up and now he was a full head taller than her. His work in the blacksmith's forge had developed his chest and arms, his muscles as powerful as those of any of the wrestlers in the travelling fairs.

He took her hands in his, drawing them to his chest, his eyes and mouth smiling. 'I've been waiting until you were fifteen,' he said, and it didn't strike either of them as strange that he was talking as though he was a full-grown man rather than a youth who'd only had his own fifteenth birthday a few weeks before. 'I want to ask your da if we can start courting now. What do you think?'

She had dreamt about this moment, prayed it would happen, but now the mention of her da brought back the worry.

'What's the matter?'

Seeing the look on his face, she said hastily, 'I want to, of course I want to; it isn't that, but Da and the lads have gone on a job and I don't know when they'll be back. And—'

'What?' He was still holding her hands.

'I've got a feeling on me, a bad feeling. Oh' – she shook her head – 'I'm being silly, that's all.' Pulling her fingers free, she shook her head again. 'I'm tired, I suppose. I didn't get much sleep last night. There was a' – she shrugged her shoulders – 'not a row exactly, but me an' Da had words about the bread knife.'

'The bread knife?'

Now a smile touched her lips for a moment at his tone. She made a pot of tea while she told him what had transpired, bringing out the fruit cake she'd baked that afternoon and cutting Jacob a generous slice as she poured out her fears and concern along with the tea.

'Don't worry, Lucy.' Sensing a need for reassurance rather than more kisses, Jacob reconciled himself to the fact with good grace. Now things were out in the open, they had all the time in the world after all. 'I'll keep you company till they get back, all right? An' don't put too much store by this "feeling", either. Mam has plenty of those, and nine times out of ten they're nowt.'

But what if this was the tenth time?

Lucy's face must have spoken for itself because Jacob reached across the table, taking her hand in his. 'Didn't they tell you anything about this job?'

'Nothing apart from it's better that I don't know.'

Jacob kept his expression noncommittal, but his mind was racing. He was suddenly sure Tom was behind this, although he wasn't about to say that to Lucy. Tom had been looking for a way to inveigle himself into Lucy's family for years and he knew why. Oh aye, he knew why, all right. He looked into Lucy's lovely face and his guts twisted. He'd see Tom dead before he'd let him lay a hand on her. His brother thought himself the big 'I am' with his fine house on The Green in Southwick, and he certainly had his da and the others licking his boots, but underneath the gentlemanly exterior that Tom liked to project these days he was still the same vicious, conniving bully he'd always been.

Becoming aware Lucy was waiting for him to say something, he forced a smile. 'Everyone's doing a bit on the side these days to get through, and your da and the lads are big enough and ugly enough to look after themselves. They'll be all right.'

'You're not. Doing a bit on the side, I mean.'

'No. Well, perhaps I'm the stupid one.'

'I don't think you're stupid,' she said softly.

'Oh, Lucy.' Forgetting his noble intentions of a minute or so before, Jacob stood up and moved round the table, taking her into his arms for the second time. When he felt her return the kiss he pulled her closer and they stood swaying together in the dim light from the oil lamp for endless moments.

It was Jacob who broke the embrace. He was finding that although the spirit was willing, the flesh was weak, and a certain part of his anatomy had a mind of its own. Fighting against the desire that threatened to make him lose control, he raised his head and took a step backwards, catching hold of her hand as he did so. 'It's a beautiful evening. Come and look at the stars.'

'The stars?'

'Aye, come on.' He took her shawl from the back of a chair and wrapped it round her shoulders before pulling her into the scullery and opening the back door. The rain of the morning had cleared and now the sky was high and devoid of the merest cloud, a sharp frost already scattering the flagstones with diamond dust, and the blackness above alive with twinkling stars and a crystal-clear white moon.

'Grand, isn't it?' Jacob kept his arm round her. 'When

I can't sleep I spend hours looking at the sky. That's the Milky Way up there – see that faint band of stars spanning the sky? And there's hundreds of millions of stars in the universe; even the sun is a star, although people think it's a planet, whereas a shooting star isn't a star at all, but dust particles that get burned up in the atmosphere.'

Lucy stared at him, amazed. 'How do you know all this?'

He grinned sheepishly. 'I bought myself a book about astronomy a while back. I was never much of a reader at school, but I like to find out about things. I got Jules Verne's book *From the Earth to the Moon* out of the library, and I reckon one day people will go into space for real in a rocket. There's men who've been looking at liquid-fuelled rockets for years and—' He broke off, smiling at the expression on her face. 'You don't believe me.'

Lucy looked up into the velvet-black sky. 'It's not that I don't believe you exactly, but . . .'

'Would our grandparents have ever dreamt men would build aeroplanes that would fly, but it's happening.' He was glad he'd taken her mind off her father and brothers for a few minutes. 'And now the talkies have come in at the pictures, and more and more folk are getting a wireless in their homes.' He paused again – this was a sore point. Tom had made a great show of buying his mam and da a wireless for Christmas, and his mam was over the moon. Not that he begrudged his mother the pleasure the set gave her; it was just galling to have Tom held up as akin to God Almighty.

As though his thoughts had conjured it into being, he became aware of the strains of 'Among My Souvenirs', a hit of the previous year, filtering out from next door. He glanced down at Lucy. She looked tired and he knew she was thinking of her father and brothers again. The back yards were still and quiet, everyone was indoors on such a cold and frosty night, but the moonlight cast a silvery glow that injected magic into the air. Acting on an impulse that later amazed him when he thought about it, he turned her round to face him. 'May I request the pleasure of this dance?'

Before she had time to answer, he took her into his arms and began to whirl her round the yard, one arm at her waist and his other hand holding hers.

Lucy gazed up into Jacob's face, and she was laughing. It seemed as though they both had two left feet. But then, as Jacob grinned at her, they began to flow into a natural rhythm and she felt as though she was floating as her laughter died away.

The crisp cold air, the warmth of Jacob's breath on her face, the thrill of being held in his arms after all the times she'd imagined what it would be like, and not least the way his dark eyes were devouring her and sending the blood coursing through her veins – all this caused a strange kind of happiness that was almost painful.

She wouldn't be able to bear it if anything should happen to separate them, she told herself dazedly. If he stopped loving her, she'd never love anyone else. But this was Jacob; he'd told her he loved her and he wanted her to be his lass. They were meant to be together. Feeling the way they did, nothing could come between them . . .

In the back lane beyond the yards and concealed by the privy next door, a pair of burning eyes stared at the couple dancing in the moonlight.

Tom Crawford had thought he'd timed his visit perfectly. When Walter Fallow had come to him cap in hand the night before, he'd barely been able to conceal his delight.

Lucy's father begging him to put some work his way. He'd long since given up hoping that day would come, in spite of the way the family had struggled over the last couple of years. Walter was as stubborn as a donkey and try as he might – and he had tried, over and over – he'd been unable to persuade the brothers to go against the father. But now he'd been handed entry into the Fallow household on a plate, or he thought he had.

He ground his teeth, his hands clenched into fists at his side, as he watched Lucy in Jacob's arms.

With the father and brothers in the palm of his hand, he'd known Lucy would do as she was told, and he didn't intend to play silly beggars, either. No, he'd do it the right way with Lucy because she was the one he'd chosen as his wife and the mother of his children. She stood out from the other lasses in these parts like a rose on a dung hill, and her shyness and the way she kept herself to herself had only increased his determination to have her. He could think of any number of lasses who'd jump at the chance to become Mrs Tom Crawford, but none of them could hold a candle to Lucy. When he rose to where he wanted to be in this town, she had the beauty and natural grace to rise with him and not be an embarrassment.

He'd come here tonight to start the process without her father and brothers looking on. He'd intended to charm her and begin paving the way. He'd been patient, the devil knows he'd been patient.

He heard Jacob murmur something or other and then Lucy's breathless laugh, and it was all he could do not to leap out at them. He'd always known Jacob liked her, but he'd thought she had more about her than to bother with his pipsqueak of a brother, looking like she did. But then Jacob had changed. Tom's gaze narrowed. It had been more than twelve months since he'd laid eyes on his youngest brother. When he called to see his mother it tended to be a morning visit, for his business in the docks and brothels and gambling establishments mostly took place later in the day and evenings. At fifteen, Jacob had the appearance of a fully grown man, and the way he was holding Lucy had none of the fumbling awkwardness of a callow youth.

He'd kill him. Tom's fingers curled as though they were already fastened round Jacob's throat. Unbeknown to him, he mirrored Jacob's earlier thought. He'd kill him before he'd let him have her.

They were still dancing when Tom merged into the black shadows on the far side of the back lane, walking swiftly and silently on the frozen ground until he reached the street. The lamplighter had been at work and, as Tom stood for a moment to catch his breath, a cat scurried through the dim light cast by the street lamp, carrying a dead rat in its mouth.

He stared after the animal, pulling the collar of his expensive greatcoat up round his neck and adjusting the fine cashmere scarf tucked round his throat. Jacob might think he'd been clever, but in a contest between the two of them his brother had as much chance of surviving as that rat. He'd see his day with Jacob, and in the none-too-distant future. Things were going his way with the Fallows at long last and he didn't intend anything – or anyone – to get in his way.

Chapter Six

Walter's arms felt as though they'd been torn out of their sockets, his neck and shoulder muscles were strained and burning and his back was breaking, and they still had more crates to unload and carry to the waggon waiting out of sight in one of the alleys close to the wharf. He bent and fiddled with the cord that bound his trousers below the knee to gain himself a few moments, straightening again with difficulty.

Damn it, but he was feeling his age. Once upon a time he could have done what was expected of him tonight as easy as winking, but he simply couldn't drum up the strength or wherewithal now. He looked to where Ernie and Donald and another lad Tom Crawford had got in for the job were manhandling a large, cumbersome wooden crate onto the dock and sighed heavily. The others were young and strong – that was what was needed here, and they knew that as well as he did, although no one had said. Tom had explained the night before that he paid on tonnage for the unloading and it would be split four ways, but the others weren't getting a square deal with him. He had to go and do his bit, but he didn't know how he was going to put one foot in front of the other.

Ernie glanced at his father as Walter emerged from the shadows where he'd supposedly gone to relieve himself. His da wasn't fooling anyone. He was done in, but Ernie knew better than to suggest it. 'All right, Da?'

'Aye, lad.'

The very quietness of his father's voice was an indication of how he was feeling. It prompted Ernie to say, 'You can see why they use the crane for these jobs. Them crates were never meant to be unloaded by hand.'

No, they weren't, but then they weren't meant to be knocked off, either, Walter thought wryly. But Tom Crawford was a cunning blighter, he'd give him that. He never swiped an entire hold of stuff, just enough so that when the gaffer Tom had got in his pocket said there'd been an accident when they were unloading and some crates had been smashed up and lost, it wasn't queried. And he chose the 'accidents' carefully so that no one owner was hit too often and got suspicious. Maurice Banks, the lad who was working with them, had been filling them in about Tom Crawford and with a certain amount of respect too. It was clear Tom was held in awe and not a little fear, but then anyone who was pally with the Kane brothers would be treated that way.

The sickness in Walter's belly, which had begun earlier that night when he'd realized what he'd let his sons in for, mounted. He had spent his entire life bringing them up as decent law-abiding citizens, and one night had wiped it away because – again as the lad had told them – once you were working for Tom Crawford you didn't walk away. Donald had laughed when he'd heard that and the lad had rounded on him, proceeding to tell a couple of stories to illustrate his point, which had made their hair curl.

Tom Crawford was more than a racketeer. Walter's face was as grim as his thoughts as he followed the other three onto the boat again and down into the crammed hold. Tom was a gangster, like that bloke in America who'd been in the papers recently. Al Capone. He stumbled, exhaustion making him clumsy.

'Da, why don't you go and keep watch on the dock?'

Ernie tried to keep the concern and pity out of his voice, but some must have got through because Walter glared at him. 'I thought he' – Walter jerked his head towards Maurice Banks, who was standing with Donald – 'said the night watchman that Tom's got on the payroll is doing that?'

'Aye, he is, but two pairs of eyes are always better than one, and I thought . . .' Ernie's voice trailed away. If looks could kill, his father's would have him six feet under. 'Let's get on with it then,' he said, nodding to the other two to get the opposite side of the crate as he and Walter positioned themselves. The container was the top one of three and shoulder-height. They began to lever it so that all four men could support the weight – like coffin-bearers, as Donald had joked earlier with dark humour.

It happened in a moment. As Walter took his full share of the weight his trembling knees buckled and he staggered. The container tipped and then toppled at an angle, smashing down on his head with sickening force. Ernie was sent flying backwards, but not far enough to save his lower torso and legs.

Donald froze for a second and then sprang forward. It was immediately clear his father was dead. Walter's crushed skull, from which his brains were protruding, caused the bile to rise in his son's throat. Ernie was panting high-pitched, animal-like whimpers, his lips drawn back from his teeth.

'We've got to get this off him.' Donald clawed and heaved at the crate along with Maurice, who was swearing profusely, but they couldn't move it. After a few fruitless moments, Donald knelt down and cradled his brother's head in his hands. 'Go and get someone,' he panted to Maurice. 'An' quick. We can't lift it by ourselves.'

'Tom'll go mad.' Maurice was as white as a sheet as he gazed at Donald with terrified eyes. 'He don't like no mistakes. It was your da's fault, he weren't up to it. You an' your brother should never have brought him along.' Now it was Donald who swore, causing Maurice to back away as he muttered, 'All right, all right, I'm goin'.'

'Don?' An ever-spreading pool of red was seeping out from beneath Ernie's broken body. 'D-Da?'

'Da'll be all right, an' so will you.' Donald couldn't believe how much blood there was. 'Maurice has gone to get help. Just lie still.'

'I'm d-dying, man.' Ernie reached out blindly to his brother. 'Oh God – God, help me.'

'You're not dying, I won't let you. Just hang on and we'll get this off you. Ernie, man, can you hear me? Don't give up.' As Ernie gave a long, choked cry, straining upwards, the sinews in his neck bulging, Donald glanced about him desperately. And then his brother went limp in his arms, his head lolling, and there was nothing but a deathly silence.

At eleven o'clock when her father and brothers still hadn't returned, Lucy sent Jacob home. She told him she was tired and wanted to go to bed.

Once he had gone, she tidied the kitchen and put a pan of porridge to soak for breakfast. She banked down the fire with damp slack and tea leaves and then settled herself at the table with a pile of mending. She'd lied to Jacob. She had no intention of going upstairs until the menfolk were home, but her father would throw a blue fit if he came back to find Jacob keeping her company after a respectable hour. And she didn't want her da to spoil what had been a magical evening.

She sat darning socks, which were more holes than wool, her mind going over every word she and Jacob had exchanged. Every look, every touch, every kiss. When they'd come in from the yard, he'd been very proper. She smiled, hugging the memory. They had sat drinking tea and chatting. Jacob had told her funny stories about the smithy and the things that went on among the customers.

He could always make her laugh. She didn't know if half of the stories were true – especially the one about a farmer's wife who was a little queer in the head and had a pony called Buttercup, which she insisted was a reincarnation of her late mother – but that didn't matter. She just loved being with Jacob. She smiled again, her thick darning needle flying in and out as she pictured his face and the look in his dark eyes when he smiled at her.

By three o'clock in the morning, however, the last remnants of enchantment had long since melted away. Lucy paced the floor, beside herself with worry. Surely they should be home by now? Then again, how could she tell? It had been stupid and cruel for her da to keep her in the dark about the night's happenings the way he had, and she would tell him so when he got back. Never mind the ruckus that would cause. She wasn't a little bairn who couldn't be trusted to keep her mouth shut. She'd been doing the work of a woman for years and should be treated accordingly.

The minutes ticked by. When the wooden clock on the kitchen mantelpiece chimed four o'clock the anger Lucy had drummed up to combat the fear was gone. She was sitting with her arms crossed at her waist as she swayed back and forth, when she heard the latch on the back door. Relief made her feel faint. She had to hold onto the back of the chair as she stood up.

The scullery door opened and Donald stood there. She stared at him. His clothes were covered in blood and she froze. His hands hung slack at his sides and his face was chalk-white, but it was the look in his eyes that terrified her. She moved her head from side to side several times before she could say, 'Da and Ernie? Where are they?'

He didn't speak and she was conscious of the ticking of the clock on the kitchen mantelpiece, although she hadn't been aware of the sound earlier. Again she said, 'Da and Ernie, where are they?'

'There was an accident.'

It was a whisper, so faint she could barely hear him. For the third time she said, 'Where are they? In the hospital, is that it? What kind of accident, Don? Are they badly hurt? Are you hurt?'

Her voice had risen and Donald reached out to her, holding her against him. 'I'm all right, but it – it's bad, Lucy.'

Her legs felt weak and she clutched him. She could smell the blood. 'How bad?'

'They're gone, lass. There was nothing I could do.'

'*No*.' She tried to free herself, but he wouldn't let her pull away. 'No, no, it's not true. They were all right when they left here. You're lying.'

'I wish I was. I wish this night had never happened.' His voice broke. 'We were unloading some crates when it happened. I think it was too heavy for Da, and he fell and it got Ernie too.'

She fought him in earnest then, but he held her tight until the storm broke and she collapsed against him, her strength gone.

A long time later, when they were both cried out, they

sat together at the kitchen table and she said dully, 'Tell me. Tell me everything. *Everything*, mind. I want to know.'

Donald bowed his head and began to speak. His voice was quivering and every so often a sob would break through and he had to pause before he could go on.

'I want to see them.' The silence had stretched for some minutes after Donald had finished. 'Now, Don. I must.'

He took in a deep breath before he answered, 'No – remember them as they were, Lucy. It's what Da would have wanted.'

'I don't care. This is my fault. If I hadn't pawned the bread knife none of this would have happened. I have to see them. To – to say I'm sorry.' She gasped against the pain. 'I won't make a scene, I promise, but I have to see them one last time.'

He turned his gaze from her, his head drooping. 'You can't, lass.'

'I can. Please, I must.'

'No, I mean – I mean—'

'What do you mean?' They stared at each other and now she said softly, 'It's all right, don't look like that. What do you mean?', thinking he was losing his mind, if the look in his eyes was anything to go by.

'We – we couldn't leave them there, in the hold. They got Tom, and he said everything had to look normal, so no one would know anything had been taken. He – he had some of his lackeys with him and there was no arguing the toss, he was spitting bricks as it was. There couldn't be any trace of anything, that's what he said.'

She sat as still as stone.

'Bodies are found in the water all the time,' Donald murmured wretchedly. 'There's always fights down at the docks after closing time. It – it was for the best, lass.'

'That's what Tom said, is it?' Her voice rose. 'How could you let him do that to Da and Ernie?'

'I didn't want to.'

There was no defensiveness in his tone, merely misery, and it was this that made her say quickly, 'I know, I know, I'm not blaming you. It's me. Oh, Don, I can't bear it.' The tears were streaming down her face again. 'What are we going to do?'

'Nothing. Tom said we do nothing. He's got a couple of blokes who'll swear blind they saw Da and Ernie drinking in one of the riverside pubs, and a landlord who'll back 'em up and say Da and Ernie were the worse for wear when they left. The coppers will make a few enquiries, but they're not going to be bothered about a couple of men on the dole who had one too many and either got into a fight or fell into the dock in the dark. The working class is expendable.'

The bitterness was palpable, and it struck Lucy that her brother seemed a different person from the young man who'd left the house just a few hours earlier, joking and laughing with Ernie. Staring at him, she wiped her face with the back of her hand and tried to think. She'd remembered that Jacob knew her da and the lads had been out together. 'Jacob was here.'

'Jacob? You didn't tell him anything?'

'Just – just that you were out together on some kind of job.'

Donald groaned. 'You shouldn't have. Is that all you said, nothing more?'

'I didn't *know* anything more.'

'Listen to me, Lucy.' Donald licked his lips, his face ashen. 'You can't tell anyone about this job, and especially not about Tom. Do you understand? He'd kill me if word got out. I mean it.'

'But Jacob—'

'*No one*. I'll go and see Jacob. I'll say Da had heard about some work and we had to meet a bloke in a pub, but he never turned up. I'll make out I left Da and Ernie drinking and I came home cos of a gippy tummy. What time did Jacob leave here?'

'Eleven.' In response to his frown, she added, 'I was worried, and he was telling me stories about the smithy and his work to take my mind off things.' A sob caught in her throat. 'I *knew* something was wrong.'

'All right, all right. I'll say I got in about ten past, and Lucy' – he leaned across the table and gripped her forearms – 'you have to say the same, even to Jacob. You can't mention Tom or anything about tonight.'

'Let me go, you're hurting me.' She shook off his hands, frightened by the look on his face.

Donald leaned back in his chair, his voice grim. 'That's nothing to what Tom'll do to me, if any word of this gets out. Believe me.'

Chapter Seven

Jacob stood silent and still in the misty cold drizzle of the April night. His gaze was focused on the substantial square-windowed house in front of him on the north side of The Green in Southwick. A four-foot-high stone wall and small front garden separated the house from the wide pavement, and the general air of this part of Southwick was one of prosperity. He had watched the churchgoers who had attended a Rechabite meeting in the hall at the back of the Wesleyan church further along The Green disperse a short while ago and now all was quiet, as befitted a rainy Sunday night. He had been standing for over an hour in the rain, which had slowly penetrated his jacket through to his shirt and vest, but he wasn't conscious of the cold. His whole being was tied up with the coming confrontation with Tom.

A motor car came trundling along the street and he tensed, every muscle alert, but it continued on its way without stopping and soon the quiet was absolute once again.

It had been the housekeeper who had answered his knock at the door an hour before. Tom's housekeeper. Jacob's lip curled. They'd heard of nothing else for weeks when Tom had first told their mam he'd got a housekeeper. His mother had seemed to think it was the height of success and she'd rammed the fact down their throats, until even his da had had enough and told her to put a sock in it. But the woman who'd told him Tom was out and wouldn't be home for an hour or two had seemed a nice enough soul, with her rosy-red cheeks and tightly curled grey hair and wide smile. Not what he'd expected somehow. He'd imagined a shrewd, hard-faced worldly type, but thinking about it, he should have known Tom would choose someone to support his stance of respectability.

It was another thirty minutes before a tall figure with a large black umbrella came into view and even from a distance Jacob knew immediately it was Tom. It was the arrogance of the walk.

He moved out of the shadows and crossed the road, watching his brother approach. There was one moment when the imperious footsteps faltered – presumably when Tom recognized him – but by the time his brother reached him Tom was perfectly in control. 'Jacob.' The tone was one of amused condescension. 'You look like a drowned rat.'

Don't let him rile you, don't give him the satisfaction. 'I want a word with you. In private.'

'By all means, but I've no intention of standing out

here. Come inside. I'm sure Mrs Hedley will forgive you for dripping all over her nice clean floor.'

Without waiting for an answer Tom opened the garden gate and walked to the front door, opening it with a key. This alone brought home to Jacob the different lives they led. No one in his street locked doors; none of them had anything worth stealing, for a start, but it just wouldn't have occurred to them.

He stood hesitating for a moment. He hadn't wanted to go into the house. Not just because he didn't want the possibility of the housekeeper overhearing their conversation, but because he knew his brother would take a secret satisfaction in being able to show off his standard of living. The rest of the family had visited on occasion and he had been included in the invitation to the lavish New Year's Eve party that Tom had held, but he had stayed away. He'd got it in the neck from his mam in the days leading up to the party, but he hadn't budged. Now, though, it would seem he had no option.

Tom was taking off his hat and coat as Jacob followed him into what was a spacious but dark hall, the wood panelling such a dark brown as to be almost black. He watched his brother sling his hat onto the marble-and-gilt hallstand and hand his coat to the housekeeper, who had come hurrying through. 'This is my brother, Jacob, Mrs Hedley. As you can see, he's a little wet. Could you take his things to dry in front of the range before you bring a tray through to the drawing room?'

'I'm not stopping.' Jacob stood awkwardly, aware of the pool of water at his feet, his shabby jacket and wet trousers, and his big hobnailed boots. Tom, on the other hand, was dressed like the well-to-do businessman he now purported to be. 'I'll keep me things on, thank you very much.' It sounded crass, but he couldn't help that.

Tom shrugged. 'As you like.' He turned and opened a door and, as Jacob followed him into the drawing room, he had to stop himself gaping. From the long velvet drapes at the two windows to the fine pieces of furniture dotted about, it was clear no expense had been spared. The heavily patterned carpet in varying shades of red and blue stretched to the four corners of the room and the blazing fire in the ornate fireplace glinted on the gold-framed picture above the mantelpiece. There were other paintings adorning the walls and a cabriole-legged display cabinet held several delicate pieces of porcelain in the space between the two bay windows.

Tom walked across to the fire, turning and lifting up the bottom of his suit jacket as he warmed his backside, his feet slightly apart as he looked at his brother, brows raised. 'So?'

Tom had put on some weight; it added to his prosperous air. Clearing his mind, Jacob said, 'I need to talk to you.'

'Aye, so you said. About what?'

'You've heard Lucy's da and brother were found yesterday, I suppose? They fished them out of the docks.'

Tom's expression became grave. 'Bad business. How's she taking it?'

Ignoring this, Jacob said, 'What do you know about it?'

'Me? Same as you, I should think. Mam said they'd been drinking and left some pub or other three sheets to the wind.'

'They weren't drinking. They were on a job.'

Tom straightened. 'Oh aye? Who told you that?'

'I was round at Lucy's the night they went missing and she said her da and the lads had got some work, but they wouldn't tell her what it was. She was worried, as well she might have been, as it's turned out.'

Mrs Hedley knocked and came bustling in with a tray of coffee and there was silence until she had left after pouring two cups. Tom gestured to the tray. 'Help yourself. I always have a tot of brandy in mine at this time of night. Care to join me?'

'They were working for you that night, weren't they,' Jacob said with quiet certainty. 'This thing stinks of you.'

'Me? Don't be barmy. Walter wasn't pally with me, as well you know, and I thought you just said Lucy was worried about the three of them? Well, Donald's alive and kicking, isn't he? And according to Mam, he told the law he'd left them in the pub after some fella didn't turn up. Why would he say that if it isn't true?'

'Cos he's scared witless.' Jacob had remained standing just inside the room, but now he walked up to his brother until they were eyeball-to-eyeball. 'Of you.'

It was Tom who broke the stare, ostensibly to reach for the decanter of brandy next to the coffee tray. He poured a measure of the spirit into his coffee cup and then sat down in one of the elaborately upholstered chairs the room held. He stretched out his legs in front of him and took a long swallow of the coffee, smacking his lips as he finished. 'I know we've never got on, but don't you think this is taking your dislike of me a little too far, baby brother? Accusations like the one you've just made should come with proof or they could be very dangerous indeed.'

Jacob breathed out slowly. 'For me or for you?'

Tom didn't speak for some moments, but when he raised his head and looked at him, Jacob found himself thinking: He's sold his soul to the devil, that's what he's done; because there was something straight from the pit staring out of Tom's eyes. When Tom spoke, his words came slow and deep: 'You dare to threaten me in my own home? You're scum and you'll always remain scum, and do you know why? Because you're content to wallow in the gutter, that's why, like the rest of the herd. You try and bring me down and you'll wish you'd never been born, I promise you. No one crosses me and gets away with it. Now get out of my house.'

More shaken than he would care to admit, Jacob concentrated on hiding the fact. Men like Tom preyed on weakness. 'If there *is* proof you're involved, I'll find it,' he said quietly. 'And your threats don't frighten me. I intend to get to the bottom of this, for Lucy's sake, if nothing else.'

'Since when did you become her keeper?'

Jacob's chin lifted. 'We've got an understanding.'

'An understanding?' Tom laughed harshly. 'You think someone like you could hold a lass like that? Think again. You're old Williamson's skivvy, a nowt.'

Jacob held onto his temper, but there was a tightness in his jaw that was painful as he gritted his teeth. He wanted to wipe the smile off Tom's face. Although he knew he probably wouldn't win a fight with his brother, they were definitely better matched than they'd ever been in the past.

His mind was racing, warring with animal instinct.

But that was what Tom wanted him to do – to fight. It would give Tom the upper hand. It was the language he understood, that of might over right.

Slowly, deliberately, Jacob reined in the bloodlust. His voice deep in his throat, he said, 'I don't care a monkey's cuss what you think of me, I never have. I've known what you are from when I was a bairn. But for the record, Lucy and I love each other. And you're right on one thing: I'm not good enough for her, but I thank God she doesn't see it that way. So say what you want and be damned. And I'll keep digging about her da and Ernie. Someone, somewhere knows the truth.'

He had turned and reached the drawing-room door before the low growl halted him in his tracks. 'You'll never have her, boy. I'll make sure of it.'

Jacob only paused for an infinitesimal moment before quietly opening the door and as quietly shutting it behind him, but he could still hear the curses that followed him when he walked towards the front door, ignoring the housekeeper who came fluttering after him. Once outside in the cold fresh air, he stood for a second, breathing it in in great gulps to rid himself of the contamination of Tom's presence. Then he squared his shoulders and walked away.

Chapter Eight

'I won't let Tom Crawford pay for the funeral.' Lucy faced Donald, her face as white as lint and her hands clenched into fists. 'You can go straight back and tell him that.'

'Be reasonable, lass.' Donald's voice verged on tearful.

'*Reasonable?*' Lucy stared at him, this brother she felt she didn't know any more. At first she had put Donald's withdrawal and long silences down to shock at what he'd experienced. He and Ernie had always been close, only two years separating them, and she knew Donald had hero-worshipped his big brother, content to follow where Ernie had led. Now it seemed as though Donald's mainspring had snapped. And she felt sorry for him, she knew he was suffering too. That's why she had let him sit huddled in front of the range day after day, cloaked in a silence even the twins hadn't tried to penetrate.

Donald and Jacob had gone to the mortuary together to officially identify the bodies, both adamant that she remained at home. And she had agreed to this, mainly because the grim-faced policeman who had called at the house to tell them about Walter and Ernie had made it clear the identification would be harrowing. There had been some sort of an investigation, but the verdict had been that the two men had fallen into the docks while intoxicated and been crushed by one of the vessels in the water. Now the police had released the bodies for burial.

Lucy took a deep breath, lowering her voice as she said, 'It's not a matter of being reasonable, Donald. Tom Crawford is responsible for Da and Ernie dying, and you know that as well as I do, and I don't care how much you try and say different. And to do what he did afterwards, branding them as drunkards and throwing them in the—' She stopped abruptly, her throat filling. It was some moments before she could continue and, when she did, her voice was resolute. 'I don't want anything from him. We'll manage.' Somehow.

She turned back to the vegetables she was preparing for the rabbit broth they were having later that day for dinner. Jacob had dropped the rabbits in the night before, already cut into joints, and she had accepted them gratefully. The money Tom had given her father was gone and Donald's dole money didn't go far. They were weeks behind with the rent. The police investigation had delayed the funeral. It was now three weeks since her father and Ernie had died, but Lucy had used the time to sell the brass bed in the front room along with her father's and Ernie's Sunday suits and shirts. She had kept the proceeds to pay for the funeral. Even so, her father's and Ernie's send-off would be a poor affair and there would be no wake afterwards, not when the cupboards were bare of food and she didn't know where the next penny was coming from. If only Donald would look for work, or at the very least go beachcombing or hunting for rabbits or pigeons in the countryside. But no, he sat on his backside in front of the range with his head in his hands.

What were they going to do? Panic swept over her and she swallowed against the tightness in her throat. Jacob had tried to reassure her that Donald would pull himself together once the funeral was over, but she had sensed he didn't believe what he was saying. Neither did she. But she was praying it was so.

The joint service for Walter and his son was held a few days later on a sunny May morning that seemed to mock the family's grief. Whether it was the shadow of impropriety over the manner of the deaths that discouraged attendance or the absence of a wake, Lucy didn't know, but numbers were few. She didn't mind this. Several of Ernie's friends and a couple of her father's old pals were at the church, along with one or two neighbours, but everyone seemed awkward and uncomfortable. Lucy had insisted that she was present and Donald hadn't argued. Enid had stayed behind to look after Ruby, John and the twins, and Lucy stood between Donald and Jacob during the short service, but she was vitally aware of Tom Crawford the whole time. He stood with his father and other brothers in the opposite pew and barely took his eyes off her. He had called at the house twice since the night of the accident: the first time to offer his condolences, and the second when he offered to cover the expenses for the double funeral – a 'private arrangement' he had said. On both occasions Lucy had refused to see him and Donald had spoken to him at the door.

They emerged from the church into bright sunlight and followed the pallbearers to the gravesides. A hundred memories were burning in Lucy's mind of happier days, moments that had seemed unimportant at the time, but which now held a poignancy that made them unbearable. Her da tramping into the countryside to pick a bunch of wild flowers for her mam when she'd first got sick; Ernie spending umpteen evenings whittling a small carved wooden boat for John's birthday the year before and sitting up with her through one long night when Flora was delirous with a fever . . .

The clods of earth hit the coffins and she flinched visibly, glad of Jacob's solid bulk at the side of her. She knew exactly where Tom was standing. He had come up behind them as they had left the church and caught Donald's arm. The two men were now side by side some yards away, although a minute or two ago they'd been whispering together. For a brief moment she wondered what they had been discussing, then she told herself she didn't care.

Her fingers searched for and found the little silver heart nestled in the hollow of her throat and the token of Jacob's love warmed her for a moment, even as she wondered how two brothers could be so different. She found herself wishing she was a man, a big tough man with fists like hammers, so she could batter Tom Crawford into a pulp. She'd said those very words to Donald, and her brother had had a blue fit. He was scared to death of Tom, she accepted that now. Ernie had been a different kettle of fish from Donald; she hadn't realized that until the last three weeks, or appreciated how much she loved him, and her da too, of course. But it was too late to tell them. Were they with her mam now, reunited at last? Oh, she wished this day was over, this endless, terrible day.

Donald was longing for the same thing, although for different reasons. He had known Tom wouldn't leave him alone. Deep down he had been sure he was caught like a fish on a hook and sooner or later Tom would reel him in. Sure enough, Tom had made it clear he was on the payroll a minute ago. Tom had even made out he was doing him a favour when he'd mentioned the job he'd got arranged the following night, but they'd both known it was a warning that Donald toed the line or else.

Dammit, he didn't want to end up like his da and Ernie. Donald's tongue flicked at the film of perspiration on his upper lip, caused more by the man at his side than the hot sunshine. But what could he do? That night at the docks Maurice Banks had made it clear that no one said no to Tom Crawford. Some of the tales he'd told – he still couldn't sleep for thinking of them.

Donald shut his eyes and bowed his head as the vicar

began to intone the last prayer for the newly departed, but Donald's frantic prayers were for himself.

It was just gone ten o'clock in the evening that same day and Jacob was finishing work in the forge. He hadn't liked leaving Lucy at the churchyard earlier. He'd have preferred to see her home, but the blacksmith had been generous in giving him time off for a funeral that didn't involve a family member and he hadn't wanted to take advantage of the man's kindness, particularly as they were busy on an important job. One of the big houses on the edge of Castletown west of Southwick had commissioned a large number of iron railings, enough to enclose some half-acre of grounds, along with two fancy gates in an intricate design complete with the family crest. He'd promised Mr Williamson he'd stay late the next few evenings and for the last couple of hours they'd been working by lamplight. The blacksmith had disappeared into his cottage for his supper a little while ago, but Jacob had refused his employer's offer of a meal and bed for the night, on the grounds his mother would worry if he didn't go home. This was true enough, but the real reason was that he wanted to see Lucy if he could.

He'd finished clearing up and now he closed the gates to the forge. Stretching his aching back, he looked up into the black sky alive with twinkling stars. It was a bonny night.

The winding lane leading from the blacksmith's cottage and forge to the North Hylton Road was dark and full of dense shadow in the silvery moonlight, its thick fringe of trees and hedgerow scented with the sweetness of May blossom and bluebells. Jacob breathed in the cool air, its balmy fragrance soothing after the heat and smells of the forge, but his mind was on Lucy.

He had faced the fact that this latest blow to the Fallow family had caused a hiccup in his plans to court and marry her as soon as possible. There was no doubt now that when he and Lucy wed, he would be taking on a ready-made family comprising Ruby and John and the twins. Donald had gone to pieces; he couldn't be relied upon to take care of the little ones. But, somehow, he and Lucy would manage. She was a grand little housewife and an idea that had been brewing in the back of his mind for some time had taken shape over the last days. The blacksmith's cottage and forge were on a plot of land that included a dilapidated dwelling on the edge of it, an old tumbledown place close to the blacksmith's stables. At present it was used for storage and had mice and beetles aplenty, but the roof was sound enough. It would take time and effort to get it habitable, but once restored it would boast two good-sized bedrooms upstairs and a large living area downstairs. It would be a start. Later on he could build more rooms onto the back of it, but that would be in the future. He knew Mr Williamson would agree to the proposal when he put it to him, for his employer would see the benefits of having him living on the job as it were, and Dolly, his wife, would be tickled pink. She was a canny little body who loved bairns; her biggest regret was in having none of her own to mother and worry over. She and Lucy would get on like a house on fire.

Deep in his thoughts, he didn't sense the two dark shadows that detached themselves from the blackness on either side of the lane just behind him. The first he knew of their presence was when something struck him on the back of his head with enough force to fell him to the ground. He must have rolled over, because when a hob-nailed boot caught him under his jaw it seemed to snap his head from his body, a red mist exploding in his brain. After that he knew nothing about the two big men continuing to use their feet on him, laughing as they belted into him time and time again until, panting and sweating, they rolled him into a ditch at the side of the lane and unhurriedly walked away.

The silence of the night settled once more, the odd bird that had been sent squawking out of its roosting place quiet now, and only the hoot of an owl in the distance disturbing the peace. And some miles away in the house on The Green, Tom Crawford sat devising the next stage of his plan like a hungry spider in the middle of its sticky web.

Lucy awoke the following morning feeling more optimistic than she had for a long time. Donald would rally now, she knew he would, and Sid Chapman's son had taken her to one side on leaving the churchyard and told her that as far as it lay in his father's power, Mr Chapman would see to it that Donald was in line for some regular shifts at the shipyard. She hadn't had a chance to discuss it with her brother yesterday. Donald had left straight afterwards with some of his and Ernie's pals who had come to the funeral, returning at teatime for a bite, whereupon he'd gone out again, but she knew he'd be pleased. And the twins started school in September. With them off her hands for most of the day, it meant she could look for work doing some cooking and cleaning, or even taking in washing. Her da had gone through the roof when she had mentioned taking in washing before, but he wasn't here now and needs must. It didn't pay much, no women's work paid much, but every penny would help. And maybe, if Donald was willing, they could take in a lodger now that the front room was empty. They could move what had been her mam's bed down from the boys' room and she could put a table and chair in there.

Dressing quickly, she made her way downstairs, glad the dark and bitterly cold winter mornings had given way at long last. It had been a harsh few months in many ways and she would give anything to turn back the clock to before she'd pawned the bread knife and have her da and Ernie here, but she had the little ones to see to and thoughts like that were weakening.

She saw the note as soon as she entered the kitchen. It was scrawled on a scrap of brown paper, which was propped against the teapot in the middle of the table.

Lucy's stomach turned over as she recognized Donald's handwriting. Sitting down, she began to read:

Dear Lucy,

By the time you read this I'll be long gone. If I
stay, it'd mean working for Crawford and I'd rather
take my chance down south than end up six foot
under like Da and Ernie. You can put the bairns
in the workhouse, where they'll be fed and looked
after, it's the only way, lass. You'll be all right,
there's always jobs going for live-in helps and such.
Mark Baxter's sister got took on just the other week
and you know how dim she is. You've got to look
out for number one now, and in time you'll see I'm
doing you a favour and this is all for the best. So
long and look after yourself.

Love, Donald

He'd left them. She moved her head slowly from side to
side, beyond tears as she read the note again. Without
talking to her, without saying goodbye face-to-face. How
could he? And to suggest putting the little ones in the
workhouse.

Nausea rose into her throat and she had to swallow
hard. He must have lost his mind; all this with their da
and Ernie, and Donald seeing it happen had turned his
brain. But it was more than that.

She screwed the paper into a tight ball in her fist.

It was him: Tom Crawford. He'd driven Donald away.
What had he said to her brother yesterday to make him
abandon them?

How long she sat there she didn't know, but when a

knock came at the back door and Enid's voice called, 'Lucy? Lucy, lass? Are you there?' her limbs felt as stiff as an old woman's as she stood up. The moment Enid thrust open the door from the scullery, she said, 'Have you seen him? Our Jacob?'

'Jacob?' Lucy stared at Enid as she tried to marshal her thoughts. 'I saw him yesterday, Mrs Crawford. At the funeral.'

'He hasn't been home all night, his bed hasn't been slept in. I knew he was going to be late cos he'd said he'd be making up a bit of time, what with the funeral and all, and he'd said to leave him something cold under a plate if he wasn't back afore we went to bed. But it's still there, on the table. Where's your Donald? He might know something.'

Lucy had never seen her mother's old friend in such a state. Gently she said, 'If he was working late, he could have eaten with the blacksmith and his wife – you know how fond of him they are, and likely they've put him up for the night.'

Enid stared at her and then let out her breath in a sigh of relief. 'Oh aye, lass, why didn't I think of that? Aye, that could be it, though it's not like our Jake to do something that might worry us. I'll clip his ear when I see him, big as he is. I'll get our Frank or Ralph to take him a bite for his lunch a bit later just to be sure, but when your Donald's up ask him if he knows anything anyway, will you, though I suspect you've hit the nail on the head.'

Lucy nodded, but said nothing. She didn't want to explain about Donald yet, not until she'd had time to think about it and tell Ruby and the others. And now there was the added worry about Jacob, although she felt sure he'd done exactly what she had said and stayed with the blacksmith and his wife. There had been another occasion near Christmas last year when he and the blacksmith had worked till midnight and they'd tried to persuade Jacob to stay, although in the end he had tramped home and got soaking wet and chilled to the bone, which had resulted in a feverish cold. She had made him promise he wouldn't be so silly again.

Lucy said this now to Enid, adding, 'Don't worry, Mrs Crawford, Jacob will be all right. They've got this big job on at the forge, haven't they? Besides the normal work, I mean.'

'Aye, aye, they have, that's true enough.' Enid was looking more herself. 'I expect that's it. Well, my lot'll be shouting for their breakfast once they're up, so I'd better go and see to it, but I'll be round later, lass, with a bit of treacle toffee for the bairns. To cheer 'em up, like. They always like my treacle toffee, bless 'em.'

Lucy forced a smile. She felt numb. All the time she had been talking to Mrs Crawford it had felt like someone else speaking.

After Enid had left, Lucy went upstairs. She found Donald had taken every scrap of clothing he owned and any personal possessions, including the cut-throat razor he had shared with their father and Ernie. He had really gone for good. It was unbelievable, impossible, but it had happened.

Blindly she left the lads' bedroom where John was still curled up under the covers fast asleep. Stumbling down the stairs, she sat down at the kitchen table. Then, dropping her head onto her arms, she gave way to a paroxysm of weeping, which continued until Ruby woke up and came downstairs an hour later.

Chapter Nine

Jacob was found at eight o'clock that morning by a farmer bringing his shire horse to be shod at the smithy. Or rather, as the farmer had pointed out to the police, the lad had been discovered by his two sheepdogs, which had jumped off the back of the cart as they'd passed the ditch and continued to bark until their master had been forced to investigate.

Abe Williamson had identified Jacob by his clothes – the bluey-black, grossly swollen head was unrecognizable. Both the blacksmith and the farmer had thought Jacob was dead when they had first lifted him out of the ditch. It was Dolly Williamson who had knelt down on the ground and put her ear to the bloody chest and heard his faintly fluttering heart.

And now Jacob was in Sunderland Infirmary and not expected to last the day. It was an ashen-faced Frank who had come round to tell Lucy the news. The two constables who had called at the house had taken Enid and Aaron straight to the hospital.

Lucy stared at Jacob's brother, a thundering in her ears, and she must have looked like she felt, because he quickly pulled out a chair and made her sit down, squatting beside her and chafing her hands. 'I'm sorry, lass, but there was no easy way to say it. Take some deep breaths, that's right. Mam was the same when they told her.'

Because of all the upset that morning about Donald, Lucy had kept Ruby and John off school. She now looked at her sister and the others, who were staring wide-eyed at Frank, and said weakly, 'Go outside and play for a while till I call you, and don't get mucky, John. I mean it.' When the back door had closed behind them, she turned to Frank. 'Can I see him?'

'They won't let anyone in 'cept Mam and Dad, even me an' Ralph an' Tom.'

Lucy closed her eyes, rocking back and forth as the tears came. 'Who would do something like that, and why?'

'I don't know, lass. The coppers reckon someone might have been trying to pinch something from the forge and Jacob tried to stop 'em, but I can't see it meself. According to Abe Williamson, the forge gates were shut and nothing was missing, and anyway Jacob was in a ditch halfway up the lane. But some so-an'-so did a number on him all right. Look, I've got to go, but I'll let you know when he – when we know something.'

Lucy opened her eyes. Frank had been about to say he'd let her know when Jacob died, she knew he had. Feeling sick, she whispered, 'Thank you.'

'Will you be all right? Where's Donald? Shall I call him?'

'No, he – he's not here, but I'll be fine. You go, and tell your mam . . .' She stared helplessly at Frank, who nodded grimly and patted her hand. There were some things for which there were no words.

Somehow she got through the endless day. Yesterday had been Donald's dole day, but when she looked in the jar on the mantelpiece she found he had taken every penny. They had nothing to eat in the house and for a moment she felt like throwing a paddy like the twins did, screaming and crying and drumming her heels on the floor, as she gazed in the empty jar. Instead she went upstairs and stripped the double bed in the lads' room, gathering up the sheets along with the blankets and the eiderdown for winter, which was stored on top of the wardrobe. Parcelling the lot together on the kitchen table, she was aware of Ruby and John and the twins watching her silently, and when Ruby said protestingly, 'He might come back tonight or tomorrow' it took all Lucy's self-control to say quietly, 'He won't.'

'But he might, *you* don't know, and what'll he say if you've pawned everything? An' anyway' – Ruby's chin lifted belligerently – '*I* wanted to sleep in that bed; ours is too crowded, an' Flora and Bess are always kicking me.'

It was the last straw. Rounding on her sister, Lucy hissed, 'Do you want to eat tonight? *Do* you?' And at Ruby's sulky nod: 'Then get your backside down to old Lonnie's with that lot.'

'Me?' Ruby glared at her. 'I'm not going. You always go to the pawn.'

'Well, today you're going, madam.' She didn't want to be away from the house in case Frank came round.

'That's not *fair*.' Ruby stamped her foot. 'You're horrible, our Lucy. I don't blame Donald for going. I wish I could.'

Lucy's hand shot out and the sound of the slap echoed in the kitchen.

Ruby was so surprised that Lucy – gentle, sweet-tempered Lucy – had smacked her that for a moment or two she remained open-mouthed and unmoving. And her surprise was compounded when, instead of saying she was sorry, Lucy picked up the parcel of bedding and dumped it in her sister's arms. 'John will go with you,' she said tersely, 'and you can get some shopping on the way back with what Lonnie gives you.' She gave John a list and the basket. 'And you come straight home, no messing about.'

John hadn't said a word, but when Ruby flounced out of the kitchen he put his small hand on Lucy's arm for a moment before following Ruby into the back yard. The brief gesture of comfort was almost too much, but aware of the twins' big eyes on her, Lucy pulled herself together. A few weeks ago she had thought life was a struggle, but then she'd had her da and brothers, and Jacob had been fit and well. She hadn't known how lucky she was.

She caressed the little silver heart as she fought back the tears, the tangible link with Jacob infinitely precious now. He couldn't die, he couldn't, not her Jacob. She pictured him as he'd been the day before, so strong and tall, so alive, so *hers*. Now he was fighting for his life and she wasn't even allowed to go to him. She couldn't bear it. And Donald was gone, their only means of support. Her world had fragmented and she didn't know what to do.

Ruby's round face was set in a puggish frown as she plodded along cradling the parcel in her arms, John trailing behind her. O'Leary's the pawnshop, known locally as 'old Lonnie's', was situated at the end of Dock Street just a short walk away and deep in the heart of Monkwearmouth. Since the unemployment had worsened it was a regular route for some, and the growing Depression meant there were always groups of men lounging about at street corners watching passers-by with hooded eyes. Ruby didn't mind them if she was going to school or out playing, but she knew every one of them would see the package she was carrying and know she was going to the pawn.

Her scowl deepened. Hopefully all her friends were in school, but she'd die if she saw any of them. She couldn't have verbalized the stigma associated with visiting old Lonnie's. She only knew it was something spoken about with long faces and shakes of the head, but with a certain amount of covert satisfaction by those who weren't reduced to gracing the shop in Dock Street when they gossiped about their less-fortunate neighbours.

She hated their Lucy. She swung round to John, her voice a snarl as she spat, 'Come on, you.'

Never one to be intimidated, and especially not by Ruby, John made a face. 'Shut up, Ratbag Ruby.' He'd coined this particular form of address some time ago and the results had been so gratifying that he'd continued to use it, knowing it drove his sister demented.

In the present circumstances it really hit the spot. Ruby was on the verge of dropping the parcel and going for him, when a voice above her head said coolly, 'Hello there, what are you up to? Shouldn't you be at school? On an errand, are we?'

Ruby froze. Tom Crawford was her idol. He was so good-looking for one thing, and he always dressed like a gentleman, his clothes being a notch or two above what the other men in the streets round about wore. His mam, Mrs Crawford, was forever going on about his fancy house and his housekeeper and whatnot, and now this . . . this *god* was here, at the height of her humiliation. Wishing the ground would open and swallow her, Ruby gave up all hope of pretending things were other than they were. Her idol's words had revealed that he knew what she was about. 'Hello, Mr Crawford,' she said woodenly.

'So?' Tom waited for John to join his sister, whereupon he tweaked the boy's cap over his eyes. 'Playing the wag, are you?'

'No.' John was indignant. He didn't mind taking the blame when he'd been caught fair and square, but he was blowed if he was being blamed when he hadn't done anything. Unwittingly he added to his sister's mortification, saying, 'Our Lucy's sent us to old Lonnie's, an' we've got shopping to do after.'

Tom nodded, but didn't comment and, needing to explain, Ruby muttered, 'It's Donald's fault. If he hadn't gone we'd have been all right.' She didn't know if this was true, but it sounded better. The Crawfords had never visited old Lonnie's in their life, and her shame was intensified by the vague feeling that if the Crawfords could manage, so should they.

Tom stiffened, but his voice sounded the same when he said, 'Donald's gone? Gone where?'

'We don't know. Down south somewhere; he left a note for Lucy this morning and he took every penny Lucy had.'

'I see.' Tom ruffled the child's hair, but beneath his calm facade his mind was racing. Struggling to hide his elation, he fished in his pocket and sorted through his change. 'Here.' He handed the two of them a shiny sixpence each. 'You go and get yourselves a comic and some sweets when you do the shopping.'

Ruby and John stared at the coin in their hands and then at Tom, who was smiling down on them benevolently. They both thanked him and Ruby's voice reflected her adulation in a way that caused his smile to widen. He'd have no problem with these two, and the twins were too young to be of account. It couldn't have worked out better. In two or three years Ruby would finish school and could be put into service, and John a couple of years after that. He wouldn't mind providing for them till then. And the twins would be no trouble. Taking on the family would be seen as an act of altruism, which would do no harm at all to his standing in the community. He'd set his mind on becoming a town councillor in the next few years. He'd seen how backhanders could smooth the way and he would make sure no scandal queered his pitch. To all intents and purposes he was a businessman; he'd been meticulous in setting up a legitimate front, and those who knew differently would look the other way. He had the backing of the Kanes, after all.

He stood staring down the street long after the two children had disappeared, excitement causing his heart to thud. Should he go and see Lucy right now? He was sure to get a warmer reception than the last two times he'd called, because she'd had Donald then, or so she'd imagined. Now the last prop had been pulled from underneath her and she was his for the taking – Jacob having been satisfactorily dealt with.

The thought of Jacob caused him to frown. He was on his way to his mother's to play the dutiful brother; it wouldn't look good if he was seen sniffing around Lucy. Better to wait until it was quieter, without folk about. If he visited under cover of darkness the children would be asleep, another bonus. He would have her to himself. The palms of his hands were damp and he rubbed them down the sides of his trousers, his body involuntarily hardening in relish at the coming encounter.

*

'You didn't oughta 've said about Donald. Lucy said not to tell anyone.' Ruby and John had paused outside old Lonnie's to look in the dusty shop window. Watches, clocks, all manner of jewellery and knick-knacks on one side were divided from an assortment of clothes on the other – moleskin trousers, stiffly starched shirts, dresses, smocks and baby clothes – by a mahogany-framed silk-embroidered fire screen, the fine embroidery in silver and pale rose tones on a blue background enchanting. Unfortunately the effect was somewhat spoilt by the couple of pairs of great sailors' boots parked in front of the screen.

Ruby dragged her eyes away from a gold locket to look at her brother. 'Well, she won't know, will she?' she said meaningfully, adding, when John looked uncoop-erative, 'if you say we saw Tom, we'll have to tell about the sixpences he gave us, and she'll have them.'

John considered this. 'Not if we've spent them,' he said practically.

'And then she'd go mad, you know she would.'

'We don't *have* to tell her about the sixpences.'

'If you tell on me, I shall say about them.'

John's brown eyes mirrored his dilemma. Honesty against the unheard-of good fortune of a sixpence all to himself.

'We could buy a box of chocolates and eat them on the way home,' Ruby wheedled. They had never tasted the different centres in a box of chocolates, only ever having had the odd ha'penny or penny to spend on sweets or a comic in the past, when their father or one of their brothers had slipped them a coin. It did the trick. John nodded. 'All right. I won't say nowt.'

Ruby smiled. She had known that her blackmail would prevail. Besides, what harm was there in telling Tom Crawford about Donald leaving them? Everyone was going to know sooner or later – they couldn't keep it a secret forever.

Chapter Ten

Lucy sat at the kitchen table feeling too tired to move. She should go to bed, she told herself. It was close on midnight and she wouldn't hear anything further about Jacob until tomorrow. Frank had been as good as his word and had popped round shortly before ten o'clock to say that his da had just got back and there was no change. Jacob was in a coma and it didn't look good. His mam, he'd added, was refusing to budge, and nothing his da or the hospital staff had said had been able to convince Enid to come home and rest.

'Is there no hope?' she'd asked Frank, hearing the pleading in her voice and feeling ashamed for putting added pressure on him at such a time. But she'd had to ask.

Frank had rubbed his mouth. 'From what they've said to Da, it might be better if he goes quick, lass. Oh, I'm sorry, Lucy, don't look like that, but if he got over this, the odds are he'd be left in a right mess. Broken bones heal, but he could be blind or deaf and unable to walk, talk, feed himself even. They can't tell yet, but it don't look good.'

After Frank had gone she'd cried until she was cried-out. Now a kind of stupor had come over her and her mind had retreated into a dull numbness. All day her mind had grappled with ways of keeping the family together until she'd driven herself mad.

When she heard the back door into the scullery open, for a wild, breathless moment she thought Donald had come home. Not breathing, she watched the door into the kitchen open, but it wasn't her brother who stood framed in the doorway.

Tom Crawford's face was unsmiling and his voice was deep in his throat as he said, 'I saw the light, so I knew you were still up.'

Lucy rose, clutching the back of her chair for support. 'Is it Jacob? He's not . . .'

'Jacob?' he asked on a note of surprise, before saying, 'Oh, Jacob. No, no it's not Jacob,' an edge to his voice. 'Look,' he said after a moment's pause, and now his tone was commiserating, 'I know how you're fixed – Donald leaving and everything – and I'm sorry, lass. Heart-sorry. You must be worried sick with the little ones to look after.'

As he came further into the room every muscle in Lucy's body tensed. The fear and unease she'd felt in his presence before were stronger, and it was this that made her say, 'I don't know what you mean.'

'So Donald hasn't upped and gone?'

'No, he's here.' She looked up at the ceiling. 'Asleep in bed.'

'You're a terrible liar.' He smiled as he stopped a foot or so away. 'Did anyone ever tell you that?'

She shivered inside, but now that the shock was receding, her voice was stronger as she said, 'I tell you, he's here. Where else would he be?'

'Then would you mind waking him, so I can have a word? He was supposed to do a job for me tonight and he didn't turn up.'

Her brain refused to work quickly enough and she gazed at him dumbly.

'I thought so.' His smile widened. 'And don't get me wrong – I like it that you don't lie well. So many girls have got it down to a fine art. But then you're not like any other lass. Not to me, anyway,' he added, and his voice had a funny quiver to it.

She knew she had to get him to leave, but she didn't know how. Gathering her scattered wits, she tried to inject authority into her voice. 'It's late and I think you ought to go. It's not right you're here at this time of night.'

'I haven't told you why I've come.'

'I don't want to know. I want you to leave.'

He stared at her, his smile dying as his jaw reacted to her stance by tensing a muscle in his cheek. 'So I'm shown the door, while Jacob's made welcome any time. Is that it? I've seen you, dancing with him out there.' He flicked his head towards the yard. 'Well, you can forget Jacob now. If he lasts the night it'll be a miracle, and the way

I see it, that's what *you* need – a miracle, or it'll be the workhouse for the bairns for sure.'

A terrible suspicion was taking form in Lucy's mind. One part of her was saying: No, no, he wouldn't do that, not to his own brother; but there had been something in Tom's voice when he'd spoken Jacob's name . . . 'What do you know about the attack on Jacob?' she whispered, her hand at her throat.

Tom shrugged. 'He'd clearly riled someone, but then Jacob has a talent in that direction. Maybe they decided he needed to be taught a lesson, I don't know. Frankly, I don't care. I'm not going to pretend there's any love lost between us. Anyway, I'm not here to talk about him. Lucy' – he reached out and took her hands in his before she could stop him – 'I'm prepared to take care of you and the others. I want you, I always have, and if you marry me I'll be good to you, I swear it. You'll want for nothing.'

'Marry *you*?' The thought was abhorrent, repugnant, and in her naivety she let him see the truth, even before she tugged her hands from his.

His nostrils flared, but his voice was low when he said, 'Aye, me, and let me tell you there's plenty who'd bite my hand off, so quick would they say yes.'

'It was you who got my da and brother killed. You threw their bodies in the dock and everyone thinks they're drunkards, and you've frightened Donald to death so he's run away.' She took a deep pull of air, backing away from him until she found herself against the wall.

'I did no such thing.' He followed her, still talking

quietly, but with red-hot colour searing his cheekbones. 'Your father and brother got themselves killed, remember that. Your father came to me begging me to put something his way; it wasn't my fault he couldn't handle it. And I covered up for them after. Or would you have preferred they be branded as thieves and Donald sent down the line, eh? Because that's what would have happened if they'd been found in the hold of the ship.'

'You did it for yourself, not them.'

'Is that so?'

She knew she was inflaming his fury, but she couldn't stop herself. The bitter anger and hurt had been kept in too long, and now here he was – the man she hated and despised – and he still wouldn't admit what he'd done or show any remorse. 'Yes, it is so, and you know it. Jacob's always known what you're really like, and he wouldn't dance to your tune like the others, would he? That's what you couldn't bear.'

'Shut up about Jacob.' He raised his hand as though he was going to slap her, but as she faced him, wide-eyed and trembling, he groaned, 'Aw, lass, don't be like this. I've said I'll marry you, haven't I, an' take on the young 'uns an' all. What more do you want?'

'I wouldn't marry you if you were the last man on Earth.' She tried to make a run for it, thinking that if she could get to the hall and call out, Ruby and John would hear, but he caught her arm, jerking her to him before she'd even taken a step.

'Oh aye, you will,' he ground out thickly. 'I want you,

and you'll come crawling on your knees begging me to marry you before I'm finished.'

'No!' His mouth closing over hers smothered her protest as he bent her backwards, but as her fingers came up to his face and her nails rent his skin, he swore, his leg whipping her knees from under her so that they fell to the floor.

Now one hand was over her mouth and the other tearing at her clothes as he seemed to go mad. Lucy continued to scratch and kick, but the muscled weight of him made it futile. Tom was a tall, heavy, well-built man in his prime and her slender body still had to fill out into the full curves of womanhood, so her struggles made no impact on him except to excite him more. For minutes she fought, even when she was all but naked. His mouth at her small breasts, his exploring, pinching fingers, the indignities he was heaping on her – it was as though hell had opened and swallowed her. A hell much worse than anything Parson Shawe had preached about.

When her body was suddenly rent in two by indescribable pain – a pain that went on and on as Tom hammered into her – even the hand across her mouth couldn't prevent the agonized screams, but they were muffled and choked. And then he gave a great shuddering groan and collapsed on top of her, his fingers moving with the motion and covering her nose too so that combined with the crushing weight of him, she couldn't breathe. But she struggled no more, not caring at that instant if she lived or died.

When, after a moment or two, the weight lifted, Lucy couldn't move. Not until he stood looking down at her did she find the strength to pull the torn remnants of her skirt about her and roll onto her face.

His voice harsh, he muttered, 'You brought this on yourself, you know that, don't you? I wanted to do it right, but you'd have none of it. Well, my offer still stands. I'll marry you an' take the bairns on an' all, and there's not many who'd put up their hand for that, so think on.' He waited a moment and, when there was no movement or word from the figure at his feet, walked to the door. 'I'll be back when you've had time to see reason.' He hesitated, then walked to the table and flung a handful of coins on its wooden surface. 'That's to tide you over,' he said gruffly. 'You'll find I'm not tight-fisted, not with me own and, like I said before, you'll want for nothing. But I won't be played for a fool. And I tell you something: I want no more talk of Jacob. You look at another man and I'll do for 'em. Remember that.'

It wasn't until Lucy heard the back door close that she painfully dragged herself to her knees. Holding onto a kitchen chair for support, she stood up and stumbled out into the scullery. The bolts on the door were rusty and stiff, but eventually she managed to work them into place. Then, shaking from head to foot, her legs gave way and she slid onto the floor, her face awash with the tears racking her body.

At two o'clock in the morning she brought the tin bath into the kitchen. She painstakingly filled it to the brim with kettle after kettle of hot water and then stripped off her tattered clothes. Before stepping into the steaming bath she burned every last scrap of clothing on the range fire and then used the scrubbing brush to scour her skin until it was red and raw.

This, then, was what her mam had told her about, the thing that happened between a man and a woman. Her blue eyes wide and tear-bleared, she shuddered. She couldn't imagine being married and it happening over and over. She never wanted a man to touch her again, and the thought of Tom Crawford made her skin crawl. She would kill herself rather than marry him.

She sat in the water for a long time before drying herself. Then, with the towel wrapped round her, she crept upstairs. Ruby and the twins were fast asleep. She stood for a moment, staring down at them. They were the same. The nightmare that had happened to her downstairs hadn't touched them, but it had changed her forever. And if anyone found out they would say she was bad, that she'd given him the eye and got what she'd asked for. It was always the same – her mam had told her that. Men could have umpteen girls and folk smiled and said they were sowing their wild oats and it was natural, but if a girl got taken down, it was a different kettle of fish. And that's what had happened. *She'd been taken down.*

She covered her face with her hands and swayed back and forth for a few moments before becoming still.

She couldn't let anyone know and, even if she could, who would she tell? Mrs Crawford would have been the natural person she would have run to, but she was Tom's mother, she wouldn't believe he had forced her. And just supposing she did, what would be the outcome? He would say he wanted to marry her, and she would rather go to the river this night and end it than endure that.

Shivering, she silently pulled on the only other clothes she possessed – her Sunday frock and spare set of underclothes. Once downstairs again, she disposed of the bath water and sat down at the table. The shivering had stopped and her mind had become clear. She knew exactly what she was going to do.

Her gaze fell on the pile of coins Tom Crawford had left on the table. There were two shiny half-crowns and a number of shillings and sixpences along with the copper. A small fortune to her, and yet to him just loose change in his pocket.

Shame and self-disgust rose in a hot flood. He had paid for her, like men did with women of the night. Her body was still throbbing and aching from his brutality, and with a low cry she swiped the coins onto the floor, where they rolled in all directions. And there they would stay. She wouldn't touch a penny of his money.

She wanted to cry again. Instead she sat down and wrote a note, which she placed in the middle of the table.

We're leaving but the sale of the table and chairs and the beds and everything will pay the rent we owe.
Lucy Fallow.

*

The few sticks of furniture they had left weren't much, but at least she wouldn't be worried the landlord would send his 'collector' after them. He was different from the rent man, the collector, and although she'd never seen him she knew of him from the neighbours. One family a door or two along the street had done a moonlight flit a few months ago and the collector had found them and broken the father's kneecaps.

The note written, she placed the pan of stew she had made the day before on the hob to warm and sliced a loaf of bread to go with it. The pawn money that old Lonnie had dished out to Ruby and John had bought some scrag of mutton and a bag of vegetables and two loaves of bread, and she had a shilling over. A shilling between them and starvation. She glanced at the bread knife. It was the source of her troubles, or that's how she felt, but as the last link to her mam and da, she'd rather have walked on hot coals than let it go again. In its own way it was as precious as Jacob's necklace.

Her hand went to her throat and then she froze. The tiny heart and chain had gone. She glanced about her wildly. It must have come off when she was fighting Tom.

Going down on her hands and knees, she searched every inch of the kitchen floor by the light of the oil lamp, moving the lamp so that she could peer into the crevices between the stone flags. Nothing. She sat back on her heels after a while, beyond tears. Had it become caught in her tattered clothes and she'd unknowingly thrown it into the fire? She gave a dry sob. It was the last straw, a loss of gigantic magnitude.

Without much hope she went into the tiny scullery and there, by the back door where she had sat for a long time after she had secured the bolts, she caught a gleam of silver. The tiny clasp had come undone, that was all. Tremblingly she picked the precious necklace up and, with her hand against her chest and her eyes closed, the tears of relief flowed. If she had lost Jacob's little heart it would have been the end of everything, that's how she'd felt.

She roused Ruby first. Bringing her sister downstairs to the kitchen, she sat her at the table. 'We have to leave here, now, today,' she said without any preamble. 'We're behind with the rent and, once they know Donald's gone, they'll put you and John and the twins in the workhouse. Look, this is what Donald wrote.' She had screwed up his note initially, not wanting the others to know the fate he'd consigned them to, but as an afterthought had straightened out the paper and hid it. Now she was glad she had. In Ruby's eyes it backed up her words like nothing else could have done.

White-faced, Ruby read her brother's scrawled words and for once her bumptiousness was absent. 'You – you wouldn't do what he said, would you?' she whispered fearfully, the terrible tales her parents had told of their beginnings in that dreaded place filling her mind.

'I don't want to, so that's why we have to go. But you'll have to help me, Ruby. I'll try and get a job somewhere, but you'll have to take care of the little ones.'

Ruby stared at her. 'But where will we live?'

It was a good question. Until this very moment she hadn't fully acknowledged that at the back of her mind she'd known Jacob wouldn't see them destitute and neither would his mother. But now, in the space of twenty-four hours, everything had changed. Jacob had been beaten nearly to death and was lost to her, and so was Mrs Crawford in a different way. They were on their own.

'Once I get a job we'll find a room somewhere.' As times had worsened, it wasn't unusual for families of ten or more to rent one room in a house. Somehow they'd manage. She closed her mind as to how she was going to feed the five of them. 'We need to take everything we can carry between us because we're not coming back, not ever. You understand that, don't you?'

Ruby nodded. She was frightened, not just by the situation, but by Lucy too. Her sister had a strange look on her face and her voice was wooden, odd. Whispering again, she said, 'Are you all right?'

She would never be all right again, but she couldn't tell Ruby what Tom had done. She couldn't tell anyone. No one must ever know. She answered Ruby with a nod. 'Go and get dressed and tell John what's happening. It'll be light soon and we need to get away once we've had something to eat. Make it a game with the twins, I don't want them crying or creating as we leave.'

'What's that?' Ruby had been about to do as she was told when her gaze fell on one of the half-crowns, which had rolled into a corner of the room. 'It's money, Lucy, and look, there's more,' she said excitedly as her sharp eyes spotted other coins.

As she sprang forward, Lucy's arm shot out and pulled her back. 'Leave them,' she said fiercely.

'Leave them?' Ruby's voice was high with surprise. 'But it's money, lots of money. Where's it come from?'

'That doesn't matter, but I don't want you picking it up, do you understand me? It's not ours.'

'Whose is it then?'

Lucy didn't answer this. What she did say was, and in a voice that made Ruby take a step backwards, 'You touch any of that money – just one penny – and I'll put you in the workhouse sooner than you can say Jack Robinson.'

Ruby stared at her sister. Slowly she edged past her and scampered out of the kitchen and up the stairs to John's room. Her brother was curled under the blankets like a dormouse and didn't take kindly to being woken by Ruby shaking his shoulders like a dog with a rat. 'Get off me,' he muttered irritably, trying to pull the covers over himself again. 'Leave me alone.'

'Wake up, John, now.' Ruby wrenched the blankets right off the bed. 'Our Lucy's gone stark-staring barmy and there's money all over the kitchen floor and she won't let us pick it up.'

'Wh-what?' John sat up, rubbing his eyes and yawning.

'Donald left a note and we've got to get away or they'll put us in the workhouse, but Lucy's gone queer in the head. She's acting all funny and there's money everywhere,' said Ruby, exaggerating as she often did to get her brother's attention.

John held his sister's feverish gaze. 'It's not only Lucy who's gone queer in the head, if you ask me,' he said stolidly, knowing his lack of reaction would drive Ruby crazy.

Ruby glared at him. 'All right, be like that then, but Lucy says you've got to get dressed an' be quick about it.' And with that she flounced out of the room, deeply offended.

John smiled to himself. It was his chief pleasure in life, thwarting Ruby, however and whenever he could. Nevertheless she had whetted his curiosity, particularly with the tale about the money, and he slid off the bed and began dressing. He needed to see what was what.

Within the hour, just as the first blush of dawn was stealing across the sky, they were ready to leave. Ruby and John and the twins were each wearing their Sunday clothes and spare underclothes on top of their everyday ones. It saved packing them. Lucy had brought the old trunk, which had stood at the foot of her parents' bed in happier times, into the kitchen, and it was crammed full. Between the blankets and double eiderdown lay a saucepan, the black frying pan, the bread knife, five plates and mugs and some knives and forks, and a few other bits and pieces. It weighed a ton.

John had his father's old knapsack on his back, which held a towel, a piece of blue-veined soap, their hairbrushes and the wooden boat Ernie had carved for John's seventh birthday. Although Lucy had told them they could only take what was absolutely necessary, she hadn't demurred when he had squeezed it into the knapsack. Flora and Bess held their raggy dolls.

They emerged into the back yard quietly, for Lucy had warned them not to make a sound. Flora and Bess didn't really understand what was happening, but Ruby and John were subdued and tearful at leaving the only home they'd ever known. Not so Lucy. She was aware of feeling numb and odd, distant from everyone, as though she was outside herself looking at them all through an invisible divide. This feeling had grown through the preparations to leave, but far from fighting it, she'd welcomed the strength that the deadening of her emotions was providing.

Once in the back lane they fell into a natural formation. Lucy and Ruby led the way, carrying the heavy trunk between them. Flora and Bess followed and John made up the rear. It was still too early for many folk to be about, just the odd blackbird or two eyeing them from the top of the walls bordering the back yards, and a dog barking somewhere in the distance.

At the end of the lane Lucy turned and looked back whence they'd come. Again there was no nostalgia in her thoughts, merely a numb acceptance that a stage of her life was over and she was leaving Zetland Street for good. How they would manage, and what she was going to do with four other hungry mouths to feed, she didn't know. But she couldn't think about the difficulties ahead. For now it was enough that they had to make their way over the bridge into the busy, bustling anonymity of Bishopwearmouth, where no one would know her. She didn't let herself think about Tom Crawford in the last thought, or acknowledge it was Enid's eldest son she was fleeing from. For the time being a section of her brain had closed off. She was functioning mechanically, her actions as basic as putting one foot in front of the other.

Ruby glanced up at her sister, intending to complain that her arm was being pulled out of its socket by the weight of the trunk and it wasn't fair that John only had the knapsack to carry. But the words never left her mouth. In the half-light Lucy had taken on the appearance of a stranger, her mouth set in a tight line and her face rigid.

Enid arrived home at noon that same day. Jacob had passed the critical stage, according to the doctor, but would likely remain in a coma for days and when he awoke – the doctor had shrugged – who knew how he would be? When a man survives a battering like the one his patient had been subjected to, there was no knowing what irreversible damage would result. But they must hope and pray, he'd added, taking pity on the stricken woman in front of him. Only God Himself knew the future for any one of them. And for the present Enid could do no good here. Better to go home and eat and rest, because one thing was certain: she would need her strength in the days that lay ahead.

She had walked home in the May sunshine rather than

catching the tram, the desire to stretch her legs and get the antiseptic smell of the hospital out of her nostrils stronger than her tiredness. And when she walked into the kitchen and found her husband and two sons cooking themselves bacon and eggs she knew her life truly had been turned upside down. Not one of her menfolk had so much as raised a finger in the home before. And this feeling was compounded when Aaron told her to sit down and put her feet up and Frank poured her a cup of tea while she told them what the doctor had said.

'Jacob'll be all right,' Ralph muttered without a shred of conviction in his voice. 'They didn't expect him to last the night, did they, and he's still here.'

Enid said nothing. The figure lying so very still with his head swathed in bandages and distorted to twice the size bore no resemblance to her son, her baby. It was as though he'd already gone from her. She felt sick to her stomach that someone would want to hurt her lad like this and she knew Aaron was thinking the same, even before he ground out, 'I'd like five minutes alone with the bloke or blokes who did it, me an' a dirty great sledgehammer.'

It was Frank, aiming to take the stricken look from his mother's face by getting her to think of something other than Jacob, who said, 'Them next door have skedaddled by the way, Mam. I popped round this morning to see if Lucy was all right cos she was pretty cut up about Jake last night, and they'd left a note saying they'd gone. I brought it back to give to the rent man. Funny thing, though, there was some money on the floor. Perhaps it was meant to be with the note for the rent man.'

Enid sat up straighter. 'Where's the note? Show me.'

Frank fetched the note from behind the clock on the mantelpiece where he'd placed it with the pile of coins. 'It don't say, but Donald's talked about going south once or twice.'

Enid's eyes scanned the brief words twice. She sighed heavily as she handed the piece of paper back to Frank. She felt bitterly disappointed in Lucy. She'd have thought the lass would have hung on for a bit to see how Jacob was, and to say goodbye properly before she left, but likely Donald had put pressure on her to go, she told herself. The lad had been a different man since the accident with his da and Ernie. Still, at least it seemed he'd got off his backside at last and had taken responsibility for the family, and not before time. Lucy had looked worried to death for weeks, and all Donald had done was sit about like a big lump of nowt.

She looked at the others. 'Folk have to steer their own course through stormy waters,' she said flatly.

'Aye, but to leave without a word—'

'I don't want to discuss it, Frank.' She took a sip of her tea, but it nearly choked her because of the lump in her throat.

And then, to the amazement and consternation of her menfolk, Enid did the unheard of – she put her head in her hands and broke into a storm of weeping that rocked them to their foundations.

PART THREE

Rising from the Ashes

1928

Chapter Eleven

Five days later Lucy was desperate. With the Depression biting she had expected work to be scarce, but the fact that she was dragging four children about with her and had to admit they had no fixed abode had been the death knell to potential jobs. By the third day she had stopped taking them with her, but by then she knew she was not looking her best after two nights sleeping rough. Nevertheless, she had been offered work in a hotel as a kitchen maid, but it was live-in, and as soon as she had mentioned Ruby and the others that had been the end of that. A laundry had said they'd have to see her parents or guardian before they could take her on and she could tell the woman hadn't believed her when she'd said she was fifteen years old. At another place, a kipper factory, the man who had interviewed her had frightened her badly when, after some pertinent questioning, she had admitted she was the sole carer of her siblings and he'd gone to call the authorities. She had known what that meant. She could see the workhouse doors opening wide in her mind's eye. She had climbed out of the window of his office at the front of the factory while he was gone and run as though the devil himself was after her.

And now it was the morning of the fifth day and the unusually warm May weather, which had been a life-saver over the last nights, had given way to a cold drizzling rain and chilling northeast wind. Lucy awoke first in the little shelter she and Ruby and John had made at the end of an alley deep in the labyrinth of Sunderland's East End. They'd opened the lid of the trunk and then hooked the eiderdown over it to provide a low tent-like roof, before wrapping themselves in a blanket and crawling underneath, but no matter how mild the day, it became very cold in the hours before dawn. And now it was beginning to rain and, instead of just being damp, the eiderdown was dripping. None of them had eaten in the last twenty-four hours and the day before that Lucy had gone without, so that the twins and Ruby and John could share a bowl of soup and a bag of chitterlings she'd bought from the pie shop with the last of their money. The twins had developed the persistent hacking coughs of winter once more and the little girls had cried themselves to sleep last night, their small tummies growling with hunger.

What was she going to do? So cold and tired she could barely think, Lucy lay stiff and still so as to not awaken the others. Every minute they were asleep was a minute they weren't hungry and cold and miserable.

Should she take them to the workhouse? They would be fed and clothed there, of sorts, and it was better than starving to death. She could get them out, once she found work and got a room somewhere. It would give her a breathing space.

And then she immediately dismissed the idea. She would never be able to get them out once they were admitted, not unless she could show she could provide a proper home, along with feeding and clothing them. And the authorities would insist that one room wasn't a home. John would be separated from the girls and consigned to the male part of the building, and if her parents' experiences were anything to go by, each day would be hell on Earth. No, she'd rather the five of them *did* starve to death than that. At least they would go together.

But she wouldn't let that happen.

Suddenly angry with herself for even thinking along those lines, she gritted her teeth. She would find work today – any work. She would, *she would*. It was up to her to make it happen.

A rustling at the edge of their sodden shelter brought Lucy jerking upwards. A big grey rat peered in at her, so close she could see its whiskers twitching. As Ruby and John began to stir it disappeared, but its appearance confirmed Lucy's worse suspicions – she'd heard more and more rustlings as the nights had gone on. The rats were becoming bolder. It was common knowledge that in the tenements and hovels of the East End the rodents thought nothing of climbing into babies' cots and taking chunks out of them while they slept. And here they were, out in the open. Easy pickings. The rats had clearly got their measure; they would have to move from here.

Within the hour she had marshalled her little brood, although it had taken some cajoling to persuade Flora and Bess to forsake their cocoons, damp though they were. The twins were reluctant to stand up, let alone walk, but as Lucy and Ruby carried the trunk between them and John had the knapsack on his back, there was no one to carry the two little girls. This didn't prevent them whining and crying as they left the alley, but looking at their small white faces, Lucy hadn't got the heart to admonish them.

Until now, she had resisted venturing into the roughest part of the East End by the docks. There the brothels, gin shops and spit-and-sawdust public houses did a roaring trade, night and day, and the pimps, pickpockets and other ne'er-do-wells were always on the lookout for new victims. It was a place Lucy had heard her father warning Donald and Ernie to steer clear of when they began earning their own money, and although she didn't understand the full import of what went on, she knew enough to appreciate it was dangerous. Today, though, it was the last hope of finding work and she had no option.

Before they made their way in that direction, she led them to the old market, which was a short distance from the alley, entering its confines through the entrance in James William Street, one of three such entries. In the centre of the market was a tap with a lead basin and a lead cup attached to it, fastened with a heavy thick chain.

It was here they had sated their thirst over the last days, and once or twice John had managed to find the odd mushy piece of fruit or spotted apple under the stalls when the traders had packed up for the night. The old market had happy memories for Lucy. Before the twins had been born and her mother had become bedridden, her parents had brought them to the Michaelmas Day celebrations in Mowbray Park, and they'd called in at the old market on the way home.

It had been full of people that night and noisy, bright and lively. Lucy had thought it was the most fascinating place on Earth. There had been a boxing contest going on, and a stall where you had to kick footballs through holes. Ernie and Donald had won two rag dolls, which they had given to her and Ruby and had now been passed down to Flora and Bess. Duke's roundabout sat at the top of the market and although it was expensive, at a penny a ride on the horses that went up and down for five minutes, her da had treated them all to a go. Three-year-old John had sat on his mam's lap and squealed with delight the whole time, and then they'd looked at the stalls. Besides the ones selling second-hand clothes and the like, there was a tripe stall, sweet stalls, a hot-pie stall and umpteen others. Her da had bought two ha'penny bags of nuts and raisins from a man with a big barrel and they'd eaten them listening to the accordion player and the buskers.

It had been a magical night. For a moment Lucy wasn't standing in the harsh light of day, supervising Flora and

Bess at the basin so that they didn't soak themselves. She was back to an autumnal evening when the gas lamps were creating rings of blue light and turning the cobblestones blue too, and her father was smiling at her mother in that special way he'd kept just for her. And then, just for a second, she felt a warm breath on her cheek and her mother's voice whispering, 'Don't despair, hinny. It's always darkest just before dawn.' It had been one of her mother's favourite sayings.

Lucy shut her eyes tightly and breathed out a slow sigh. She'd sensed her mother close once or twice in the last days and she didn't care if that meant she was going barmy, she thought painfully. She needed those brief moments of comfort.

'Lucy, Flora's got wet again.' She was brought back to the present by John's aggrieved voice. 'I *told* her to press the button gently and then count to three until she heard the pipe thump before she pressed again, but she pushed too hard, so it came out in a rush. *Tell* her,' he added, as Flora found the energy to punch her brother with one small fist before bursting into tears.

'Here, lass.' They had been standing a few yards from a hot-pie stall and Lucy hadn't been aware that the owner, a stout matron of indeterminate years, had been watching them. 'These were left over from last night and I can't sell 'em in case they've gone off, but I dare bet you won't be too fussy, eh?'

Lucy knew they looked a sorry sight, but even if she hadn't, the look on the woman's face as she handed Lucy the bag would have confirmed it. But the woman's smile was kind and Lucy took the bag gratefully, thanking her before they moved off to a quiet corner. The pies, one for each of them, were cold and broken, with congealed grease in places, but Lucy knew that to her dying day nothing would taste so good again. They finished every crumb, licking their fingers over and over, and then half-laughing at each other.

It was a sign, Lucy told herself. Hearing her mam, and then the pies. It was a sign she would get work today. It had to be.

Enid and Aaron, along with their three other sons, were sitting round Jacob's bed in the hospital. It was Jacob's first day of sitting up, and although Enid had waxed lyrical about how much better he looked when they had arrived at his bedside, inside she wanted to cry. Lying down he had looked dreadful, but sitting up he appeared even worse. His bruises had turned every colour of the rainbow and his face was so swollen that his eyes were slits in the mounds of flesh. Every breath was agony for him, the nurses had told them that, saying that until the broken ribs healed he would be in constant pain. And now and again he would shut his eyes and fall asleep for a few minutes. But he had recognized them all and spoken coherently for the first time – a minor miracle, according to the doctor, although Enid didn't think there was anything minor about it. Now she knew Jacob could hear and see and that his mind was his own, she realized just how much she had prepared herself for the worst. The relief had caused a flood of emotion, which she was endeavouring to hide behind her usual forthright manner.

Jacob had just asked how long he'd been in hospital and Enid's voice was brisk when she said, 'A week, lad. And most of that time you've been away with the fairies and worrying us all to death. The doctor said you can't remember anything about what happened or who attacked you. Is that right?'

'Aye.' Jacob didn't move his head as he spoke. Since regaining consciousness in the early hours of the morning he'd learned that if he stayed completely still the pain was more or less bearable. Now he stared at his mother through aching eyes and repeated the question he'd asked twice before since his family had arrived: 'When is Lucy coming in to see me?' They had palmed him off without really answering, but he was determined to know.

The doctor had told them he might repeat things for a while and his memory wouldn't be up to scratch, but that it would improve each day, so Enid's voice was patient when she said, 'I told you, lad. Only family are allowed at the moment.'

'Lucy *is* family.'

Dear gussy, he had a bee in his bonnet about the lass and it wasn't surprising – they'd grown up together after all and were close, like brother and sister, Enid thought. But they had decided to say nothing about the Fallows disappearing down south until he was well on the mend.

And then Jacob completely disabused his mother of

the 'brother and sister' idea when he said, very clearly, 'We love each other, Mam. We always have. She's my lass.'

Enid's eyes opened wide. 'Your lass? Oh, lad, I don't think – I mean—' She glanced helplessly at the others. 'Don't set too much store by what might have been said in the past,' she finished weakly.

Jacob squinted at his mother as best he could. His bloodshot eyes kept smarting and running. One of the nurses had said he was lucky not to have lost any teeth, and he'd made her giggle when he'd wryly replied that 'lucky' was not the word he'd apply to himself right now. This particular nurse reminded him of Lucy. Not in her looks – Nurse Hardy was a mousy little thing – but in her gentle manner and sweet smile. 'All right, Mam,' he said quietly, 'let's have it. What's going on? And don't give me any soft-soap. I'm not a bairn.'

'He's right.' Tom sat forward on his hard wooden chair, his face impassive. 'Tell him.'

'Tell me what?' Panic curdled deep in Jacob's stomach, but he fought from letting it show as his gaze moved to each face in turn. When no one replied, he said again, 'Mam? Tell me what?'

It was Tom who answered. 'The Fallows have cleared off down south. They scarpered in the middle of the night and left owing umpteen weeks' rent.'

'It wasn't like that.' Enid shot her eldest an angry glance. 'And we don't know they've gone down south for sure; that's just surmising, because of what Donald had said to one or two folk. They left a note and the furniture to pay off the back-rent, you know that as well as I do, Tom.' She turned back to the figure in the bed, her voice softening. 'It don't look like they intended to come back though, lad.'

He felt funny, odd. Jacob felt himself slipping back into the dark muzziness he'd lain in for the last few days as everything in him called 'Lucy, Lucy', but no sound passed his lips. He was vaguely aware of his mother calling for help and of Nurse Hardy's voice sounding firmer than usual as she ushered the family away, saying he needed rest, before returning to him and drawing the curtains round the bed. Then the heavy blanket of exhaustion drew him down into the darkness and he went into it, the soundless cry echoing in his head.

'What did you have to go and say it like that for?' Enid glared at Tom as the five of them made their way out of the infirmary.

'Like what?'

'You know what I mean, so don't come the old soldier, not with me. We'd agreed that when we told him about Lucy and the others leaving we'd break it gently.'

'How many ways can you say it, Mam? Look, I know you're worried about him, but some things are best faced head-on. He'd just have worried away at it like a dog with a bone, you know he would. He sensed we were keeping something from him. Why do you think he kept on about her?'

It sounded reasonable and she wanted to believe he'd had Jacob's best interests at heart, but had he? She had never been able to fathom why, but there had always been a strong animosity between her eldest and her youngest. Not that it was all down to Tom. Jacob had disliked his brother from the moment he could crawl and had made it obvious, too.

Enid checked herself. Why was she making excuses for Tom again? She had to face it, there was a hardness in him that wasn't in the others. Mind, with things as they were, that was perhaps no bad thing. Tom had the will and determination to make something of himself and, as a family, they were reaping the benefit of it. No one could say different.

Why did she love Tom more than her other bairns? She had used to tell herself it was because he was her firstborn, or that she felt guilty he'd been conceived outside the sanctity of marriage and had to make it up to him in some way. The truth of it was that from the first moment she'd looked at his bonny little face she'd been captivated, and as time had gone on she'd realized she would never love anyone else in the same way. She knew he was no angel, but then what lad was? And he'd always looked after her – she knew she came first with him. She'd only have to mention she'd got her eye on something and it was hers, although she'd had to be careful lately. Aaron had got the hump good and proper when Tom had bought her the wireless. They had argued bitterly about that and she'd accused him of being jealous of their son. When

Jacob had taken his father's side, and Frank and Ralph had followed suit, she had said too much, something she regretted now, because the house had never been the same since.

Quietly now Enid said, 'Donald and Lucy and the bairns might come back anyway. The grass isn't always greener, and the pull of your beginnings is strong.'

'Aye, they might,' Tom agreed with seeming disinterest.

Aaron and his other two sons said nothing; they rarely did in front of Tom. They might have him over between the three of them, but each held his tongue in Tom's presence. They would have walked on hot coals before they admitted the truth: that they were scared of their own flesh and blood.

Once outside the hospital grounds, Tom dipped his hand into the pocket of his fine tweed jacket, handing his mother a note. 'Here, Mam, get a cab home.'

'You're not coming back for a cup of tea?' Enid didn't hide her disappointment.

'Another time.' Tom bent his head and kissed her brow.

It was something no one else did, not even Aaron. He only kissed her as a prelude to the sexual act itself, and then under cover of darkness in the seclusion of their double bed. Tom's caress never failed to warm Enid's heart and she smiled at him.

'I've some business to see to,' Tom said quietly. 'I've let things slip, coming in to see Jacob every afternoon.'

'Oh, I understand, lad, course I do, and it's been good of you to come every day.' In fact Enid had been surprised at her eldest's solicitousness, considering the way things were between the two brothers. It just showed – blood was thicker than water.

Tom smiled at her, confirming the thought when he said, 'I come as much for you as for Jake, Mam. Families needed to stick together at times like this. But you needn't worry now, all right? He's on the mend and in his right mind, more than we could have expected.' Turning to his father and brothers, he added, 'I'll see you three tonight. Nine sharp.'

His tone could have been described as one giving orders to menials, and the muscles in Aaron's jaw clenched. Nevertheless he nodded.

The four of them stood watching Tom for a moment as he strode off. He cut a fine figure in his tweed jacket and cap, the quality of his trousers and shining leather shoes evident at a glance. Enid gazed after him fondly, before turning with the ten-shilling note in her hand. 'We'd best pick up a cab at the corner.'

'You go ahead, I haven't lost the use of me feet yet,' said Aaron flatly, 'an' if I want a ride, a tram's good enough for me.'

Enid's gaze sharpened. 'What's the matter with you then?'

'What's the matter with me? If you don't know, there's no point in me saying, is there?'

'Just because our Tom gave us the money for a cab, is that it?'

'Our Tom, our Tom. It's always our Tom. The sun's

shone out of his backside since the day he was born, hasn't it? An' he gave *you* the money for the cab, not me. Let's be clear about that.' He glared at his wife for a moment more before growling, 'Oh, to hell with it.' He stomped off, his hands thrust into the pockets of his trousers.

When Frank and Ralph followed him, after a muttered 'Sorry, Mam', Enid stood gazing after them until they were out of sight. Sickness churned in her stomach. There was a time when Aaron wouldn't have dreamt of leaving her standing in the street, and not so long ago either. And Frank and Ralph couldn't have made it clearer whose side they were on. *Sides*. She shook her head. What was happening to them?

Slowly she began to walk towards the corner of Chester Road where she could pick up a cab, and as she did so, she looked down at the note in her hand. They were better off than they'd ever been, thanks to Tom, but they'd been a darn sight happier a few years back when Aaron and the lads worked at the shipyard. But times change. Would she want her menfolk standing in line at the dole queue like so many of their neighbours or living in fear of the workhouse? She shuddered. Tom wasn't stingy with what he paid out to Aaron and his brothers; it wouldn't hurt them to show a little gratitude rather than the moroseness that had settled on the three of them of late. They were in clover compared to some, and she'd tell them that. Look what had happened to the Fallows.

Thinking of Lucy brought her mind to Jacob and what

had transpired in the hospital. Again she shook her head. The pair were little more than bairns and to talk of love . . . Besides, even with Lucy doing her bit and looking after the little ones, Donald was going to have his work cut out to feed and clothe them and keep a roof over their heads for the next umpteen years. There would be no talk of lads or lassies for Lucy or Donald for a good long while, because who'd want to saddle themselves with their sweetheart's brothers and sisters? It had upset her that Lucy had left without a word, but if her Jacob had been thinking along the lines he'd spoken of, perhaps it was all for the best. Like Tom had said, some things are best faced head-on and at least Jacob knew what was what now. Tom had been right to tell Jacob straight out, and she'd had a go at him for it, bless him.

Guilt was now added to the host of emotions swirling in Enid's breast. Feeling that she couldn't win or please anyone, no matter what she did, and – ridiculously – suddenly missing her mother who had been dead for more than twenty years, she plodded on, blinking back hot tears and feeling very alone.

When Tom had left the others outside the hospital he had gone into the nearest pub and ordered a double whisky, which he had swallowed down in a couple of gulps, before ordering another. Now, gazing into the glass, he swirled the amber liquid around a few times. As yet Jacob didn't suspect he'd had anything to do with the beating, that much had been clear. And even if he put two and two together, he couldn't prove anything, and who'd believe him anyhow? It had been a nasty moment when he'd arrived at the ward and found Jacob back in the land of the living, though.

He narrowed his eyes and tipped more whisky down his throat. Nine out of ten blokes wouldn't have survived half of what his brother had had done to him, but that was Jacob all over. Drop him in a muck heap and he'd come up smelling of roses.

He finished his drink and left the pub, and now his mind had moved on from the annoying problem of Jacob's recovery and was focusing on the matter that had consumed him over the last days. Where was Lucy? When he'd called to see her the day after he'd had his way with her, he'd expected to find her broken and submissive and ready to see reason. Instead the house had been empty and, when he'd gone next door, his mam had been all of a dither, showing him the note Lucy had left and telling him she'd gone off with Donald. He hadn't disabused her of this idea. It suited his purposes to let everyone assume Donald had taken the family down south while he made his own investigations. But to date he'd come up with nothing.

But he would. His jaw tightened. She'd had no money; Frank had shown him what he'd found scattered over the kitchen floor and it was most, if not all, of what he had given her. So she wouldn't have got far. And Sunderland wasn't so big she could hide forever, not with four bairns hanging onto her skirts.

He smiled grimly to himself. He'd been spitting bricks that first day, especially at her implied insult regarding the money. He was still angry, but he had to admit a sneaking respect for her – a first for him where a woman was concerned. She had surprised him too – another first. She had appeared crushed when he'd left that night, but she had more spirit than he'd credited to her. Life with her wouldn't be dull. Of course she would do what she was told, if push came to shove, but with Lucy he'd make allowances: the iron hand in the velvet glove. That was after he'd brought her to heel for leading him a merry dance, mind you.

He nodded at the thought, not feeling the fine rain on his face as he walked on, imagining what he would do to her when he got her into his bed, and after a few moments he began humming a hit of the year before, 'Ain't she sweet', and he was smiling.

Chapter Twelve

It was seven o'clock in the evening. The rain had become more persistent over the last hour and the hope of the morning was no more. Lucy was beside herself. It seemed no one was prepared to offer even the meanest work to a young lass with bairns in tow. 'It's this way, lass,' the last prospective employer – a grand name for the owner of the little pie shop with a notice in the window saying 'Help wanted' – had said, 'I need someone I know isn't going to let me down. An' with that lot' – she'd flicked her head towards the four standing at the entrance to the shop – 'you've got your hands full already.'

Lucy had nodded dully at the familiar refrain. Now, as she joined the others huddled together against the driving rain and they began to walk away, she was surprised when the shop owner came hurrying after them.

'Look, lass,' the woman said a little breathlessly – she was as round as she was tall, which was a good advertisement for her pies – 'I know of a bloke who's in a bit of a fix, a friend of mine. Do you know Perce Alridge, the fishmonger in Long Bank?' Lucy shook her head. She knew Long Bank joined High Street and Low Street, because she'd applied for a job at the kipper-curing house there, but that was all.

'Well, me an' Ada, Perce Alridge's late wife, have been pals since school, but she died a couple of months back havin' their third. The bab died an' all, and he's bin left with two little 'uns and the shop to run. Ada did a bit in there an' all and, to tell you the truth, Perce don't know if he's on foot or horseback. He had a young lad helping him till yesterday, when he caught him thieving from the till. It might be worth calling there and seeing what's what, if nothing else.'

'Oh, I will, I will, and thank you. I'll go there now.'

Lucy's smile lit up her tired face and, after looking at her for a moment, the woman said, 'You tell Perce that Maggie sent you. All right, lass? An' steer clear of the pubs on the waterfront, if you don't get no joy with Perce. Some of the foreign sailors are drunk morning to night, when they're not on the boats, and lookin' like you do they'd eat you alive. Havin' the bairns with you would make no difference to them, they're like animals.'

Her face straight now, Lucy nodded. 'Thank you,' she said again, her stomach trembling at the thought of what the woman meant. She knew about two-legged animals and being eaten alive. The bruises on her body and the stinging and pain between her legs had all but gone now, but she only had to close her eyes at night and she was reliving the nightmare.

It was only a short distance to Long Bank and the rain had cleared the street of the normal scattering of snotty-nosed infants playing their games. John had described the Bank as a higgledy-piggledy street earlier that day, when they had gone to the kipper-curing establishment, and he was right. Certainly coming from the regimented rows of two-up, two-down streets where they had lived, it seemed so. Some of the buildings were two-storey and some three- with different-sized doors and windows and jutting-out pieces here and there. The overriding smell was one of fish, which wasn't surprising, located as it was within a stone's throw of the docks; and pubs, shops and tenement dwellings lived in noisy, dirty disharmony. The brothels did a roaring trade of a night in this part of the East End, and for those customers who weren't too particular about who serviced them, the dock dollies did the job for half the price in the stinking alleys and narrow courts that made up much of the area.

They found the fishmonger's shop halfway along the street, and in spite of the relatively late hour there was a small queue leading to the marble counter, behind which a harassed-looking man was serving. Not quite knowing how to proceed, Lucy stationed the others outside under the shop's awning. The twins immediately started to cry. They were wet and cold and hungry, and they didn't like the window containing rows of gaping-mouthed, glassy-eyed fish. Telling Ruby to take care of them, Lucy joined the line of housewives, most of whom were carrying buckets or stained, evil-smelling baskets.

A couple of the women eyed her curiously, the one in front of her turning to say, 'Haven't seen you round here afore, lass?'

Trying not to breathe in too deeply, Lucy said, 'No, we used to live over the river in Monkwearmouth.'

'Oh aye, Monkwearmouth, was it?' The woman nodded, glancing at the four huddled by the window. 'Times are hard, sure enough, hinny,' she said, the roughness of her voice softened by a note of compassion. 'You here for the halibut heads an' bloaters an' whatnot? Keeps my lot going, the end-of-day bits Perce knocks out cheap. I reckon he does more trade in the last hour than he does the rest of the day put together.'

She chuckled, and another of the women chimed in, 'I got a nice lot of herrings a couple of nights back, Flo. Nowt like a bit of roe on toast in the mornin' to keep you goin' all day, an' we had the herrings soused in vinegar an' some pickling spice our Rory come by. Handsome they were.'

'Your Rory oughta be careful, lass. He'll be sent along the line if he's caught, or to the House of Correction leastways.'

'He won't get caught, not our Rory. Cunnin' as a cartload of monkeys, he is, an' twice as nimble.'

'Aye, so was Sarah's lad – Larry, wasn't it? – but he got nabbed.'

'But he was a pickpocket, Flo. You can't compare my Rory with him.' The woman sounded affronted. 'My Rory don't go in for the thievin' proper.'

The conversation continued in the same vein as the queue shortened, and after a few minutes Lucy had a clear view of the fishmonger. He was a big man, not so much in height as in breadth. His head seemed to flow into his broad shoulders and his chest was massive, straining against the shirt and heavily stained apron covering it. The rolled-up sleeves of his shirt showed hairy, muscled arms and his hands were hairy too, and large. Very large. His hair was short and his face ruddy, and as he served his customers he kept up a flow of banter, which didn't detract from the speed with which each woman was sent on her way clutching her purchases and, in the main, smiling.

The closer she got to the counter, the more Lucy wanted to turn on her heels and run. Something about the fishmonger repulsed her and caused a trembling inside, although she didn't know what it was.

And then she was in front of him and a pair of mild blue eyes held hers. 'Aye, lass?' he said a tinge impatiently, when she didn't speak. 'What can I get you?'

Lucy opened her mouth, but no words came out. His shirt collar was undone and a tuft of thick curly hair showed; she had never seen such a hairy man before or such a threateningly male one. He terrified her. She took a step backwards and trod on the toe of the woman behind her, who swore loudly and pushed her in the back, propelling her forward again. Somehow, through her embarrassment and panic, she heard herself say, 'Maggie sent me, Mr Alridge. She – she said you were looking for someone to help out.'

The woman behind her made a ribald comment, which caused the others to titter. Not so Percival Alridge. He watched the young lass in front of him colour to the roots of her hair, a fact that, if Lucy had but known, amazed him. In this part of the East End the fairer sex didn't blush; most of the young lassies and women round about had tongues on them that would put a sailor to shame.

Wondering how on earth Maggie had come across such an innocent – and a bonny one at that, he added to himself – he cast a warning glance at the woman behind Lucy before saying quietly, 'A lad, lass. It's a lad I'm after. This is a fishmonger's and it's hard work at the best of times.'

His manner had assuaged the blind fear to some extent, and paramount now was the knowledge that if she didn't get this job they were done for. 'I'm used to hard work. I can do anything a lad can do,' she said quickly.

'Aye, an' more besides,' the woman behind her quipped, causing another ripple of laughter in the shop.

Keeping his amusement from showing, Perce began, 'I'm sorry, lass, but—'

'*Please.*' Throwing pride and caution to the wind, Lucy stepped right up to the counter. 'Please, Mr Alridge, I need this job. I'll work harder than any lad, I promise, and I'm stronger than I look. I've tried everywhere—' Her voice caught in her throat and, willing herself not to cry, she said weakly, 'Please let me prove it to you.'

'Oh, give the lass a chance,' the woman behind her said now. 'She can't be worse than Norman. You said yourself he was a lazy little blighter, Perce.'

'Aye, an' light-fingered into the bargain,' another woman piped up. 'He was lucky to get away with the good hiding you gave him, Perce. Many a man would have called the law, an' rightly so. But this lass has got an honest face. You are honest, aren't you, hinny?' she called to Lucy. 'Course you are.'

Lucy nodded, her eyes on the fishmonger, who was scowling at the customers.

'Let me mind me own business and you mind yours,' he growled to the shop in general. 'All right? An' you, lass' – his gaze fastened on Lucy for a moment – 'you wait at the back till I'm finished and we'll see, but I'm not promising anything, mind.'

Lucy nodded again. She couldn't have spoken through the surge of hope which had risen up in a big lump in her throat.

It took half an hour for the customers to dwindle, but at eight o'clock Perce called out that he was closing to any more who tried to enter, and served the last few. After washing his hands in a bowl of water behind the counter he came round the other side and shut and bolted the door. It was then that he glanced at Lucy, who was standing where he'd told her to. 'You'd better come up for a minute so's we can talk proper,' he said gruffly.

'Thank you.' Conscious of four distinctly alarmed faces outside the window, Lucy summoned up her courage.

Dancing in the Moonlight

She'd nipped out earlier and told them what was happening, but the bolting of the door had clearly unnerved them. 'Could my brother and sisters wait inside, Mr Alridge? They won't touch anything.'

Perce followed her gaze to where the four children were: the twins sitting on the trunk and Ruby and John standing behind them. All four looked wet and cold, and Flora and Bess were crying.

'They're yours?' His voice was high with astonishment. 'I thought they were waitin' for someone.'

'They are. Me.'

'Why did you bring them with you if you're looking for work?'

It was the question she'd dreaded while she had been standing at the back of the shop. 'I had to. There's nowhere else for them,' she said flatly.

'Couldn't you have left 'em at home with your mam an' da?'

She stared at him and after a moment he said, 'So that's why you're cartin' that damn great trunk about?' He swore softly. 'I'll let 'em in, and you can all come up an' have a warm while you tell me what's what. And the truth, mind. I might not be the sharpest card in the pack, but I know when I'm being lied to.'

'I don't lie, Mr Alridge.'

'Is that so?' He looked down into the great deep-blue eyes. 'Then you're the first of your sex I've come across who don't, and that includes me dear old mam, God rest her soul.'

They followed the fishmonger across the shop into the rear of the premises where the smell of fish was even stronger, and then up a flight of narrow stairs to a small landing. He unlocked what looked like a front door and, as he opened it, a small child flung himself at the fishmonger's legs, crying, 'Da, Da, Charley's wet himself again an' he wouldn't let me change him, an' he's gone to sleep on the mat.'

'All right, all right.' He scooped the child into his arms, turning to Lucy and saying, 'This is me eldest, Matthew. Say hello to the visitors, Matthew,' as he ushered them all past him into a large sitting room-cum-kitchen.

Lucy blinked as the smell – a combination of stale urine and fish and other things besides – met her nostrils, but as she glanced around she could imagine that in former days, when the fishmonger's wife was alive, it had been a bonny home.

A suite of patterned plush stood angled round the small fireplace, which had no fire burning in the grate, and a beautiful leaf-carved mahogany bracket clock ticked the minutes by on the mantelpiece, with a large number of brass ornaments keeping it company. It looked as though every item of furniture had been chosen with care, from the mirror-back sideboard with a central bow-fronted cupboard to a pair of bun-feet display tables on either side of the window, which had dead-looking aspidistras on them. One wall had a number of plaques of different designs and shapes covering it – a large central plaque decorated with the Virgin Mary and Child between winged putti within a garland of lemons and vines taking pride of place. Against another wall a large display cabinet held pretty porcelain figurines. This, along with everything else, was covered in a thick layer of dust, and the floor was strewn with toys and clothes and bits of food and other debris.

The kitchen area was even more grubby. A large leather-topped table was covered with the remains of many meals, as were two smaller tables, and an enormous dresser was almost devoid of its crockery and kitchenware, which was scattered in piles on any available surface. A black-leaded range took up most of the far wall and in front of this, on a thick clippy mat, a small child lay curled up sleeping.

The fishmonger must have noticed Lucy's expression because his voice was defensive when he said, 'It's a bit of a mess. I've got me work cut out in the shop. It was the wife who used to take care of things up here an' see to the bairns. I pay a neighbour to bring in one hot meal a day for us an' see to the weekly wash, but the rest of it . . .' He waved a beefy hand at the chaos.

'Who looks after your little lads?' Lucy asked quietly.

The fishmonger ruffled the hair of the child nestled in his arms. 'Matthew's a big boy, aren't you?' he said to his son, who didn't look a day over five. 'He looks after the little 'un an' I pop upstairs when I can. I need to keep me business going or we're all in queer street,' he added when Lucy continued to stare at him.

She nodded quickly, hoping she hadn't offended him. 'Of course. How old are the bairns?'

'I'm nearly five an' he's three,' said Matthew from his perch, pointing at his brother. 'Charley was dry in the day afore Mam went to heaven, but he wets himself all the time now. He makes himself sick an' screams a lot an' all, an' yesterday he bit me. Look.' He held out a skinny arm and Lucy saw where a set of small teeth had punctured and bruised the skin.

Lucy looked from the child to his father, who stared at her helplessly. She was very aware of Ruby and John and the twins huddled together just inside the doorway, but she didn't glance their way. This was what her mam had meant; this was why she'd heard her voice this morning. She had to grab this opportunity with both hands or . . . She couldn't follow through on the 'or'. *This had to work.* Quietly, keeping the excitement from showing, she said, 'It strikes me you need someone up here more than in the shop, but if you took us on, we could all help out. I could see to things up here an' look after the bairns when you weren't too busy below, an' once my sister and brother are back from school they could work in the shop till it closes. Those women said you're busier in the evenings than at any other time, is that right? The twins could play with Charley and keep him happy – they like little ones – and be friends for Matthew too.'

'Take you on?' There was utter bewilderment in his tone. 'The five of you? Here? Livin' here, you mean? Are you barmy, lass?'

'We'd work for our bed and board, you wouldn't have

to pay us anything, and you'd save paying out to the neighbour and the wage for someone in the shop. I could get things nice in here and your bairns would be well looked after, I promise. It – it'd be a home again for you an' them.' In spite of herself she couldn't stop the pleading note from sounding in her voice. 'And for us,' she finished weakly.

Ruby and the others had the sense to keep absolutely quiet. It was the little boy, Matthew, who spoke, twisting round in his father's arms to put his small hands either side of the florid face as he whispered, 'I don't want to look after Charley all the time an' be locked in, Da. Can they come? Please?'

Percival Alridge was not a man who was easily nonplussed, but, as he put it to himself, right at this moment he didn't know which end of him was up. People would think he'd gone stark staring mad if he took five more bairns on – and right at this moment Lucy appeared little more than a bairn to him – but there was a grain of sense, more than a grain, in what the lass had said. But five of them . . . Brusquely he said, 'How old are you, lass? An' the truth, mind.'

'Fifteen. And Ruby there is eleven, John's eight, coming up for nine, and the twins have just turned five. Ruby is big for her age and John's as strong as a horse. We're good workers, Mr Alridge, and—'

'Enough.' He raised a hand, palm upwards to her. 'Let me think.' A gust of rain hammered at the window, waking the little boy on the mat, who rolled over, crying even before he opened his eyes as he whimpered, 'Mammy, Mammy.'

Whether it was this that decided in her favour Lucy would never know, but as he gazed at his son, Perce muttered, 'I must want me head testing for even considerin' such a daft notion.' Then he turned to her. 'Look, lass, the lot of you can stay the night and I'll listen to your story. I'm not saying more than that. Now there's a pot roast in the oven, but Mrs Mallard's only made enough for me an' the lads, so I'll go down an' sort out some cod and haddock for you to do for your lot, all right? I dare say you're peckish.'

'Thank you, oh, thank you.' Telling herself she mustn't cry, Lucy tried desperately to keep her eyes from filling up.

'Aye, well . . .' The fishmonger cleared his throat twice. 'Like I said, I'll hear your story once the bairns are settled.' Even as he spoke, Perce knew he'd lost the battle. It wasn't so much the pickle he was in since Ada had died, or even the fact that he couldn't deny Charley was going from bad to worse and Matthew's little shoulders couldn't continue to carry the load. It was the look in the young lass's eyes when she'd thanked him.

The flat had three bedrooms, but the third was still kitted out as Ada's sewing and ironing room. After they had eaten their fill and John had been bedded down with the brothers in their double bed, and Ruby and the twins on a big eiderdown on the floor of the sewing room with a heap of blankets over them, Lucy and Perce had their chat. Lucy said nothing about Jacob, or Tom Crawford forcing himself upon her. She found she couldn't even bring herself to mention his name when she spoke of the man who had been instrumental in causing the deaths of her father and brother, and Donald to leave Sunderland.

Contrary to his nature, Perce listened without asking any questions or interrupting the flow. He was aware this child-woman was nervous – even frightened – of him. She had recoiled when their hands had touched accidently as she'd handed him a cup of tea and she was as tense as a coiled spring as she spoke. It made him wonder if there was more to her story than she was telling him. Was she in trouble with the law? Was that the real reason for the moonlight flit?

He immediately dismissed the idea. Lucy was honest. He'd bet his life on it. And after all she'd gone through she was bound to be worked up. One thing was for sure: if she and her brood were prepared to work for their bed and board, he couldn't lose on the deal. He was paying through the nose for what Mrs Mallard did and she wasn't even much of a cook, and if he didn't have to fork out for another lad to help in the shop, he'd be quids in. More than that, he was sick of living in a pigsty and it'd be a weight off his mind to have Charley and Matthew looked after. Ada would turn in her grave if she could see her home the way it was. She'd been houseproud to a fault, had Ada.

Lucy had finished her story and was sitting quietly

with her hands in her lap, her great eyes fixed on his face as he came out of his reverie.

He looked at her for a moment without speaking. He'd never seen peepers like hers, he thought. She was a bonny lass altogether. Give it a year or two and she'd grow into a beautiful woman, one who'd turn heads wherever she went. There was a sweetness to her face that got you somehow.

Running a hand through his bristly hair, he leaned forward slightly and again noticed the almost imperceptible movement of her body away from him. Always one for calling a spade a spade, he said quietly, 'Do I frighten you, lass?'

Lucy blinked, the colour suffusing her face almost scarlet. She wanted to deny it; he'd hardly take them on if she admitted the truth, but the words wouldn't come.

He nodded slowly as if she had affirmed it. 'Look, lass, I might be a bit rough an' ready, but you've nothing to fear from me, all right? It's me way to be a bit bumptious and mouthy. Well, you saw me in the shop, didn't you, and the customers like it, that's the thing. But I wouldn't harm a hair on your head. Nor the little 'uns.'

Lucy nodded, her throat full. He was a nice man, she could see that, and it wasn't his fault he was so big and hairy and sweaty. Swallowing hard, she said shakily, 'I know. Really, I know.'

He nodded again. 'So, the way I see it, you're in a pickle and I'm in a bit of a one meself. My Ada was a good wife an' mother, an' the bairns miss her, especially Charley. I was thinkin' I might have to get someone in to mind 'em and to see to the house full-time, a housekeeper you might say, but to tell you the truth I couldn't afford what they'd ask, not with paying a lad down in the shop an' all. If you an' the others are prepared to work for your keep – not the two little 'uns of course, I don't mean them – I think we might have got ourselves a satisfactory arrangement all round. Your brother an' sister can help me downstairs once they're back from school of an evenin', an' in the mornin' for a couple of hours afore they go, an' if I need you during the day I can shout up and you can come down for a bit. That shouldn't happen too often, but you can never tell what a day'll bring.'

He stopped, clearing his throat – something Lucy was to learn was a habit when he was embarrassed or out of his depth – before he said, 'There, there, lass, don't take on, there's nowt to cry about.'

'You – you're so kind.' The tears streaming down her face, Lucy tried to pull herself together.

'Aye, well, I don't know about that, you'll have your hands full an' no mistake.' He smiled at her, revealing surprisingly white, even teeth. 'We'll see about a couple of beds for you an' your sisters, an' you can organize that room how you want it. You'll find a stack of material in there. Ada was always buying bits that caught her eye and makin' something or other. I dare say you can use a sewing machine?' – Lucy couldn't, but she nodded anyway, telling herself she would soon learn – 'so you can run a few things up for yourself and the bairns when you've time.'

Lucy nodded again. She was well aware they looked a motley crew. 'We've some things in the trunk,' she said quietly. 'Blankets and a few bits from home.'

'Aye, well, everything'll come in useful, lass. I'll bring it up later and you can sort out tomorrow. For now' – he rose ponderously to his feet – 'you get away to bed. You're goin' to be busy tomorrow sure enough.'

'Thank you.' Lucy had stood up when he did and now she faced him, wetting her lips before she said, 'That's not enough, to say thank you, but I promise you won't regret taking us in, Mr Alridge. We'll work day and night to pay you back.' Even as she said it she wondered how she was going to make Ruby come up to scratch.

'Aye, well, you can start paying me back by forgetting the "Mr Alridge", lass. Makes me feel old enough to meet my Maker, that does. The name's Perce, short for Percival. Ada always used to call me Percy, but she was the only one who did.'

Realizing she ought to have said it before, Lucy murmured, 'I'm sorry about your wife, Mr – Perce.'

'So am I, lass. So am I.' There was a depth of sadness in his voice. 'Known each other from bairns, me an' Ada, an' she was one of the best.' Briskly now he turned from her, saying over his shoulder, 'I've things to do downstairs for mornin', so I'll say goodnight.'

Lucy stood staring after him when he had gone. She had seen his eyes fill up just before he'd left; he must have loved his wife very much. The thought was comforting and for the first time since she had walked into the shop she found herself relaxing a little. Letting out her breath in a great sigh, she glanced round the room. It was grubby and messy, and the square of carpet in the sitting room and the clippy mat in front of the range stank from where Charley had wet himself numerous times. The smell in the boys' bedroom had knocked her backwards too.

In spite of her exhaustion she itched to get started on transforming the fishmonger's home back to how it used to be, but telling herself that tomorrow was another day – one more of her mother's aphorisms – she crept into the room where Ruby and the twins were sleeping. Just as she was, she crawled under the blankets next to Ruby, who was snoring softly, and in spite of the hard floor, which the eiderdown did little to alleviate, she was asleep within moments.

Chapter Thirteen

The next weeks were ones of hard work and adjustment for the occupants of the house-cum-shop in Long Bank, but by the middle of June, when suffragists were mourning the death of Emmeline Pankhurst, the First Lady of women's suffrage, Lucy and her brother and sisters were settled into a routine. Lucy had resisted attempting to find out news of Jacob, although she thought of him all the time. There was little possibility he'd pulled through, but if he had, he was still lost to her as finally as if he were dead. Tom Crawford was dangerous – just how dangerous she hadn't fully realized until that night in May – and his last words rang in her ears when she thought of Jacob. Tom would kill Jacob if she went to him. She'd heard the truth in his voice when he'd threatened her and she believed absolutely he would do it. She had to forget her old life and make this new one work. There was no other choice.

Getting the rooms above the shop clean and sweet-smelling – along with the privy in the yard, which had stunk to high heaven – had taken time, especially because Lucy had found the fishmonger's boys very demanding at first. Traumatized by their mother's untimely demise and the long periods when they'd been locked in the flat alone by their harassed father, they were confused and frightened. Charley wet himself constantly and Matthew had nightmares several times a night, his screams so blood-curdling that poor Flora and Bess wailed and whimpered under the bedclothes.

After making the decision to put Charley back into nappies for the time being and allowing him a pap bottle whenever he asked, there was a marked improvement in his wellbeing. Flora and Bess regarded him as a live doll and spoiled him outrageously, something Charley lapped up, and within a few days he was toddling about and laughing and getting up to mischief like any normal three-year-old.

Matthew was a different kettle of fish. Try as they might, Flora and Bess found they couldn't persuade him to join in their play, no matter what they said or did. He watched Charley and the twins silently most of the time, sucking his thumb and answering in monosyllables when the little girls talked to him. He was never rude or hostile, merely totally uncommunicative. Every so often he would dissolve in tears for no apparent reason and at those times couldn't be comforted.

Lucy had found Matthew to be an intelligent and thoughtful child with a sensitivity beyond his years, the very antithesis of his rough-and-ready father. Maybe he took after his mother or even his grandparents, but as both the boys' paternal and maternal grandparents were dead and Ada's two sisters had long since moved away from the district, there was no one she could ask. Certainly it was clear that although Matthew loved his father, they were not close, and Perce had a limited understanding of his son.

She encouraged Matthew to help her in little jobs about the house, seeking to draw him out of himself, but although there was the occasional breakthrough, it was obvious the child was troubled and very unhappy. Some of this was to be expected, for he had lost his mother recently after all, but Lucy felt there was more to it than that. She couldn't put her finger on what it was, but sometimes she thought he was living in a state of terror, and then she would ask herself if she was seeing her own state of mind in the little boy, as an answer to his problem. The thought of Tom Crawford finding her, of knowing where she was living, was a constant fear.

And then came the night when, after a particularly bad nightmare, she lifted Matthew out of bed and took him into the sitting room, determined to get to the bottom of what was troubling him. He had always refused to talk about his night terrors and she hadn't pushed him, feeling it was early days and she needed to tread carefully with the boys, but on this occasion his white, pinched face and stricken eyes persuaded her differently.

Perce was snoring loudly in the third bedroom. He never woke, whatever the din, and she wondered how many times Matthew had lain, rigid with fright and crying, since his mother had died. She held him for a long time until he stopped shaking and his sobs diminished, and then said softly, 'Tell me what the dream was about, Matthew. If you talk about it, it won't be so bad. I promise.'

The reply came choked by tears. 'It will.'

One small hand was resting on hers, dimples where knuckles would be one day, and her heart went out to him. 'If you share it with me, I will know how to help if it comes again, won't I? And although it's scary and horrible, it's best to tell someone. Do you want me to call your da so you can tell him, hinny?'

'No.' His hand clutched at her. 'I – I'll tell you.'

'Good lad.' When he didn't speak for a few moments she prompted, 'Is it always the same dream or different ones?'

'The same.' He sniffed and rubbed his nose. 'It starts off being very dark, like when you close your eyes, an' I know I've got to open the door.' He gave a great heave of a sob. 'So I find the handle, but when I open the door the dark's turned red and me mam's there an' she's screaming at me. There's – there's blood everywhere, an' she comes at me like this' – he held out his arms, making his hands into claws – 'and the blood's coming out of her mouth. An' I see Charley on the floor an' she's done for him an' I know she's going to get me too. I scream and scream' – he took a shuddering breath – 'an' then I wake up.'

'Oh, Matthew . . .' Appalled, she pulled him closer as

the sobs racked his body, rocking him back and forth. He burrowed into her like a baby animal seeking protection and for a few minutes they remained like that, only his quiet weeping and the ticking of the clock on the mantelpiece breaking the silence.

She spoke again, even more softly, her voice scarcely above a whisper as a thought occurred to her. 'On the night your mam went to heaven, did you see her?'

There was a long pause and when his voice came it was so faint she could barely make out the words. 'Charley was asleep, and me da had told me to stay in bed, but Mam was making this noise and I wanted to see if she was all right. She – she was lying on the bed and' – he shook his head as if it was too terrible to explain – 'then Mrs Dodds took something out of her and it was all bloody and it was a babbie. And then Mam was quiet and me da was crying.'

'Did they know you were there, your da and Mrs Dodds?'

'No.' His head whipped up and again he was clutching at her. 'You mustn't tell me da, Lucy. He'd said for me to stay in bed. He'll say it was my fault if he knows.'

'Your fault? Of course he won't. Your mam – what happened wasn't your fault, hinny. You mustn't think that.'

'I was supposed to stay in bed.'

'Matthew, something went wrong when your mam was having the baby, something inside her, and it was nothing to do with you or anyone else. It wasn't her fault

– she loved the baby like she loved you and Charley, and it certainly wasn't your fault, either. Her and the baby are in heaven now and one day you'll see her again, like she used to be before that night, because that's how she looks, I promise, but for now your da and you and Charley have to take care of each other. That's what your mam would want, because she loves you all, very much.'

'If – if I'd done what Da said, she wouldn't have died, nor the babbie. I was naughty—'

'No.' She stopped his choked words. 'No, Matthew, that's not true, and your da would tell you so if he knew what you're thinking. You have to believe me.' Desperately she searched for words to take away the images he should never have seen, images that haunted his days and turned his nights into horror. 'What happened was an accident, Matthew. Like when John cut himself the other evening on your da's big knife in the shop. Do you remember? He came up here and I had to put a bandage on his hand and it kept bleeding for ages. But it was an accident, like your mam's. But she's safe now with the baby in heaven, and you're safe here with your da and Charley.'

'And you.' It was a whisper. 'You're going to stay, aren't you, Lucy? I want you to stay.'

'Of course I'm going to stay.' She kissed the top of his small head. 'I promise. Now do you want some warm milk to help you sleep?'

He nodded. 'Can I have it in a bottle like Charley does, on your lap?'

She hugged him tightly. If he had but known, he could have had anything he wanted right at that moment.

She held him close while he drank the warm milk and when he drifted off to sleep she didn't disturb him, settling herself in the chair and dozing on and off until morning when Perce came out of his bedroom. Shushing him before his deep booming voice woke the child on her lap, she filled him in on what Matthew had said, both the nightmare and what had followed.

'Damn and blast it!' Perce was appalled, his voice uncharacteristically weak, and he sat down heavily. 'He saw it? Matthew saw that bloodbath?'

'He not only saw it, but he's got it into his head it was his fault his mam died. These nightmares, when his mam's trying to get him, it's all mixed up with the night she died. He needs reassurance that he's not to blame. From you, his da.'

'Aye.' Perce nodded, staring at her a trifle vacantly. 'But what'll I say?' He rubbed his nose, much as Matthew had done earlier. 'I'm – I'm not any good with words.'

The last emotion Lucy would have expected to feel for this great hulking man was compassion, but it was that which was filling her now. She still shrank from him, especially when she heard some of his coarse banter in the shop with the more earthy of his customers – although he never spoke like that with her. And physically she found him repulsive, she couldn't help it. But over the last weeks she had come to understand that while he wasn't simple or backward, he wasn't too bright, either.

As Perce himself was apt to say – with an element of pride too – what he was short of in brain power he made up for in brawn. The fact that he had been an only child and his late parents had left him a thriving business had been his good fortune, lifting him above the average man in the street. Quietly now she said, 'We'll go over it, but it's important that *you* do the talking with him, all right?'

'Aye, all right,' he answered obediently. 'An' thanks, thanks, lass.'

All this had happened just over a week ago, and since the morning Perce had spoken with Matthew it was obvious: a weight had been lifted from the child's shoulders. He enjoyed playing with his brother and the twins now, and was undoubtedly the leader in their games. He was sleeping better and his appetite had grown, but he rarely let Lucy out of his sight, and on the occasions Perce called her to help in the shop for a while, Matthew was forever up and down the stairs checking she was there. Lucy had flatly refused to lock the door to the flat at those times, assuring Perce that the twins would keep little Charley with them upstairs, but that Matthew needed to know he was free to come downstairs when he wanted to.

To Lucy's relief she found she didn't have to cajole or threaten Ruby in order for her sister to pull her weight in the shop. From the first day, Ruby had taken to the work like a duck to water. She cheerfully did her stint before school every morning and just as happily at night once she was home, learning the names of the different kinds of fish and their prices and becoming a favourite with the customers. John did his share stoically, but he didn't enjoy it and neither did Lucy when she helped out. The serried ranks of cod, whiting, plaice, catfish, dogfish, monkfish, haddock, mackerel and the rest, all with blank eyes staring blindly, depressed her, and the huge tubs of live eels caused her stomach to churn. The smell, the slime on Perce's great marble slabs and the buckets behind the counter full of guts and innards and blood sickened her, and although she kept telling herself she had to get used to it and it would get better as time went on, it didn't. In fact it got steadily worse.

And then, at the beginning of a July that promised to be a scorcher, Lucy finally faced the fact that the sickness that had grown worse over the last week, until now she was actually vomiting, wasn't so much to do with the fish as with her own body. She had flown downstairs that morning, her hand over her mouth, and once in the privy had retched and retched until she was sweating and shaking.

She had seen her mam like this. The knowledge that she'd been refusing to let into her consciousness could no longer be kept at bay, and she laid her head against the rough brick wall of the small outbuilding. *Before Ruby and John were born, and again with the twins.*

She was carrying a bairn. Tom Crawford's bairn.

Perce had been up when she had hurriedly left the bedroom and shot down the stairs, and as she leaned against the wall of the privy she heard him outside. After a moment he called, 'Lucy? Lucy, lass? Are you all right?'

She shut her eyes tightly. She doubted at this moment if she would ever be all right again. Only bad girls got themselves in the family way without a wedding ring on their finger. The lives of such girls were blighted, and no decent man would look the side they were on. Charlotte Woodrow's face was vivid on the screen of her mind. Charlotte, who'd been so bonny that the little seven-year-old girl Lucy had been then had looked at her in awe. Charlotte had gone into service at a grand house in the country, and when she had returned home eighteen months later there had been an almighty rumpus one night when her da had leathered her to within an inch of her life. A few months later a fine bouncing baby boy had arrived. Her parents had kept their grandson, but thrown their daughter out, and it was well known that Charlotte had been reduced to servicing sailors down at the docks for a bob a go.

'Lucy?' Perce's voice came again, louder. 'Say something.'

Opening her eyes, she wiped her mouth with the back of her hand. She wanted to say that she wished she was dead – would that satisfy him? Instead she slid the bolt on the door and stepped into the yard.

Perce surveyed her white face for a moment. 'Belly upset?'

It would have been easy to say yes, but what was the

point? She was only delaying the inevitable. Would he turn them out, lock, stock and barrel? She wouldn't blame him, but if he did it would be the end. Her fight to keep them all out of the workhouse would have been for nothing. Perhaps she would be able to persuade him to keep Ruby and John and the twins, if she made herself scarce and agreed to disappear for good? She knew where she would go then – and it wouldn't be the living death of the workhouse. But she wouldn't end it round these parts; she'd get as far away as she could, so there was no chance of Ruby and the others finding out and being distressed. Ruby and John worked hard and well in the shop, Perce was always saying so, and the twins were good for Charley and Matthew. Would Perce see that when he'd had time to think?

Looking him full in the face, she said simply, 'I think I'm expecting a baby.'

Perce's slack mouth fell open and it testified to his amazement that for once he had nothing to say.

After a moment she said dully, 'It wasn't my fault, he – he forced me. I don't expect you to believe that, but it's the truth. After Donald had gone, and he knew I was alone with the bairns, he came to the house late at night when they were asleep and I was in the kitchen. That's when he . . .' She swallowed hard. 'Me and the bairns got away the next morning because I knew he'd come back again. I'm – I'm not bad. I'm not.'

Perce stared at the little lass he'd come to admire and rely on over the last weeks. She had turned the flat into a home again, and had worked wonders with the lads. His life was back on an even keel and running as smoothly as when Ada was alive and he was grateful for it. Furthermore she was bright up top, and as bonny as a summer's day, and she and her siblings did the work of twice their number. He knew he needn't fret or worry that they had sticky fingers; he could leave Lucy or the other two in the shop without having to concern himself that the till would be short at the end of the day. But this: a *bairn*. He hadn't reckoned on this.

Feeling as though he'd just been punched hard in the stomach, he cleared his throat twice. 'Who is he? This bloke?'

There was no reply from her, only a downward movement of her head.

'You can tell me, lass.'

'No.' She shook her head. 'I can't.'

'Do' – again he cleared his throat – 'do you love him?'

'*No.*'

There was something in the one word which settled that notion once and for all in his mind, and with it came the conviction that she was telling the truth; she had been used against her will. As coarse and earthy as he was, Perce found the idea repugnant. What sort of scum would take a nice little lass like Lucy and treat her like that? His big hands clenched into fists at his sides. 'Lass, if you tell me his name, I'll go and see him. He needs to be told—'

'No.' She made a sound that was something between

a groan and a whimper. 'I can't. He mustn't know where I am.'

'You're frightened of him.' It was a flat statement. 'Did he threaten you afterwards? Cos I'll knock his block off—'

'No.' Again she interrupted him and now she was wringing her hands in her anxiety. 'You don't understand. He's dangerous, Perce, and he wants me. If he knew I was expecting, he'd be pleased because he'd think he'd got me. Oh, I can't explain, but if he knew, I'd never get away again. He'd think he'd got a hold on me and somehow he'd make me marry him. I know he would.'

Perce's simple face stretched in puzzlement as he stared at her. 'But there's the bairn,' he said, as though whatever had gone before was of no account. 'If he'd marry you . . .'

'I'd rather die than have him lay a hand on me again. And I don't want his bairn, I can't bear the thought of it. I wish it was dead. I wish *I* was dead.'

'Don't talk like that, lass.'

'Why?' She suddenly rounded on him, her eyes wild. 'He's a vile, horrible man and he hurt me, and you think I should still marry him because of the baby? I hate him, I've always hated him and I think my mam knew what he was like all along. She never liked him.' She burst into tears, turning away from Perce to stand with her face in her hands as her body shook.

Perce stood looking at her helplessly, not knowing what to say or do. A sudden thought struck him. 'Is this bloke the same one who got your da an' brother killed, an' frightened Donald away down south?'

Lucy tried to pull herself together. Her voice a sob, she said brokenly, 'Yes', scrubbing at her eyes with the backs of her hands. 'Like I said, he's dangerous. No one can stand up to him.'

They were looking at each other when they heard the back door in the house next door open and someone clatter into the yard, divided from theirs by a seven-foot-high wall. A long and profoundly loud eruption from the unfortunate's nether regions was followed by a male voice yelling, 'Beattie? There's no lav paper again. I thought you were goin' to get the bairns to cut up a few more newspapers?'

An equally irate female voice yelled back, 'I did! There's more backsides in this house than just yours, Arthur Briggs.'

'Aye, well, be that as it may, I'm sittin' here with me trousers round me ankles an' this particular backside in need of wipin', so if it's not too much trouble' – this was said with great sarcasm – 'a couple of pages of yesterday's *Echo* would be appreciated.'

Lucy had shut her eyes during the exchange, but she opened them now when Perce said gruffly, 'Get yourself inside an' we'll talk of this later, all right?'

She nodded, walking past him into the back room of the shop and making for the stairs which led to the flat, before turning on the first step. 'I know this has put you in a spot, but would you see your way clear to keeping Ruby and John and the twins on? Ruby can help in the house as well as the shop and John's a good worker, you know he is, and the twins . . .' She floundered; he'd think the twins were too young to be of account. 'The twins help with Charley and keep Matthew company,' she finished weakly. 'I promise I'll disappear and not bother you again, and no one will know about the – the bairn.'

He said nothing, staring at her across the room for a full ten seconds. Then he wetted his lips: 'Like I said, we'll talk later, lass, but for now there's the day's business to get on with, an' the bairns'll be wanting their breakfast.'

She nodded again, but as he disappeared into the front of the shop called softly, 'It'd be the workhouse, you see. That's the thing.'

There was silence for a few moments and then she heard him begin to open up in readiness for the crates of fish and seafood that were delivered fresh every morning once it was light. Feeling as though she was walking in ten-ton boots, she made her way upstairs to begin what had become her routine, since living at the fishmonger's premises.

This might be the last morning she would wake up here, she told herself as she opened the front door of the flat, and it dawned on her, as she gazed around, how much of a home it had become. She had tried to pretend to herself that life could be normal again, that she could forget what Tom Crawford had done, and live here quietly looking after the house and the bairns, but that dream was over. She had something growing inside her. Not a tumour, like poor Gladys Lyndon had had. Gladys's mam and da had gone mad at first when her belly had begun to swell. But when they'd marched her to the doctor's and he'd told them she hadn't misbehaved as they'd assumed, Gladys's mam had come to see her mam and she'd been crying and saying she wished Gladys *had* been expecting, because the doctor had only given her a few months to live.

Lucy's hand brushed her still-flat stomach and her mouth tightened. She'd give anything to have a tumour rather than a piece of Tom Crawford inside her. She couldn't bear it, she'd go mad. But no, she wouldn't have to bear it. Once the bairns were settled one way or the other, she would do what she had to do. There were places where the river flowed deep and fast, and undercurrents and debris made sure whatever went down never came up. If Jacob had died, would she see him, her mam and da and Ernie too? Or would she go straight to hell because what she was going to do was a sin? Whatever, it made no difference. She was tired. Tired of fighting and trying. She had never felt so tired in her life, come to think of it. Or so sick and ill.

Rallying herself, she got Ruby and John up and sent them down to help Perce in the shop as usual, before tidying up and preparing breakfast for the household. Then she woke Charley and changed his nappy and dressed him, before rousing Matthew and the twins. Once the four were sitting at the kitchen table she called Ruby and John. The children always had their breakfast together, before Ruby and John disappeared downstairs to hold the fort while Perce came upstairs for his meal. Usually she sat at the table and ate with him, but today she set no place for herself, something he noticed as soon as he came up.

'You not eatin'?' He frowned at her.

'I'm not hungry.'

'Hungry or not, you need somethin' in your belly, lass.' Then, realizing it was probably the worse thing he could have said in the circumstances, he covered himself by blustering, 'Everyone needs to stoke the boilers at the beginnin' of the day, sets you up, so it does. Sit yourself down an' have a bite of somethin' with a sup tea. Come on, lass, I mean it.'

She sat, only because she was feeling distinctly ill again and it was easier than arguing.

His voice softer, Perce murmured, 'A dry biscuit or two always used to settle Ada at the beginning of the morning when she was . . . you know. An' then an hour or so later she'd be ready for something more. Little an' often, lass. That does it.'

The kindness was almost too much. Knowing that if she started to cry she wouldn't be able to stop, Lucy nodded and did as he suggested. Funnily enough, after a few minutes the nausea receded enough for her to enjoy a cup of tea.

Perce ate his usual breakfast of a plate of smoked kippers with great chunks of buttered bread with every appearance of enjoyment, and once he had finished he clomped off downstairs so that Ruby and John could get ready for school. The school was at the back of Holy

Trinity Church in Church Street East just a short distance away, but Ruby, who would much have preferred to stay working in the shop with Perce than sit in a classroom doing her lessons, always left the house at the last minute. Usually Lucy was patient with her sister's dawdling, but today she found herself snapping at Ruby several times. Ruby eventually left the house in a flounce with a face like thunder.

An hour later, with the four younger children playing happily, Lucy collected the dirty washing and took it down to the wash-house in the yard. A copper boiler stood in one corner with a tin bath turned upright in another, and a table for scrubbing ran along one wall. There was room for the mangle and poss-tub too. When Lucy had first entered the wash-house some weeks back she had considered it the height of luxury to be able to do the washing away from the flat, and it made bathing so much easier too.

Today, though, desolation and despair coloured her surroundings, sucking every last vestige of hope and courage from her spirit. She leaned her head against the brick wall of the wash-house, shutting her eyes as she gave in to the dread filling her mind. *What was to become of them?* She touched the small silver heart in the hollow of her throat, her soul reaching out to Jacob as the tears trickled down her face.

'I love you,' she whispered as she stood there, feeling very small and very alone. 'For always, and I'm sorry. I'm so so, sorry . . .'

Chapter Fourteen

It had been three weeks before Enid and Aaron could bring Jacob home, and another two before his broken ribs would allow him to breathe easily, but now, at the beginning of July, he was looking and feeling more like his old self. His nose would never be the same again, but not being a vain individual, its crookedness bothered him not a jot, nor was he concerned about the scar which ran from his right eyebrow to his ear. A tiny fraction one way and he might have lost his eye, but he had been spared that misfortune. He was lucky. Everyone kept telling him so. And he could have believed it if Lucy was next door.

He thought of her all the time and his thoughts were a torment to him, especially through the long night hours when the rest of the world was sleeping. Used to the hard physical work in the forge, his enforced idleness was a subtle torture. Only the fact that the doctors had warned him that he could put himself back into hospital if he tried to rush his recovery prevented him from returning to the blacksmith's.

Over the last couple of weeks he had begun to take slow but lengthy walks, as much to get away from the house and his mother's eagle eyes as to get his damaged body into shape. It had been a day or two before he allowed himself to acknowledge that during these walks he was constantly searching every face for that one dear one. Crazy, he knew, because she was away down south somewhere, but he couldn't help it. And every moment his mind was giving him hell. She had gone. Without a word. Without a last goodbye even. He had been as near death as damn it, and she hadn't waited to see if he pulled through. He had said as much to his mother, and she had put the blame on Donald for making Lucy leave, but he couldn't altogether buy that. If she had loved him like he loved her, she would have waited. Hell, he'd been on the point of asking her to marry him and taking on the lot of them, hadn't he? More fool him. Aye, more fool him. Well, now he knew. She wasn't the lass he had thought she was.

He was thinking along these lines as he sat eating his dinner with his parents and Frank and Ralph, lost in a morose brooding, which the other four couldn't fail to notice, but which they'd learned through experience they couldn't jolly him out of. He was with them but not with them, and it was worrying Enid to death. She glanced at him now out of the corner of her eye, wondering where her happy, cheerful son who always had a quip hovering on his lips had gone. It was as though a light had gone out, she told herself, forcing food past the hard lump in her throat that such thoughts always produced. And she didn't know what to do or how to help him. He'd nearly bitten her head off when she'd made the mistake of saying that there were other fish in the sea besides Lucy, and since that time they'd all been careful not to speak her name or to allude to their old neighbours in any way. But he couldn't go on like this. It was as though he'd given up – that's what frightened her. He needed something, anything, to snap him out of the dark place he was in.

The blacksmith and his wife came to the house an hour later. It wasn't unusual for Abe Williamson to drop by; he'd called several times since Jacob had been at home, but not with his wife. Jacob was sitting on a chair in the yard and the others were listening to the wireless when the knock came at the front door, sending Enid into a tizz. Only Jacob's employer, Dr Pearson and the vicar would knock on the front door; everyone else used the back. And when she opened the door and Abe's homely face smiled at her she was relieved. The blacksmith might be Jacob's boss, but he was one of them – an ordinary bloke – unlike the doctor and the vicar; and with the dinner dishes still to see to and Aaron and the lads in their slippers with their shirtsleeves rolled up, she'd have been mortified if it was either of the other two.

Hiding her surprise that Dolly Williamson had accompanied her husband, Enid swung the door wide. 'Come in, come in,' she said warmly. 'It's good of you to call, Mr Williamson, and you too, Mrs Williamson. Jacob's been a bit down the last day or two. It'll gladden him to see you.'

They didn't step up into the house straight away, and it was Dolly who said, her voice subdued, 'We wondered if we could see Jacob alone, Mrs Crawford? If you don't mind, of course.'

'Mind? Why would I mind?' Enid smiled broadly, even as she thought: What now? Don't they know my lad is at the end of his tether? If they've come to give him the old heave-ho, it's bad timing at best, and I'll have something to say about it. Say what you like, the blokes who set upon him had their eye on the bits and pieces in the smithy, and Jacob was in the way. It's as plain as the nose on your face, and they owe him something for that.

Keeping the smile on her face with some effort, Enid showed the visitors into the front room, sending up thanks that it had received its weekly dusting that very day and was looking its best. She was thrilled with her front room. She had told Tom exactly what she wanted in there and he'd done her proud, bless him. 'I'll get Jacob,' she said, a trifle stiffly in spite of herself.

When Jacob walked into the room a minute or two later after a hasty conversation with his mother, which had resulted in him warning her to hold her tongue regardless of what his employer had to say, he found Abe and Dolly sitting side by side on the elaborate brocade couch, which would have been more suited to a grand drawing room than a terraced front room. He could see what had disturbed his mother – the pair clearly had something to say. Unlike Enid, however, he felt no trepidation about the forthcoming conversation. Due to the beating, he'd already had several weeks off work and the blacksmith couldn't be expected to keep his job open indefinitely. It would be another couple of weeks, maybe three or four, before Jacob was able to commence his duties and even then the doctor had warned he might not feel up to it. Abe Williamson knew this; Jacob had told the doctors to explain the facts to him. There was no point in being anything but completely honest. Maybe if the very worst hadn't happened, maybe if Lucy hadn't left him, he'd be feeling differently right now, but if he was being truthful, he found he simply didn't care about his job or anything else.

He smiled at the couple, who had always been very fair with him. If they had come to tell him they were letting him go, he wanted the meeting to end well and for them to part as friends. Stepping forward, he shook Abe's hand as the blacksmith stood up, saying, 'Hello, Mr Williamson, it's good of you to come again' and then was touched when Dolly sprang to her feet and hugged him.

'You look a lot better than the last time I saw you,' she said, a little tearfully. 'Frightened us to death, you did. I'd have laid odds you were going to snuff it.'

Jacob grinned, his first natural smile in weeks. You always got the truth from Dolly. 'I'm clearly tougher than I look.'

'And just look at your poor nose,' she continued worriedly. 'Does it hurt?'

'Not any more.' He tapped the offending article to prove the point. 'I think it looks pretty good, like one of the boxers in the travelling fairs, don't you think?'

'Oh, go on with you.' Dolly hugged him again before sitting down as Enid bustled in with a tray of tea and biscuits, making a great show of shutting the door behind her as she left and not saying a word.

'Oh dear, have we offended your mother by asking to speak to you privately?' Abe said ruefully. 'It's just that we felt it only right to talk to you first.'

'Don't worry about Mam.' Jacob sat down in a chair opposite the couch as the blacksmith seated himself again. 'She's a bit het-up at the moment. Only natural, I suppose.'

'Oh aye, aye.' Dolly nodded vigorously. 'She must have been beside herself, I know I have been. What a thing to happen and on our own doorstep, so to speak. If I live to be a hundred, I'll never forget the way you looked when we lifted you from that ditch.' Her lip quivered as her voice faltered.

'Aye, well, we're not goin' down that road,' said Abe hastily. 'Look, lad, we've both come the night because we've a proposition to put to you, as you might say.'

He paused, and when he seemingly found it difficult to go on, Dolly spoke again, but softly now. 'I think you know we've always looked on you as the son we never had, Jacob, right from the time you first came to work at the smithy for a bob or two on a Saturday. We're fond of you, more than fond, and we always intended to do what we're about to say, but this terrible attack on you has prompted our hand. We want to get everything straight, so we all know where we stand.'

Jacob stared at the couple. He didn't have a clue where this was leading, but if it was a prelude to giving him the sack it was a funny way to go about it.

'I went to see me solicitor in Bishopwearmouth last week, lad.' Abe took over again. 'Stamp & Stamp in the High Street – do you know 'em?'

Jacob shook his head, somewhat bemused.

'I changed things, so when I pop me clogs everything comes to you, with a stipulation that you look after Dolly as you would your own mam, and let her live in the house as long as she's alive, with a monthly allowance. We've a fair bit in the bank; never had nowt to spend it on, having no bairns, I suppose, and with the business and all, I think it's fair to say you'll be set up for life.'

Jacob was sitting bolt upright in the chair now, his face portraying what he was feeling. 'But – but – I'm no relation. I mean, there must be someone else closer.' He shook his head, bewilderment and amazement vying with disbelief. 'It's very good of you, Mr Williamson, more than good, but . . .' Again he shook his head, his eyes stretched wide. 'I – I can't let you do it.'

'It's done, lad.' Abe grinned at him. 'And it's as the pair of us would want. But I think you could call us Abe and Dolly now, don't you think? Seeing as we're nearly family.'

Jacob stared at the couple, who were beaming at his obvious surprise and shock. He had known they thought a lot of him, but this, this was . . . He could find no words to describe it. They had said they thought of him as a son, and in truth for a long time now they'd been more than just employers to him. He got to his feet and they rose with him, and when he stammered, 'I-I don't – know what to say,' Dolly stepped forward and took him into her arms, saying, 'Don't say anything, lad. Just get better, that's all we want.'

'Thank you.' He was hugging her and as Abe joined them the three of them stood together, their arms round each other. 'Thank you, thank you so much. I can't believe it.' He didn't know if he was laughing or crying; maybe it was a bit of both, and certainly Dolly's face was wet by the time they drew away.

'It's up to you, lad, but we wondered if you'd find it easier to move in with us at home rather than make the journey back and forth, when you're able to come back? You could perhaps come and see your folks at the weekend. That way I could go through matters appertaining to the business in the evenings when we've had our meal, show you the paperwork and the financial side and things like that. It's just a thought; sleep on it and let us know. We've plenty of room – four big bedrooms, as you know – so we won't be on top of each other.'

Jacob looked into the kindly face of the blacksmith. He didn't have to think about the offer, it was just what he needed. He had been dreading continuing to live next door to where Lucy had been. There were too many memories, too many things to remind him every moment of what he had lost. It wasn't too extreme to say there had been times when he'd thought he was losing his mind over the last weeks, instances when he could have sworn he heard her voice through the wall or calling from the yard outside. Of course, the fact he wasn't sleeping most nights didn't help. His mam said he was low physically and mentally because of what had happened, and it was early days. She was probably right, but he knew he would never be the same now that Lucy had vanished. That was the nub of how he was feeling, and perhaps moving away from Zetland Street and making a new start would give him peace of mind.

A new start . . . As he stood on the doorstep waving goodbye to Abe and Dolly some time later, the words reverberated in Jacob's mind. That was the way he had to look at things from this day forth. Whatever Lucy had felt for him, or not felt, didn't matter now. He had to forget her. He'd thought he knew her as well as himself, but it had been a delusion. It was a lesson for the future: once bitten, twice shy. He nodded at the thought, his mouth grim.

He squared his shoulders, waving once more as Abe and Dolly turned the corner. Then he stepped back into the house, shutting the door behind him.

Abe and Dolly had asked him to wait until they had gone before he broke the news to his family and he wasn't surprised to see his mother peering round the kitchen door. Her brow was creased with worry for him, and a sudden rush of love for her took him by surprise. He grinned at her. 'Stop frettin', they weren't here to give me the push, all right? Just the opposite, if anything. It's good news for a change. Put the kettle on, I could do with another cup of tea and I'll tell you all about it.'

They listened with open mouths, and then came a storm of questions and congratulations and, from his mother, a few tears of joy. 'Who'd have thought it, our baby brother a man of means,' Frank said to Ralph, winking as he did so.

'And him nothing more than a whippersnapper.' Ralph shook his head. 'And gormless into the bargain, don't forget that.'

'Oh aye, definitely gormless. I'm surprised he knows one end of a horse from the other when he's shoeing 'em, but then with two legs at each end he can't go far wrong.'

The chaffing and laughing were at their height when Tom walked into the kitchen from the hall a minute or two later. He had recently acquired a motor car, which he parked in the street under the gas lamp, and Enid had promptly given him a key so that he could use the front door when he visited. He stood just inside the doorway as he glanced around, his voice faintly patronizing as he said, 'Had a few the night, have we?'

'Not a one, lad, not a one.' Enid almost danced over to him. 'It's our Jacob, you'll never guess. Abe was here, and he's making Jacob his heir. Look on him as a son, they do. Everything'll be his one day. The house, the forge, everything. What do you think about that?'

Tom's eyes shot to his brother and Jacob returned the

look, straight and unblinking. He knew exactly what Tom would think about it. Frank and Ralph had pulled his leg, but he knew they were chuffed for him, and his mam and da were over the moon. Not so Tom. Oh no. He'd be spitting bricks inside.

There was a moment's silence and then Tom raised his eyebrows, coming further into the kitchen. 'Is that so?' He smiled at Jacob, his mouth wide, but his eyes cold. 'Well, aren't you the dark horse. How did you pull that one off?'

Jacob made himself smile back. He wasn't about to give Tom the satisfaction of rising to the bait, although he was aware of the insult beneath the friendly-sounding words spoken in a jocular fashion. 'The sun shines on the righteous, Tom.' He forced a natural-sounding chuckle as though the exchange was nothing more than one brother ribbing another. 'But I don't suppose you know much about that.'

For a moment Tom lost his smile and the facade slipped, and Jacob glimpsed what was beneath. It reminded him of the evening he had gone to his brother's house, an evening that had prompted all sorts of thoughts during the long painful days and nights when he was lying in the hospital wondering who had done this to him. Could Tom have been lying in wait for him that dark May night, prepared to beat him to death in cold blood? Or had he sent his minions to do his dirty work? It was possible. Jacob wouldn't put anything past his brother these days. But he had come to the conclusion that, for all his faults,

Tom wouldn't put their mother through the agony of losing a son. Tom had always thought a bit of their mam, he'd give him that.

But he could be wrong. The fine hairs on the back of Jacob's neck prickled. Looking at his brother now, he could be wrong. Whatever, once he was back at the forge he'd be on his guard, and he'd made up his mind he'd talk to Abe and Dolly about getting a couple of guard dogs. Big brutes. The bigger, the better.

The brothers stared at each other a moment longer, but when Tom turned to face the rest of the family his smile was back and it was reflected in the tone of his voice when he said, 'They say every cloud has a silver lining, but I reckon Jake's must be lined with gold. How about a drink to celebrate? You got any of that French brandy left that I brought a couple of weeks ago?'

'Aye, one bottle, lad. I'll get it.' Enid bustled out of the kitchen to fetch the brandy from the sideboard in her hallowed front room, beaming as she went. It was good to see her eldest and youngest getting on at last. They said God works in mysterious ways, and she wouldn't have wished Jacob to be beaten within an inch of his life to bring about the reconciliation, but the way Tom had visited the hospital every day spoke for itself. Blood will out. She nodded happily at the old adage.

In the kitchen, Tom spoke quietly and quickly once his mother was out of earshot. 'I want you three at Potato Garth at ten tomorrow night. Jed's sending a couple of his blokes and they're in charge, all right?'

Aaron's jaw tightened. 'I don't like working with any of them lot across the river, I've told you that.'

'You'll do as you're told and keep your mouth shut.' Tom's voice was low, but deadly. 'You don't like it, you know what to do, but the dole pays peanuts, Da. Don't forget that, and things are getting tighter. I've got a list of men as long as my arm who'd be glad of the work I put your way – all of you' – his gaze included Frank and Ralph, who hadn't opened their mouths – 'so think on.'

Aaron stared at his son, his teeth digging into the flesh of his lower lip so that the action seemed to drag his head down and his shoulders with it. 'I didn't say I didn't want the work. I didn't mean that. We do. We all do.'

Jacob couldn't witness the humiliation a moment longer. He stood up, his voice curt as he said, 'I'm tired, I'm going to bed.'

He met his mother in the hall, returning with the bottle of brandy, and she caught his arm. 'You not having a drink, lad?' And as he shook his head her voice changed, becoming sharper. 'He's falling over backwards to be nice, but you don't make it easy for him, Jacob. One drink wouldn't hurt, now then.'

He loved his mother very much, but he wanted to shake her till her teeth rattled. For years she'd chosen to close her eyes to the way Tom spoke to their da and the rest of them, and there were none so blind as those who didn't want to see. And yet he couldn't put the blame wholly at his mam's feet. His da had gone into it with his eyes open, he was reaping what he'd sown. Damn it, he was sick of the lot of them. If he hadn't been going to Abe's he'd have moved out anyway. 'I'm tired, Mam. It's been a long day,' he said shortly.

'Aye, all right.' Telling herself it was still early days in his recovery, Enid said no more, but her annoyance was evident in that she didn't wish him goodnight, but marched past him into the kitchen where she shut the door with unnecessary force.

Jacob stood for a moment or two staring after her. A few months ago, even a few weeks, he wouldn't have liked to go to bed at odds with his mother, and it disturbed him that this made no impact on his emotions now. He was changing, he told himself. He *had* changed, and he wasn't sure if he liked the new Jacob.

Then he shrugged the thought away. Everyone changed – it was part of life's pattern – and maybe this was just the final stage of severing the umbilical cord. The attack, Lucy leaving him, and everything he'd hoped for the future being blown to smithereens was part of it, but the other side of the coin was Abe and Dolly and all they were offering him. The Sister in charge of his ward at the hospital, a stern, gimlet-eyed woman who had inspired fear in her staff and patients alike, had come and sat on his bed one night in the early hours when he couldn't sleep and had got himself into a bit of a state. He'd told her about Lucy, blubbering like a baby to his shame, and she'd been kindness itself, holding him like his mam would have done and waiting until he'd pulled himself together. She'd fetched him a cup of tea and one for herself, sitting by the side of the bed and talking of this and that to pull him out of his misery. Just before she'd resumed her duties she'd leaned across and brushed the hair from his brow. 'You're young, Jacob,' she'd said softly, 'and for now you can't see the wood for the trees, but believe me when I say that when one door closes another opens. I've been a nurse for more years than I care to remember and I've seen it time and time again. Concentrate on getting well and wait for that door to open and, when it does, you walk through it, lad. All right?'

He had nodded, not really believing her, but after she'd disappeared to see to another patient he'd found he could settle down for sleep, and it had been his first long, deep sleep since he had come round from the coma.

And now that door *had* opened. Tom's loud laugh came from the kitchen followed by an obedient chorus from his family, grating on his nerves. It had opened and he was going to walk through it and make a good life for himself, or his name wasn't Jacob Crawford.

And Lucy? He would forget her. In time.

Tom was thinking along different lines as he drove home later that night. There was barely an hour that passed when he wasn't thinking about Lucy – the desire that had been a fixation from when she was little more than a child having grown into an obsession with her rejection of him. He had been sure she would see reason and come back with her tail between her legs, within a day or so of leaving. With four bairns in tow and Donald having washed his hands of them, was there any other choice? But the days had turned into weeks and still no word from her. No word for *him*. He could scarcely believe it.

After a month he had paid a visit to the Sunderland workhouse in Bishopwearmouth after it had occurred to him that that was the answer. She'd placed the youngsters into the house and gone off to find work of some kind, but Lucy being Lucy, she would go to see them on visiting days. He could trace her through her siblings and, with her soft heart and caring nature, she was probably thinking she had made a terrible mistake by now in leaving them there. He would use that.

He had been excited that day when he'd gone to see the master of the workhouse and, having convinced himself he was right, was bitterly disappointed and angry when he was proved wrong. Vowing to himself he'd take it out on her hide when he did find her, he was forced to accept that he was back at square one.

But he could be patient. He nodded at the thought as he drove into The Green and came to a stop, continuing to sit in the car as he stared blindly through the windscreen. He had been the first, and Lucy was his. She was leading him a hell of a dance right enough, but that was part of the game. Say what you like, she had wanted him that night deep down. They were all the same, playing the coquette while telling you with their eyes they were ripe for it.

He eased himself out of the car, standing for a moment as his eyes swept his surroundings. He'd come a long way since he was a snotty-nosed bairn playing in the back lanes around Zetland Street and he intended to go further still. She would be the wife of a wealthy and influential man and, once that ring was on her finger, he'd bring her to heel.

His body hardened as he visualized exactly how he would subdue and subjugate her, and as he turned towards the house he stopped. He wouldn't be able to sleep. His loins were burning for a woman and he knew the very one who would do. Kitty had been as innocent as they come when she'd first been brought to the brothel by the father who'd sold her for a good sum to the Kanes, but she'd learned fast and didn't mind a bit of rough stuff as long as she was kept supplied with the white powder she craved. Aye, a servicing by Kitty would help him sleep, and the good thing about a whore was that they didn't mind whose name you called out when you were using them.

He got back in the car, driving round the deserted green and turning in the direction of Monkwearmouth. As he drove, his mind was on the pleasures of the next hour or two, but it wasn't Kitty he was envisaging beneath him, but the girl who continued to elude him and torment his waking and sleeping hours.

Chapter Fifteen

'So, what do you say, lass?' Perce sat, his great red hands on his knees and his eyes fixed on Lucy's white face. It was ten o'clock in the evening. The children were asleep and, a few minutes before, Lucy had sat down with the fishmonger to hear their fate. She had been praying all day that Perce would find it in his heart to keep Ruby and John and the twins, but never in her wildest imaginings had she considered him saying what he had.

'But . . .' She swallowed past the constriction in her throat. 'Why would you want to marry me?'

There was an inflection in her voice that made Perce sit up straighter. 'It's not for that, lass,' he said hastily. 'I mean, not with you carryin' the bairn an' all. I wouldn't expect—' He had turned as red as a beetroot. 'What I mean to say is: that side of things wouldn't happen until after the bairn comes an' you're feelin' all right.'

She wanted to get up and run out of the room, out of the house, to keep running and running. Instead, she said tremblingly, 'Then why?'

Perce cleared his throat. 'Seems to me you're in a fix,' he said, stating the obvious. 'An' me, well, you know how it was with the bairns when you first came. Matthew, he's took to you, an' I don't know how he'd be if you went now. An' Charley, he already looks on you like his own mam. You've put things right again, that's how I see it, an' young Ruby and John are good little workers an' all.' He waved his hands helplessly, not knowing how much to say. He had been thinking hard all day and, although he'd loved his Ada, he knew Lucy was a cut above. He'd never get the chance to marry a bonny, bright lass like her again. Course, it was too soon after Ada and the tongues would wag, especially when Lucy started to show, but he'd weather the storm.

'But if you feel like that, couldn't I stay and things remain as they are?' Immediately Lucy had spoken she knew she had shocked him.

'With you in the family way? No, lass, no. There's already been a bit of gossip, you know how folks are, but with you bein' a slip of a lass an' me just havin' lost Ada, it was somethin' and nothin'. But this' – he gestured towards her stomach – 'this makes everything different. Folk'd say it was mine, and me name would be mud if I didn't do the right thing an' marry you.'

'But it's not yours.'

'Aye, well, you know that an' I know it, but the rest of 'em.' He shook his head. 'I've got Charley an' Matthew to think of, lass. I don't want them hearin' somethin' when they're older and thinkin' the less of me. Besides'

– he hesitated, and then ploughed on – 'even if folk did believe the bairn wasn't mine, they wouldn't expect me to keep you on, not with you havin' fallen outside wedlock. I'm sorry, lass, but that's the way it is. You'd have earned a name for yourself.'

She nodded. She knew full well what people would think of her. Gossip would be rife.

'Knowin' what happened, that it wasn't your fault, I'd be prepared to bring up the bairn as mine. Give it me name, I mean, an' treat it like the others.'

The bairn. *Tom Crawford's bairn.* She wanted it ripped from her body, this monstrosity growing inside her. Her voice so low it was a whisper, she murmured, 'I could see someone. Have – have it taken away.' She knew there were such women who would do the job for a price, everyone did, but not who they were or how much it would cost. Would Perce lend her the money?

His next words hit that hope on the head. 'Never, lass, an' don't talk of it. It's a sin against God an' nature, an' I know of more than one lass who's gone down that route and lived to regret it.'

'I don't want his baby, Perce.' She gulped, tears trickling down her cheeks. 'I feel dirty, unclean, contaminated.'

Perce drew in breath through his nose and then sighed loudly. 'The way I see it, lass, you've got no choice. And it's your baby too. An' mine, if we get wed. Him' – he searched for the right words – 'him fathering it is nowt in the long run; it's what happens after it's here that counts.'

Lucy stared at the man she had privately termed as slow at best, and simple at worst, and knew a moment's deep shame at her opinion of him. His words had struck a chord in her – she had never looked at it like that before. But what if it looked like Tom Crawford when it was born? Worse, what if it had his nature? But she couldn't cross that bridge now; a day at a time was enough. And in that moment she knew she was going to accept Perce's offer of marriage. How she would face the other side of marriage, once the child was born, she didn't know. It made her flesh creep to think of lying with him and letting him touch her, but again she told herself: a day at a time. She wanted to be here for the twins and Ruby and John; Matthew and Charley too, come to it. They needed her, all of them. And if she was being truthful, the thought of ending it all was terrifying. She just didn't know if it was more terrifying than continuing on.

'Are you sure you want to do this, Perce?' she whispered, part of her hoping he would say no and that he had changed his mind. 'You said how people would talk. Don't you mind?'

Perce stared into the lovely young face in front of him. He might not have much up top, he reflected, but he knew human nature and he recognized a good girl when he saw one. If she left this place she wouldn't live long, she'd see to that. She was an innocent. In spite of what had happened, she was an innocent in the true sense of the word and he found that he wanted to protect and take care of her in a way he never had with Ada. Ada had been a product of the East End, tough and hard-bitten and vigorous, like him, and he had loved her, but she had never aroused the desire to shield her from the harsher side of life like Lucy did. He didn't know how this was going to turn out; he only knew he was going to have a damn good try to make it work.

Without any hesitation, he said, 'I'm sure, lass, and they can say what they want. What they don't know they tend to make up, and while they're having us over they're leavin' some other poor blighter alone.'

They were married very quietly by special licence within two weeks, not at the Holy Trinity Church in Church Street, where Perce and Ada had been wed some years before, but at a small Methodist church where the minister had been very happy to do the job for the handsome donation Perce had made towards the fund for the failing church roof. Only the children were present and the minister's wife and grown-up daughter, who agreed to act as witnesses, again for a generous handout by Perce.

Perce closed the shop for a while, and in no more than an hour and a half they were back home, Ruby and John delighted with the bonus of a day off school, and Ruby eager to help Perce in the shop. After Perce had changed out of his Sunday suit and had a quick bite to eat, the three of them disappeared downstairs, leaving Lucy with the four younger children. They hadn't really appreciated what was going on. For the twins the short ceremony meant they could live in their new home forever and would never be cold and wet and hungry again, because that was what Lucy had told them. Matthew understood that Lucy had agreed to become his new mother and that she would never leave, because that was what Perce had told him. Charley was just happy that the other three were happy and took his cue from them.

Lucy sat watching them play, ostensibly while tackling a basketful of mending, but in reality her hands were still.

She was a married woman. She felt sick, but more in her spirit than her body. She was tied for life to Perce and, when the child was born, she would become his wife in deed as well as word.

But that was a long way off, she comforted herself quickly. Months and months. For now things would remain the same as they had been, except that she would no longer be sleeping in the bedroom with Ruby and the twins, but would join Perce in the room he had shared with his first wife. He had made it clear that was what he expected, making the point that Ruby and John were old enough to ask awkward questions if they did otherwise, and she'd been forced to agree with him.

In truth she had been surprised that Ruby and John had accepted her marrying Perce so easily, but then they both liked the big, tough fishmonger very much, so perhaps it wasn't so strange. She had told them nothing about the position she found herself in. They would leave announcing that she was expecting a baby as long as they could, and when they did tell the children, the baby would be Perce's.

That was what they'd agreed. The child would come early of course, but that happened on occasion, and if some folk assumed they'd jumped the gun, that wouldn't matter now they were married.

She glanced down at the thin gold band on the third finger of her left hand and shuddered. It felt alien and curiously heavy.

There were plenty of couples who enjoyed the wedding night before the wedding, as Perce had put it, adding that he and Ada had been at it for more than a year before they were wed.

It. Lucy's stomach turned over and she tasted bile in her mouth. It was because of *it* that she was here now, Tom Crawford's seed growing inside her womb and her life ruined. And there was still the night to come and the close proximity of Perce in their marital bed . . .

She had always disappeared into the bedroom she shared with Ruby and the twins before Perce went to bed, leaving him sitting contentedly puffing his pipe and reading the paper most nights. She knew he went downstairs after she'd turned in, presumably to use the privy and check the bolts on the doors, because she had heard him, but she was always asleep before his heavy tread came up the stairs once more.

This evening was different. Her nightdress was lying on top of the double bed in Perce's room and her personal items and clothes were in the big oak wardrobe and chest of drawers. The room itself was familiar to her. She dusted it, changed the sheets and pillowcases on the bed when necessary, and took the thick shop-bought rug at the foot of the bed downstairs to the yard to shake every so often. It was a nice room, reflecting Ada's good taste, like the rest of the flat. Tonight, though, the thought of it was terrifying.

Lucy felt frozen to her chair on one side of the fireplace as she pretended to read the *Woman's Weekly* magazine Perce had bought her that day. He often presented her with one of the weekly or monthly periodicals – *Good Housekeeping*, *People's Friend* or the newer *Woman and Home* which had only been published for a couple of years and had been Ada's favourite – and she usually read them eagerly from cover to cover, never having had such a luxury at home. Tonight, though, the words and pictures danced in front of her eyes, making no sense. All she could see was the big brass bed.

She glanced at Perce, hidden behind his paper with the odd curl or two of smoke rising above it now and again. She liked the smell of his pipe; if nothing else, it masked the sickly aroma of fish that clung to his hair and skin. It was a warm evening and she knew his face would have beads of perspiration glistening on it and that his bristly hair would be damp. She had never come across a man who sweated so much.

She felt a soft ball of nausea rise up into her throat, which had nothing to do with the morning sickness that seemed to linger most of the day, and swallowed hard. She had to make the best of this. There weren't many men who would have done what Perce had done and she was grateful to him; she was, but . . .

She jumped visibly as the newspaper lowered. 'You need to use the privy afore we turn in, lass?' Perce said quietly.

'Aye, yes, th-thank you.' She virtually scampered from the room, but once outside in the yard she didn't go directly into the privy, which she kept smelling as sweet as plenty of buckets of ash and a daily scrubbing could make it.

The humid summer's night bore no resemblance to the frosty cold evening when Jacob had held her in his arms and told her about the stars, but suddenly she was back there again, dancing in the moonlight as she looked up into the black velvet sky studded with twinkling lights. Her arms tight around her waist, she moaned out loud. She *had* to find out if he was dead or alive, she couldn't go on wondering. If he was alive and in his right mind she would be content, she could put up with anything then.

But almost immediately reason kicked in. If he was dead, nothing could bring him back. But if, somehow, he had been spared and, in her trying to find out, Tom got to know where she was, then . . . She shook her head, her heart thudding. Who knew what Tom would do? And if Jacob discovered her whereabouts, what could she say to him? That his own brother had forced her and she was pregnant with Tom's child? He wouldn't believe her story that she had married Perce freely and was expecting the fishmonger's baby – she wouldn't be able to lie that convincingly to Jacob. He would confront his brother and all hell would be let loose, and somehow Tom would see to it that Jacob was done away with. She believed that absolutely, and the more she had thought about the attack on Jacob by person or persons unknown, the more she'd wondered.

She lowered her head, her eyes dry, but her heart bleeding tears. The best thing she could do for Jacob was stay out of his life. Anyway – she turned and looked at the building behind her – she was married now. She wasn't the young, innocent girl Jacob had loved. He would probably be disgusted to see her now; she was used goods, tarnished and second-hand. He might even think she had led Tom on and got what she'd asked for.

No. She moved her head. Jacob wouldn't think that. Not her Jacob.

But he wasn't her Jacob any longer. A voice in her mind spoke clearly and coldly. Today she had stood at the altar with Perce and taken her marriage vows. Perce had offered her a way out and she had taken it. In doing so, she had made her bed and now she had to lie on it. Literally.

Perce was still reading the paper when she came back into the sitting room. He didn't lower it or look up when she said in a small voice, 'I'll get ready for bed now', merely saying, 'Aye, all right, lass. I'll be in shortly.'

Alone in the bedroom, she stared at herself in the long cheval mirror and for a moment thought of Ada. What would Perce's wife think of another woman taking her role so soon after she had passed away? But then if Ada knew, she'd also know that Perce hadn't married her because he loved her, but because, as he'd termed it, she was in a fix, and also because he needed a mother for his two boys. 'I promise I'll keep your memory alive for them,' she said softly. 'I'm not taking your place, not really.' And then she heard a noise from the sitting room and all thoughts of Ada went out of her head. She tore off her clothes in a panic and pulled on her nightdress, climbing into the strange bed, which felt much softer than it looked, and lying on the very edge of the side Perce had told her was hers. She had changed the sheets and pillowcases that afternoon and the somewhat unyielding cotton smelt fresh and clean as she pulled the covers up to her chin.

Then she remembered her hair was still pinned up in the tight bun she'd taken to wearing. Sitting up and keeping her gaze fixed on the door, she extracted the pins and combed out her hair with her fingers, before quickly plaiting it and lying down once more. Her body rigid and her heart thumping fit to burst, she waited.

Perce was a surprisingly long time and when at last she heard him outside the door, she had composed herself to some extent. When he came into the room she stared at him in surprise. He was already in his nightshirt and, by the look of it, had had a shave. Catching her look, he said a little sheepishly, 'Ada wouldn't let me in the bed until I'd had a shave an' wash down. She said she had to put up with the smell of fish all day, an' she was blowed if she was puttin' up with it all night an' all.'

Lucy nodded. She wanted to say something, but her mouth was too dry with fear. She watched him extinguish the oil lamp on top of the chest of drawers, sending the room into a darkness that was both welcome and unnerving, and then his great bulk caused the bed to sag and creak as he slid in beside her. As taut as a piano wire, she held her breath.

Aware of the stiff woodenness of the slender figure on the other side of the bed and the reason for it, Perce spoke the words he would have found it impossible to say, but for the darkness. 'Lass, I'll say this once an' then we'll not talk of it again, all right? I know you wouldn't have looked the side I was on, but for your misfortune, an' it's heart-sorry I am that a nice lass like you was taken advantage of by scum like him, but not all blokes are like that. I don't pretend to be what I'm not, an' I know I'm no young maiden's prayer, but I can promise you right now I'll not hurt you or misuse you. There'll be no funny business, so you can rest your mind on that score. An' after the babby's born it'll be up to you when . . . you know.'

He cleared his throat, his face scarlet in the blackness.

'What I mean to say is, I'll wait till you're ready, however long that is. I don't want nowt but what's freely given; it'd stick in me craw otherwise. Do you believe me, lass, cos it's important you do?'

His words were warm, soothing oil on an open sore.

Lucy couldn't have expressed the comfort and ease they brought to her mind and body, or how his humility had melted the core of fear that had been at the heart of her since she had first set eyes on him. With a bolt of revelation she realized Perce was finding this difficult and embarrassing too, and it was from that moment on that something approaching tenderness came into her for the big, lumbering man who had taken her and her siblings in. Her voice a whisper, she said, 'I believe you.' He didn't smell like the Perce of daylight hours; instead the only odour was one of carbolic soap and the faint aroma of pipe smoke. 'And I'm grateful, we all are, for what you've done for us.'

'Well, the way I see it, you've done plenty for me an' the bairns an' all, lass, so we'll call it quits, eh?' Perce's voice expressed his relief that the conversation he'd been working himself up to all night was over. 'I'll say goodnight then. I've got to open up earlier than usual tomorrow. Seamus Riley is comin' with a load, an' he's always here at the crack of dawn, but he's a canny old blighter, is Seamus. Always seems to fish where the best catches are, not like some of the young 'uns.'

'Goodnight.'

The reply was timid, but the trembling note that had been at the back of her voice during the wedding service and thereafter was gone, and Perce smiled to himself. It was a rum do, he thought to himself, that his wedding night had been spent reassuring his young bride that he had no intention of laying a finger on her. When he and

Ada had got wed they'd been at it for half the night, but then they'd had plenty of practice beforehand and Ada had liked her oats. She'd been a big lass and lusty; he missed her more than a bit, God rest her soul.

He turned over onto his side with his back to Lucy and shut his eyes. Things would pan out in time, they always did. No use fretting or wishing for something different.

The simple, homespun philosophy that was such a part of him had him sleeping like a baby within a moment or two, and as he began to snore Lucy found herself relaxing into the soft warmth of the feather-and-down mattress. Even when, a few minutes later, he moved, one great brawny shoulder coming to rest against her, she didn't flinch or adjust her position. She trusted him, she thought with a stab of wonder. More than that, she felt safe for the first time since the night Tom Crawford had come to the house. Perce wouldn't let anything, or anyone, hurt her.

PART FOUR

The Fishmonger's Wife

1929

Chapter Sixteen

It had been a long, hard winter. Snow, sleet, blizzards and packed ice had meant week upon week when Lucy ventured no further than the back yard and saw no one but Perce and the children. He had refused to let her work in the shop once they were married; initially because he'd realized the sight and smell of the fish, eels and other seafood made the nausea worse, and then because, as her shape changed, they agreed it would add more credence to the story about the baby coming early if her belly wasn't monitored by the housewives who came into the shop.

Normally the enforced seclusion would have driven Lucy mad, but owing to the fact that the nausea remained persistent, along with a consuming tiredness that saw her falling asleep by the fireside every afternoon when Charley had his nap, she was grateful for it. The twins and Matthew had started school together at the end of the summer and trotted off with Ruby and John every morning, but even so her days were full with washing and ironing and cooking, along with keeping the rooms above the shop spick and span and caring for Charley. It didn't help that she was carrying the child in her womb all at the front, either. From the back she didn't look any different, but by the beginning of February her stomach appeared ready to explode and she was reduced to waddling like a duck, as she remarked bitterly to Perce. But none of this would have mattered if the baby wasn't Tom Crawford's. As her belly had grown, so had her aversion to and revulsion of this 'thing' – she couldn't think of it in any other way – that was his.

Every time the child moved or kicked, she wanted to tear it out of her; it was as though its father was violating her again and it was a constant reminder of what had happened. Each night she prayed it would be stillborn. In truth she had little hope that a holy God would answer such a prayer, but she prayed it nonetheless in spite of her immortal soul. She wouldn't let herself think about what she would do if He refused her.

By her calculations the baby was due in the middle of February, but the time came and went, and it was on a bitterly cold morning at the end of the month in the middle of a snowstorm that she had her first pains. Ruby and John had already left with Matthew and the twins, for which Lucy was thankful. She and Perce had kept her pregnancy from the children as long as they could, suspecting it might bring back bad memories for Matthew, and they had been right to be concerned. His little face had turned chalk-white when they had broken the news and he hadn't been himself since; the nightmares had returned and, added to that, he had taken to sleepwalking. One night just after Christmas John had awoken in the early hours to find the window open and Matthew sitting on the ledge, still deeply asleep, but with his eyes wide open as he'd gazed into nothing. John had had the presence of mind to quietly guide the child back into bed and close the window, and when he'd informed them about it in the morning, Perce had wasted no time in nailing the window shut. But it had upset them both, particularly Lucy, who felt wholly responsible for the little boy's misery.

Now, as she stood looking out of the window into the swirling snow, she prayed another prayer and this one was for the little child she'd come to love. 'Let this be quick, God, so it's all done and dusted by the time he comes home from school. Don't let him be here. Spare him that.'

This time God answered in a way that had Perce running for the midwife within a couple of hours, and at two in the afternoon Lucy gave one last push and a small but perfect baby girl made her appearance into the world on a gush of liquid as her mother's waters broke at the moment of birth, splashing the midwife in the process.

'By, lass,' the good woman said, wiping her face before she cut the cord, 'this one is going to be a child of the sea all right, but then with her da bein' a fishmonger that's as should be. An' a nice quick labour an' all – you're goin' to have 'em as easy as shellin' peas.' Wrapping the crying baby in a towel, she dumped her in Lucy's arms, not noticing the new mother's instinctive recoil, and began to wash her hands in the bowl of water Perce had brought up earlier.

Her arms stiff, Lucy made herself look down at her daughter. A pair of blue-grey eyes in a tiny sweet face stared back at her and one little hand with minute fingers escaped the towel and reached up, as though asking for reassurance. And Lucy fell in love. As swiftly and completely as that.

With tears of joy and relief and wonder, and a whole host of other emotions she couldn't have named, streaming down her face, she kissed the tiny hand and then each tiny finger, barely aware of the midwife at her elbow. She couldn't remember much about Ruby being born, but John and the twins had been wrinkled and red and squashed-looking. This baby, *her* baby, was beautiful, she thought mistily. So sweet, so pure, so exquisite.

'Let me have her for a minute, lass, an' I'll get her cleaned up afore her da comes in, an' you an' all,' said the midwife briskly, whisking the baby away before Lucy could protest. 'She's a bonny one all right,' she added chattily as she began to see to her tiny charge, who showed her disapproval of the proceedings by squawking loudly. 'On the small side, but then you'd expect that with her comin' early.'

Lucy looked hard at the midwife, but the woman didn't appear to mean anything other than what she'd said, and had clearly accepted that the child was a few weeks premature. 'What does she weigh?'

'Just under six pounds, but she's breathin' all right so don't worry about it.'

The midwife flashed her a reassuring smile, which made Lucy feel guilty, and she said softly, 'Thank you, Mrs Todd. You've been so good.'

'Aw, go on with you, lass, you did it by yourself. I wish all my ladies were like you, but you'll have to watch out with the next one. If you had your first this quick, a good sneeze'll do it next time.' She chuckled at her little joke and Lucy smiled weakly. It was a reminder of something she didn't want to think about. She liked Perce, and over the last months since the wedding her fear and repulsion had been replaced by a deep gratitude and warmth towards the big man who had taken them in, but that other side of their union – the intimacy which so far had been put on hold – was something different. Just the thought of being touched and handled made her feel physically sick.

The midwife continued to chat as she swiftly changed the bed and helped Lucy into a clean nightdress, settling her against the heaped pillows and handing her the baby before she went to call Perce. 'He'll be tickled pink,' she said before leaving the bedroom, 'a little lassie after two lads, an' one that's the spittin' image of her mam.'

Was she? Lucy gazed down into the sleeping face of her daughter, searching each tiny feature of this perfect little being that belonged to her, awe and wonderment flooding her once more.

'Thank you, God, thank you,' she murmured through

fresh tears, knowing she was thanking Him more for not answering her prayers than anything else. If her child had been born dead . . . But she hadn't been, she hadn't been. She clutched the warm little body tighter to her. And she would make it up to her. All those wicked things she had prayed, all the times she had wanted to pound her belly until the evidence of Tom Crawford was gone, she'd make it up to her daughter somehow. And this child was hers, only hers. Fierce maternal love swept through her. She had Perce's name, and she would always be grateful to him for that, but this little person was wholly hers and she would fight to the death to protect her.

Perce opened the door with Charley in the crook of one arm. He tiptoed over to the bed slowly, in a somewhat ludicrous manner, his big red face abeam. 'It's a little lassie then?' Lucy nodded, turning the baby so that Perce could see her properly and opening her other arm for Charley, who snuggled beside her.

'By, lass, she's a beauty,' he said reverently. 'She don't look real. She puts me in mind of one of those dolls in Tollett's toyshop window, an' Mrs Todd's right, she's goin' to take after you. How do you feel?' he added awkwardly. 'All right now?'

Anyone else might have thought he was asking after her physical condition, but Perce was the only one who had known how she had struggled with the child growing inside her. Lucy smiled at the man she'd come to see as a gentle giant. 'I love her,' she said simply.

His face mirrored his relief. 'Aye, well, that's as it

should be. You thought of a name yet?' She had refused to discuss possible names before the birth, for it had panicked her.

Lucy looked down at the delicate little face. 'Daisy,' she murmured softly. 'I've always thought they are the most beautiful little flowers, so dainty and perfect. Daisy Agnes, after my mam. She – she would have liked that.'

'Daisy it is then,' said Perce gruffly, pretending not to see the tear accompanying her mother's name. Shows of emotion always embarrassed him.

Mrs Todd bustled into the room, her round homely face benevolent as she looked at the four of them. 'Didn't I tell you she's the bonniest bab this side of Durham?' she said to Perce. 'Now I'm off for a bit to put the dinner on for my lot, but I'll be back come evening, an' you' – here she spoke to Lucy – 'you get some rest, lass. All right? An', Perce, you make sure she stays in bed for a good few days. You say her sister is goin' to take charge for a bit?'

'Aye,' nodded Perce. This had come about some weeks before when he'd announced his intention to pay a neighbour to come in during Lucy's lying-in period. Ruby had vehemently protested and insisted that she would see to things, saying a few days off school was neither here nor there as she hated every minute anyway. Perce had agreed to it when Lucy had admitted to him that she had been dreading another woman in the house. She knew full well that, without exception, Perce's friends and neighbours had been shocked to the core at him taking another wife so soon after Ada's death. The gossip had been vicious, especially when it became known that she was expecting a baby. Perce had weathered the storm in his usual good-natured fashion. Having a thick skin, he hadn't been unduly perturbed, but after Ruby had repeated the odd remark that she had heard in the shop Lucy had been doubly glad she didn't have to meet the hostility before her baby was born.

Tired as she was, Lucy found she couldn't sleep until the children were home from school. She needed to see for herself that Matthew's fears had been fully laid to rest when he saw little Daisy and herself alive and well, and that he was happy about the baby. She had grown so close to Perce's firstborn over the last months that she didn't want the little boy to feel pushed aside or uncertain about the future and his place in her affections.

She was sitting up in bed with her hair brushed and a ribbon threaded through the plait, and Daisy fast asleep in the bassinet, when she heard them. The crib had been Matthew's and Charley's and it was a good one. Perce had placed it at an angle to the glowing fire in the bedroom's small fireplace.

The twins and Charley bounded into the room first, followed by John and then Ruby, who was telling the little ones to be quiet and behave themselves. For a minute or two Lucy was smothered by the younger three, who jumped on to the bed, flinging their arms round her before Ruby marshalled them off. When the pandemonium had died down and Ruby was supervising the others who were peering into the crib, Lucy looked to the doorway where Perce was standing with Matthew in his arms.

The little boy's eyes were wide and he was very still in his father's embrace as Perce said softly, 'There she is, Matthew. I told you she was all right, didn't I? And you've a baby sister an' all. Do you want to have a look at her?'

The glance he gave at the bassinet was almost fearful and Lucy said gently, 'He'll see her in a minute. Come and sit with me first, Matthew, and tell me what you've been doing at school today.'

Perce carried the child to her, placing him beside her, and as Lucy put her arm round him she felt him quiver. His eyes enormous, he whispered, 'The baby's out of your tummy now?'

'Yes, she's in the crib over there.'

'So she's been borned?'

'Yes, she's born, and now she'll grow and get bigger like the rest of you.'

'So she won't' – the child swallowed painfully – 'she won't have to be borned again? Not ever?'

'No.' Lucy wanted to gather him to her and rock him, but she forced her voice to be matter-of-fact. 'She's here, Matthew. She's out of my tummy and she's safe, and so am I. This is a happy night. A very happy night for all of us.'

She felt the small tense shoulders relax as he leaned against her. 'Richard Duffy says you can't have two mams.'

The statement, apropos of nothing they had been talking about, threw her for a moment.

Matthew went on, 'He said you only have one mam and one da ever, but he's wrong, isn't he?'

Now she did pull him closer, kissing the top of his head. 'Aye, he's wrong. You and Charley are living proof of it. You have your first mam in heaven, where she's living with the baby who's your little brother, and you have me, your second mam, here with you. And I'm not going anywhere.'

He sat for a moment more and then wriggled to the edge of the bed. 'Can I see her? My baby sister?'

The others made room for him round the crib and after a second or two he turned, looking at Lucy as he said excitedly, 'She's got fingernails, like a real person.'

'That's because she *is* a real person.' Lucy smiled. 'Just a very small one.'

'Can I hold her?'

Lucy looked at his eager face and breathed out slowly. It was going to be all right. *He* was going to be all right. 'Come and sit beside me again and your da will bring her then.' And as the others began to clamour, she added, 'Each of you can have a turn after Matthew.'

The children came clambering onto the bed as Perce picked Daisy out of the bassinet. He carried the little bundle over to Lucy, who had Matthew beside her, and very gently placed the baby into his son's arms, which Lucy had positioned to hold the infant. As he straightened, his eyes met hers and the look they exchanged was one of harmonious accord and unity, like any other couple concerned about their children.

Lucy blinked. For the first time she felt they were a family, and the tenderness this rough, hulking, simple man induced in her went up a notch. Telling herself she couldn't cry, for hadn't she told Matthew this was a happy night, she glanced at the row of fascinated faces at the end of the bed. Every pair of eyes was fixed on Daisy, even Ruby's, and a soothing warmth filled her soul. Again she thought: It's going to be all right; but this time she wasn't referring to Matthew.

The next few weeks were tiring. Being a small baby, Daisy demanded feeding every two or three hours, night and day, and in spite of her fragile appearance, everyone in the house soon came to understand that what Daisy wanted, Daisy saw to it that she got. But Lucy didn't mind. Even on the odd bad day when the infant seemed forever glued to her breasts until her nipples became cracked and sore, Lucy relished motherhood. And gradually, as the snow and ice and sleet gave way to milder weather and the time between feeds stretched until Daisy was sleeping through the night, Lucy faced the fact that she couldn't ask Perce to be patient any longer.

He had come to care for her. Love her. She knew this, although he had never spoken of it, that wasn't Perce's style. Instead he showed his affection in a hundred little practical ways that often caused a painful sensation to come into her throat because she knew that if she lived to be a hundred she could never love him. Not in that way. Nevertheless, she had a duty to fulfil and a debt to pay, a debt that meant she had to make Perce as happy as she could all their married life. But for him, Ruby and the others might well be in the workhouse and she would never have seen her sixteenth birthday. It seemed incredible now that she had contemplated ending it all and that she had been in such anguish about Daisy – the light of her life. But she had. And Perce had saved her, saved them all, and in so doing had allowed Daisy to come into the world. If only for that one thing alone, nothing he asked of her would be too much.

This was the nature of her thoughts in the cold light of day and she meant every word. But on a cool night towards the end of May, a month after her birthday, which had gone unnoticed by everyone, she stood shivering and shaking in the wash-house in the yard. She had filled the tin bath with plenty of warm water and had bought a tablet of scented soap for the occasion, and now she forced herself to strip completely.

Half an hour later she couldn't put off returning to the flat any longer. Perce raised his head from his paper when she walked into the sitting room. 'All right, lass? You've been a while.'

It was beyond her to do more than nod before she scuttled into the bedroom. After checking Daisy, who was fast asleep in the bassinet in a corner of the room, she sat down on the bed. She knew Perce would go downstairs and have his nightly wash-down and shave shortly, and she waited until she heard him clomp down the stairs before she stood up and began to undress.

Instead of pulling on her old calico nightdress on top of her shift and drawers, she stripped completely. Then she reached under her pillow and drew out the new nightdress she'd made herself with a roll of material she'd bought from the Old Market especially for the purpose. The soft white lawn had been a pleasure to sew and now, as she pulled the nightdress over her head, she stood looking at herself in the mirror. The garment was sleeveless and quite plain, except for a wide blue ribbon which gathered the bust into a ruched effect. It showed off her new curves in a way that caused hot colour to flood her cheeks and the trembling to begin once more.

Taking down her hair, she brushed the golden-brown waves until they shone and rippled in the light of the oil lamp. For the first time since her marriage she didn't plait it, but left it loose to flow over her shoulders.

The last thing she did was to unfasten the thin silver chain holding the little heart from around her neck. Very deliberately, she wrapped it in a piece of paper and placed it under her clothes in the chest of drawers. She would never wear it again. From this night forth she was someone else's wife. Some might say she had been Perce's wife from the day she was wed, but she knew differently. Inside, where her heart and soul lay, she had still been Jacob's. What she was about to do tonight would alter that. It had to. And it was this last act, rather than anything else that had gone before, which completed her transformation into a woman.

Instead of seeking cover under the bedclothes, she made

herself sit quietly on top of the bed awaiting his appearance. The first move in this would need to come from her, she was aware of that, and Perce being Perce, she would have to make her intentions abundantly clear, because subtlety was lost on him.

In spite of herself and the panic that was coursing through her, the thought brought a weak smile. Who would have imagined that, after nearly eleven months of marriage and with a baby daughter to boot, she would be seducing her own husband? Not that Perce would take much seducing, she knew that. She understood the reason for his restless tossing and turning over the last months and the odd burst of temper that his frustation caused.

She heard his footsteps on the stairs, then in the room outside. The bedroom door opened and still she sat on the bed as she looked across the room to where he stood surveying her, his face stretched in comical surprise. His big arms hung loosely by his sides and he didn't move, nor did he speak. Strangely, his bewilderment eased her shyness and fear of what lay ahead. Softly, she said, 'Why don't you turn out the lamp and come to bed and love me?'

It hadn't been anything like she had expected. In spite of herself and her desire to ease the craving of his body, she had become stiff and unyielding once he was in bed beside her. When his arms had gone about her, the trembling of her body had increased. She forgot that this was Perce and that he cared about her, she was only conscious of feeling smothered and helpless, but he had begun to talk to her, to stroke and pet her, his voice deep and unhurried.

Slowly, very slowly, her tensely held shoulders and limbs relaxed and her hands, which had been knotted against his huge chest, uncurled. She could do this, she told herself fiercely. It wasn't so bad. Perce wouldn't hurt her more than he had to.

In the event, he didn't hurt her at all. When he had at last nudged her thighs apart she had braced herself for the pain and discomfort, but there was only a brief sensation of tightness as he entered her. And it had been over quickly.

Now she lay in the darkness listening to him snore beside her, knowing this was to be her lot from now on. It wasn't what she would have chosen, but she had Daisy, and Perce loved her. Of that she had no doubt. She had known so before tonight, but the things he had said under cover of darkness had confirmed it. And he asked so little of her in comparison to what he gave.

Her pent-up breath escaped in a tiny swoosh of sound.

She would make Perce happy and ensure their home would be a good place for Daisy and Matthew and the others. And, in doing so, she would be happy too – as long as she didn't let herself think of Jacob and that other life that could have been.

Chapter Seventeen

The summer was a warm one and Daisy flourished, growing more enchanting with each week that passed. Her cot was now in the girls' room and, although Lucy missed having her near, she felt she owed it to Perce to make their bedroom their own again. She had ceased inspecting her daughter's baby features for any sign of Tom Crawford. Daisy was a replica of herself, everyone said so, and Lucy was content. Perce was besotted with the infant – if Daisy had truly been his, he couldn't have loved her more – and the flat above the fishmonger's shop *was* a happy place.

Summer mellowed into a crisp autumn with sharp white frosts and high blue skies, and the Wall Street Crash over the ocean in America at the end of October barely impacted on Lucy's life. The papers were full of the news that the bursting of the stock-market bubble meant the withdrawal of American loans to foreign countries and other such financial details, but Lucy, still only sixteen years old, couldn't drum up interest about such faraway happenings. By the time the weather worsened, though, both she and Perce had become aware that the domino effect of the collapse of the American money market had plunged Britain into a recession that made the previous years look like a walk in the park.

November was a raw month of bitterly cold winds and fierce snow showers, and the queues at the end of the day for the cheap fish and odds and ends grew daily as the recession bit harder. Inevitably at close of business there were folk who were turned away with empty baskets.

The amount of dole given to a family was supposed to be related to their 'needs', but Lucy knew this meant a standard of bare subsistence and inadequate diet. She hated to see the thin, poorly clad men, women and children trudging out into the winter's night empty-handed and desperate.

She was thinking about the problem as she sat with Perce in front of the fire one evening at the beginning of December, her hands busy with a basketful of darning, but her mind occupied elsewhere. 'We could provide hot soup,' she said, out of the blue. 'Just in the last couple of hours before you shut up shop.'

Perce's newspaper lowered and he stared at her. 'What?'

'All the end-of-day bits and pieces that you sell cheap, we could use them by making soup. They'd go further and most, if not all, of the customers could have something. People could bring their own bowls and pans and what-have-you; I don't mean they'd eat in the shop, but they could take away something hot, to see them through the night at least. We could price it at a quart costing a penny, or something like that. There's room for a good-sized range in the back of the shop where you store things, so we keep it separate from here. It'd be another kitchen so to speak, and you'd make more by selling soup like that than you ever do in selling the odds and ends to folk. What do you think?'

Perce shook his head doubtfully. 'It'd be a lot of extra work.'

'Not really. I could prepare it gradually throughout the day when I've time, and make sure it's ready. With the Depression worsening it'd be another string to our bow, now wouldn't it? And we'd be helping people. I – I know what it's like to be hungry and at your wits' end.'

'All right, all right, I'll think about it,' said Perce hastily. 'Don't get all worked up.'

Lucy smiled. She knew what that meant. Perce refused her nothing that it was in his power to give.

Over the next two or three weeks Lucy bought a good second-hand range and various pots and pans and utensils, and Perce transformed part of his storeroom into a working kitchen. He put his foot down on delaying the new venture until after Christmas, however, feeling that with seven children in the house, six of whom were under ten years old, Lucy had enough to do over the holiday period. She was happy to go along with this. The year before she had been feeling desperately unhappy about her condition and hugely cumbersome to boot; this year she wanted Christmas to be a time of family fun and joy.

To that end, she and Ruby decided to take John and the little ones into the town to Fawcett Street, where all the big shops were lit up and sparkling with fairy lights and decorations on Christmas Eve. It had been snowing on and off for the last week, but over the past two days no fresh fall had occurred and the snow was packed hard on the ground, making it easier to negotiate Daisy's perambulator through the streets. Just as they were leaving, Perce called Lucy into the shop where he was busy serving customers and slipped a couple of notes into her hand. 'Take them to tea at Binns,' he said, squeezing her arm. 'An' don't rush back, neither. I can manage here. Enjoy yourself.'

She smiled at him, her eyes glowing, as excited by the little adventure as though she was going as far afield as Newcastle. On impulse she reached up and kissed him on the cheek, careless of his grimy apron and the smell of fish. His round, rough face flushed with pleasure and, to cover his delight, he said gruffly, 'Go on with you, they're waiting.'

It was a merry little party that made its way into the main part of town as an early twilight began to fall. The festive season seemed to have infected everyone with its magic. Although most folk were laden with parcels and last-minute shopping, they were, on the whole, bright-faced and jovial, and Daisy, sitting up in her perambulator clad in a small white furry coat and matching bonnet that Lucy had made for her, drew many a smile and a nod.

They didn't hurry as they wandered along in the bitterly

cold, crisp air. The children were well wrapped up against the chill and John had the twins on either side of him, whilst Ruby held tight to Matthew and Charley's hands. It was the first time Lucy had come into the centre of town since Perce had taken them in and now she berated herself for not having the courage to do so before. Hidden away at home with Perce close by, she had felt safe and secure, and for a long time that had been all she'd wanted. The fear of seeing someone she knew, of seeing *him* – Tom Crawford – had kept her in a kind of prison, she realized now, as she gazed at the crowds and the lights. And she was no longer the penniless young girl of yesteryear. She was a married woman. She had a husband and a child, a whole family.

It was gone six o'clock when they left Binns, after a sumptuous tea of wafer-thin sandwiches, little pastries and cream cakes. Each of the children – even Ruby – was clutching a small chocolate bell wrapped in silver paper with a picture of the store on it, which had been complimentary with the tea. Lucy had tried to prise Daisy's away from her, fearing she would try to eat the silver paper, but to no avail. Now Lucy smiled at her daughter as she wrapped her up warmly in the perambulator, which they had left just inside the entrance to the shop in the care of the friendly doorman. Daisy might look like a tiny angel with her halo of golden-brown curls and huge blue eyes, but she had a mind of her own.

It was as they emerged as a laughing, chattering group into the icy-cold air in which the odd desultory snowflake was floating that a voice behind her brought Lucy spinning round.

'Lucy, lass?' Enid Crawford was staring at her, amazement stretching her face. 'It *is* you, as I live an' breathe. And Ruby and John and the twins too. Well, I never.'

For a moment Lucy could only stare back. Her heart was pumping so violently it seemed to vibrate her ribs and fill her head.

It was Ruby who broke the awkward moment, her face beaming as she recognized their old neighbour. 'Hello, Mrs Crawford,' she said brightly, as though they'd only spoken the day before. 'We've just been to tea in Binns and it was grand.'

'It was a special treat for the bairns, it being Christmas Eve and all.' Lucy found her voice as she stitched a smile on her face. 'How are you, Mrs Crawford?'

'Me, lass? Same as ever.' Enid answered her, but her gaze had become riveted on Daisy. 'The bab?' she said bemusedly, for no one could mistake who her mother was. 'She's yours?'

'Aye, yes.' They were blocking the path, causing people to step off the pavement to pass them, and now, as Lucy turned the pram, she said weakly, 'I think we're in the way. It was nice seeing you, Mrs Crawford.'

Enid was not going to be dismissed so easily. 'I'll walk along with you a way, lass. Our Tom brought me in, he'd got a spot of business to see to, and I'm meeting him shortly at the corner of Bridge Street. He's got his own car now, you know. Doing nicely for himself.'

Lucy said nothing. The mention of Tom's name made her want to take to her heels and run, but that was impossible.

'But enough of that,' Enid continued, looking back at the others who were trailing behind them. She smiled, then turned to Lucy once more. 'How long have you been back, lass?'

'Back?' Through the swirling panic, Lucy knew she had to stop and turn off into a side-street soon. She couldn't walk on with Tom's mother and risk seeing him.

'Aye. You an' Donald and the bairns went down south, didn't you? When you left so suddenly?'

Lucy caught the edge to the last words and, strangely, it put iron in her backbone. She knew it wasn't Tom's mother's fault that he'd forced himself on her and caused them to flee their home, but for a moment it felt like it. Mrs Crawford had no right to judge her. No right at all.

She stopped so abruptly that John and the twins, who were behind her, cannoned into her and Enid walked on a few paces without realizing.

When Enid turned, it was to see Lucy staring at her with a tight face. 'We didn't go down south, Mrs Crawford,' she said flatly. 'Not me and the bairns. Donald did. He left us. I knew I had to find work and a room somewhere for us or it'd have been the workhouse for the bairns.'

'But' – Enid's brow wrinkled – 'you could have come to me, lass. We'd have worked something out. To take off like that—'

'There were reasons.'

'Oh aye?' Enid raised an eyebrow.

Lucy ignored the question. Instead she said, 'I didn't like to leave with Jacob in the hospital, but I had to.'

Enid remained still for a time as she stared into Lucy's face, then nodded slowly. 'Seems you landed on your feet right enough.' Now her voice was as flat as Lucy's had been. 'Jacob's done all right for himself too. He's old Williamson's legal heir now. It all happened after he come out of the hospital.'

Jacob was alive. Lucy was glad of the pram handle to hang onto. Weakly, she said, 'I'm glad.'

'How old's the bairn?'

Lucy was surprised at the steadiness of her voice when she lied. 'Six months.' Mrs Crawford would report meeting her to Tom and the others and she couldn't prevent it, whatever she said. She understood her mother's old friend well enough to know that. Besides, she could give no legitimate reason to ask her to do otherwise. The most she could do was say that Daisy was younger, just in case Tom put two and two together. 'I got married in July last year and fell for Daisy quite soon after.' Thankfully Daisy, tired out after the excitement of the outing and with a full stomach, had fallen asleep clutching her silver bell and, being petite and fragile-looking, could easily pass for six months when sleeping.

'She's bonny, like her mam.'

The words should have been friendly, but the edge was back and stronger.

Aiming to steer the conversation away from Daisy, Lucy gestured towards Matthew and Charley. 'These are my husband's boys from his first marriage.'

'Oh aye, a widower, was he? What's he do for a living then?'

The snow was falling in big fat flakes now and it was the perfect excuse for Lucy to deflect the question. 'I'm sorry, Mrs Crawford, I must get them home.' As she spoke she began to walk, turning the pram into St Thomas Street to her left as she said, 'Happy Christmas, Mrs Crawford.'

Enid had walked a few steps with her and now she stood as the others trooped by her, Ruby and John echoing Lucy as they passed. Enid said not a word.

Lucy walked as quickly as she could, the others slipping and sliding behind her on the packed snow. It was like a skating rink in places where children had been playing their games. She found that she was holding her breath and let it out in a silent sigh when Ruby's voice came, saying, 'Wait for us then. Where's the fire?'

They were halfway along St Thomas Street, which, being a side-street, was not lit up like the main thorough-fare, with just the odd street lamp casting yellow pools of light on the snow, but when Lucy glanced behind her as she waited for the others, she could see Enid's figure still watching them. As Ruby reached her, her sister said, 'Why did you tell Mrs Crawford Daisy's only six months old, our Lucy?'

Lucy stared at her, unable to think of one reason that would satisfy Ruby. 'It's complicated,' she said at last, beginning to walk on.

'I don't see why.'

'I have my reasons.'

'Lucy, I'm not a bairn. You can trust me, you know.'

Lucy stopped again. Ruby's voice hadn't been belligerent, merely hurt. The two of them had become closer since Daisy's birth, when Ruby had taken care of her for a week or two and seen to the house and the children. She had worked hard and from the first had proved to be a devoted aunty, as besotted with Daisy as they all were. But whatever Ruby said, she *was* still a bairn at twelve years old; besides which, the truth was so humiliating, so horrible, that Lucy didn't know if she could voice it, even to her sister.

And then Ruby said something that startled her. 'It's something to do with you marrying Perce so quick, isn't it?'

The snow was falling thickly and each of them had a layer of white on their hats and shoulders, apart from Daisy who was snug and warm. Lucy blinked a flake from her eyelashes, her voice low when she said, 'We'll talk at home when the others are in bed. I promise.'

Ruby nodded. Her voice equally hushed, she murmured, 'Whatever you say, you know I'm for you, don't you, Lucy? I've never really said it before, but I know there's not many people who'd have done what you did when Donald scarpered. Like he said in that note, you could have put us in the workhouse and looked after number one, but you didn't. I'll always remember that.'

If Ruby had taken her clothes off and danced the fandango, Lucy couldn't have been more surprised. And it was then she realized with a shock that Ruby was right: her sister wasn't a child any longer. At some point in the last eighteen months Ruby had grown up and her age was irrelevant. Furthermore, her sister had turned into a friend and she hadn't even realized it. Softly she said, 'Thanks, lass.'

'When you two have quite finished whispering, can we start walking again?' John's voice was aggrieved. He had been attempting to stop Matthew and Charley and the twins from breaking their necks sliding on a sheet of ice that the neighbourhood children had polished to a glassy finish during the afternoon, and which was lethal. 'I want to get home, if no one else does.'

As Ruby and John took the four younger ones by the hands again, Lucy glanced down the street. Mrs Crawford had gone. But how much longer would it be before Tom discovered where she lived and made his presence known? Because he would, she knew it as sure as night follows day. It was merely a matter of time now.

She began to walk on. And Jacob: what would he think when he heard she was married with a baby? Did he hate her for leaving when he was so ill? She didn't blame him. And maybe he had a lass now. A sweetheart who had taken her place in his affections. Someone young and pure, a lass with no dark secrets.

And then she glanced into the pram, Daisy's sleeping face lit briefly by the street lamp they were passing. A love so strong that it made her chest ache gripped her.

Daisy was worth every single thing she had gone through, she told herself fiercely. Even if she could turn back the clock and set a different course, if it meant losing her precious little girl, she wouldn't do it. Not for a second.

But still, a chill had settled on her heart, and a sense of foreboding that made her shiver.

Chapter Eighteen

Enid Crawford was full of righteous indignation as she continued to walk towards the corner of Bridge Street where Tom was picking her up. She was a little late, for running into Lucy had delayed her, but with her shopping bags full of this and that and the pavements treacherous, she didn't dare rush, although with her head full of the last few minutes she nearly went headlong a couple of times.

You live and learn, she told herself grimly. Oh aye, you live and learn all right. She would have bet money that Donald had dragged Lucy and the others down south against the lass's wishes, and that Lucy would have come to see her immediately she was up north again, should they return this way. But no. If she'd heard her right, Lucy had never left these parts. Jacob had been grieving for her, fair tearing himself apart in the early days, and all the time she'd been making a life for herself with some widower or other and having his baby.

Edith's eyes narrowed as she peered through the snow-filled air towards the corner of Bridge Street up ahead, but there were too many bustling shoppers coming and going to see if Tom's car was waiting for her.

And the way Lucy had been with her too, barely giving her the time of day, if truth be told. She'd always had a soft spot for the lass and she'd imagined Lucy thought a bit of her too, but today she felt like she'd been kicked in the teeth. And on Christmas Eve an' all. She wished now she'd stayed in Monkwearmouth and got her last bits there, but with Tom offering to bring her in and things so bad at home, she'd fancied getting out for a bit.

For a moment Lucy's cursory treatment of her was pushed aside as she thought of Aaron and the lads. Miserable as sin these days, Aaron was, and Frank and Ralph weren't much better. She didn't understand them, she didn't straight. Thanks to Tom, they were bringing in good money at a time when most folk didn't know where their next meal was coming from, but were they grateful? Were they heck. Faces as long as old Meg's backside from dawn to dusk.

She sighed her disapproval, her mouth set in a grim line.

She cooked and cleaned and washed for them, and barely got a civil word. It felt as though they were blaming her for something, but she'd done nowt wrong. And when she'd lost patience the week before as they were sitting at the evening meal, and told them they ought to count their blessings, Aaron had turned on her. Like a loony, he'd been. And the lads had said nothing as he'd raved and ranted.

She stopped for a moment, adjusting her shopping bags and catching her breath, every word Aaron had flung at her burnt on her mind. 'You can say that? Count me blessings? Blessings!' He'd turned to glance at Frank and Ralph and they'd lowered their eyes to their plates. 'You've no idea, have you, woman? And why? Because you don't want to see. As long as you have your new front room and your gramophone and wireless and the rest of it, you keep your head buried in the sand. He's bought you – lock, stock and barrel – and to hell with the rest of us. Well, you can't spit in the face of the Almighty and get away with it forever. There'll be a day of reckoning, sure enough. Remember that, when I go the same way as Walter and Ernie Fallow.'

He'd stomped out of the back door, pulling on his cap as he went. She had been left staring after him. She had turned to Frank and Ralph in bewilderment. 'What did he mean? Go the same way as Walter and Ernie?'

They hadn't answered her, saying instead, 'We'd better get after him' and she had been left staring at the uneaten meals on the kitchen table. They hadn't come back till she was in bed.

She walked on and was relieved to see Tom's car waiting for her, the engine running. He jumped out and took her bags, throwing them on the back seat before helping her into the passenger seat as he said, 'I was beginning to think you'd come a cropper; the ground's like glass, and it looks like we're in for another packet. I shouldn't have let you go by yourself, but I didn't think at the time.'

She glanced at him fondly as he slid into the driver's seat. 'Don't be daft, lad. I'm all right. I'm sorry I kept you waitin,' but you'll never guess who I ran into a minute or two back.'

Tom was concentrating on pulling out into the traffic, his mind preoccupied when he said, 'Who was that then?'

'Lucy Fallow and the bairns.'

The car swerved, a loud blast of a horn from a vehicle travelling in the opposite direction causing Tom to pull the wheel sharply to the left again. He swore at the other driver before saying, 'Lucy Fallow? Are you sure?'

'Course I'm sure. She was just coming out of Binns, she'd taken the bairns in for tea apparently. Her husband must be good for a bob or two if they can afford to do that.'

'Husband?'

'Oh aye, told me she'd married some bloke or other, a widower by all accounts with a couple of bairns. Got one of her own an' all, six months old, she is.' Enid stared complacently out of the windscreen where the wipers were labouring to clear the snow. It was grand travelling in style like a lady, she thought, the luxury restoring a sense of wellbeing. 'Bonny little thing she was, the image of Lucy. Seems Donald cleared off down south like we'd thought, but Lucy and the bairns stayed in these parts. And not a word to me, when she must have known I'd be worried about 'em.' Enid's voice hardened. 'She's not the lass I thought she was, that's for sure.'

'Where does she live?'

'We didn't get on to that. Truth be told, she didn't want to know me, lad.' Enid's sniff spoke volumes. 'Couldn't wait to get away.'

Tom was gripping the steering wheel so tightly his knuckles were white. It took all his will power to relax. He wanted to turn the car round this minute and go looking for her, but of course that was impossible. But to think she had been under his nose the whole time. Fury was a white-hot ball in his stomach. But then much of his business was contained to Monkwearmouth and Southwick; he only came over the river to see the Kanes on the whole. But now he knew for sure she was in these parts, he'd ask Jed to put the feelers out. Casually he said, 'So you didn't get her married name, anything like that?'

'No. Why?'

'No particular reason, Mam. Just making conversation. I'm sorry she upset you, though, you were always good to the Fallows.' He patted her hand briefly. 'Try and forget it now. Don't let it spoil your Christmas.'

'No, you're right, lad, but when I think of her going off and getting wed, and our Jacob in the state he was about her, it makes my blood boil. I didn't realize it until he was in the hospital, but he was fair gone on her, and from what he said he'd had some encouragement that way an' all. I didn't think she was the type of lass to play fast and loose, not Lucy. She took me in good and proper.'

'You know what they say about the quiet ones who look as though butter wouldn't melt in their mouths. They're always the worst.'

Enid nodded. 'That's true enough.'

They were crossing the Wear Bridge now, and as they reached North Bridge Street, Tom said quietly, 'Might be best not to mention seeing Lucy to Jacob, Mam. You don't want to rake it up again, considering how cut up he was.'

'You think so?' Enid looked at him doubtfully. 'I thought if he knew she was married with a bairn, it'd finish any hopes he might have about her coming back one day.'

'I don't think he thinks that way. He's got on with his life, hasn't he? Even walked out with the odd lass or two. But likely it did leave a nasty taste in his mouth and what's the point in reminding him, now he's settled and happy? He thinks she's down south with Donald – leave it at that.'

'If you think that's best, lad.'

'I do.' He didn't want Jacob muddying the waters.

'Aye, all right. We don't see much of him these days anyway, as you know.' Enid glanced again at the son who was her sun, moon and stars. 'You're a good lad, bothering about him, when he's the way he is with you.'

Tom shrugged. 'He's still my brother, Mam. That's the way I look at it.'

Enid continued to ramble on about her afternoon until he dropped her off outside her front door, promising he'd be round for Christmas Day lunch the following day. He declined her offer of a drink, saying Mrs Hedley would have his dinner ready and it would take him longer to get home than usual, with the snow coming down so thickly. Once clear of Zetland Street, he pulled the car into the kerb and sat for a few minutes, staring blankly through the windscreen. His hands were shaking, he realized, holding them up in front of his face and giving a 'huh' of a growl. Stupid!

Angrily he started the engine and drove home too fast for the weather conditions, his head buzzing. Over eighteen months and not a day, not an hour, but Lucy hadn't come into his mind. But he'd never once imagined she was married.

He let loose a string of obscenities, beside himself with rage. She must have had this bloke that she had married on the go all along, that was the answer. There was no doubt she'd still been a virgin the night he'd taken her, but that didn't mean she hadn't been seeing someone on the quiet. But when would she had found the time and opportunities? She'd had her hands full with the bairns and keeping house, hadn't she? He'd thought Jacob was the fly in the ointment, but perhaps she'd been stringing them both along and had had her eye on this other bloke, this widower. She'd thought she could keep them all dangling most likely – that was the way women were.

And then she'd caught her toe with him, when he'd given her what she'd asked for.

He ground his teeth, wanting to hurt something or someone.

He'd find out what was what in the coming days, he promised himself. She thought she could treat him like a fool and then play Happy Families, did she? Well, she had another think coming. He wasn't done with Lucy Fallow. No, not by a long chalk.

Enid entered the house by the front door and as she walked along the hall she could hear Aaron holding forth about something or other. She paused outside the kitchen door, which was very slightly ajar. She couldn't have explained why she was about to eavesdrop, because she suspected she wouldn't like what she heard.

Aaron's voice was loud and slightly irritable. 'I tell you, I heard it straight from the horse's mouth. It's the same bloke who told me about Walter and Ernie, and he was there that day an' all. Maurice Banks, him that lives in Bright Street. He only talks so freely cos he knows I'm Tom's da and he thinks I know everything that goes on, being family. *Family*! Huh.'

Enid screwed up her eyes against the bitterness, but still she didn't make her presence known.

'But how does he know it was Tom who ordered the bloke to be done in?'

'Like I said, Frank, Maurice was *there*. All right? Part of it. This wasn't second- or third-hand. Tom reckoned he had it on good authority that the bloke was working for the customs, undercover like. And this isn't the first time some poor so-an'-so's disappeared or been done over so bad their own mother wouldn't recognize them. You know that as well as I do.'

'Aye, an' I also know it's not wise to talk about it.'

'Oh, come on, this is just us three. What's said in these four walls stays in 'em, but let's face facts. Tom's goin' to hell in a handcart, and I for one don't know him any more. He's no lad of mine, not these days. I've had a bellyful, I tell you straight.'

'Da, we've been over this before. There's no way out. We keep our heads down and do as we're told. There's the Kane lot, don't forget. No one in their right mind goes up against them, and Tom's as thick as thieves with Jed.'

'Thieves is about right, but I wouldn't mind if it was just the thieving. It's the rest of it that sticks in my craw.'

'Aye, well, that don't concern us. Like I said, we do our bit an' keep quiet. The rest is just hearsay, when all's said and done. He's never asked us to do anything like that.'

'And if he did?'

'He won't. He knows you've got your breaking point.'

'Oh aye, very respectful of me, he is,' Aaron said with deep sarcasm.

Enid couldn't bear another moment. Creeping back up the hallway, she opened the front door, but banged it shut this time, calling out as she did so, 'I hope there's a brew on, cos I'm frozen through.'

'Hello, Mam.' Ralph opened the kitchen door as she reached the end of the hall, taking one of her bags. 'Got everything you wanted?'

'Well, what I haven't got now we'll do without. It was cold enough to cut you in two out there, but still the town was full and, when you think, it's only two days, isn't it? Day after Boxing Day it's back to normal except everyone's drank and eaten too much.' She was gabbling, she told herself. She had to act natural. Taking a deep breath, she walked across and opened the oven door to check the pot roast she'd put in before she had left with Tom. 'It's ready,' she said. 'I'll just take me things off and put away the shopping and then I'll dish up.'

'I've poured you a cup of tea, lass,' Aaron said behind her. 'Come an' have it an' get warm, the dinner can wait. The lads'll see to the shopping.'

His voice had been kind – kinder than it had been for some time – and as she turned she saw that he was pulling out a chair for her at the table. She looked at his weatherbeaten face, at the lines that years of honest, back-breaking toil to provide for his family had carved out. He had used to come back from the shipyard exhausted and spent, and often frozen to the marrow in the winter. It was no wonder he was riddled with arthritis and a hundred and one other complaints.

When the moan sounded loud in her ears she didn't realize for a moment it had burst forth from her own throat. It was shocking, like the cry of a woman in labour. And when Aaron pressed her down into a chair and then put his arm round her as she wept and wailed, murmuring, 'There, there, lass, don't take on. Nothing's worth this. Come on, me love', it made her cry even harder. He was heaping coals of fire on her head. Because she knew, through the remorse and guilt, that she wasn't going to tell him she had been listening.

Once again, she was choosing Tom.

Chapter Nineteen

Christmas came and went on a high of jollity and no one but Ruby knew that behind Lucy's smiles and gaiety was a nagging, ever-present fear. Once Perce was asleep on Christmas Eve, Lucy had crept out of bed and gone into her sister's room, where Ruby was wide awake and waiting for her. They'd sat in the sitting room and, over a mug of hot milky cocoa, Lucy had told her sister the whole story, omitting nothing. They had cried together and spent half the night talking, and Ruby had agreed to keep her eyes and ears open in the coming days for any sign of Tom Crawford sniffing about.

On New Year's Eve they celebrated the passing of the old year and the arrival of the new one quietly as a family. Ruby and John stayed up until midnight and were allowed a small glass of Perce's beer each, and Perce acted the goat and stepped outside the flat to knock on the front door as first-foot, on the initial stroke of the New Year.

Later, in the warmth of their big bed, Perce drew her gently into his arms, but not for the reason Lucy had supposed. Instead he lay quietly for some minutes holding her close before saying, 'I can't believe you're mine, lass. I looked at you tonight and it swept over me again how lucky I am. This last year since the bairn's been born, well, it's been the happiest in me life.'

'Oh, Perce.' It was at times like this that she told herself she must do everything she could to make him never regret taking them in. He was so good, so kind. 'I think I'm lucky, too, to have you.'

'Oh aye, a man twice your age, with two bairns and a face like a battered pluck.'

She could hear the smile in his voice and she giggled. 'I like your face.'

'That's all that matters then.' He kissed the top of her head before settling her more comfortably against him. 'I love you,' he whispered so softly she could barely hear him.

She could not say, 'I love you too.' Instead she turned and reached for his face, bringing his mouth to hers.

Gradually over the next days and weeks the threat of Tom Crawford was relegated to the back of Lucy's mind. It was still there, manifesting itself in the odd nightmare now and again or a jittery feeling when she left the safety of the flat to take Daisy and Charley to the park or to do some shopping, but she forced herself not to dwell on it. Her soup kitchen, as Perce called it, was a huge success and took more of her time than she'd expected, but this was welcome in the circumstances. It left her no time to brood.

On Daisy's first birthday at the end of February Perce closed the shop for the afternoon and they took the children to the Winter Garden at the rear of the Museum and Library building. The large conservatory was full of tropical plants and flowers and had a pond full of goldfish, but it was the aviary that delighted little Daisy. Even after two hours of looking at the birds she wasn't ready to leave.

It was a wonderful afternoon, and when they got home and had finished the birthday tea, Daisy put the final seal on the day by taking her first steps unaided. A proud Perce whisked her up into his arms shouting, 'That's me darling, that's me bonny babby' and everyone clapped. After that Daisy had insisted on staggering about until bedtime, delighted by the attention.

It was in the second week of a bitterly cold March, when unemployment's upward spiral had reached a new peak of one and a half million, resulting in angry demonstrators fighting with the police in some major cities, that Lucy noticed Perce deep in conversation with a customer one evening. John was keeping an eye on the little ones in the flat above the shop, and she and Ruby were busy dealing with the queue for hot soup at the far end of the marble counter, which stretched the width of the premises. They were some distance from Perce, and Lucy couldn't hear what was being said.

It wasn't unusual for Perce to chat with his customers – his hearty banter sold more fish than the reasonable prices – but something about this exchange bothered Lucy.

For one thing, the customer was a man, and in a community where women did the shopping this was out of the ordinary. And the individual concerned had a look about him – Lucy couldn't explain it to herself except to say that he appeared shifty.

This was explained to some extent when she asked Perce about the man later that night when they were alone. He looked at her a little sheepishly, lowering his voice, although there were only the two of them sitting in front of the fire now that the rest of the household were in bed, and said, 'He was after setting up a bit of business, lass. That's all.'

'What sort of business?' She was busy hand-sewing some cream lace on a little dress she'd made for Daisy for the summer, and she stopped to give him her full attention.

'He's matey with one of the skippers on the boats, and this bloke sees him all right when they've had a good haul. He's got stall in the Old Market – nothin' fancy – and oft times there's too much for him to get rid of, but he don't like to say no in case this bloke takes offence. He's offerin' to let me have any extra, for what he pays this pal of his, on the quiet like. It's half of what I can get stuff for, lass. Course, I'm not daft. I've an idea the price he's told me, tasty as it is, is not what he forks out, but if it does me a good turn and he makes a bit on the deal, that's all right.'

Lucy stared at him doubtfully. 'Do you think he's telling the truth? It could be knocked off, you know.'

Perce grinned at her. 'See no evil, hear no evil, say no evil, that's my motto, lass, and I'm not about to look a gift horse in the mouth. If he says it's all above board, that's good enough for me.'

'What about the harbour police?' she said drily. 'Would it be good enough for them?'

'You worry too much.' His smile widened. 'Let me do any worrying – that's what husbands are for.'

'So when is he bringing it?'

'Next time he gets a load. He'll tip me the wink.'

'I don't like it, Perce.'

'It might not happen, pet. Don't fret. It could well be something or nothing.' He popped his pipe in his mouth and disappeared behind his paper again, signifying the end of the discussion.

Lucy bit on her lip. They didn't need to take any risks, they were doing nicely as it was. Since Daisy had been born and she'd started feeling more herself, she had taken over the paperwork concerning the business. Perce was no scholar and he hated putting pen to paper, so everything had been in an awful mess, but gradually she'd brought order to the chaos and established a neat set of accounts, as Ada had done before her demise. The business had never made much of a profit, but enabled them to live comfortably within their means as long as they watched the pennies. Over the last two months, however, with the soup kitchen, operating profits had begun to soar. Lucy had decided to make batches of bread rolls to be sold alongside the soup, and these had gone down extremely well. She bought umpteen sacks of flour at a time, seconds, for a very good price, which were delivered free of charge to the shop for a bulk order. In spite of the chaff and inferior quality of the flour, the rolls were filling and cheap, which was what her particular clientele asked for. Soft white bread at four times the price was no good to families who hadn't got two farthings to rub together.

She glanced at Perce, but the newspaper was very firmly in place and she took the hint. She'd leave this for tonight, but the matter was by no means closed.

Hidden behind his *Echo*, Perce knew exactly the way Lucy's mind was working, which was why he hadn't let on that he'd already arranged to pay a visit to the Old Market early in the morning, before it was light, and see for himself the sort of fish the man could offer.

'Me pal dropped a load off not more than an hour ago,' the man had murmured before he'd left the shop. 'It's packed in ice for the night, but there's too much for me. You'll see what I mean when you have a look. Meet me before the market gets goin' an' there's too many folk around. Say five or thereabouts? Come to the main entrance in Coronation Street an' I'll see you all right. Me lad'll help you bring back what you want. We've got a handcart we use.'

It'd be daft not to go and at least have a look, Perce thought to himself. He lost nothing by doing that, except an hour or two's sleep. If he was canny he could be back before Lucy knew he'd gone and she'd be none the wiser.

His eyes focused on the paper. It was full of doom

and gloom, predicting a steady increase in the jobless figures, which showed no indication that the trend would change in the coming months. 'Lengthening dole queues, as the world economy slumps further after last year's Wall Street Crash, are besetting all countries, not just Britain.' the reporter had written. 'Industrial production is in rapid decline as factories close or lay off workers; farmers and small tradespeople are facing ruin and, where benefits are paid, they are rarely enough to keep families above starvation level. Mass unemployment, desperate poverty and political extremism are the best that Britain and the rest of the world can look forward to in the new decade.'

He was a right cheerful Charlie, Perce thought with dark humour, but he dared bet the bloke was right, which made it even more imperative to make the most of any opportunities that did arise. God helps those who help themselves, and in these times no one could afford to be choosy.

Having justified himself, Perce settled down to read the rest of the paper in peace. What the eye didn't see, the heart didn't grieve over, and Lucy could remain in ignorance, if he was careful. That was the way to handle this.

Stealthiness and silence didn't come easily to Perce, and he was sweating with the effort it had taken not to awaken Lucy and the rest of the household when he left the flat the next morning just before five o'clock. Creeping down the stairs to the shop with his boots in his hands, he tiptoed through Lucy's new kitchen and into the main part of the premises, where he put on his boots on. Sliding the bolts on the front door, he opened it, then locked it from the outside and pocketed the key.

It had snowed again during the night and was bitterly cold, but the mantle of shining white created its own light, making it easy to see in the darkness. The rest of the world was sleeping, and he stood for a moment on the icy doorstep, viewing the clean, pure, untouched scene in front of him, which made even Long Bank beautiful. Like the Garden of Eden before man had had to go and stick his oar in and spoil things, he thought. As he stepped down onto the pavement it came to him that he had never thought in such a way before Lucy had come into his life. She saw beauty in so many things he'd never really looked at before – the different colours of autumn leaves; the little robin that regularly came to the kitchen windowsill for the crumbs of cake she put out for him; the delicate fragility of a snowflake – and it had rubbed off on him. He smiled self-consciously. He was going soft, that was the trouble.

He hadn't even reached the end of the street and turned into High Street East when he became aware of three men standing on the corner of Bank Street. It wasn't unusual, since the slump had taken hold, to see a number of huddled figures on street corners. They stood, collars up, cap peaks down and faces morose, as they shared a Woodbine between them and railed bitterly against the government, employers, the upper classes and anyone else they blamed for the current state of affairs. What was unusual was that it was five o'clock in the morning.

Perce, anxious to get to Coronation Street, see to the business and return home before Lucy awoke, barely glanced their way as he passed. He had covered another few yards when instinct brought him swinging round. But it was too late . . .

A tap on the bedroom door brought Lucy jerking awake. Realizing Perce wasn't in bed beside her, she sat up, pushing back her hair. 'Yes? Come in,' she called, flinging the blankets aside and reaching for her dressing gown.

'We've all overslept.' Ruby stood in the doorway, Daisy in her arms and the twins either side of her. 'It's gone half-six Lucy. Why on earth hasn't Perce called us?'

'I don't know.' Taking Daisy from her sister, Lucy tried to think. 'You wake the boys and put the porridge on. I'll see what's what.'

Opening the flat's front door, she stood on the small landing and peered down the stairs. 'Perce? Are you there?'

It was eerily quiet. Furthermore no lights were showing, so the gas jets hadn't been lit. Her heart in her mouth, Lucy was about to go down the stairs when Ruby appeared at the side of her, clutching the heavy iron poker. 'Give Daisy to John, lass, and he'll keep the little 'uns up here. I'm coming down with you.'

Lucy stared at her sister, really frightened now. Silently John carried Daisy into the flat, shutting the door behind him. Not knowing what they would find, they crept down the stairs. The back door leading to the yard was still bolted, and the kitchen and shop stood empty in the morning light. The air left Lucy's lungs in a sigh of relief. 'It doesn't look as though there's been a break-in.' For a minute she'd been worried that Perce had heard something in the middle of the night and come down and been set upon. 'But where is he? Look, the door's unbolted.' Walking across, she tried it. 'It's locked. He must have gone out, but where?'

'Nothing's set up.' Ruby was as perplexed as she was. 'And the fish from the docks'll be arriving any minute.'

The words had hardly left her mouth when they heard the horse and cart that signified the day's delivery. Grabbing the spare key from behind the counter, Lucy opened the front door and took charge of the crates of fish and other seafood. They normally opened for customers at half-past seven, but after locking the door again Lucy left the Closed sign in place.

By the time Daisy had been changed and everyone was dressed and sitting down to breakfast, Lucy was wondering if Perce's early-morning sojourn had anything to do with the matter they'd discussed briefly the night before. It still didn't explain why he hadn't told her he was going out, especially if he'd thought he might be so late back, and Perce was the last person on Earth who'd do anything to worry her. She knew that. But it seemed the only explanation. She decided that, once Ruby and John had gone off to school with Matthew and the twins, she would take Daisy and Charley with her and pay a visit to the

Old Market, to see if she could spot Perce or maybe the man who'd called in at the shop. She certainly couldn't just sit around waiting, she was too het-up. As for the shop – it would have to stay closed. There was nothing else to be done.

They were still eating when there was a loud banging at the shop door. Leaving Ruby in charge of the breakfast table, Lucy shot downstairs, hoping desperately it was Perce. It was only when she saw the two policemen through the shop window that she realized Perce wouldn't have knocked. He had taken the key.

Opening the door, she stared at their grim faces and her heart jumped into her mouth. For the life of her she couldn't speak a word.

The older of the men spoke, his voice quiet. 'Mornin', lass. We're looking to speak to Mrs Alridge.'

She was vaguely aware of Ruby appearing at her elbow as she whispered, 'That's me. I'm Mrs Alridge.'

Sergeant Johnson hid his surprise. When she'd opened the door it had been on the tip of his tongue to ask her to fetch her mother. Just to make sure, he said, 'Mrs *Percival* Alridge?'

Her eyes wide and fear-filled, Lucy nodded.

'May we come in and have a word, Mrs Alridge?'

'Is it Perce? Where is he?'

'I think it would be better if we spoke inside.'

'Oh yes, yes, come in.' She trod on Ruby's foot as she backed away from the door, but neither of them noticed.

The younger policeman shut the door once they were

inside and, like his colleague, had been taken aback by the slip of a girl who was the fishmonger's wife. She was a beauty, he thought, finding it hard to take his eyes off her. But so young. And now she was a widow.

'I'm afraid it's bad news, Mrs Alridge.' Sergeant Johnson kept his voice calm and matter-of-fact. Thirty years of being a policeman had placed him in this kind of situation more than once and he'd found that an air of control helped the bereaved to accept what he had to say. 'Your husband was found in an alley off High Street East a little while ago.'

Ruby was clutching Lucy's arm, and it was she who said, 'He – he's hurt?'

Lucy knew. Even before the policeman said quietly, 'I'm afraid it's worse than that.' She listened while he went on to explain that they suspected it was a robbery that went wrong. Perce had a number of knife wounds to the chest. His pockets were empty. No one had heard or seen a thing. Perce being a big man who looked as though he could take care of himself, it was highly likely they were looking for more than one assailant. The bairns who had found the body had fetched their mother and she'd recognized him as the fishmonger who lived in Long Bank.

Lucy took in each fact that the policeman stated in his steady, carefully sympathetic voice as she enfolded Ruby in her arms, who was weeping profusely. When the Sergeant suggested they go upstairs, she explained about the children and said she would rather break the news to them herself.

She agreed to go to the police station later, whereupon they would take her to identify the body. She thanked them for coming and said she would answer any questions they had later that morning. And all the time, every moment, one name was burning in her mind. *Tom Crawford*. He had found them. Found her. And he had done what he'd threatened that night. He had warned her he wouldn't let another man have her, and now he had killed Perce. She knew it as surely as if he was standing in front of her and saying so himself. But no one would believe her. She hadn't laid eyes on him for nigh on two years and he hadn't contacted her in any way, but she knew – she *knew* – Perce's murder was no bungled robbery. That man yesterday, he hadn't wanted to sell cheap fish. He'd lured Perce to his death.

Oh, Perce, Perce. After everything he had done for her. He had given her back her life and, in doing so, had saved Daisy too. And he had never judged her. If only she had told him that she loved him. That was what he'd wanted, she knew that. And she hadn't, and now she'd never see him again, she couldn't make it right. She couldn't bear it – she'd go mad.

Through the agony of her thoughts, she made herself look at the two policemen. 'I'm sorry, but could you go now? I need to take care of my sister and then we have to tell the bairns.'

Sergeant Johnson's gaze narrowed on the beautiful white face in front of him. Instinct told him that her shock over her husband's demise had been genuine, but she was a cool one sure enough. Cool as a cucumber, and not a tear for the poor devil. He understood from the mother of the bairns who'd found the body that this one was the fishmonger's second wife, and it didn't take the Brain of Britain to work out that he'd wanted a bonny young thing to warm his bed and she'd seen him as a meal ticket. Still, the ins and outs were nothing to do with him, but he'd bear it in mind in his investigations – not that he thought she had anything to do with what had happened. But you never knew.

Nodding politely, he said, 'Certainly, Mrs Alridge, and we'll see you later. Are you sure you're all right to be left?'

'Quite sure.' Lucy hesitated, then, her voice a whisper, she said, 'Would – would he have suffered much?'

She met his eyes as she spoke and the Sergeant found himself recanting his earlier thoughts and feeling ashamed. His voice uncharacteristically gentle, he lied softly, 'No, lass, no. He'd barely have known a thing.'

She didn't believe him. As Lucy shut the door behind the two policemen, her eyes were dry, but she was weeping from every pore of her body. She had to make the others believe it. It was the only comfort she could give them.

Chapter Twenty

The murder was on the front page of the *Echo*. A local shopkeeper, a respectable, God-fearing man with a beautiful young wife left to bring up a number of bairns, the youngest a daughter only thirteen months old – the story was a reporter's dream. And they made the most of it.

On top of her consuming grief and her worry about the children, Lucy had to bear the fact that her past was winkled out and held up to scrutiny. Not that the reporters were unkind. Rather, they presented her as a tragic heroine who, after the death of her menfolk, was turned out on the streets with her brother and sisters by a harsh landlord, but went on to find love and happiness with the saintly Perce, who opened up his home and his heart to them. The drama and romance were the stuff of the silver screen. Her maiden name, where she used to live, even where she went to school, were reported with avid detail. From being a nondescript fishmonger's wife, Lucy was elevated to the ranks of the legendary overnight.

Much as she hated the loss of privacy, it was the particulars about Daisy that frightened her. She had told Tom's mother that her daughter was six months old, and here it was in black-and-white that Daisy was double that. If Tom hadn't known before that there was a good chance Daisy was his, he'd put two and two together now.

She had no hope that the perpetrators of the attack on Perce would be brought to justice. Whether Tom had done the deed himself or got others to murder Perce, the tracks were well and truly covered. He would make sure of that. He was evil, but in a cold, clever, calculating way. How he came to be Jacob's brother she would never fathom.

She had trained herself not to think of Jacob when Perce was alive. To do so seemed a betrayal of the man she owed so much to. Now it was harder. The old fear that Tom would do Jacob harm was back, tenfold, after what had happened to Perce. Not that Jacob would necessarily want anything to do with her, though. He must think she had left Zetland Street not caring if he lived or died, and had then promptly married someone else and had their baby. He'd probably washed his hands of her. Painful though that was, she hoped it was true. It was the only way he would be safe.

Lucy had expected Matthew to take his father's death worse than anyone else after the way he'd lost his mother, but although the child was sad and cried a lot, it was Ruby who proved almost inconsolable. Lucy had kept her suspicions about Tom Crawford to herself, but Ruby's mind had apparently been working along the same lines. On the evening of the third day following a visit from Perce's solicitor, when he told Lucy that Perce had left everything to her, lock, stock and barrel, the two sisters were sitting quietly in front of the fire, the rest of the household fast asleep. Out of the blue Ruby said, 'Do you think *he* had anything to do with it?'

Lucy didn't have to ask who she meant. There followed a stillness, and it was broken by her saying tentatively, 'Do you?'

Ruby nodded. 'Mrs Crawford would have told him she'd seen us that time. I think he found out where you lived and decided to do Perce in. You said he'd threatened to do the same to Jacob the night he – well, you know.'

Lucy looked into her sister's swollen, pink-rimmed eyes, wondering if Ruby was blaming her for Perce's death. It was more than possible; certainly she was blaming herself. If Perce hadn't taken them in, if he hadn't married her, he'd be alive now, she told herself wretchedly. And Ruby had loved Perce. She hadn't realized it before, she'd been too caught up in running the house and seeing to the family's needs, as well as working in the shop and starting the soup side of the business, but Perce had become father and older brother and a knight in shining armour to her sister. And now Ruby was bereft. 'I wouldn't have married him if I'd thought for a second anything like this might happen,' she said, her voice breaking. 'I'm so sorry, lass.'

'It's not your fault.' Ruby took her hand. 'And we

don't know for sure it's him.' They sat quietly for a minute or two, each lost in thought, and it was only when the burning coals shifted in the fire, creating a shower of red sparks, that Ruby roused herself to say, 'We'll have to be on our guard from now on. You can't be here by yourself with Daisy and Charley when we're at school. Perhaps we ought to leave after the funeral.'

'I'm not letting Tom Crawford frighten us from our home for a second time.' Lucy's head had shot up and now her chin tilted at a fighting angle. 'We're going to stay here, Ruby. I'm going to run the business, because I know that's what Perce would have wanted for his boys. He was proud that his grandfather set up the shop with next to nothing and then his da carried it on. I'm not letting Tom Crawford erase even his memory. The sign out there is Alridge & Son. The only difference will be an "s" added. Oh, and I'm changing the locks,' she added grimly. The missing key had begun to play on her mind.

Ruby's face was a picture. '*You're* going to run the business? Lass, you can't. How will you cope with the shop, and Daisy and Charley and everything, when I'm at school?'

'I don't know, I haven't thought about the details yet.'

'You know nothing about the different sorts of fish and what's entailed. And what about dealing with Perce's suppliers and the rest of it?'

'I'll learn. I learned how to manage the books, didn't I?'

'Lass, the books are a tiny part of it.'

'Tiny part or not, it's something I already know, so that's a start. Next year you'll be leaving school in the summer, so that'll make things easier.'

'That's still a long way off. What about now?'

'I'll put a notice in the shop window tomorrow, saying "Assistant required".'

Ruby stared at her sister. Lucy had insisted that Perce's solicitor spoke to both of them, saying she had no secrets from Ruby, so she had been party to the details. Mr Bainbridge, a dour individual, had informed them that, in accordance with the new will Mr Alridge had made when he'd married her, the present Mrs Alridge owned the shop and flat outright, but the nest egg Perce's late parents had built up had dwindled away to virtually nothing in previous years.

'The former Mrs Alridge had expensive tastes,' the tall, bony man had said thinly, his long, narrow nose quivering with disapproval. 'I attempted to explain to Mr Alridge on a number of occasions that it is prudent for inflow to cover outflow, but to no avail. Nevertheless, it was my duty to try.'

Thinking of this now, Ruby said, 'How will you pay an assistant? There's no money to tide you over. And think of the hard physical work Perce did and the hours he put in, and you're just a—' She stopped abruptly.

'A lass? That's what you were going to say, isn't it?' Lucy asked without heat. 'And I understand what you're saying, Ruby. I do, really. But I have to do this.'

Ruby shook her head. This was madness. Women didn't

go into business. They should sell up and get as far away from here as they could. 'But *why*?'

'For Perce. And Matthew and Charley. The shop's their name, their birthright. And – and me.'

Lucy bowed her head, biting on her lip to control the welling emotion. She didn't know if she could explain how she felt in words. 'After Tom Crawford used me that night, I felt so dirty and ashamed. And helpless. That was perhaps the worst thing of all. I hadn't been able to fight him off or stop him. He could do that, he could do anything he wanted, and then just walk away and carry on, or even come back and do it again.'

She stood up and began to pace the room.

'I hadn't thought I was a weak person before that night, but I've never been so frightened of anything or anyone as him.'

'With good cause, lass, and I don't call that being weak.'

'But then Perce took us in and, even when I found out about Daisy, he still cared about what happened to me. He made me feel safe again and I can't tell you what it meant. He was such a good, good man.'

'Oh, lass, don't cry.'

As Ruby made to stand up, Lucy flapped her hand for her sister to remain seated. Wiping her eyes, she composed herself. 'Since Sergeant Johnson knocked on the door I've been frightened, terrified. And I hate that I'm scared. Last night I dreamt we were back in the alley with the rats, and I even ached in my dream where Tom Crawford hurt me. Then I woke up and I was so thankful, but the fear was still there. And now Perce can't protect me. So' – she took a deep breath – 'I have to protect myself and Daisy too, and it starts in here.' She tapped her forehead. 'If I leave here, if we run again, I'll be scared for the rest of my life. Forever looking over my shoulder. I won't let scum like Tom Crawford do that to me.'

Ruby nodded, tears streaming down her face.

'I *will* make a success of the shop. I've promised Perce. And I've got you and the bairns and my Daisy. I'm going to count my blessings, like Mam always said.'

Ruby scrubbed at her eyes with her handkerchief and then blew her nose loudly. 'What if he comes here? To the house? He's cocky enough. And changing the locks won't stop him.'

In spite of herself, a shiver snaked down Lucy's spine. 'Like you said, we'll be on our guard from now on. That's the most we can do.' That and wait, she thought grimly. Because if there was one thing in life she was sure about, it was that Tom Crawford would confront her sooner or later.

She didn't have to wait long. She had agreed that Ruby and the others could remain at home until after the funeral, which was to take place the following week, and the morning after her conversation with her sister Lucy rose early. There had been no deliveries of fish to the shop since the day after Perce's body had been found. She had to go to the docks and see the fishermen concerned, and tell them she was opening for business the day after the funeral.

After placing the advertisement for an assistant in the front window of the shop, she walked along Long Bank and down into the harbour, where the quays were. Quite a few boats were in, moored from Low Quay on the left of the harbour right along to Mark's Quay on the right, with various quays in between. The dockside was heaving with fishwives collecting their fish in great baskets, boys with barrowloads, trawlermen and the odd customs official in dispute about something or other, and over everything – like a great, thick, invisible blanket – was the consuming odour of the waterfront. Fishwives gutted and cleaned their wares; eels and crabs and lobsters fought to escape big buckets; and the odd fish flapped out the last few moments of its life among its dead companions. The noise and bustle could be overwhelming to the uninitiated and Lucy felt conspicuously out of place, but she pressed on to Ettrick's Quay where Seamus Riley could be found. She had spoken to this particular fisherman a number of times when he had made deliveries to the shop and had found him to be a friendly and garrulous old man, which would be welcome in the circumstances.

Seamus and his sons were unloading their catch when she called to him, and after expressing his condolences he agreed to resume his deliveries after the funeral. An idea had been brewing in Lucy's mind over the last twenty-four hours. Perce had always bought his supply of seafood from more than one source, saying that he didn't want to have all his eggs – or, in this case, fish, as he'd joked with a grin – in one basket, but even before her husband's demise Lucy had been wondering if this was the best practice. Gathering her courage, she put the proposition she'd been rehearsing since she had awoken that morning to Seamus. 'If I agree to buy all my fish and seafood from you from now on, and I'll guarantee to take a certain amount, what sort of deal can you do for me?' she said, hoping she sounded more sure of herself than she felt.

Seamus stared in amazement at the bonny young piece – as he privately termed Perce's wife – and chewed for a moment on his baccy. 'I was doing the best price I could for Perce, lass,' he said. 'He never complained.'

Lucy nodded. 'Perce always said your fish were the best he had, Mr Riley,' she said briskly, 'but I'll be taking more, a lot more, and giving you my undivided loyalty. That's worth something, surely? I'm on my own now and I've got seven hungry mouths to feed at home. I can't afford to pay a penny more than I have to.'

Seamus's mouth gaped for a moment, showing his stained brown teeth. Perce had been easy-going to a fault and not much of a businessman – everyone on the quays knew that and had taken advantage of it, to a greater or lesser extent. But the slip of a lass in front of him was a different kettle of fish. She had fire in her belly, this one. He'd thought at first, when Perce had married her, she was a decorative piece who'd reeled Perce in so that she could sit back and have a life of leisure, but he was wrong. Doing a quick mental sum in his head, he named a price that was reasonable, and such was his surprise at the turn of events that when Lucy knocked him down still further, he surrendered with barely a murmur.

After bidding Seamus a good morning, Lucy made her way back along the crowded dockside, pausing for a few moments to watch one of the River Wear divers being helped into his suit. It was a heavy, one-piece affair made of canvas, with rubber rings round the wrists and a great copper breastplate and lead weights on his chest and back. The boat was going out to service the buoys in the river, and she wondered how the diver could do anything, with the weight of the suit to cope with, along with his copper helmet and massive great boots. She looked at the air pump, the handles of which would have to be turned as long as the diver was under the water, and shivered. Since her father and Ernie had been fished out of the dock, the River Wear had lost any appeal it might have had, and the river ships, steamships, paddle tugs and paddle steamers no longer held any fascination for her. The dark, deep water was an alien place, an abyss of grim secrets and lost dreams, and she hated it.

The morning was cold but bright, the March sun holding no warmth, but causing the heavy frost of the night before to twinkle like stardust. Snow had been forecast for the last day or two, but as yet there had been no sign of it, although the icy blue sky was starting to cloud over. She walked home slowly, taking care not to slip. There was no need to rush. Ruby would have seen to Daisy and marshalled the others into getting dressed, and before they'd retired the previous evening she had told her sister to give the children their breakfast if they were hungry before she was back.

She had reached the shop and was about to open the door when some sixth sense caused her to turn before inserting the key in the lock. Tom Crawford was no more than six feet away. They stared at each other and she found that she couldn't move a muscle.

'Hello, Lucy,' he said very softly.

Still she found she couldn't respond, not until he took a step towards her, and then she said, 'Don't you come near me. You come any closer and I'll scream – I mean it.'

'Don't be silly, you'd only make a fool of yourself.' But he had stopped. 'I only want to say how sorry I am about your trouble. That's all.'

'I don't want your condolences.'

'Now that's not very nice, is it?'

Her voice had been shrill with fear. Now Lucy took a deep breath and spoke flatly, saying what she'd promised herself she'd say if she saw him face-to-face. 'Did you have anything to do with my husband's death?'

Her directness threw him, she could see it in his face, but almost immediately he recovered. 'Me? How could I? No one knew where you lived after you left Zetland Street.'

He'd done it. She knew so without a shadow of a doubt. The truth had been there for a split second in the cold eyes. He'd killed her Perce. Fury blotted out the fear.

'You wicked, evil monster.' She wanted to leap at him, to tear him limb from limb. 'You killed him, I know you did.'

'Don't be ridiculous, I wasn't even in Sunderland the day it happened. I'd stayed overnight in Newcastle and there are any number of people who can confirm that.'

If he had meant to convince her of his innocence, it had the opposite effect. 'So you had your alibi while your lackeys did your dirty work.' She had known, hadn't she? From the first moment the police had called, she'd known it was Tom Crawford who was responsible. But how could she prove it?

As though he could read her mind, Tom said softly, 'It's dangerous to besmirch a man's good name without proof, lass, so be careful. Be very careful what you say.'

'Good name!' She was beyond caution. 'You're filthy, putrid, you always have been. My da called you scum, and he was right.'

His nostrils flared and colour seared his cheekbones, but still he didn't raise his voice. 'Is that so? Well, I seem to remember you weren't above giving me the eye at one time.'

'You liar!'

'A liar, am I?' He moved swiftly, gripping her arms above the elbows and shaking her once, very hard. 'And what are you? What was that story you gave my mother about the bairn being six months old?' He gave a bark of a laugh. 'Once I'd found out where you were, it didn't take me two minutes to find out the truth. Did you tell

him? The sap you married? Did you tell him it was mine?'
He shook her again. 'Because she is, isn't she?'

A couple of men who were passing by on the opposite
side of the street stopped, and one called out, 'You all
right, lass?'

Tom let go of her, swinging round to snarl, 'Sling your
hook. This is nothing to do with you.'

'I'm fine.' A brawl in the street because of her would
be the final straw. She was already notorious as the wife
of the man who'd been brutally murdered, and Lucy knew
the old rumours about her swift marriage to Perce and
Daisy's subsequent arrival had been stirred into flames
once more. 'Really, I'm all right.'

The men still hesitated. 'You sure, lass?'

'You heard her, didn't you?' Tom took a step in their
direction at the same time as Lucy said, 'Yes, I'm sure.'

As the men ambled off he turned back to her. 'I know
when she was born and I'm not daft. Why would you lie
about it to Mam, unless you didn't want me to find out?
It wasn't very clever, lass, now was it?'

'I don't know what you're talking about.' Lucy didn't
falter. 'I never told your mother my daughter was six
months old, she must have misheard me.' Terror of what
might happen if he didn't believe her gave her voice a
ring of truth, and she saw that she'd disconcerted him.
'Daisy was early, as it happens, but she was my husband's
child.'

'I don't believe you. My mother doesn't get things like
that wrong.' His voice had changed to a deep growl.

'I don't care what you believe.' Lucy's face was devoid of colour, but adrenaline born of fear kept her back straight. She was fighting for Daisy rather than herself; she would not have this fiend lay any claim to her daughter.

'Is that so?' Tom gritted his teeth, struggling to control himself. He didn't want a scene any more than Lucy did. He was aiming to become a town councillor in the not-too-distant future, and mud had a habit of sticking.

'Aye, it is and, whatever you say, I think you had a hand in Perce's death like you did in my da's and Ernie's.'

'That was an accident, for crying out loud.'

'Accident or not, you were responsible.'

He swore, his voice low but vicious. 'What's the matter with you anyway? You could have had a life of ease with me, decked out like a lady and not having to lift a finger. Instead you chose to live in these filthy streets, with a stinking fishmonger pawing you about.'

'Perce was ten times – a hundred times – the man you are.' She glared her hate, wanting to puncture the inflated ego. 'And he didn't have to rape me to get what he wanted.'

For a moment she thought he was going to strike her. His face livid, Tom seemed unable to speak for a moment and she watched his hands bunch at his side as he resisted felling her to the ground. Then, with the words hissed through his teeth, he said, 'But he's dead and I'm alive. Remember that. And I'll be watching you from now on, wherever you go.'

He had turned on his heel before she said, her voice

shaking now, 'I'm not answerable to you, Tom Crawford. I'm not answerable to anyone.'

He swung round, his eyes gimlet-hard. 'Keep it that way. I don't know if the bairn's mine, not for sure, you've seen to that, but my mam's not hard of hearing and she doesn't often make mistakes, so I'll draw me own conclusions, if it's all the same to you. And no one takes what's mine. Keep that in mind if you get the notion to play Happy Families again, all right?'

The sky had clouded over, the blue all gone and grey taking its place. 'You killed him, didn't you?' she said dully. 'You killed him because of me.'

He didn't answer, but after a few moments of staring at her face, he smiled.

She had her answer.

That same day, at two in the afternoon, as the first fat snowflakes began to fall from a laden sky, Lucy had another visitor. Ruby and John were minding the little ones upstairs and Lucy was scrubbing the shop from top to bottom. She had been working since she had come in from the encounter with Tom Crawford, needing the hard physical exercise to counter the consuming guilt and grief she was feeling about Perce's death. Why had she married him? she asked herself over and over again. If she had gone right away from Sunderland, Perce would still be alive. But how could she have done? She'd had no money and there had been Ruby and John and the twins to consider. And if she'd gone when she'd found out she was expecting

Daisy, her daughter wouldn't be here now, because the way she had been feeling then, the river was the only answer. And why – *why* – had she told Enid Crawford that Daisy was so much younger? In Tom Crawford's eyes it had been tantamount to admitting Daisy was his, once he'd asked around and found out her true age. It had been stupid, so stupid, but she'd panicked that evening and in attempting to throw him off the trail had made everything a hundred times worse. And Perce had paid the price.

So the recriminations reverberated in her head hour after hour until she felt she was going mad. And that feeling was heightened when she heard a tap at the window and straightened up, to see Jacob standing outside the shop.

For a moment Lucy couldn't move; she just stared at him. He was taller than she remembered and well built, a man already at seventeen with no vestige of the boy or youth left. Of course that would be his work in the forge, she told herself numbly. And he was well dressed. Not as his brother had been, acting the toff, but Jacob's overcoat hung full and thick and was the same dark grey as his cap.

Somehow she made herself walk to the door and turn the key, and now her heart was pounding like a sledgehammer and threatening to jump out of her chest. As his eyes swept her from head to foot she was acutely conscious of the big calico apron she'd pulled on over her dress to do the cleaning and of the wisps of hair that her exertion had loosened from the piled coils on top of her head.

His voice was just the same, though, deep with a slight catch of huskiness in it, which had always thrilled her in the past, as he said quietly, 'It's been a long time, Lucy.'

She nodded. 'Yes.' It was a whisper.

'I didn't hear about what had happened until last night – we don't have a newspaper every day. I'm sorry. About your husband.'

Again she nodded, not knowing what to say or do. The snow was beginning to settle on his cap and shoulders and, opening the door wider, she said, 'Would you like to come in?'

He hesitated, and Lucy wasn't to know that the sight of her was tearing Jacob apart inside. From the moment he'd read the paper the night before, he'd been beside himself. 'Still no light on the murder of the fishmonger in Long Bank,' the reporter had written. And then had followed a list of the fishmonger's dependants, starting with his young wife, Lucy – his second wife, the article had emphasized – and her sisters, Ruby, Flora and Bess, and brother, John, and the fishmonger's two children by his first wife, along with a thirteen-month-old daughter by the present Mrs Alridge. A family deprived of their breadwinner was always tragic, the article had gone on, but under such violent circumstances doubly so. It had finished with the usual, 'If anyone knows anything about the events of . . .' and so on.

He'd read it twice, the blood thundering in his ears,

and he must have looked like he felt, because Dolly had glanced up from her knitting and given a start, saying, 'What is it, lad? What's wrong?'

It had been a long night and he'd counted every minute of it as he'd paced the floor of his room. It had to be her, which meant she had never left Sunderland and gone down south after all. She'd been in the town and she was married with a bairn. He had been at death's door and eating his heart out for her, and she had been canoodling with some bloke or other and getting wed.

Round and round he had walked, every emotion under the sun searing his breast, until he thought he'd lose his mind. By the time he'd come down to breakfast he'd known what he had to do. It wasn't wise, he'd known that even before he'd told Abe and Dolly his intentions and they'd advised him to hold his horses and wait a while, but he had to see her today. And now here she was. In front of him. And if the fifteen-year-old girl had been lovely, the young woman she'd become was breathtaking.

He had thought he was managing fine without her, that Lucy was his past and he was content for her to remain there. He was his own man now, wasn't he? A partner in a good, solid business that one day would be his. He'd even bitten the bullet and started courting steady. Felicity was a nice lass, bonny, but not forward. He'd come to terms with the fact that the Lucy he'd danced with in the moonlight was not what she'd seemed, that he'd made a huge mistake and was better out of it. Events had proved that he hadn't really known her. No use crying over spilt milk, that was a mug's game, and at least he wouldn't be fooled again.

But he had been fooling *himself*. He looked into the azure-blue eyes, which he had never thought to see again, and nothing mattered. Not her betrayal, not her marriage to another man, nothing. He loved her. Still. It was like she was part of him. 'Why did you leave the way you did, when I was in hospital?' He hadn't meant to say it. He'd told himself on the way here that, if he saw her, he would be polite but formal, express his condolences whilst letting her know that he didn't think much of her treatment of him. Draw a line under things – that's what he'd intended.

'I had to.' Her eyes had fallen from his. 'Donald had left us and the little ones would have been put in the workhouse.'

'You must have known my mam wouldn't have let that happen.'

'They were my responsibility, no one else's.'

He could not take his eyes from her face, but still he didn't move from the doorstep. 'You didn't come to the hospital or even write to say where you were. We thought Donald had made you go down south with him.' She did not reply, and he went on, stating the obvious, 'But you were here in Sunderland with this man, the fishmonger. I didn't know you knew him. You'd never mentioned him.' Steeling himself, he asked the question that had tormented him all night. 'Did you love him?'

She made a little movement of her head, which could have meant anything. Her voice a whisper, she said, 'Please don't do this, Jacob.'

Don't do this? After all she had put him through, she said: Don't do this? He had the right to ask, damn it. 'Did you? Did you love him?'

She raised her head, her blue eyes looking straight into his and her voice stronger. 'Perce was a good man, a fine man. The very best.'

Jacob nodded slowly, hurt afresh and wanting to hurt back. 'And twice your age. A widower, the paper said, with two bairns, and his wife still warm in her grave when he wed you. Seems this good, fine man didn't waste any time in making sure his needs were provided for.'

She blinked, her face turning a shade paler. 'It wasn't like that.'

'No?' When she remained silent, he said tersely, 'I understand you have a daughter. Thirteen months, isn't she? And you say it wasn't like that?'

She wanted to take the look out of his eyes, to confess everything, tell him the truth, but to do so would be a death sentence for him and maybe for her too, and there was Daisy to think of. He would go looking for his brother. Whether he killed Tom, or Tom killed him, the end result would be the same. Jacob would either be dead or would swing at the end of a rope. If she gave him the slightest inkling, fresh blood would be on her hands. This had to end. Now. Her voice hardly audible, she said, 'You shouldn't have come here today, Jacob.'

She actually registered in her own body the flinch he gave. She was near tears, but she told herself she must not give way because, if she did, she would be lost. Enough people had been sacrificed because of her. First her father and Ernie, then Perce, but if Jacob was attacked a second time, he would not survive it. Tom would make sure of that. From the moment she'd seen Tom today she had been absolutely sure he'd arranged the beating Jacob had taken that night two years ago, and that he'd expected his brother to die. Maybe she had always known it deep down.

Jacob stood looking down at her bowed head. He heard himself say stiffly, 'I can see that', while his mind shouted at him, 'Tell her how you feel, man. What does it matter about her husband – he's dead and gone. Tell her you love her.'

But what was the use? And why humiliate himself further? Everything about her stated that she wanted him gone. He was an embarrassment, a reminder of things best forgotten, as far as she was concerned. She had said he shouldn't have come. Well, she needn't worry. Hell would freeze over before he'd come again. The finality of the thought came through in his voice when he said quietly, 'Goodbye, Lucy.'

He turned, striding away through the snow, which was now swirling and dancing in an already white world, and he didn't look back. It would have served no purpose if he did. He could barely see a thing through the mist of tears blinding his eyes.

PART FIVE

We Shall Fight Them on the Beaches

1939

Chapter Twenty-One

Lucy closed her eyes to shut out the words in the newspaper she was reading – it was all bad news as usual. In the nine years that had passed since the day she'd sent Jacob away her life had changed dramatically, along with the world as a whole.

She moved restlessly in her chair, her mind in turmoil. The world had become a place of boiling emotions as peace became more and more fragile, and lately she'd found it increasingly hard to sleep at night, for thoughts of what the unrest might mean for her menfolk. War was a terrible possibility.

In Russia, Joseph Stalin – presented as the father of his people, like the tsars of old, in the media – exercised forced collectivization and incessant purges of all possible opposition to his plan of economic development. Lucy couldn't see that he was anything other than a monster. Hadn't he destroyed millions of lives and eliminated ten million of the wealthier Russian peasants, or kulaks as they were called? His slogan was 'Liquidate the kulaks as a class', but some newspapers reported that Stalin wasn't just declaring war on the kulaks, but on the hundred million peasant farmers the country contained, both large and small. She felt for the ordinary men, women and children caught up in Stalin's campaign of terror, and in Germany the rise of Adolf Hitler had followed the same ruthless lines.

Once in power, Hitler had abolished democracy and begun to impose his racial policies against the Jews, Gypsies and other minorities. She swallowed hard; it made her feel sick to think of it. All those poor people, trapped in a country that had turned against them.

Five years ago it had been reported that concentration camps had been set up in Germany for political dissidents, under the control of the black-uniformed Schutzstaffel or SS, and the June of that year had seen the 'Night of the Long Knives'. Publicly, the Führer usually took pains to observe the legalities of a civilized society, but the ruthless purge of the brown-shirted SA – an army under the leadership of Ernst Röhm, who apparently had never fully accepted the supremacy of Hitler – had been an act of sheer gangsterism worthy of Al Capone. Just last year Hitler had again been in the news when he'd invaded Austria and brought the country into the German Reich, and no European nations had united to oppose him.

Lucy shook her head, remembering what Matthew had said at the time. 'He's just a bully,' her stepson had declared. 'And if you don't stand up to bullies, they think they're unstoppable.' Young as he was, Matthew had been right.

And if her precious boy could see that, along with millions of ordinary men and women, why couldn't the so-called experts in high places? But man's need to conquer and subjugate was everywhere. Might against right. And the evil ones were banding together. Mussolini had publicly deplored Hitler's anti-Semitism before the Italian leader had invaded Abyssinia four years ago. He'd been seen as a potential ally of France and Britain against the growing threat of the Nazis, but once the League of Nations had denounced Mussolini as an aggressor and had imposed sanctions on Italy, he'd changed his tune.

Really, Lucy thought, it was like children in a playground with their separate gangs, but these 'children' had the power to destroy millions of people. Hitler, seeing his opportunity, had begun to court his old enemy with flattery and now Mussolini, emboldened by German support, had invaded Albania only this year. And the two leaders had got together and signed a 'Pact of Steel'. Pact of Steel! What was that, if it wasn't declaring: You're in my gang now?

She opened her eyes and looked down at the newspaper. The papers and the news reports on the wireless held a terrible fascination for her, even as they filled her with dread. She wished she could close her eyes to what was happening, but she couldn't. World peace was crumbling. In the Far East the war between two of the world's ancient civilizations, China and Japan, grew more bloody, and the civil war in Spain had ruined the country. Stalin and Hitler, hitherto bitter enemies, had their unholy alliance, and Britain and other countries sought to appease the Nazis by sacrificing a free nation, Czechoslovakia. How could God keep this country safe when they acted like that? She, like thousands of other ordinary folk, saw what Mr Chamberlain seemed determined not to see: Adolf Hitler wanted war, and John and many other young men would go away to fight . . .

Her hand went to her throat and she worried at the skin there, before she realized what she was doing and brought her hands together in her lap. All she'd done over the last difficult years – the wealth and standing in the town she had carved out with blood, sweat and tears – would count as nothing, for she wouldn't be able to save him. Every time she thought about what was happening abroad she visualized the women – mothers, sisters, wives, sweethearts – who'd been forced by their governments to send their menfolk into goodness knew what, and it chilled her blood. She had thought, when she'd made their family unit secure and affluent, that her loved ones were set up for life, but she couldn't protect them if the worst happened and this war became a reality.

Her mind wandered back over the last decade, which had been one of unrelenting grind, but through hard work and determination she'd expanded the business several times. Early on she'd seen the need to gain the custom of the well-to-do upper crust of Sunderland society in their grand houses, along with the large hotels, realizing that if she limited her sales to the mean streets of the East End, as Perce had done, profits would always be poor.

With that in mind, within the first year she borrowed against the fishmonger's property and bought a reliable second-hand van. By the time she felt confident to drive, Ruby had left school and she put her sister in charge of the shop, with a full-time assistant to help her. The soup venture had become so successful that Lucy hired a lad part-time to help her in the evenings, but during the day she drummed up business in the town, travelling as far afield as Hendon and Ryhope.

Each morning saw Lucy setting off with the day's deliveries, dressed in the attractive blue-and-white outfit she had made herself, complete with a pretty little mop cap. She knew a number of her customers had been tickled pink when she had first approached them. 'A mere wee slip of a lass' one hotelier had called her, when she had knocked on his door, not unkindly but rather disbelievingly, when she had insisted that she could supply him with produce that was second to none – and for a competitive price. But she had persuaded him to give her a chance and slowly she had gained a reputation in the district for punctual deliveries, excellent seafood and, not least, a smile to brighten the dullest morning. It had proved to be a winning combination.

In the stricken North and the poorer parts of most cities the slums seethed like coral reefs with predators and prey, Lucy thought grimly. Small fry were all but fleshless, but their vast numbers were enough to ensure the attention of money-lending sharks, by whom no bone was left unpicked. She had wanted to take the children out of an environment that she considered rife with danger, and she knew it was no good looking to the government for help. For those families eligible for the dole – a married couple with three children could claim one pound, nine shillings and thrupence – it meant running a gauntlet of petty officialdom and nosy neighbours, and the dreaded Means Test was purely an exercise in cruelty.

She pictured the Hepburns in her mind. Little Tommy had got himself a paper round to help out his mother; he knew she often went hungry so that his da and the rest of them could eat, and a combination of exhaustion and undernourishment had left Mrs Hepburn prey to illness – anaemia, varicose veins and rotten teeth were the least of the poor woman's problems. The family hadn't declared the few pennies Tommy brought in, knowing it would be deducted from their allowance, but a neighbour had informed the authorities. The result had been the workhouse for the lot of them, where healthy children of pauper parents were often placed in the company of the senile, and physically and mentally sick adults, with devastating consequences for the innocent. There was barely a day that passed in which she didn't think of Tommy and his nine siblings.

Lucy shook herself. She had been determined they wouldn't go the way of the Hepburns and so many others. Perce had provided her with an opportunity, and with it had come a deep conviction that she had to capitalize on what she had. Four years after starting the soup kitchen she'd opened similar premises in the heart of Bishopwearmouth. Due to the shallower financial waters of the slump, the building societies had trimmed the deposits required by mortgagers from 25 per cent to 5 per cent. Properties would never be so cheap again and she'd recognized this. The following year she'd moved the family out of the flat and into a large five-bedroomed terraced house on the outskirts of Bishopwearmouth, situated in a prime position overlooking Barnes Park, with gardens front and back.

By this last act her standing as a respected business-woman took a huge leap forward, and opening a further two shops within the next three years confirmed her position in the town. She made no effort to buy property over the river in Monkwearmouth or Southwick, however, no matter how attractive the price. Nor did she venture that way on the Sunday jaunts that she and Daisy and the others frequently enjoyed. It was enemy territory.

Lucy shivered. Every so often, without fail, Tom Crawford would make sure she was aware of his brooding presence on the perimeter of her life. Occasionally she actually caught a glimpse of him, but more often than not she was simply aware of being watched by invisible eyes. It played on her nerves, especially after he became a town councillor and was accepted into the upper strata of Sunderland society.

Of Jacob she had seen and heard nothing. Jacob could be on the other side of the world rather than the other side of the River Wear.

She knew the family blamed her inability to relax and

her insomnia on overwork. All, that is, except Ruby. Only Ruby knew what ailed her, and the reason for the rule that Daisy never left the house unchaperoned. The problem was Tom Crawford and, while he drew breath, tension and anxiety would always be constant companions. It didn't help that as Daisy had grown, so had certain traits become apparent that could be linked to the man who'd sired her. Not in a physical sense. In looks, Daisy was a carbon copy of her, Lucy thought thankfully, but from a toddler her daughter had displayed an iron-like will that was disconcerting in one so young and especially a girl. There was no spirit of compromise in Daisy, either, no inclination to meet an adversary halfway to avoid confrontation. When her daughter had made up her mind about a matter, she became blind and deaf to reason.

But – Lucy's eyes softened – Daisy was also kind and compassionate, which helped to balance that other side. From a toddler she'd hero-worshipped Charley, following him around whenever she could, and although the two of them fought like cat and dog on occasion, Lucy knew they were close. And she herself had a special bond with her daughter, even though they had many a battle over this or that. Another of Daisy's endearing qualities was that she was incapable of remaining cross for long or of holding a grudge, and in spite of her daughter's complicated nature, which seemed to cause the child to war against herself as much as anyone else, theirs was a deeply loving relationship.

She stretched and stood up, glancing round her sitting

room, where the French windows were open to the warm twilight of the August evening. It was a beautiful room; she had furnished it herself exactly how she wanted it – she was lucky, so lucky, to have all this, and most of the family working in the business. The East End property was run by a husband-and-wife team and their two grown-up daughters who lived in the flat over the shop, but the other shops were managed by Ruby and John. Ruby was in charge of the one off High Street West, and Flora and Bess helped her along with another assistant, and John was responsible for the remaining two properties and had a staff of seven employees answering to him. Matthew had left school the previous year and had joined Lucy to learn about the supply and delivery side of the business, which was now extremely lucrative, as her bank balance testified. Her requirements had long since overtaken what Seamus could provide; she now had several sources of supply and a fleet of three vans. She still drove one herself because she enjoyed it, but once Matthew was old enough to pass his driving test he would take her place and be in charge of the other van drivers. At least that had been the plan, before talk of this wretched war. She'd imagined that within a few years she would be able to leave the business in the hands of the family and take Daisy to Europe, away at last from the reach of Tom Crawford. The private nest egg she'd accumulated would have meant they could have travelled and broadened their minds, before settling somewhere and making a new life in the country of Daisy's choice. Free from the past.

She walked out into the quiet garden, needing its serenity. The evening was soft, the air filled with the scent of roses and fragrant mignonette and jasmine. The birds were singing and the eight-foot-high walls covered in ivy and climbing roses represented safety. She glanced at the beds of sweet peas, larkspurs, pinks and all manner of sweetly perfumed flowers, but tonight the garden didn't work its magic. Her eyes focused on the sections of the air-raid shelter they'd been provided with, which were currently placed against the wall of the house. The lads had wanted to erect the steel-built, tunnel-shaped shelter weeks ago, but it needed to be partly sunk into the ground and would have meant destroying some of the garden. She'd told them that if – *if* – war was announced, they could do their worst, but not before.

She'd been fooling herself. It had been clear from the beginning of the year, when the government had begun to distribute air-raid shelters and had announced that the Territorial Army was to be doubled, what was in store. The country was bracing itself, and talk of plans to introduce conscription and of farmers ploughing up grazing pastures to increase the proportion of food produced at home was just the beginning. Only this month it had been announced that everyone was to have an identity card and number, and many movable treasures had been taken to safety from the major museums and galleries and even from Westminster Abbey. The Polish crisis was deepening, and folk were saying that by the end of the month the Army and RAF reserves would be called up and the Royal Navy mobilized.

John was already declaring that he wanted to teach the dirty Nazis a lesson, and when she'd chastised him for such talk, he'd told her flatly that he wouldn't wait to be called up before he did his bit.

Lucy bit down hard on her lip, her stomach churning. Such talk terrified her. John was nineteen years old and he hadn't got an aggressive bone in his body. He had no idea what he'd be letting himself in for. He spoke as though it was an exciting game. Just last Sunday he and Matthew had disappeared for hours and come home full of watching a practice of the gas decontamination unit in operation. But war wasn't a game; it was vile, savage, barbaric.

Her dark thoughts were broken by voices calling her name. The others had gone to the cinema, the Ritz in Holmeside, which had only been open a couple of years and had been fitted out lavishly with chandeliers and deep-pile carpets. She'd pleaded a headache to avoid going, but really she had wanted to go over some accounts in peace and quiet and, she admitted to herself, when she wasn't at work she preferred to be within the security of her own four walls.

They came surging through the French doors into the garden, crowding around her and laughing and chattering as they described the Astaire and Rogers musical, interrupting each other constantly. Ruby and John's voices rose above the others as they disagreed over something. Lucy smiled ruefully. She'd never imagined she would find her brother's and sister's bickering comforting, but just at the moment the normality of it was balm to her soul.

Just over a week later, on Sunday September 3rd, at eleven-fifteen in the morning, the eight of them were clustered together again, but this time there was no laughter as they sat listening to the radio broadcast by the Prime Minister, Neville Chamberlain.

'I am speaking to you from the Cabinet Room of 10 Downing Street. This morning the British Ambassador in Berlin handed the German Government a final note stating that unless we had heard from them by eleven o'clock that they were prepared to withdraw their troops from Poland, a state of war would exist between us. I have to tell you now that no such undertaking has been received, and that consequently this nation is at war with Germany.'

Lucy's face was chalk-white, her heart thudding so hard it was painful, but as she glanced at the others, no one spoke and even John was motionless. And then the sound of the air-raid sirens outside shattered the stillness and sent everyone diving under the kitchen table, amid shrieks and frightened squeals from Daisy, Flora and Bess.

It was only after the noise had dwindled away a little while later, the expected aerial onslaught being un-forthcoming, that Lucy said flatly, 'I think you lads had better get started on the air-raid shelter this afternoon.'

Chapter Twenty-Two

'But I don't understand, lad. They'll call you up soon enough, you can rest assured on that. Why go and willingly stick your head in the noose?'

Jacob smiled at Dolly. She'd said she didn't understand his decision, but the truth of it was he couldn't explain what he didn't fully understand himself. He was no hero, and he wasn't even sure if he was doing it for King and country. He just knew that the last nine years or so had been different from what he'd expected. Before he had seen Lucy again, after her husband had been murdered, he'd begun to settle into a life without her. Afterwards, well, he'd gone mad for a while, he thought ruefully. Wine, women and song. He knew Abe and Dolly had been worried to death. Then one morning he'd woken up to find yet another pool of vomit by the bed and had staggered to the mirror to look at his bleary-eyed face. He'd stared for a long time at a reflection he barely recognized, remembering nothing of the night before, but some woman's cheap perfume was rank on his clothes and he hadn't a penny left in his pockets.

From that day to this he hadn't touched a drop of liquor, and he'd started courting the nice lass he'd taken up with before he'd seen Lucy again. It hadn't lasted – Felicity had told him one day, when they'd been walking out for a year or more, that she felt she couldn't compete with the perfect memory he held of his childhood sweetheart, and he hadn't disabused her that his memory of Lucy was far from perfect now. Which had said a lot about how he felt about Felicity, in hindsight.

And so he had taken to working longer and longer hours in the forge, burning off his dissatisfaction and sense of loss, and not least his sexual frustration, with physical hard work. And it had helped, to some extent.

There had been the odd occasion when he'd longed to go out and get drunk, usually after a family get-together at Christmas or New Year, which he showed up at to please his mother, who was forever complaining she didn't see him from one year to the next. At those times when Tom was present, his brother inevitably commented on Lucy's meteoric rise within the community and deliberated on what she must be worth now, letting Jacob know that she was well out of his league. Tom needn't have bothered, if he had but known. That one meeting with her had told him whatever she'd felt for him when they were youngsters was gone, and there was nothing so dead as the cold ashes of love.

Shaking away his thoughts, Jacob took Dolly's plump little hand in his and looked into her worried face. He was closer to this little woman than he was to his own mother and over the years he'd come to love her dearly. And he knew Dolly thought the world of him. Growing up, he had always been aware that there was no one like Tom for their mam and, child-like, he'd accepted it. Ralph and Frank hadn't seemed to mind, but then the pair of them had always been thick with their da. He had been the odd one out somehow, but having Lucy, it hadn't seemed to matter. It was only when he was lying in the hospital after Tom had told him Lucy had left that he fully realized that, in siphoning off the major part of her affection for Tom, his mam had done the rest of them down, including his da.

'I have to do this, Dolly,' he said softly now. He didn't say, 'I need to find myself' because she wouldn't have understood that. What he did say was, 'But I want you to know something – something I should have said years ago. You're the mam I always wanted, and I couldn't have got through without knowing that you and Abe were behind me in the bad times. My mother is a good woman and she brought me into the world, but I've never thought of her as I think of you. I'm proud to be your son.'

'Oh, lad.' The tears were running down her rosy cheeks and she couldn't say more, and when Jacob took her into his arms they stood together for some time with her face pressed against his shirt front.

*

The town was quieter than usual when Jacob walked into Bishopwearmouth later that day. Children were being evacuated to safe areas in the country and Sunderland's exodus had begun the day before, on September 10th. Clutching their few personal possessions and gas masks, the little ones had gathered at specific times at the train stations, their weepy relatives waving them off. Few parents knew where their children would end up, although the government had said they'd be told as soon as possible. Jacob wondered if Lucy had sent her daughter away. The child must be nine years old now, old enough to have an opinion about whether she went or stayed. Several of their customers had related details of the rumpus caused at home when evacuation had been mentioned to the older children, and although some of them had won the battle to stay, it seemed that the little ones were packed off willy-nilly.

He walked through the warm dusty streets, feeling it could well be the calm before the storm. Everyone was on tenterhooks for the expected bombing to begin and some people he passed were carrying their gas masks. Air-raid shelters had grown up everywhere, he noticed: the Anderson shelter for those who had a garden and could dig some three feet down and then cover the corrugated-steel roof with earth, along with turf and flowers in some cases; and a brick-surface shelter where households only had a back yard. For those folk without even their own back yard there was the Morrison shelter. He had been in a friend's house recently that had one, and the oblong box, which served well as a table, had proved to be a great den for the children. He'd peeped inside after hearing giggles when he was sitting having a cup of tea, and found four cheeky little faces grinning at him. The children had been snuggled up among the cushions and blankets that the shelter contained, reading picture books by torchlight. Their harassed mother, who'd recently given birth to twin boys, had remarked that it kept the older ones occupied for hours, and every cloud – even the war – had a silver lining.

The afternoon was a mellow one. The sky was high and blue and the air warm, but without the fierce heat of July or August. A breeze caressed his face as he walked and he stopped, taking his cap off for a moment and running his fingers through his curly brown hair. On such a quintessential English day it seemed impossible that across the ocean Warsaw, a town of ordinary men and women and children like the ones here, was enduring days of nightmarish bombing, which was devastating the city and killing tens of thousands. At the end of August the news reports had spoken of France and Britain's confidence that, if the worst happened, the Poles would hold Nazi Germany in the east and the superior strength of the old First World War Allies would produce a victory. Now even the most optimistic could see that Poland was doomed. And it could happen here. They had underestimated Hitler.

He shivered, but the chill was from within. Which was why he had to see Lucy one last time before he enlisted.

It wasn't rational, and when he had told Dolly she had been horrified, reminding him of the downward spiral their last meeting had provoked, but he couldn't leave without saying goodbye. That was all he wanted to do. He expected nothing, he would ask for nothing. But he *had* to see her. If she wasn't in, if she was away, then he would delay enlisting until she was back, because once you'd signed up they had you off to training camp quicker than a dose of salts, from what he'd heard.

He knew where she lived. Well, the address at least, he corrected himself. He'd never been there. But the houses round Barnes Park were a cut above. She'd done well for herself, but then Lucy had always been top of the class at school and had left the rest of them standing. He remembered the hours she had spent going over fractions and decimals with him, when the intricacies of arithmetic had been beyond him and Mr Gilbert had made him wear the dunce's cap three days running. In front of the other bairns in the playground he'd acted big and challenged any of the lads who'd needled him about it to a fight, saying real men didn't need learning and it was a load of rubbish. Inside he'd been dying. When they were alone, Lucy had put her arms round him and he'd cried like a baby, and even then, at the age of nine or ten, he'd wondered why it cost him nothing in pride to admit the truth to her.

He stopped abruptly. What was he doing? Dolly was right, he was indulging in some form of masochism in trying to see Lucy again. He closed his eyes as he raised his face for a moment, letting the sun glow red behind his eyelids. What cruel quirk of human nature allowed people to go on loving when they weren't loved in return? There should be some sort of safety mechanism built into every human heart that could turn off the flow when required. He should turn round right now and make his way back over the river. It was the sensible thing to do.

But when had sense ever come into the feelings that he had for Lucy? A grim smile touching his lips, he walked briskly on.

The trees in Barnes Park and the surrounding streets were in the last flush of summer, green and lush before the first autumnal frosts set about changing their raiment to gold and red and brown. This western suburb of Bishop-wearmouth was leafy and quiet and an air of restrained, good-mannered prosperity prevailed. Jacob stood looking towards the front garden of the house he knew to be Lucy's and was struck by how just a few furlongs could change an area. The neat square of lawn was surrounded by small orderly shrubs, and a path at the side led to the front door, which had stained glass in the top section. The three-storey terraced house was shipshape and smart from the outside, as were its neighbours, and it struck him afresh just how much she'd risen in the world.

As he watched from the other side of the road a car drew up a few doors down and two well-dressed women alighted. When the door of the house they entered was opened by a maid in a black-and-white uniform with a lacy cap perched on top of her head, it took him aback.

A maid. It was further proof of the great divide that existed between him and this new Lucy. Did she have a maid? Maybe a cook too?

He almost turned and walked away there and then, beset by a number of emotions and none of them encouraging.

He stood dithering for a long time – how long he didn't keep track of – but when the two ladies exited the house again and one of them said something to her companion and they both looked his way, it gave him the impetus to cross the road and walk up Lucy's path, his heart thumping. He rang the bell several times and knocked on the door, but no one answered from within. He glanced at his watch. Half-past four. He would wait until five and then walk back into the town and get a bite to eat somewhere and return later this evening, once dinner was over. Aye, that's what he'd do, if he didn't have his collar felt by the local bobby in the meantime that was. Those two women had clearly wondered if he was up to no good. He smiled with black humour. That would put the tin lid on this whole daft episode – him ending up in gaol.

He walked down the path back to the pavement, screwing up his face as he rubbed between his eyebrows where a niggling headache had started. When he raised his head, she was walking towards him and by her side was a child who could only be her daughter. The likeness was remarkable. Transfixed, he stared at them. Lucy stared back and he was aware of the little girl saying something to her mother, but Lucy didn't seem to hear her.

They were within a yard or two before he pulled himself together enough to say, 'Hello, Lucy.'

'Jacob.'

The sound of his name on her lips impacted on him like a physical pain and the force of the feeling startled him. He wondered how he had managed to keep away from her for so long, but the answer was standing by her side. The child was the embodiment of the decision she'd made to exit his life without a backward glance at a time when he'd needed her most. *She didn't love him.* His head had accepted it long ago, it was his heart that had the problem.

And then the little girl stepped forward, holding out her hand with a confidence that took him by surprise in one so young. 'I'm Daisy.' She smiled at him and it was Lucy's smile in Lucy's face. And yet, not quite. The mouth was different, wider, not as full and bow-shaped as her mother's, and Lucy had never displayed the self-assurance and aplomb that seemed to come naturally to her daughter. 'How do you do.'

'I'm Jacob.' He took the small hand and shook it. 'I'm an old friend of your mother's. We used to live next door to each other when we were bairns.'

'Did you?' The smile widened. 'You must have known my Grandma and Granda Fallow then? They died before I was born, and my Uncle Ernie too. I haven't got any grandparents because my da's parents died long ago, but

I have got uncles and aunts, and two brothers. That's not the same as grandparents, though.'

'Daisy.' Lucy checked her daughter by touching the child's shoulder. 'I'm sorry,' she said to Jacob. 'Daisy has always thought it most remiss of me not to provide her with at least one set of grandparents.'

'Oh, Mam.' Daisy leaned against her mother and the smile they exchanged was warm.

Jacob felt awkward and it reinforced the doubts he'd had about coming. They were strangers now, poles apart. What had he been thinking of? He'd embarrassed her and she clearly couldn't wait to get rid of him. He was trying to think how to finish the conversation and retain some dignity when Lucy said, 'We've been to visit the Winter Garden, it's one of Daisy's favourite places. They've extended the summer break for the time being, but I suppose the schools will reopen soon. We were just going to have some tea and toast. Would – would you care to join us?'

Jacob couldn't believe his ears. He must have looked as surprised as he felt because Lucy was blushing as she said, 'We can't stand talking out here, and I presume you came to see me? I – I saw you at the door. I mean, you weren't just walking past, were you?'

Her discomposure steadied him. Suddenly she seemed more like the Lucy he had known and less like the prosperous businesswoman whose success had become the stuff of legends locally. 'No, I wasn't walking past, and a cup of tea would be nice.'

They stared at each other a moment more, as though the invitation and its acceptance had been momentous, and then he found himself following the pair of them as Lucy led the way into the house. The hall was spacious, but that was all he took in before Lucy said, 'Daisy, show Mr Crawford into the sitting room and open the French doors – it's bound to be too warm in there.' She glanced at Jacob. 'It's south-facing.'

He nodded. He hadn't liked the 'Mr Crawford'.

'I'll go and put the kettle on, and Daisy' – her gaze returned to the child – 'come and help me set the tea tray in a moment, please.'

In other words she didn't want the girl talking to him if she wasn't present. Feeling as though he was on one of the rides at the Michaelmas Fair that went up and down at an alarming rate, Jacob followed Daisy across the hall, past the foot of the stairs and through a door to his left. He watched the child as she ran across the room and flung open a pair of small-paned glass doors. The room had struck him as a mite stuffy, but immediately the breeze brought in the scent of flowers and sunshine. Turning back to him and speaking as though they were carrying on a conversation that had been uninterrupted, Daisy said, 'My second name is the same as my grandma's, my mam's mother. Agnes. It's a nice name, isn't it? Did you like her, my Grandma Fallow?'

A little unsure of himself with this fairy-like child, Jacob nodded. 'Aye, yes, I did.'

Daisy considered him for a moment, her head tilted

to one side and her big straw hat shading her face and turning her blue eyes almost black. 'I suppose you'd have to say that, wouldn't you?' she reflected thoughtfully. 'It would be rude not to.'

A great desire to laugh out loud came over him. Stifling it, he returned in like vein: 'You could say that, but in this case I meant what I said. I was very fond of your grandma, everyone was. She was a kind, gentle soul.'

'Like my mam.' Before he could reply, she went on, 'I'm not like my mother. Oh, I know we look like each other, but I'm not patient or kind like she is, not all the time anyway. Sometimes not a bit. There's a boy at my school and he's a bully – he's always tormenting the little ones or anyone who's shy or quiet, you know? Miss Price, that's my teacher, took us on a nature ramble before school broke up for the summer holidays and I saw Lawrence holding Alfred Bell, who's got bowed legs like a frog, at the top of a high bank, threatening to push him down into the stream at the bottom. He was laughing.'

The blue eyes held his and Jacob found that he was holding his breath as he listened to this beautiful sprite of a child.

'I crept up and Lawrence didn't know I was there. I pulled Alfred away from him and pushed Lawrence down the bank. I couldn't have done it if he'd known I was there, as he's much bigger than I am, so I didn't shout first and tell him to let Alfred go. He wouldn't have done so anyway, he was enjoying making him cry,' she said matter-of-factly. 'Lawrence broke his ankle and hollered enough to wake the dead. Miss Price said I should have fetched her to deal with it, but as I was only trying to help Alfred and it was an accident and she knew I was sorry, we'd say no more about it.'

'That seems fair,' said Jacob, completely out of his depth.

'But I wasn't sorry. Lawrence deserved everything he got. I hate boys like him.'

'Right.'

'My mam would have fetched Miss Price, wouldn't she? My grandma too.'

'Possibly. Aye, probably in fact.'

Daisy nodded. 'But by then it might have been Alfred who ended up with the broken ankle, and Lawrence would have lied and said they were only larking about. And because Alfred's so scared of him he wouldn't dare say different. So I'm not sorry.'

Gently Jacob murmured, 'But you might have got hurt too.'

Daisy stared at him for a long moment. 'I hate boys like Lawrence,' she repeated. 'They pull the wings off butterflies and cut up worms for fun, and the teachers say not to tell tales, if you report them. Lads think they're superior to lassies, but they're not.'

Jacob looked into the earnest little face. By, she was one of this new breed of females – feminists they called them – already, at the age of nine, but he liked her spirit. 'I would say that you're more like your mother and grandmother than you think. You couldn't stand by and see Alfred tormented and hurt. What's that, if not kindness? You just deal with things in a different way from what your mother might do, maybe.'

Daisy took a moment to consider this. It was clear she hadn't looked at it this way before. 'So you think I'm like my Grandma Agnes?'

It seemed to mean a lot to the child, so Jacob gave a definite inclination of his head, going a step further when he said, 'She would have loved you, that's for sure.'

His reward was a smile that lit up her face.

'I'd better go and help Mam,' Daisy said, skipping to the door, 'but I just wanted to ask you about my grandma. I don't know anyone who remembers her 'cept for my Aunty Ruby and Uncle John, but they just say what they think I want them to say, like Mam.'

She left him staring after her. What an extraordinary bairn, he thought soberly. A child of great determination and strong passions, almost certainly, but tempered by a compassion and kind heart for the underdog, which she'd inherited from her mother. Had she got that fierce side from her father? He would have liked to have met him. And then immediately he repudiated the thought. No, no, he wouldn't. Hell, what a stupid thing to imagine – it was the last thing he'd have wanted. But he had often wondered about the man whom Lucy had loved and married, the man who'd given her a bairn and, having met that bairn, he wondered all the more.

He stood, cap in hand, looking around the room. This was Lucy's home; he felt he was seeing her personality reflected in the elegant lines of the furniture it held and the calm, quiet colour scheme. The carpet and curtains were a pale green and the walls dove-grey, and there was little in the way of knick-knacks, apart from a number of china figures – ladies in crinolines mostly – standing on the wide mantelpiece over the fireplace. His mother would have called the room plain and sparse, in a disparaging fashion, but the cream couches and chairs (without a fringe to be seen) complemented the whole perfectly. An occasional table was covered in magazines and papers, and a knitting bag sat by one chair, a couple of homely touches.

He walked over to the French doors and looked out into the garden. A well-camouflaged and protected Anderson shelter had been built at the very rear of it, a blast wall standing in front of the entrance. A blackbird was busy digging for worms in the layer of dirt and turf that had been placed over the domed roof and he smiled to himself. That bird wasn't going to let the likelihood of Hitler's bombs put him off searching for his supper.

'The lads built the shelter a week ago. They've done a good job, haven't they?'

He hadn't heard Lucy come into the room and now he swung round to see her standing with a tray. 'Here, let me.' He took the tray from her while she cleared the magazines and papers on the table into one corner. There were two cups and two plates of well-buttered toast and, seeing his glance, Lucy said quickly, 'Charley, my youngest stepson, has just got in and Daisy's eating with him in the kitchen. He's been out fishing the whole day with his pals and he always manages to get mucky.'

He didn't comment on this. 'I wondered if you'd have a maid,' he said, sitting down in the chair Lucy indicated with a wave of her hand. 'It seems the sort of area.'

'No, no. We all have our jobs to do, and the girls and I take turns with cooking and so on. I wouldn't like a maid.'

She poured him a cup of tea and handed it to him across the table, and as she did so the cup rattled slightly in the saucer. The brief betrayal of her nervousness was comforting. She was wearing a cream dress and her wonderful hair was fixed in some fancy way or other on top of her head, and she impersonified cool control. But she was nervous, nevertheless. Like him.

Jacob found that he didn't know how to begin, or what to say when he did. There followed a silence during which their eyes met and then dropped away and, gathering his courage, he opened his mouth. 'I probably shouldn't have come here today, I'm aware of that, but I felt the last time we met it didn't end well, for all sorts of reasons. We were close as bairns and I've always remembered that time with great affection.' That was good, striking the right note, and emboldened he went on, 'The thing is, I'm going to enlist and I didn't want to leave Sunderland without explaining' – he had been going to say 'how I feel', but realizing that was the last thing he could do in all truthfulness, he changed it to – 'I don't want any hard feelings between us.'

'You're going to enlist?' She had put down her cup as he had spoken and now sat facing him with her hands clasped in her lap, her face white. 'Why, Jacob? Why not wait and see when, or if, you're called up? Something might happen. The war might be over soon.'

'No one believes that now. Not the way things are going for Poland. And I'd rather jump before I'm pushed. That's the only way I can put it. He's an evil so-an'-so, old Hitler, and when you read about what's going on in the concentration camps like Dachau and Buchenwald it brings home what you're fighting against.'

Lucy couldn't argue with that. The inexplicable sadistic cruelty of SS camp guards, who were reported to be revelling and vying with each other in the authorized regime of brutality and terror, made grim reading. But Jacob going away to fight . . . She had felt dizzy and faint when she'd first seen him standing there outside, beset by such a flood of emotion that she'd felt she was drowning. And now, sitting talking to him like this, being able to look at his dear face and hear his voice, she wanted each moment to last forever. But he was talking again . . .

'This war won't be like the last one. This time the Nazis will make sure they crush us from the air before their army invades British soil, unless we stop them. They've got more bombers and fighters, more everything. They've been preparing for this for a long time while our government licked their backsides and talked peace.' He stopped abruptly. 'Sorry.'

She made a throwaway movement with one hand. 'When will you go?'

He shrugged, forcing a smile. 'I hear your signature isn't dry before they're shipping you off to training camp.'

She wanted to ask him to stay a day, a week, a month, and spend it with her. They could go away somewhere, to another town and find a hotel and be together. To quell the madness she said, 'Have you told your mother?' And it was only in that moment that the thought hit that he could have a wife and bairns, a sweetheart at least.

Jacob shook his head. 'Only Dolly and Abe. I don't see much of Mam and the rest of them these days, not now I live at the forge, but I'll call in once it's signed and sealed. It'll be better that way. Fait accompli.'

She had to know. She was wondering how to phrase it when a voice from the doorway said, 'Jacob Crawford? It is you, isn't it?'

They both started at the sound of Ruby's voice and, as she and Flora and Bess came into the room, Jacob said, 'Aye, it's me, Ruby, and these two young ladies must be the twins. You were both knee-high to a grasshopper the last time I saw you.'

Hastily Lucy said, 'Flora and Bess, this is Jacob. He used to live next door to us in Zetland Street, but I don't suppose you remember.'

'I do.' Flora was more forward than Bess and had discovered the attraction of the opposite sex in the last year or two. Now she made what Ruby always termed disparagingly her 'cow's eyes' at Jacob. 'You used to come with us when we went to the beach and you had two brothers. No, three. And your mam used to feed us treacle toffee when we came round.'

Jacob smiled. 'And you and your sister always hid some in your pinny pockets for later and you thought my mam didn't know.'

'Did we?' Flora giggled. 'How awful. What other terrible things can you remember?'

The moment to ask him had gone. Lucy joined in the ensuing conversation, but within a few minutes Jacob stood up and took his leave of the others before she walked him to the door. Once they were alone in the hall he said quietly, 'I'm glad we're parting as friends, Lucy. I've thought of you often over the last years.'

She wanted to tell him there hadn't been one day when he hadn't been in her thoughts, but the spectre of his brother was there suddenly, dark and threatening. Besides, if he had a wife or a sweetheart she'd embarrass him, and herself too. He had said he had come because he didn't want any hard feelings between them – that was all. The control it took to keep her voice from trembling made it sound stiff when she said, 'Of course we're friends, Jacob.'

She wished Ruby and the twins hadn't come home when they had, but it had been she who had insisted they close the shop early now that the blackout was causing so many accidents. Once it began to get dark, with no street lamps lit and black curtains at every window so that not the slightest chink of light could escape, cars were crashing and people were slipping off kerbs and walking into lamp posts. But perhaps it was for the best that they had been interrupted. She'd been about to make a fool of herself.

Her tone of voice wasn't lost on him. He stared at her for a moment more, drinking in every detail of her face, and then opened the door himself, stepping down into the dusky twilight that had fallen since he'd been in the house. He turned, and found that by standing on the bottom step as he was, his head was on the same level as Lucy's. He had intended to shake her hand and tell her to take care of herself. Instead he leaned forward and brushed her lips with his own.

'Jacob . . . '

He spoke over her breathless protest, his voice husky. 'Write to me, Lucy? While I'm away? Please?'

'I – there must be someone who'll write to you? I – I mean someone special—'

'I'm looking at her.'

'But—'

'I tried. Heaven knows I tried, but women always know when you're short-changing them.'

She mustn't do this. Somehow Tom would know, and even if Jacob was away fighting he wouldn't be safe from his brother. But he was going away to war. Safety didn't come into it. And he'd said he had little contact with his family. And, most of all, she wanted to write to him. To reach out and touch him with pen and paper and be touched in return. That wasn't too much to ask, was it?

'Take the day you know and leave the morrer to God, hinny . . .' Her mother's voice caressed her as the warm evening breeze ruffled her hair.

It had been years, over a decade, since she had heard that beloved voice in a moment of crisis. She had never thought to hear it again. Without thinking any more, she reached out and touched his face. 'I'll write,' she breathed softly.

This time the kiss was long and deep as he stepped up to take her into his arms, and when he raised his head he looked at her for a long time before letting her go. When he walked down the path and the twilight swallowed him up, no promises had been made. How could they? No one knew what the next day or week, let alone month, would bring. Or even if they would see each other again.

It was enough, though. For now, it was enough.

Chapter Twenty-Three

'Well, I think you ought to be ashamed of yourself, besmirching Tom's good name like this, and you his da.' Enid sat glaring at her husband over the kitchen table, where they were eating their evening meal and listening to the reports of the war on the wireless. 'Who are you to say that he hasn't got a bad heart, if he's a doctor's certificate to prove it?'

'Give me patience!' Aaron lifted his eyes to heaven as he ground his teeth. 'You're not a stupid woman, Enid, so don't act like one. Doctors can be bought, if you know the right people, and our Tom knows the right people sure enough. He's no more got a bad heart than our other three. There's Jacob, who signed up in the first month, and Frank and Ralph both prepared to do their bit if it comes to it, in spite of having a wife and family apiece, but Tom' – he flicked his hand in a gesture of disgust – 'he's a nowt.'

'You're wicked, Aaron Crawford. That's what you are.' Enid's voice was trembling. 'And are you saying you want Frank and Ralph to go over the water? Is that it?'

'Don't talk silly. Of course I don't, but they're willing to if needs must. At the moment they're serving King and country better in the shipyard and it might be like that till the end of the war, but who knows? What I'm saying is that they're not lily-livered.'

'And Tom is?'

'Aye. He is. An' it gives me no pleasure to say it about me own, whatever you might think to the contrary. He's bad, Enid. Through and through. And you've had a hand in that. Spoiling the lad from the day he was born and shutting your eyes to what you didn't want to see. I could wallop the others when they were bairns and misbehaved, but if I raised my hand to Tom, the roof went off the house. And he was the one who needed it, not Frank and Ralph and Jacob.'

'There you have it in a nutshell.' Enid stood up, flinging back her chair so that it rocked on its legs for a moment before toppling over. 'You never took to our Tom, not from when he was a babby. He kept this family going in the Depression before the government needed the shipyard workers back on side, but were you grateful? Not a bit of it. And you've turned Ralph and Frank against him. They've never got a good word for the lad these days.'

'He's not a lad, Enid. He's a full-grown man and one who chose his own road a long time back – a dirty road. And aye, it is to my shame I walked it an' all. I'm not proud of meself. But as to Ralph and Frank, they've made their own minds up about their brother, so don't try an' put that one on me. You want to ask them sometime what they know about him, and I don't mean hearsay either, but you wouldn't do that, would you? It might open the can of worms you've laboured for years to keep closed.'

Aaron pushed his plate away from him, reaching for his jacket and stuffing his cap on his head. 'I'm going down the pub, an' don't wait up.'

After the door had banged behind him, Enid walked slowly to the table and sat down again. She didn't finish the rest of her meal, but sat staring into space. She was tired, she thought dully. Tired of the state of war which existed in this house and was worse than the 'phoney war' that the nation had endured for the last eight months. After war had been declared, weeks of anxiety, false alarms and uncertainty had followed, and then the country had settled down for a wartime winter. The government had warned they were expecting tens of thousands of casualties during the first two or three months, and hospitals had been cleared in preparation for the wounded civilians, mortuaries stacked with piles of cardboard coffins, and lime pits dug to cope with the dead. It had struck terror into everyone. Every home had been issued with a hand-operated stirrup-pump and long-handled shovel to deal with the incendiary bombs that the government was sure would come raining down from the Luftwaffe, and every night folk had slept with one ear cocked for the air-raid sirens. But the blitzkrieg hadn't happened.

Enid reached for her cup of tea and drank it slowly. Instead they'd been bombarded by regulations, exhortations and petty officialdom, and the blackout had become public enemy number one. On New Year's Eve the headline in the papers had been the news that more than 4000 men, women and children had died in blackout accidents, whereas during the same period only three members of the British Expeditionary Force had been killed in action. By February more than half of the evacuees who had fled in September were home again, and this added to the feeling of normality that had grown as bairns played their games in the streets and back alleys once more.

Enid put down her cup and sighed heavily. But inside this house there'd been no relief or laughter. It had been bad enough between her and Aaron before Frank and then Ralph had left to get wed and set up house with their wives, but now . . . She brushed a wisp of grey hair from her brow. She just didn't know what to say to him any more.

Take tonight. She'd waited until she'd dished up the dinner and they were sitting eating, before she'd mentioned about Tom calling round earlier. Tom hadn't wanted to worry them, she'd said, but he'd felt it only right to let them know what the doctor had found when he'd been to see him. She had expected Aaron to show some concern, she'd even hoped it might mellow him towards their firstborn, but he'd looked at her as though she was mad. And yet another row had followed.

She poured herself a second cup of tea.

And this on the heels of learning that the British and

French were suffering heavy losses in their attempt to intervene against Germany's invasion of Denmark and Norway. She didn't understand strategy and the rest of it, but even she could see the war had suddenly hotted up. And her lad was out there, her Jacob. Aaron gave her no credit for worrying to death about him. Instead he'd gone on about Ralph and Frank going out there to join in the bloodbath. Men were a different species. Oh aye, they were.

She shut her eyes, rocking backwards and forwards on her chair a while, her arms wrapped round her waist. She missed Agnes. It had been over fourteen years since she'd gone, but she missed her old friend like it was yesterday. She had never got thick with any of the other neighbours, she hadn't wanted to – nosy blighters the lot of them – and Ralph's and Frank's wives were nice lassies, but they had their own mams.

A moment of searing loneliness brought a pain to her chest. Only Tom loved her. The rest of them . . . She shook her head, a tear seeping from under her closed eyelids. No, only Tom cared, and she wasn't going to pretend that she wasn't glad he'd be staying close, rather than being shipped off over the sea to be blown to smithereens or used as fodder for German machine guns, whether he'd bought his way out of fighting or not.

She stopped her rocking, wiping her eyes and reaching for her tea.

She wasn't daft, whatever Aaron might think. Deep down she'd wondered what was what, when her lad had shown her the certificate signed by some doctor or other she'd never heard of. *But she didn't care.*

She expelled a long breath. No, she didn't care how Tom had come by it because it was his ticket to stay out of the war. She knew that if Tom had been called up she'd have become unhinged; there was only so much she could bear. The others she'd grieve over, but her lad . . .

Across town, on the other side of the river, Lucy found herself glued to the wireless whenever she was home. The winter had been a savagely cold one, the worst for a long time according to the old-timers, and when John had been called up in January as one of two million nineteen- to twenty-seven-year-olds, she had been beside herself. But there had been nothing she could do about it, not least because John was raring to go. After that, the winter had been a time of petty irritations set against a background of endless waiting – for what exactly no one was quite sure. And then, as April turned into May, they found out.

Jacob had written every week since he had landed in France as part of the British Expeditionary Force. With French troops occupying the Maginot Line, the British Army had proceeded smoothly to their positions along the Franco-Belgian border, where they'd built pillboxes and dug trenches. Once the Poles had been defeated, the German divisions had moved swiftly back across their country to the Siegfried Line.

'It's surreal,' Jacob had written in one of his first letters, 'but the general feeling among everyone here, French and

British alike, is that the Germans have no intention of attacking us. Insults are exchanged daily through loud-speakers, but not a shot has been fired, and it seems the weather is the common enemy. Nevertheless, and I hope I'm wrong, I can't help feeling that Hitler is playing cat-and-mouse again, like he did before the war.'

He had been right. As the ice and arctic winds and snow became a distant memory and cloudless blue skies took their place, Germany invaded Holland, Belgium and Luxembourg on May 10th. The 'phoney war' was over. In Britain, Neville Chamberlain had been totally discredited and forced to resign and Winston Churchill had taken his place as Prime Minister, forming an all-party coalition government, but many feared it was too late for their loved ones in France, who were facing a military catas-trophe. The wireless had become an instrument of subtle torture overnight for Lucy and she barely ate or slept.

Lucy hadn't heard from either Jacob or John for three weeks when, in the middle of May, the Secretary of State for War, Anthony Eden, announced to the nation that the formation of the Local Defence Volunteers was taking place with immediate effect. Matthew signed that same day. With German forces now streaming across France and the Low Countries, an invasion of British soil was imminent, and in spite of little equipment and even less training, the LDV were prepared to wage a guerrilla war in their own streets. Matthew went off to the training centre after work armed with a pickaxe, along with many others, but what he and the rest of the LDV lacked in weaponry they made up for in spirit. And strangely, although the thought of Matthew engaging a German soldier in face-to-face combat was terrifying, Lucy was grateful to the newly formed organization. Since John had been called up, Matthew had been champing at the bit to do *something*, as he groaned umpteen times an hour. The elderly Sergeant Major who was in charge of the unit was treating as a soldier every old-timer, farmer, shipyard worker, miner, shopkeeper or young lad wet behind the ears who was under his command, drilling his ragtag-and-bobtail army ruthlessly.

Matthew came home late at night full of the evening's activities and with many a tale to tell. There was talk of the government kitting out the LDV with standard-issue army uniforms and guns in time, but for now most of the recruits merely sported a forage cap and an armband, and carried pitchforks, broom handles, hand scythes or, as in Matthew's case, pickaxes. One old gentleman, Matthew had told them gleefully, had turned up for duty with an enamel colander tied to his bald head with a scarf. He claimed that his wife had insisted he have some protection from falling bombs. When the Sergeant Major had pointed out through gritted teeth that as yet there *were* no falling bombs, the henpecked husband had retorted that the Sergeant Major could take that up with his wife, because he certainly wasn't going to argue with her.

Such light moments were rare in a month that turned increasingly desperate for the Allies, and sickeningly worrying for their loved ones at home. By the last week of May every thinking man and woman in England could see that the suicidal decision by the Allies to leave the defensive positions they'd spent the bitterly cold winter so arduously preparing, and move forward to join the Belgian Army to form a defensive line running along the Dyle and Meuse rivers, was disastrous. They'd been lured into a cunning trap and driven back towards the coast by a large German force. Thousands of soldiers and refugees were mercilessly bombed and machine-gunned from the air as they tried to escape along the packed roads.

It was this that was occupying Lucy's mind as she left one of the shops John had had the responsibility of overseeing late one night. As yet she had been unable to replace him, so she had stepped into the role, which had meant an increase in her working hours to something like twelve to fourteen hours a day. Her head full of the latest report that the tanks and infantry of the German panzers had punched through the French defences and reached Boulogne and that British forces were heroically defending a doomed Calais, she didn't notice a figure detach itself from the shadows and begin following her.

It was only when the soft footsteps behind her quickened, and a sixth sense caused the fine hairs on the back of her neck to prickle, that the intense darkness of the blackout became frightening. She had seen Tom Crawford twice since Jacob had called at the house. Once, just before Christmas, his car had been parked across the road when she had returned home from a shopping trip with Daisy one Saturday afternoon. He had waited until he was sure she had seen him, doffing his hat as he'd smiled at her through the window, and then driven off, leaving her white and shaken. 'Who was that?' Daisy had asked, her eyes following the car as it sped into the distance.

'No one.' She'd steadied her voice, smiling at her daughter, but inside she'd been trembling. He was getting bolder.

The next time had been a few weeks ago. She had met Ruby in town for lunch, as they did sometimes, there being a cafe across the road from the shop Ruby managed that they both liked, and as they had left the building he'd been there, straight in front of them.

'Hello, ladies. Fancy bumping into you.' His words had been casual, even jocular, but the look he'd given her had been long and concentrated, stripping away the last decade or more and reducing her to a terrified young girl inside. She had stared back at him, not trusting herself to speak, and it had been Ruby who said, 'Leave her alone. She doesn't want anything to do with you, Tom Crawford.'

His eyes had shot to her sister and after a moment he had nodded slowly. 'Ah, I see. A little bird has been whispering its lies in your ear. You shouldn't believe everything you're told, Ruby. There are two sides to every story.'

Ruby hadn't grown much over the past few years but

she'd seemed to grow in stature as she'd said, 'I know what I know, and nothing you could say would make me believe any different.'

'Is that so?' His voice was low, flat. 'Did she tell you I wanted to marry her? Eh? That I was prepared to take the lot of you on and do right by her, even after she'd led me a dance and carried on with other blokes?'

'I never led you on. I never wanted anything to do with you, ever, and you know it. You keep harassing me and I'll get the police involved. I mean it.' Lucy's heart had been pounding in her chest fit to burst, but she'd been pleased at how strong her voice had sounded.

'What will you tell them, Lucy? That you bumped into an old friend in the street? An old friend who happens to be a town councillor and a man with a great deal of influence in the town? Be my guest, but they'll laugh you out of court.'

'Come on.' Ruby had taken her arm and pulled her away, but once they were safely in the fishmonger's shop she'd steered her through to the room at the rear of the premises and shut the door so that they couldn't be overheard. Then she had hugged Lucy, before stepping back and looking into her eyes. 'Has he done this before, lass? Waylaid you?'

'Not exactly.' Seeing Tom so close, the sheer bulk and broadness of him, had left her thoroughly unnerved. 'Not like today. He usually just lets me know he's there, from a distance. Sometimes I haven't even seen him, but I've felt he's around.'

'Why haven't you *said*?' Ruby had stared at her aghast. 'You should have told me. How long has it been going on? Months? Years?'

'Since he came to the shop that day after Perce died.'

'And you never said.'

'I didn't want to worry you for no good reason. It's not like he wants me any more, in that way. He doesn't know for sure that Daisy is his and, like I told you at the time, he looked at me as if he hated me when he left that day. As long as I don't get involved with anyone – a man – he won't do anything.'

Ruby looked more appalled, if anything. 'But you can't live like that, Lucy. And you're wrong. He does still want you, it was plain in his face. He's risen high and he's never been thwarted by anything in his life, that's the trouble. The fact that you've refused him is what spurs him on, don't you see? If you weren't the way you are, he'd have lost interest years ago. He's a nutcase, lass, twisted, and to have pursued you all these years, tracking you like an animal, proves it.'

Ruby's words were ringing in her ears as she walked faster now, berating herself for doing the very thing she'd made the others promise not to do – walking alone in the blackout. But for once she hadn't been thinking about the threat of Tom Crawford, not with Jacob and John possibly lying dead or injured so far away on foreign soil. She didn't dare run – the last thing she wanted was to go sprawling and twist her ankle or something – but the footsteps were right behind her now. Gathering her courage she swung around, her voice shrill as she cried, 'One step more and I'm going to scream.'

'Lucy? It's me.'

The voice wasn't Tom Crawford's, but neither did it belong to the scrawny, emaciated stranger she could just make out one or two yards away. Her stomach in knots, she peered through the darkness as she told herself her memory was playing tricks on her. 'Who are you?'

'It's me. Your brother, Donald.'

'*Donald?*' The voice was his, but the man in front of her looked old, at least double the thirty years of age Donald would be now. And yet the voice . . . She took a step nearer. 'Donald,' she whispered, shocked beyond measure as she recognized a trace of the familiar face in the skeletal features of the skull-like head. 'What's happened?'

'I'm sick, lass.'

'Sick?' She stood dazed for a moment more and then as full realization dawned, she flung her arms around him. 'Donald, oh, Donald. It's you, it's really you.'

It was a second before he responded, and then his arms went round her, too, and she was hugged as he'd never hugged her in the past. 'I'm sorry, lass, I'm so sorry,' he murmured over and over again, his voice breaking. 'I shouldn't have done what I did, I shouldn't have left you. Can you forgive me?'

'You're back, that's all that matters.' And it was, it really was.

'Oh, lass.' He was sobbing, crying like a baby, and

now she was the one hugging him as he wept out his deprecation of himself, incoherently in the main.

It was some minutes before they drew apart, Donald rubbing at his face with his coat sleeves and Lucy wiping her eyes with her handkerchief. 'I can't believe it's you.' She reached out and touched his cheek with her hand and he caught her fingers, pressing them against his skin. 'You said you're sick? What's the matter?'

'It's me stomach, lass, but don't let's talk about that now. I've got me pills, so I'm all right, but – I wanted to see you. I've been back a couple of days, but I couldn't drum up the courage to come to the house after I found out where you lived. Not after what I did. I – I thought you'd slam the door in my face.'

'Why would I do that?' she said softly. 'I love you.' They looked at each other, their smiles shaky. Then Lucy slipped her arm through his. 'Come on,' she said, even more softly. 'Let's go home.'

Chapter Twenty-Four

'This is it, matey. This is the end. Would you look at that? We're done for this time.'

Jacob didn't turn to look at the man who had spoken – Willy Armstrong, his friend and the battalion's comedian. But Willy wasn't cracking one of his endless jokes now.

They had been marching more than forty miles a day for three days to the coast, fleeing refugees constantly hampering their movements, and bombs and machine-gun bullets from the air picking them off like ducks at a fairground stall. Jacob had become numb to the roadside human debris of the retreat, bodies and bits of bodies becoming just more obstacles to step over. Their Sergeant had told them evacuation from Dunkirk to England was the only hope they had, and ultimately the only hope the nation had, if Germany invaded its shores. Without the British Expeditionary Force, which contained the majority of Britain's most experienced troops, who would defend their mothers and wives and sweethearts and children from Hitler's Nazis?

'Keep that in your minds, along with putting one foot in front of the other,' Sergeant Fraser had bellowed, reminding them of it at frequent intervals until a German bomb had separated his head from his body.

And now they were within sight of their objective – or what was left of it. Much of Dunkirk was on fire and the smell of burning machinery and corpses hung oppressively in the choking air. Above the heavy black pall of smoke, German and British planes were engaged in a fight to the death, but the limited resources of the RAF couldn't compete with the enemy's low-flying Stukas, which were ripping into the endless columns of British troops on the undefended beaches and blowing them to kingdom come.

Even as they watched disbelievingly, a bomb blew a mighty crater into the sand, a number of soldiers fell into it, dead and alive, and another bomb covered them over.

'It's a slaughter!' Willy's filthy, dust-caked face was stretched in horror. 'They've brought us here to finish us off. No one's going to get out of this alive.'

Privately Jacob agreed with him, but they were standing with a couple of young conscripts who looked as though they should still be in short trousers and who were plainly terrified. 'We'll get out,' he said quietly. 'The Corporal said it's not just the Royal Navy that's coming for us, but fishing boats and the like. We'll show Hitler what's what. We look after our own.' He called to the Corporal, who was a few yards away. 'Isn't that right, Corp? We'll live to fight another day.'

The Corporal, who had taken over when Sergeant

Fraser was decapitated the day before, limped over to them. He'd had a machine-gun bullet lodged deep in his foot for the last five days, but had still led the marching. He was a Newcastle lad, born and bred, and in happier days he and Jacob had had many a friendly, if heated, discussion about their respective town's football teams. 'Oh aye, man,' he said now, grinning. 'We'll all live to see Newcastle knock the living daylights out of Sunderland, that's for sure. Now get lively and dig a trench; it'll be a while before it's our turn to depart these fair shores and there's no need to make the Germans' job simple for them by providing easy targets, is there? There's been enough griping that you want a rest, over the last few days. Now's your chance. An' once you've got a brew on, I'll have two sugars in mine, all right? An' a couple of Garibaldis to go with it.' Jacob grinned back. They had no supplies and no one had eaten for three days. Even their drinking water had come from streams and rivers, and, in the last resort, muddy ditches.

Over the next forty-eight hours, amidst the bombing and shelling, all they could do was wait their turn and watch what was happening. Hunger was a worse enemy than the Luftwaffe's attempted annihilation, and Jacob wondered if they were simply going to starve where they sat or stood.

Dunkirk's bomb-damaged breakwater was still serviceable, allowing some of the waiting troops to be taken off by larger boats. The rest were picked up directly from a ten-mile stretch of beach by small craft largely manned by amateur sailors. British, French and Belgian ships of all sizes – from destroyers to private motor cruisers – were part of the operation. But it wasn't easy. Both large and small craft had difficulty getting their human cargo out to the waiting British destroyers, because they were quite a long way out, due to the shallow waters of the harbour. And the German bombs rained down incessantly.

Before their rescue, the waiting troops were forced to stand out in the water waiting for the boats and small craft to take them on board. When Corporal Potts came limping over to marshal them into position, Jacob had to will himself to move forward. The sea was running red in places, with body parts and dead bodies floating side by side, and the thought of just standing there – so near and yet so far from rescue – was worse than the endless hours of waiting their turn on the beach.

But if he wanted to get back home, back to Lucy, he had to take the chance. And he wanted to, more than life itself. One thing had crystallized in his mind over the last hellish weeks. He was going to tell her how he felt. Spell it out. No talk of friends or old times' sake or any of the other rubbish he'd been hiding behind. He was going to tell her he loved her and always would, that she was the only woman on Earth for him and he wanted her to wait for him. He didn't care that she was wealthy and could no doubt buy him ten – twenty – times over. After what he'd seen and had to do, that was so unimportant it was laughable. He had let his hurt that she'd disappeared from his life and married another man and had his baby, and his pride that she had become too wealthy and successful to approach, keep him silent. She might not love him like she'd clearly loved her husband, but she did have some feeling for him. He had seen it in her face and heard it in her voice that last afternoon before he had left. He had let her slip through his fingers once, admittedly through no fault of his own, he qualified, but he had spent nearly half of his life to date without her.

So much wasted time.

They had reached the end of their line now and were standing waist-deep in salty water, the soldiers in front of them scrambling into the small boat waiting for them. Willy climbed aboard, and as he did so the skipper of the vessel said to Jacob, 'Sorry, pal, he's the last one I can take.'

Jacob nodded, but the next moment Willy had splashed down into the waves again, saying, 'No offence, matey, but he's me lucky mascot.' He called to one of the youngsters, 'Here, mate, you go in this one. I'll wait for the next bus. There's bound to be one along sooner or later.'

He joined Jacob, saying somewhat sheepishly, 'We've been shoulder-to-shoulder thus far, that's the way I see it. All right?'

Touched, but knowing better than to show it, as Willy was embarrassed enough, Jacob grinned. They'd watched each other's backs from day one, but he didn't know if he would have refused the boat. 'I thought for a minute there I was going to be spared your jokes on the way home.'

'Is that so?' Willy pulled his helmet more firmly over his forehead. 'Did you hear the one about—'

It took them both by surprise. One moment the little boat had been speeding away with its occupants sandwiched in like sardines in a can, and the next it was blown out of the water by a direct hit, fragmenting into a hundred pieces as bodies flew through the air.

Willy swore softly, but didn't say another word. There were no words to say, after all. The lad who had taken his place had been a baby-faced, gangly youth, who had thanked him as he'd climbed into the small motor cruiser.

When their turn came, it was a fishing boat that picked them up and the gnarled fisherman and his son who were manning the craft that was their livelihood were characters. 'Let's be having you, boyos,' the fisherman shouted as, weary unto death, they climbed aboard. 'You're an orderly lot and no mistake. There's more pushing and shoving in the queue outside the pie shop of a Friday night. An' just so you know, I've got no intention of going to meet my Maker courtesy of Jerry, so you'll be back on British soil afore too long.'

It was comforting. Bravado, most certainly, but comforting nonetheless.

'We've lost two destroyers four or five miles out in the last twenty-four hours, so I'm giving you a ride home meself. That's if there's no objections? No, I thought not. All right, we're chock-full, so the next stop is England, boys.'

Exhausted, cold and wet through, his teeth chattering from standing in the icy French sea, Jacob shut his eyes for a minute or two as the boat began to chug away, but then he turned his head and looked back towards the beach. They were leaving column upon column of British troops waiting for evacuation, and from a distance it reminded him of stone walls dividing miles of fields; some of the formations were in squares and others were simply long lines. They had been told that British soldiers were sharing with French formations in holding the rearguard, fighting furiously to the south end of the bridgehead to keep the Germans back from pouring into Dunkirk and storming the beach. They were either going to be killed or captured, he thought wearily, and if he got out of this slaughter alive he would owe his life to those men he'd never meet or be able to thank.

It was a big 'if', though. German aircraft, torpedo boats and U-boats were operating in the Channel and even if they cleared this mess and got out to sea, it wouldn't be plain sailing. Not by a long chalk. But anything was better than waiting on that damn beach being bombed and machine-gunned by an enemy in the sky above them, who was faceless and without pity. If anyone had told him a few years back that he would be capable of hating men he had never seen and of wishing every last man, woman and child of a nation to deepest hell, he wouldn't have believed them.

'Here, mate.' He came out of the black morass of his thoughts to find Willy snapping a small bar of chocolate in two and handing him half.

'What the . . .?' Jacob stared at his friend in amazement. 'Where did that come from?'

'I've been keeping it for this moment.' Willy grinned at the expression on Jacob's dumbfounded face. 'For a little celebration if we ever got away. I swopped my watch for it, with that French kid we were talking to on the last day of the march before we got to Dunkirk.'

'You've had it all that time?' Jacob thought of the endless days on the beach when he'd been near fainting with hunger. 'What if we'd been killed before we reached the boat?'

'Then we wouldn't have needed it any more anyway.' Willy was delighted with Jacob's reaction, being forever the showman. 'And you'd have been none the wiser.' He watched as Jacob crammed the whole four squares of his share into his mouth, not chewing, but just letting them melt in an ecstasy of taste. 'Now, aren't you glad I waited till now?'

Strangely he was. Not simply because of the taste and smell and wonderful sensation of the smooth warm chocolate filling his mouth, but because a moment ago he'd been in the darkest place he could ever remember, filled with a hatred so strong it had blotted out everything good in the world. A reaction, maybe, to the waiting and fear and the massacre going on around him, but he had wanted to kill and destroy, and take satisfaction from it.

And that wasn't him, that wasn't Jacob Crawford. He wasn't an animal.

He let his tongue savour the sticky sweetness as the boat chugged further out to sea, so tired he could barely register the explosions going on around him. Willy could have kept the whole bar to himself and eaten it without him knowing – it would have been easy. But he hadn't. And why? Because he was a good man, a fine man. Along with many others. The world wasn't all bad. It stood to reason that even among the Germans there were good men, although he couldn't see that right now.

Willy's eyes were shut and his head was lolling on his chest, a smear of chocolate at the side of his mouth. Jacob smiled wearily, his last conscious thought before he fell asleep himself being, 'We're fighting for right, and with blokes like Willy on our side, we'll beat 'em yet. They don't know what they've taken on with us British.'

Twenty-four hours later, on June 4th, the beaches of Dunkirk were littered with decaying bodies and the twisted shapes of hundreds of battered vehicles and weapons of all kinds. But Operation Dynamo, the evacuation of the British Army by more than a thousand boats, varying in size from a Royal Navy anti-aircraft cruiser down to dinghies that were sailed across the Channel by their civilian owners, was complete.

Crowds, waving Union Jacks and yelling 'Well done, boys', were waiting on the shores of the south-coast ports as more than 338,000 troops who had been rescued were fed and given shelter before they were put aboard trains for barracks or home or hospitals.

Lucy had heard no word from Jacob or John as she listened to the speech of Winston Churchill that day and, like thousands of other women nationwide, she didn't know if her loved ones were coming home. She sat with Donald and the others clustered around the wireless, heartsore and tired and frightened by the threat of invasion, as the Prime Minister spoke the words she was to remember for the rest of her life:

'Even though large tracts of Europe and many old and famous States have fallen or may fall into the grip of the Gestapo and all the odious apparatus of Nazi rule, we shall not flag or fail. We shall go on to the end. We shall fight in France, we shall fight on the sea and oceans, we shall fight with growing confidence and growing strength in the air; we shall defend our island, whatever the cost may be. We shall fight on the beaches, we shall fight on the landing grounds, we shall fight in the fields and in the streets, we shall fight in the hills; we shall never surrender; and even if, which I do not for a moment believe, this island or a large part of it were subjugated and starving, then our Empire beyond the seas, armed and guarded by the British Fleet, would carry on the struggle, until, in God's good time, the New World, with all its power and might, steps forth to the rescue and liberation of the Old.'

There was a deep silence after Lucy turned the wireless off. Daisy, who had flatly refused to be evacuated to the country when war broke out, was sitting between Flora and Bess, both of whom had tears running down their cheeks. But Daisy wasn't crying, and it was she who broke the quiet when she said, her young clear voice ringing with conviction, 'I shall fight them in the streets. I'd rather die than become a Nazi slave.'

'It won't come to that.' Donald spoke, but his eyes were on Lucy. He knew she was worried to death about John and, as the days had gone on and there'd been no word, they were all fearing the worst. Matthew had just turned seventeen and she was concerned that if they lowered the call-up age to eighteen, as had been suggested once or twice in the newspapers, he would be conscripted the following year, which was an added worry. But there was something else, something he couldn't put his finger on. He knew that Jacob Crawford had come to the house before he'd gone away to fight, Ruby had told him so, but when he'd tried to broach the matter with Lucy, she had gently but firmly refused to discuss Jacob or any of the Crawfords, come to that. In Ruby's own forthright way she'd let him know they'd had to leave the day after he'd skedaddled – as she put it – and described the subsequent week or so of living rough with all its horrors, before the fishmonger had taken them in. But Lucy hadn't said a word about that time. Ruby had given him the impression Lucy had married the man to secure them a home, but when he had plucked up the courage and tentatively asked about her husband, Lucy's face had been soft and her voice warm as she said, 'He was a grand man, Donald. A wonderful man, and his boys are just like him.' That was all very well, but it didn't explain why Lucy had cut Enid Crawford out of her life so completely.

In the deep recesses of his mind – a place where he hadn't gone too often because it had stirred up the guilt and shame he'd buried about walking out on Lucy – he had known that she wouldn't abandon the others to the workhouse. But he had comforted himself with the fact that she would have gone to Enid Crawford, and the Crawfords would have helped them get by. Ruby had explained that away by saying that Jacob had been found beaten near to death the same day he'd gone and, with the Crawford house in turmoil, Lucy hadn't felt she could burden Enid with their problems. And he could buy that; but why, once Lucy was settled and happy with her fishmonger, hadn't she gone to see Enid Crawford now and again? That would have been the natural thing to do. The kind thing. And, above all else, Lucy was kind.

She raised her head now and caught his eye and, seeing her face torn with anxiety, he said again, 'It won't come to that, lass. There's the sea between us and them, we're an island, and it'll make all the difference. They won't invade British soil, you'll see.'

Conscious of Daisy's big eyes on her, Lucy made herself say, briskly and with conviction, 'I know that, Donald. Now, Daisy and Charley, you set the table and Bess, you can help me dish up. Let's eat straight away because

Matthew's away to a meeting about manning anti-aircraft batteries tonight.'

They had just stood up when the doorbell rang shrilly. As one, everyone froze, their eyes shooting to Lucy.

It didn't have to be a black-edged telegram. She kept saying the words as a prayer, as she walked out of the sitting room and into the hall, with the others following. Her hand shaking, she opened the front door.

'Hello, lass, I've lost me key,' said John, for all the world as though he was returning home after a day at work.

Dolly Williamson called at the house very early the next morning, so early in fact that the birds were barely up, let alone anyone else, but although the rest of the household was fast asleep, Lucy had been dressed and working downstairs on some paperwork for an hour or two. The previous evening had been a time of thanksgiving and merriment, John's appearance transforming the sombre atmosphere in the house and everyone being determined to make his few days of leave happy and memorable, but once she had been alone in her bed her fears for Jacob had had free rein. The more so now that she knew John was safe.

It was too much to hope that both of them had been spared. John had played down what he'd been through in front of Daisy and the twins, but she'd heard him talking to Donald late at night as the two brothers had sat together over a bottle of whisky, and what he'd described had been sheer butchery. Why should God listen to her prayers and save them both, when some families had lost all their menfolk in one fell swoop? Nevertheless, she had prayed and argued and cried out to God for hours.

She was sitting at her desk in the morning room, which overlooked the street, when she heard the clip-clop of horse's hooves stop outside the house. Peering out of the window, she saw a plump little person being helped down from the horse and cart outside and knew instantly, from Jacob's descriptions in the past, that it could only be Abe and Dolly Williamson.

She opened the door before Dolly had time to knock, and saw that her husband had climbed back into the cart and was staring straight ahead, and that Dolly's round face was unsmiling. Her heart giving a great lurch, she said, 'Is it Jacob?'

Dolly answered just as bluntly. 'I've come with a message from him, if you're Lucy?'

A message. That meant he was alive. Relief made her knees weak and she had to clutch hold of the door frame as her head swam.

Dolly looked at the woman in front of her keenly. She had asked her name, but she'd known instantly this was the girl who had bedevilled her lad for years and driven him half-barmy. She was beautiful, even more lovely than she'd prepared herself for, but at the moment she'd turned as white as a sheet and looked as though she was about to faint. In spite of herself, Dolly felt sorry for her, but then almost immediately she told herself not to be so daft. Lucy Alridge might look as fragile as a flower, but she was made of iron within; she had to be, to have lived with herself after the way she had treated Jacob. But he'd asked her to come and see Lucy and so she had come. For her lad.

Pulling herself together, Lucy said weakly, 'Won't – won't you come in?'

'No, I'll not come in.' This was said in the tone of 'I'll never set foot over *your* doorstep' and made Dolly's opinion of the proceedings abundantly clear, even before she continued, 'We got a telegram from Jacob an hour ago, saying he was back in barracks in England, but he can't get immediate leave. He said he'd be writing to you, but wanted me to let you know he was safe.'

Lucy looked from Dolly to Abe, sitting so stiff and silent in the cart, and then back to Dolly again. These two people had been like a mother and father to Jacob for most of his life and she knew he thought the world of them. But they didn't like her.

For a moment she had an overwhelming desire to tell them she wasn't the person they thought her to be, but of course that was impossible. Instead she drew herself up with a natural dignity that wasn't lost on the blacksmith's wife, her voice matching her posture when she said, 'Thank you very much for coming to see me, Mrs Williamson. It was kind of you.'

'Aye, well, like I said, Jacob asked us.' Dolly was flustered now and it showed. She looked as though she was about to say something more and then thought better of it, turning and scrambling up beside her husband before he could get down to assist her.

Lucy didn't shut the door until the horse had begun to amble off, taking its time in spite of its master's 'Come on, lass, gee up!' And then she closed it slowly, turning to lean against it.

For a minute, when she had first seen them and their faces so grim, she had thought . . . She shut her eyes against what she had thought.

But he was alive.

Of course there was still Tom, and she could never tell Jacob the truth about Daisy, and they could never be together; nothing had changed, not really, but he was alive.

PART SIX

Greater Love Hath No Man . . .

June 1940

Chapter Twenty-Five

Lucy received Jacob's letter a few days later and from the first word she was aware that the tone had changed. Before, his letters had been friendly, warm and chatty, starting with 'Dear Lucy' and finishing 'Your loving friend, Jacob'. This one began, 'My dearest Lucy' and there was no making light of the war, as in his previous correspondence. Instead, he poured out the agony and loss and heartache of what he had seen, his grief at the friends he had lost, the fear he'd had that he would never return home and see her again. This was the Jacob who had asked her to be his lass so many years ago.

She read the letter twice, her hand touching the silver heart she had taken to wearing again, hidden under the high collars of the dresses she favoured.

This time . . . this time he had written a love letter and, if she'd needed further proof, he had ended with, 'All my love, Jacob'.

She pressed the letter to her bosom, shutting her eyes as a hundred emotions tumbled one after the other through her body, causing her to tremble. This was exactly what she had feared after he had kissed her and she'd had time to reflect on the foolishness of what she'd done, but then his letters had begun to arrive and their easy, friendly style had reassured her that she hadn't led him on. Hadn't put him in danger from an enemy who was far more cunning and dangerous than the Germans – an enemy she couldn't even warn him existed. How could she tell him his own brother had killed Perce, and had probably been responsible for the attack on him when he was fifteen years old? That Tom had forced himself upon her, and Daisy was the result? And that he had continued to hound her ever since?

She couldn't. She opened her eyes, reading the letter again and touching the words he'd written, as though in doing so she could touch him. What was she going to do?

She spent the next few days in a torment of indecision and eventually wrote back along the lines she would pen to John – to a brother. She couldn't stop writing to Jacob now, it would be too cruel, and this way maybe she could say enough to let him know how things stood, without actually *saying* anything? Unsatisfactory though that was, it would have to do.

His next letter came on the Monday, after a scary weekend when the first bombs dropped on Sunderland just after midnight on a fine summer's night towards the end of June. The sirens had sounded half an hour before, sending Lucy and the others running to the Anderson shelter, shocked and disorientated after being woken so abruptly. They found out the next day that no one had been killed, although a centuries-old tithe barn had been demolished in Whitburn, killing a horse stabled there, and another of the bombs had narrowly missed the Fishermen's Cottages at The Bents. Suddenly the war had become very near, and with the French now under German occupation, everyone was frighteningly aware that the British had been left to fight the Nazis alone. The petty restrictions of the blackout and rationing, and the authoritarian attitude of the air-raid wardens, which had got up the nose of many a northerner, became unimportant overnight.

Jacob's letter was waiting for Lucy when she got home from work. It had been a long day and she was tired, and she noticed as soon as she entered the house that Donald was having a bad day. The inoperable cancer that had spread from his stomach to his kidneys had begun to take over his liver too, if the yellow tinge to his emaciated flesh was anything to go by. The doctor who had been treating him in the London hospital prior to his arrival in Sunderland had estimated that he had three, maybe four months left. That had been a day or two before he had come home in the middle of May. Looking at him today as he met her in the hall, she thought the doctor's prognosis had been optimistic.

'Looks like Jacob's written again,' said Donald, handing her the envelope with Jacob's distinctive black scrawly writing. 'Are you sure you two are just friends?'

'Quite sure.' Lucy took the envelope and stuffed it in

her pocket. 'I'll go and change and then we'll have a cup of tea in the garden before dinner.'

Donald stood staring after her long after she had disappeared up the stairs. Friends, be blowed. She'd been all of a lather the last time Jacob had written and he'd remembered the way things had been between those two when they were young. Thick as thieves, they'd been. Something had happened between them, and he suspected Jacob was the reason Lucy had cut the Crawford family out of her life. Had he let her down in some way? Hurt her? Whatever he'd done, she still loved him, or his name wasn't Donald Fallow.

The grinding-hot ache in his stomach flared into one of the explosions of pain that were becoming harder to bear, and he doubled over for a moment or two before straightening and slowly making his way into the sitting room and through to the garden. He took one of the pills from the bottle in his pocket that the doctor in London had given him and swallowed it without water.

It was a gorgeous evening, mellow and warm after a hot day, a few fleecy clouds in the bluest of blue skies. Some were saying that the beautiful summer with its clear high skies and dry weather would make things easier for the German bombers, and that might be the case, but he couldn't help feeling a secret satisfaction that his last summer was England at its best. He sat absolutely still and, as the pain settled down to the familiar gnawing ache, gradually relaxed.

Ridiculous, when he was dying, he thought, but he

was happier now than he'd been for years. Since he had left Sunderland in fact. He'd found work easy enough down south, but had poured every penny he'd earned down his throat, drinking himself into oblivion each night so that he could sleep. Without the drink, the screaming nightmares had come: his father and Ernie appearing the way they'd been that last night, smashed and bleeding, their open mouths bubbling blood as they'd tried to drag him down with them under the dank, black water of the docks. He'd known they were reproaching him for walking out on Lucy and the bairns, that they were telling him to go back, but he'd been more scared of Tom Crawford than of any ghosts that haunted his mind. And so he'd worked all day and drunk himself senseless every night, telling himself it would get better in time. But it never had. Not until the moment he had seen Lucy again and she'd given him absolution.

'Donald?' He opened his eyes to find Lucy standing in front of him and he took the cup of tea she was holding out as she said, 'You should see a doctor.'

'I did. In London.'

'Here, I mean.'

'I've told you, lass, there's nowt they can do. When I run out of my pills I'll see a quack about getting some more, but for now I'm all right.' He looked intently at her as she sat down beside him. 'How's Jacob?'

She'd been about to drink and he saw her pause for an infinitesimal moment. Then she put the cup to her lips and took a sip. 'Jacob?' It was said with studied casualness. 'He was writing to say he's coming home on leave.'

'Oh aye? That's nice. You'll be seeing him then?'

She took another sip of tea. 'I'm not sure if that's a good idea. I'm not sure if agreeing to write to him was a good idea either, to be honest.'

She was putting on a good act, but she was all of a lather again. 'Why is that then?' Donald asked quietly.

She shrugged. 'The childhood thing, us living in Zetland Street – everything – is in the past now. We're different people, but I'm not sure if Jacob sees that. I don't want to bring the past into this new life that I've built for myself, and Jacob is part of the past.'

It was too pat. As though she had rehearsed it. 'That's a bit harsh, lass, isn't it?' he said mildly. 'Me an' Ruby an' the rest of us are part of that past, too.'

'That's different. You're family.'

He was silent for a moment. 'What is it, lass? What's really bothering you?'

She shot him a quick glance before looking down at her cup. 'I've told you.'

'I don't think you have. There's something eating away at you and you're as jumpy as a kitten. You never used to be like that.'

'I had to change. I had a family to take care of.' And then she quickly put out her hand and touched his, adding, 'I don't mean anything by that, I'm not blaming you or anything.' She took a deep breath. 'I built up Perce's business with blood, sweat and tears, Donald. There were

378

days, weeks, when I barely saw Daisy when she was little. It wasn't what I wanted, but it was necessary if we were going to be secure in the future. Financially secure. I saw my chance and I took it, and I don't regret it. If you're poor and unprotected, people think they can do whatever they like, treat you however they like and get away with it, and mostly they do.'

He stared at her troubled profile, trying to understand. 'What has that got to do with seeing Jacob?'

Her smile seemed forced. 'Nothing. I'm wandering. Take no notice. Look, I'm going to hurry Bess and Flora up with the dinner; it's always late when it's their turn to cook. I'll call you when it's ready.'

Donald finished his tea and settled back in his deckchair, shutting his eyes, but although he appeared to be dozing in the warm evening sunshine, his mind was worrying at what Lucy had said, like a dog with a bone. There was more than met the eye here, but he was blowed if he could get a handle on it. The talk about Jacob belonging to the past was so much codswallop. He had asked Ruby the other day if she knew what was eating Lucy, and she'd replied airily – too airily now, when he thought about it – that Lucy was absolutely fine, but pressured with running the four shops and being involved in one or two committees in the town and caring for the family. 'But she likes to keep busy,' she had qualified in the next breath. 'That's the sort of woman she is now.'

He'd tackle Ruby again. Donald mentally nodded at the thought. He'd pick his moment and grill her until he was satisfied, but without Lucy around. He wasn't prying for prying's sake, but in the years since he had left something had happened to Lucy, he was sure of it. Something he might have been able to help with, or even prevent, if he had stayed around. He felt responsible, rightly or wrongly. And one thing was for sure: for however long he had left, Lucy and the others were his priority. He wouldn't let her down a second time.

Chapter Twenty-Six

Lucy slept badly that night, in spite of there being no sirens cutting into the quiet and sending everyone scurrying for the shelter. Jacob's letter was folded away with the others in an old chocolate box tied with a ribbon, which resided on the top of the wardrobe, but she didn't have to look at it to remember every word, which ran over and over in her mind every time she stirred:

Dearest Lucy,

The rumour is that our battalion isn't going to be one of the ones staying around to protect British shores from invasion, but we're going to be shipped off abroad to bolster troops protecting the British Empire. In case it happens to be true, I've applied for leave and will be home shortly. I have to see you – there are things I need to say that I can't write down, and if I'm going to be hundreds or thousands of miles away I can't go without making it clear how I feel, even though you probably know already. I'm not going to say anything more now and you won't have time to write back before I leave, so don't try.

All my love, Jacob

She awoke before it was light and sat at her open window with the scent of climbing roses perfuming the lazy, warm air. Every nerve in her body was sensitized and her head throbbed and her heart ached, but she knew what she had to do. He would come soon. If not today, then tomorrow or the next day. No more wild imagining that somehow things would come right and they could be together. No more wishing Tom Crawford dead, willing one of Hitler's bombs to land on him and blow him to smithereens, or a car or lorry to run over him in the blackout or – oh, a hundred scenarios she'd thought up since she had seen Jacob again and wanted what she couldn't have. Tom Crawford would live forever. In a world where the innocent were bombed and tortured and maimed, how could she hope for anything different? There was no room for hope or flights of fancy now. The bad were always stronger than the good because their consciences didn't trouble them. Tom would kill Jacob without a second thought, to prevent them being together. Ruby was right: in refusing him she had let loose a monster; he couldn't bear the thought of someone else having what he had been denied. There was no love involved, merely an egomaniacal obsession that would stop at nothing. It was the same kind of evil that had plunged the world into this war.

The first bird began to sing, pure, crystal-clear notes that rent her heart, and soon others were joining in a rich chorus composed by their Maker. Dawn was breaking, a new day was unfolding and she couldn't stop it. Couldn't stop time. Couldn't stop the moment when she would have to look into his face and send him away forever.

She leaned her head against the cold glass of the window, murmuring his name as her whole being cried out and asked for his forgiveness for what she had to do. But of course he wouldn't forgive her. He wouldn't understand and she couldn't explain, and he would hate her. He would hate her, and she would die and go on living however many years she was destined to live, for Daisy, for Ruby and the others, but all the time she would be dead inside. But even then, *even then*, it would be better than giving in to her heart.

Nothing had changed. If she told Jacob, warned him, she would have to explain what had happened and then Jacob would kill Tom, she knew he would. And hang for it. If she didn't tell him, if she kept quiet and accepted his love, then it would be the equivalent of preparing a lamb for slaughter, because Tom would kill him. Either way Jacob would die. There was no way out of it, there never had been. Tom's mania made him stronger than them all.

Lucy stood up. She felt chilled, despite the warm morning. She had to be convincing when Jacob came. There could be no tears or tender goodbyes. She must make him believe she thought of him as an old friend and that was all, that there could be nothing of a romantic nature between them, now or in the future. And because of that she must make it clear to him that she didn't want him to continue writing to her or calling at the house again when he was home on leave. She had to pretend that his forthcoming declaration had made her feel uncomfortable, and she wanted any contact to cease.

By the time she had washed and dressed and put her hair up, she had composed herself. Outwardly, at least. It was still too early for the rest of the household to be up, and she made her way silently downstairs to the sitting room, intending to sit in the garden for a while. She saw immediately that the French doors were ajar, and when she tiptoed across the room and peered outside, Donald was fast asleep in the deckchair he favoured, an empty mug at his side and yesterday's newspaper lying across his lap.

He looked so ill. She caught her breath, sorrow flooding her soul. It didn't seem fair that, having found him again, he was going to be taken away. Tom Crawford had ruined Donald's life as surely as if he'd been crushed that night, along with their da and Ernie; it was just that Donald had endured a slow, lingering, lonely demise.

And then she shook her head at her dark thoughts. Stop it, she told herself. Go and make a pot of tea. Do something positive. She and Donald could share it before the rest of them came down and she would make some hot buttered toast to go with it. Their butter ration had gone within a day or two this week, but Farmer Thornhill had slipped her a whole pat on Saturday morning in exchange for a nice few pieces of cod, and his wife's butter was the best she'd tasted. It might tempt Donald – he didn't eat enough to keep a sparrow alive.

She was crossing the hall when something, some instinct outside herself, caused her to walk to the front door and look through the stained glass into the small front garden. Jacob was sitting on their brick wall, his army cap in his hand and his face lifted to the rising sun. She didn't know if it was the coloured glass or the sunlight on his bare head, but there was an aura of rainbow light about him as he sat motionless.

She stepped back sharply, her hand going to her throat and her heart thudding in her ears. She glanced round the empty hall as though it would help her, but there were just the dancing sunbeams slanting on the far wall and the faint ticking of the grandfather clock from the dining room.

She stood for some moments until the rushing in her ears had subsided, and then stepped forward and opened the door. He was still sitting there and she saw now that his eyes were closed against the sun's glare. 'Hello, Jacob,' she said, very softly.

His eyes shot open and he sprang up, but he didn't immediately come towards her. 'Hello, Lucy,' he said, equally softly. 'Did you get my letter?'

She nodded. He had never looked more handsome; the army uniform suited him.

'I'm sorry I'm so early, but I got in late last night and

I wanted—' He paused. 'I wasn't going to knock until I was sure someone would be up.'

She nodded again. Her throat seemed to have closed up and she had to swallow, before she could say, 'You'd better come in a minute.'

Something in his face died at the tone of her voice, but she told herself not to weaken. She was about to lead the way into her morning room, but there were papers covering the desk and some files she had brought home piled on the chaise longue. Instead she walked through to the sitting room, hearing him close the front door and then follow her. She turned, waving at a chair. 'Won't you sit down?'

He ignored this. 'What's the matter?' His eyes searched her person for one of the dreaded black armbands, which had become more prevalent since Dunkirk. 'Did John make it back all right?'

'John?' For a moment she didn't understand. 'Oh yes, John. He's down on the south coast with his unit – what's left of it. But he's fine.' She stopped abruptly. She was babbling. 'Yes, he's fine,' she repeated slowly. 'How are you?'

He looked at her across the room. 'In turmoil.'

Lucy blinked. This wasn't going how she had planned it. 'It must have been terrible, we heard such horrible things.'

'I don't mean France.' He came to stand close, but still he didn't touch her. 'What's the matter?' he said again.

She had to say it, straight out, but she couldn't do so

while looking into his dear face. Turning, she walked over to the fireplace, putting one hand on the mantelpiece and keeping her back towards him as she murmured, 'I feel I might have given you the wrong impression before you left to fight, and if I did, I'm truly sorry.'

A deep silence took hold. It was a full ten seconds before he said quietly, 'What impression was that, Lucy?'

'That we could be more than just friends. Your letter suggested . . .' She had forgotten everything she'd proposed to say. 'I'm sorry,' she said again.

'Lucy?' He waited until she had turned to look at him. 'I love you, and I feel you care for me. Maybe not as I love you, that would be impossible' – he smiled, but she didn't respond and after a moment he went on – 'but there *is* something between us.'

'Friendship.'

'And much more.'

'No.' She was near to tears, but she told herself she must not allow them to flow. 'No, Jacob. I have a daughter, a family, my work, and I am content. We're not children any more.'

'I have never stopped loving you.' He paused, his look and his voice altering. 'I don't understand what drove us apart and how you could leave the way you did, but that no longer matters. I was angry and hurt for a long time, but it didn't stop me loving you. You need to know that.'

'Don't. Please don't.' She bowed her head. 'I care for you as a friend, but I don't love you.'

'Tell me that while looking into my eyes.'

She did not obey him, she couldn't, and when his hands fastened on the top of her arms, she shivered.

'There's something more, isn't there? Something you're not telling me. What are you afraid of, Lucy?'

It was so near the truth that she panicked. Jerking herself free with a strength born of desperation, she looked at him. 'I think it would be better, in the circumstances, if you didn't call here again. I don't want any unpleasantness and I wish you well, but there is absolutely no question of a future together. Do you understand me?'

He straightened as his face stiffened. 'Aye, you've made yourself perfectly clear.'

'Goodbye, Jacob.'

He looked at her for one more moment, his face as black as thunder, then without a word he turned and marched across the room, flinging open the door with enough force for it to smash against the wall. She heard his footsteps in the hall, then the front door banging behind him.

He had gone. As the enormity of it swept over her she almost ran after him, her breath escaping in a shuddering sigh. And then her longing was vocalized as Donald said from the French doors, 'Go after him, lass. Tell him you didn't mean it.'

She didn't ask how much he had heard; it didn't matter. She had completely forgotten he was in the garden. She turned to look at him, hanging onto the door frame. 'I did mean it.'

'Lass, this is me – Donald – you're talking to. Don't try and tell me you don't love him.'

'It's not as simple as that.'

'Of course it's as simple as that. What else is there? Hell's bells, lass, don't throw away a good man like Jacob because things went wrong in the past. I heard him, and he means it. He loves you. Are you thinking of Daisy? Is that what's stopping you? She'd take to him, I can guarantee it, and he'd be a grand father for her.'

She stared at him, her eyes wide and dazed, and her voice sounded dazed too as she said flatly, 'He can't be her father; he's her uncle.'

'Her what?' Donald came over to her. 'Lass, sit down. You're upset and you don't know what you're saying.'

'Jacob is Daisy's uncle.' She let him guide her to one of the sofas and he sat down beside her, taking her hands as she repeated, 'He can't be her father, you see.' She gave a strange noise, a laugh that wasn't a laugh, and as it mounted into hysteria he shook her hard, snapping her head back on her shoulders. Then an agonized cry escaped her and the tears came as she collapsed against him.

It was some time before she raised her head from Donald's chest, and as he wiped her eyes with her own handkerchief, he said quietly, 'Tell me everything, from the beginning.'

And she told him everything from the beginning.

Later that morning Donald left the house by taxi-cab. Lucy was in bed, being looked after by an anxious Ruby, to whom he'd explained the full facts. To everyone else he'd said that Lucy's collapse was due to a nasty flu-like malady and she needed complete rest and quiet, marshalling them off to their respective places of work with no argument.

He had no intention of keeping the promise he'd made to Lucy that he wouldn't tell Jacob the truth. Jacob would rise above the revelations, he knew that, but he agreed with Lucy that Jacob might do something rash regarding his brother. So he would have to make sure he reached Tom Crawford first. His fingers closed over the razor-sharp kitchen knife in his pocket. The man was an animal, a dirty stinking animal, to take down a pure young lass like that and then to terrorize her for years, having murdered the bloke who'd taken her in and given her his protection and his name. Tom Crawford deserved to die.

He climbed into the taxi, and as the driver turned round and said, 'Where to, mate?' he answered, 'The blacksmith's in Southwick, Abe Williamson. Do you know it?'

'Oh aye, I know old Abe's place, an' with petrol gettin' harder to come by, I reckon we'll all be back to horse an' cart before long. Still, if it helps keep the Nazis at bay, who's complainin', eh? You see them pictures of the blighters parading up the Champs-Elysées in Paris an' the swastika flying from the Eiffel Tower? Makes you sick to your stomach, don't it? I tell you . . . '

He continued to tell Donald every minute of the journey, but Donald was content to let the man chat on and just

put in the odd word now and again. Once he'd seen
Jacob, he intended to go straight to Tom Crawford's house.
If he wasn't in, he'd wait, and make sure Jacob didn't get
to his brother first.

He looked out of the window. It was a grand day.
Apart from the thick white lines painted on kerbs and
lamp posts to help people see where they were going in
the blackout, you'd hardly know there was a war going
on. He wouldn't mind dying on a day like today. He'd
taken two pills before he'd come out because the pain
had been crippling, but now it had died down and with
that had come strength for what he had to do. He couldn't
make right the wrong he'd done to Lucy, or the years of
living looking over her shoulder every minute after Tom
Crawford had raped her. He wasn't God. But it *was* in
his power to give her the chance of a future with the man
she loved. It was something. Not enough, but something.

When he arrived at the forge he asked the taxi driver
to wait and climbed out of the car, but he hadn't taken
more than a step or two when Dolly came bustling out
of the house with a bowl of corn in her hand for the
hens that were scratching around. Catching sight of him,
she stopped. He knew he looked bad, but if he hadn't,
then her face would have given it away, and likewise her
voice when she said with some concern, 'You all right
there? Can I help?'

'I'm looking for Jacob Crawford. He's home on leave,
isn't he?'

'Aye, he is, but he's not here, lad. He arrived late last

night, but was up and about before me an' me husband this morning. Left us a note to say he'd be back later, but he had business to attend to in the town, and he was going to call in on his mam an' all. Can Abe help?' She nodded towards the barn-like structure of the forge where Donald could hear the sound of hammering. 'He's in there.'

'No thanks, lass. I'll call again.'

He'd turned and climbed back into the taxi when she shouted, 'Who shall I say called?', but he ignored her. He didn't want Jacob turning up at the house before he'd had a chance to put him right about Lucy, and Dolly obviously hadn't recognized him, which was all to the good. Mind, his own mam wouldn't recognize him these days.

'Where to now?' The taxi driver was happy. He didn't often get a fare like this one. Most folk went straight to one place and complained bitterly if he had to stop at traffic lights.

'Zetland Street.' With any luck, Jacob would still be at his mam's. They'd think it odd, him turning up like this, but that couldn't be helped and as long as he was able to talk to Jacob, nothing else mattered. The certainty of imminent death had a way of sorting out what was important and what was not.

To the taxi driver's delight, Donald told him to wait when they pulled up outside the Crawfords' house. 'I might be a few minutes, but that's not a problem, is it?'

'Not if you're happy to pay for the meter ticking, mate.'

'I am.' He needed to be able to get to Tom's house immediately he was done here, that's if Jacob was still inside. Otherwise he'd go back to the forge and wait at the end of the lane. Either way, he needed the taxi; he couldn't walk more than a few steps today and already the pain was kicking in again.

Climbing out of the taxi, it dawned on Donald that he had never once entered the Crawfords' house through the front door. And, thinking about it, the only times he could remember using his own front door was for his mother's and then his da's and Ernie's funerals. All the coming and going had been via the back lane, even when it was claggy with thick mud or a sheet of frozen ridged ice. Amazing when you thought about it, and even more amazing that he had never queried this unwritten law.

Enid's doorstep was as white as snow and the brass door knocker in the shape of a pixie gleamed as only Brasso and elbow grease could make it gleam. Even the stiffly starched curtains at the front window were as he remembered. For a minute he'd gone back in time and was a bairn playing in the street with Ernie and the Crawford brothers. Playing the games Tom decreed, and everyone doing as they were told to avoid a bashing from his fists.

Pushing the thought aside, he knocked on the door. It was only a few moments before it opened and Enid stood framed in the doorway, staring at him without an iota of recognition. 'Hello, Mrs Crawford,' he said quietly. 'It's Donald. Donald Fallow.'

'Donald?' Her voice was high with surprise. 'Saints alive, it is you, lad. What's happened to you?' Then, remembering herself, she said, 'Come in, come in, lad. Well I never, Donald Fallow.'

He stood aside to let her pass him in the hall and she led the way to the kitchen at the back of the house, saying, 'It's funny you came today of all days, because our Jacob is here, home on leave.' She stopped before she pushed open the door that was slightly ajar, turning to him as she said quietly, 'You bad or something, lad?'

He almost smiled. As direct as ever. 'Aye, I'm bad, Mrs Crawford.'

'Dunkirk, was it?'

'No, no. It's me stomach – cancer. I've been middling for a couple of years, and it came to light when I tried to join up back in September last year.'

'I'm sorry about that, lad. Heart-sorry.'

She touched his arm and Donald was surprised by a rush of emotion. She'd looked as though she cared, really cared, and he was about to blow her little world apart, because she thought the world of Tom. And then he hardened his heart. The truth was the truth and Jacob needed to be told.

He followed Enid into the kitchen. Jacob was sitting at the table and as Enid said, 'It's Donald – Donald Fallow – lad', Jacob stared at him with the same shock that had registered on his mother's face.

Recovering himself the next moment, Jacob stood up,

holding out his hand as he said, 'Don. It's been a long time.'

'Aye, too long,' said Donald as he shook Jacob's hand.

'Sit down and have a cuppa, lad.' Enid fetched another cup and saucer as she spoke, adding, 'This one said he's not hungry, but it won't take me a minute to make you a bacon sandwich, if you'd like a bite?'

'No thanks, Mrs Crawford.' She was making him feel like a Judas and he knew he had to come straight to the point. 'It's Jacob here I've come to see, actually.'

'Oh aye?' Enid put the cup and saucer on the table, but made no effort to pour the tea. Her eyes narrowed as she said, 'Why is that then?'

'It's private, Mrs Crawford.'

'Private, is it? Well, if it's anything to do with your sister I know my lad went to see her this morning and she told him to sling his hook, same as she's made it clear she wants nowt to do with me.'

'*Mam.*' Jacob's voice was grim. 'This is nothing to do with you, and Lucy isn't obliged to see either of us. I've told you.'

Ignoring him, Enid kept her eyes on Donald. 'In a right state he was when he got here, or I don't doubt he wouldn't have said anything. Tried to palm me off with some tale or other, but I got the truth out of him.'

Donald could imagine. Enid Crawford in battle mode was frightening. Quietly he said, 'It *is* something to do with Lucy, but I would prefer to speak to Jacob alone if you don't mind, Mrs Crawford.'

Jacob stood up. 'Come into the front room.' And as his mother went to speak again, he looked at her, a long look, and she made a 'huh' in her throat, but said no more.

The front room was another step into the past. Donald could remember as a boy peeping into the Crawfords' front room and standing agog at the stiff, shiny splendour of it. Even now he felt awkward about disturbing the mausoleum-like chill. A wave of the nausea that plagued him night and day made him glad to sit down as Jacob gestured towards the sofa.

'Did Lucy send you?' Jacob remained standing, tense and still.

'No. She doesn't know I'm here, truth be told. In fact she made me promise not to tell you what I'm about to say, but I was in the garden when you came this morning and after you'd gone she – well . . .' Donald didn't know how to put it. 'She was in a state.'

'That wasn't my intention.'

'I know that.' Donald smiled gently. 'Look, would you mind sitting down? I'm getting a crick in me neck and, frankly, for what I'm about to tell you, you'd be better sitting.'

'Lucy's not ill?' Jacob's face lost some colour as he sat down.

'No, I'm the one with cancer,' Donald answered with dark humour, and at Jacob's 'I'm sorry, man' he shook his head. 'I'm not here to talk about that, it's unimportant. What is important is that you listen to me without interrupting, if you can. I didn't know any of what I'm about to say until this morning when Lucy collapsed – only Ruby's known. It's not pleasant, I warn you.'

Jacob stared at him, his jaw working. 'Let's have it.'

'The night you were attacked and left for dead all those years ago, I walked out on Lucy and the bairns and went down south,' said Donald, making no excuses for himself. 'Somehow Tom found out she had no one to protect her and the next night he went to the house and tried to force her to marry him. When she refused, he—'

'What?' said Jacob, his face now chalk-white.

'There's no easy way to say it, man. He attacked her, raped her there on the floor in the kitchen.'

The blood thundered in Jacob's ears, the agony pressing in until it swelled his whole body and erupted in an anger and murderous hatred, even as his heart cried, 'Lucy, oh, Lucy, Lucy!' His mouth spewing curses, he wrenched himself from Donald, who had stood up and was trying to press Jacob back down in his chair. 'I'll kill him. I swear I'll kill him.'

'That's exactly what Lucy was afraid of. You do that and he's won, don't you see? You'll hang for him.'

'I don't care. He's filthy – scum. He's never been normal.'

No, Tom Crawford wasn't normal. Donald's mind recalled some of the stories he'd heard from Maurice Banks and other men who'd worked for Tom and the Kanes. But 'abnormal' wasn't the right word for Jacob's brother. Tom was something more than that. When a man was mad they put him away in a lunatic asylum to protect folk, but most of them poor blighters wouldn't hurt a fly, in spite of their gibbering and jabbering. Yet the ones like Tom, the ones cunning enough to appear sane, were more dangerous than a hundred of the other kind.

Now Donald did press Jacob back into his chair, saying, 'She fled the next morning because he'd told her he'd be back, and no one was giving you any hope of making it. She couldn't go to your mam for obvious reasons. Then, after the fishmonger took 'em in out of the kindness of his heart, she found out she was carrying a bairn, Tom's bairn. The man married her to give her protection and he didn't touch her until after the bab was born, and then not until she let him. She didn't love him, but she was grateful to him for saving them all. He was a good bloke, Jacob, and your brother had him done away with.'

Jacob had been sitting with his head in his hands and now his eyes shot to Donald. 'Lucy knows that for sure?'

'Oh aye, lad. Tom threatened he'd do the same to you if she had any truck with you, and he's haunted her for years, turning up places or waiting outside the house. She's had no peace.'

Jacob ground his teeth, wiping his wet eyes with the back of his hand. 'And you say I shouldn't kill him? If I don't, she'll never be free of him, you know that.'

Aye, he knew. For a moment Donald thought about telling Jacob what he was going to do, but decided against it. Jacob would say he had to be the one to deal with his brother, and the whole purpose of him coming here today would be useless. Jacob would know soon enough that the problem had been taken care of, and without him being involved and Lucy losing the man she loved.

Quietly Donald said, 'It's Lucy who needs your attention right at this minute. I've never seen her like she was this morning after you'd gone. Go and see her. Tell her you know it all, man. She loves you; she's kept quiet all these years to protect you, because she's sure that beating you had years back was arranged by Tom.'

Jacob groaned. 'I thought she'd married the fishmonger because she loved him and that Daisy was his. How could I have doubted her?'

'God Himself would have assumed the same, if He'd been in your shoes. How were you to know?'

'I should have known. Dammit' – Jacob drove one fist into the palm of his other hand – 'what she's gone through, and all because of my brother. My *brother*, Don, my own flesh and blood. I could go stark staring mad thinking about it.'

'Then don't.'

'Easier said than done, and I shan't rest until he doesn't draw breath. When the fishmonger died and I went to see her that day, I should have known then she wouldn't have walked out on me without one hell of a good reason when I was in the hospital. But I was jealous and angry. She'd had a bairn by someone else and it burned me up inside. I took what she said that day at face value. I didn't dig deeper.'

'Look, you believing her was your protection, the way

Lucy saw it. The way she still sees it. Go and see her. I've a taxi waiting and I can drop you off before I go on to the hospital. I need more pills.' He took a bottle out of his pocket as he spoke and rattled it. The lie had come to him as he'd been talking. 'We'll talk about how to handle Tom when I get back.'

'I know how to handle him,' Jacob said grimly.

'Aye, well, I can't say I blame you, but talk to Lucy first – that's all I'm asking. She deserves that.'

Jacob nodded, but as Donald stood up he said, 'The world will be a cleaner place with him gone, Don. That's the way I see it, and she won't have to live in fear any more. It's no good trying the legal route – he's a town councillor now, a pillar of the community, with half the town in his pocket. He bought his way out of the war by means of a bent doctor, our da wrote and told me so, and you can bet he's making a packet with the black market. He's clever, that's the thing, and he can be charm itself when it suits him. He's had me mam eating out of his hand since the day he was born, and she's no fool.'

When they walked through to the kitchen Enid was stirring something or other on the stove. As she turned, Jacob said, 'I'm off, Mam.'

'You're going with him? To see her, I expect.'

'I'm going to see Lucy, aye.'

'You're a fool. The way she's treated you, I should have thought you'd learned your lesson.'

'There's more to this than you know, Mam.'

'She had that fishmonger she married on the go long

before she left here, you know. Our Tom told me so. She might be bonny enough, but she's as hard as iron, lad. She has to be, to have done what she did to you when you were at death's door in the hospital.'

'You know nothing about it.' Jacob picked up his army cap.

'That's what you think. Our Tom said—'

'Don't tell me what that filthy liar said.' Jacob swung round with such ferocity that Enid nearly jumped out of her skin. 'He's putrid, Mam. Diseased. Here, in his mind.' He tapped his forehead. 'Did he tell you he was responsible for putting me in that hospital, eh? Did he tell you that? Or that he took Lucy down, the night after Donald had left? Raped her in her own house because he didn't want her to be with me? She didn't know Perce Alridge before that. She and the bairns lived rough for a week when she fled from here, because of what Tom had done, and the man took them in out of the kindness of his heart. And the result? Tom saw to it he was done away with.'

'You're mad.' Enid's hand was clutching her throat and she looked from Jacob's livid face to Donald and then back to her son. 'Has he told you that?'

'Tom's rotten, Mam. Through and through. He always has been and he's got blood on his hands.'

'It's true, Mrs Crawford.' Donald had had to sit down on one of the kitchen chairs. 'My father and Ernie were killed doing a job for him. I was there, I saw it. The people he's mixed up with are the worst sort of villains.'

'I don't believe it.' Enid had straightened, but her face

401

was white. 'It's all lies. Just because he's got on, you're jealous – you've always been jealous of him. And Lucy knew that fishmonger all right. How else do you explain her marrying him in next to no time and having a bairn?'

'He married her because she *was* expecting a bairn, Tom's bairn, and it was either that or the workhouse. And she accepted him for the same reason. Like I said, he was a kind man.'

Their voices had been raised and no one had heard the front door open and close. It was only when a voice from the kitchen doorway spoke, saying, 'I knew it. I knew she was mine' that they became aware of Tom's presence.

Enid screamed as Jacob whirled round and sprang at his brother, but Tom had been expecting it, his great fist delivering a mighty blow under Jacob's jaw that snapped his head back and sent him crashing senseless to the floor. Donald staggered forward, the knife in his hand, but as he lunged, Tom caught the hand holding the knife and with seemingly little effort took it from him, before punching him full in the face. He, too, crumpled into a heap, blood pouring from his broken nose as he lay groaning on the floor.

Enid groped at a chair, pulling it out from beneath the kitchen table and sitting down heavily. She watched as Tom hauled Donald to his feet, but when he hit him again, protested, 'What are you doing? Stop it.'

'Stop it? He came at me with a damn knife.'

As he raised his fist once more, Enid stumbled over,

hanging on Tom's arm as she said, 'You'll kill him. Stop it, I say.'

She dragged Donald free, but he slithered unconscious to the floor next to Jacob, who was out cold. Enid looked from them to Tom, blinking as though coming out of a deep sleep. 'You said, in the doorway . . .' She took a deep breath. 'You said you knew Lucy's bairn was yours.'

'I suspected it, aye.'

'So you did take her down?'

'It wasn't like they said, Mam.' Tom was thinking fast. He'd heard enough to know that Donald and Jacob were out to get him, so he had to deal with them. Permanently. But there was his mam to consider. 'She made eyes at me, led me on.'

'But she was a bairn, a wee lass.'

'She was no bairn. I told you, she had the fishmonger on the go an' all.'

'Then why did you think the child was yours?'

He stared at her, unable to think of a reason that would hold water. 'I just did, that's all.'

'She hadn't been with a man when you took her, had she.' It was a statement, not a question. 'She was pure, a virgin. That's how you knew. I always wondered why she went without a word to me. Me, who'd been like a mam to her after Agnes passed away. But she couldn't come to me, because you're my son. So she lived on the streets till the fishmonger took them in.' She put a hand to her brow. 'Did you kill him? Her husband?'

'Don't talk soft.'

'You did, didn't you? It's true, isn't it, what they said?' She put out her hand and, like a blind person, lurched over to the table, leaning on it heavily. 'And Jacob? Did you put him in hospital that time?'

He didn't have time for this. He could deal with Donald with one hand tied behind his back, but Jacob was a different kettle of fish. He'd taken Jacob by surprise and got in the first punch, but if he came round it might be different. He had to get them in the car and take them to Jed's place, where he could deal with them and make sure they disappeared for good. 'Get me something to tie 'em up with.'

'What?'

'Before they come round. You don't want them to go for me again, do you?'

'There – there's a ball of string in that cupboard.'

She watched as he tied Jacob's hands and then his feet together. There wasn't enough string left to tie Donald's ankles as well as his hands. There was blood everywhere, most of it from Donald's broken nose. Shakily she said, 'What are you going to do?' as he finished the knot on Donald's wrists.

Tom straightened. His mother would understand. He had always known that he had her love in a way none of the others did. Heaven and hell might pass away, but his mam would be for him. Softly, with the look he reserved purely for her, he murmured, 'They're out to ruin me, Mam. You heard what they said. It's lies, it's all lies, but mud sticks and my name'll be nowt in this town if they have their say.'

Enid couldn't speak, her throat had closed up with the pain she was experiencing. Not a physical pain, that would have been bearable, however severe it was, but a pain born of the inescapable knowledge that her buried fears were out in the open and her son was bad. How bad she hadn't even guessed at in the past. How long had she refused to believe what her mind had been trying to tell her? So long that she couldn't name when it had begun. But no matter what she had sensed, or what Aaron and the others had said, she'd always given herself the answer she wanted to hear.

Taking her silence for complicity, Tom continued, 'Get me a couple of blankets to wrap them in, and then you keep watch till it's clear for me to get them in my car, all right? I'll have a word with the taxi driver and pay him what he's owed, so he clears off out of the hockey. He brought 'em both, did he?'

Numbly Enid forced out, 'No, just Donald. Jacob was already here.'

Tom nodded. He'd get the taxi registration. It might be necessary for the driver to disappear too. Jed didn't like loose ends. 'Watch them a minute.' Without waiting for a reply, he walked out of the kitchen into the hall and then she heard the front door open.

She had to stop this. Jacob was her son, her baby. But Tom wouldn't really do what she had imagined he was saying – he just intended to frighten them. To make sure they kept their mouths shut.

A voice outside herself, a harsh voice that grated in her head, repudiated the thought. He was going to kill them both. In cold blood. And it wasn't even a problem to him. Oh, God, God! She looked upwards, wringing her hands. Help me.

She heard Tom's footsteps coming back and stood up, facing him as he came through the kitchen door. 'You can't do this. We have to get the police. They attacked you, I can vouch for that. You're the' – she had been about to say 'innocent party', but couldn't bring herself to voice it, changing it to – 'offended party, lad. They'll see that.'

'I haven't got time to argue, Mam. Go and get me those blankets.'

She stared at him. 'Please, Tom, listen to me.'

'I'll get them myself.'

He turned and a moment or two later she heard him running up the stairs. Beside herself, she knelt down by Jacob, shaking his arm. 'Wake up, lad. Wake up.' Donald was stirring and groaning again; leaving Jacob, she bent over Donald and now she shook him none too gently.

'What are you doing?' Tom was back, the blankets draped over his arm.

'He – he was waking up.'

'Leave him, he's not going anywhere. I'm not bothered about him, but I need to get Jacob in the boot of the car before he comes to.' He knelt, rolling Jacob's unresisting body in the blanket. 'I'll come back for Donald in a minute. I need you to come with me and stand outside, so that you can tell me when it's clear. The boot's already open.'

'Someone will see.'

'No, they won't, not if I'm quick. It'll be all right. It's the only way, Mam. When I'm gone, you can clear up and no one will be any the wiser.'

He was really going to do it. Enid stood up as Tom hoisted the cocoon he'd made of his brother over his shoulder, and from somewhere within her being flowed a wave of resolution. Reaching behind her to the range, she grabbed the heavy iron poker that lay on the fender. 'Put Jacob down, Tom.'

'What?' A look of almost comical amazement stretched his face as he saw his mother wielding the big poker.

'Put him down, I mean it. I can't stand by and let you do this.'

'You'll not use that on me.'

'I will, if I have to.'

Jacob chose that moment to move and groan from within the blanket and several things happened in quick succession. Donald had been more alert than he had let on and, seeing Tom momentarily distracted, he used every ounce of his remaining strength to twist his body and bring his legs in a cutting motion to the back of Tom's knees. With Jacob's weight over one shoulder, it was enough to knock Tom off balance. At the same time Enid swung the poker with all her might, intending to hit Tom's other arm and make him drop Jacob. Instead the full weight of the poker smashed into his outstretched throat as he stumbled forward, his head up as he attempted to regain his balance. The impact was deadly, crushing Tom's windpipe as though it were made of eggshell and fracturing bone and rupturing muscle.

Tom crumpled, clutching his throat, as Jacob thudded to one side and a horrible gurgling sound filled the kitchen. Enid, careless of Donald struggling to sit up and of Jacob clawing his way out of the folds of the blanket, knelt down, taking Tom's head in her lap. For long seconds, his eyes bulging in terror, he fought for breath against the choking blood and bone, his legs scrabbling in his death throes against the stone slabs.

And then a silence descended. Donald sat against a table leg, looking as though he was already dead, and Enid had collapsed over Tom's still body. Jacob, having finally got his head free of the blanket, was unconscious once more. Then Enid began to scream.

Chapter Twenty-Seven

Later that day the police car that had arrived at Lucy's house an hour earlier brought her, with Ruby at her side, to the hospital where Donald and Jacob were patients and where Tom lay in the morgue. At first she hadn't been able to take in what the two policemen were telling her. But when she had, instead of breaking down as Ruby had feared, she had quietly insisted that she be taken to see her brother and Jacob.

The Detective Inspector and Detective Sergeant saw the two women to the entrance of the ward, but didn't go in. They had already questioned the injured men and were satisfied with their answers, which tied in with what the mother, Mrs Crawford, had told them. That it had opened a whole can of worms, which they were now going to have to sort out, wasn't lost on either of them.

'Rum do, this,' said the DI to his Sergeant as the doors of the ward closed behind Lucy and Ruby. 'There's been the odd whisper about Tom Crawford in the past, but then any bloke who gets on is a target for rumours. It'll upset some of the bigwigs on the town council when the muck gets aired in public, but with his own mother saying he was a wrong 'un, they won't be able to keep it quiet.'

'I wonder what made the lass's brother and Crawford's brother prepared to shop him suddenly? They must have known about it for years, and the lass's brother even worked for him for a time. I know the mother said it was because Crawford had pulled a fast one to get out of fighting for King and country, and it had been the straw that broke the camel's back – or backs, in this case – but I don't know if I buy that. Do you?'

The DI shrugged. 'Good a reason as any. It was enough to put the wind up Crawford anyway. He did the pair of them some damage, and I reckon he still might have done for the lass's brother, by the look of him. It was only the mother stepping in with the poker that stopped him. Takes some guts that, but then, as she said, she thought murder was going to be done.'

'Murder *was* done,' said the DS, grinning.

'Don't be facetious.' The DI didn't appreciate his subordinate's questionable sense of humour. 'It was self-defence. Crawford had gone stark staring barmy and likely she thought she was next.'

'It'll be interesting delving into Crawford's so-called business transactions in some detail.'

'Aye.' The DI brightened. The lass's brother had mentioned the Kanes and he'd been waiting for a long time to pin something on them. 'Aye, it will.'

*

In the ward, Lucy and Ruby were sitting with the Sister at the nurses' station. She had sat them down immediately, saying she needed to talk to them before they saw the patients. 'Mr Crawford has concussion,' she said gently, 'and we thought at first his jaw was broken, but it appears it is not.' She paused. 'I'm afraid your brother is much worse. I understand he was already ill before the assault?'

Lucy nodded. 'Donald has stomach cancer.'

'Quite so. Dr Ingram has examined him and he feels you ought to prepare yourselves. I'm very sorry.'

Lucy and Ruby held hands tightly. 'How long before . . . '

'It's hard to tell, but he's very poorly. Very poorly indeed.'

'Can we see him?'

'Dr Ingram has given him something for the pain and he will sleep for some hours now.'

Lucy gripped Ruby's hand tighter. 'We'd still like to see him, if that's possible.'

'Of course. Come this way.' The Sister rustled to her feet and led the way to one of the two beds in the ward surrounded by curtains, which were next to each other. She stopped at the first one and drew back the curtain so that Lucy and Ruby could step inside. A nurse was sitting on a chair by the head of the bed and she stood up, looking at the Sister. Lucy stared down at the colourless face on the pillow, grief overwhelming her. It was Ruby who whispered to the Sister, 'Could I stay with him? While my sister sees Jacob – Mr Crawford? I'd like to sit with him, if I may?'

The Sister's somewhat austere face softened. 'I don't see why not, my dear.' She beckoned to the nurse, who left them. Lucy touched the paper-thin hand lying so still on the starched white counterpane. It was cool and dry. Blinking back hot tears, she murmured to Ruby, 'I won't be long.'

Outside the curtains again, the Sister said, 'Mr Crawford's had something to help him sleep, too. He was very disorientated earlier, but don't be alarmed. It will pass.'

'Thank you.'

This time there was no nurse sitting by the bed. When the Sister had closed the curtains again, leaving them alone, Lucy tiptoed to Jacob's side. The lower part of his face was all bruises and badly swollen, and in contrast the rest was almost as white as the sheets, but then he opened his eyes and he became her Jacob. 'Lucy.' He blinked, as though worried she was an illusion. 'Lucy.'

'I'm here.' She took his hand. 'Don't try to talk. Just rest now.'

'Donald?'

'He's sleeping.'

'He told me, Lucy. Told – told me every-everything.'

'I know, I know. Shush now, go to sleep.'

'So – so sorry, Lucy. My own brother. Bad. Rotten.'

She brought his hand to her lips, kissing it and resting it by the side of her face. 'Don't worry, he can't hurt us any more. It's over, Jacob.'

'My mam . . . '

'I'll go and see her, if you want me to.'

He nodded, wincing as the movement hurt his head. 'Headache.'

'Shut your eyes. It will make you feel better.'

He did for a moment, opening them to say, 'I love you. I always will.'

'And I love you. I always have.'

His eyes shut again and immediately he slept, but the smile stayed in place.

Donald died just before midnight. Flora and Bess had come to join Lucy and Ruby at his bedside, Matthew and Charley remaining at home in charge of Daisy, so his four sisters were with him at the last. He had been awake a little while before, and each of them had been able to tell him how much they loved him and how precious he was.

'Don't deserve it,' he whispered to Lucy when she bent over the bed and kissed him for the umpteenth time. 'Should have stayed.'

'All forgotten, my darling.' She stroked his face gently. 'Be at peace now. You've given me Jacob, and I don't have to be frightened any more. I love you so much, we all love you.'

'Ready – ready to see Ernie now. Can look him in the face. Couldn't have before.'

'I know, I know, but you've saved me. You can tell him that, can't you, and kiss Mam and Da for me.'

A flicker of a smile touched the grey lips. 'Remember me sometimes.'

'Every day, my darling. Every single day.'

He closed his eyes, but this time he didn't open them again and it was only a minute or two later when the Sister came silently to the bedside, taking the hand that Lucy wasn't holding and checking his pulse. 'He's gone, my dears,' she said softly. 'And so peacefully. Be glad for him.'

Lucy returned alone to the hospital the following afternoon. She had gone to see Enid in the morning, who was in a terrible state. The two women had cried and talked together for a long time, and then cried some more. Enid was utterly broken, a shell of her former self. Lucy didn't think she would ever be totally whole again, but Aaron had been there and Lucy had been amazed at how gentle he was with his wife. She had left the Crawfords' house feeling terribly sad, but with Aaron's last words to her on the doorstep ringing in her ears. 'I shan't let her sink, lass, don't you fret,' he'd whispered. 'I think a bit of her you know, always have, but she didn't make room for me afore. But she needs me now an' that's not a bad thing.'

She had always thought, should a miracle happen and Tom Crawford meet his end, that she would feel like dancing and singing and shouting for joy, but curiously a great weight was pressing down on her heart. Not for him. Never for him. But the cost of his demise had been so great. Donald dying, Jacob hurt and Enid crushed so that she would never fully rise again. And the repercussions would follow them for a long time. The rumours, the gossip, the avid curiosity. Tom's evil presence would continue to overshadow them and cast a dark pall on their lives.

She had said as much to Ruby when she'd returned home for a bite of lunch before it was time to go to the hospital. Her sister's response had taken her aback and, if she was honest, had offended her a little.

'Don't talk so daft,' Ruby had said in her forthright way. 'I know you're grieving for Donald, we all are, and it can't have been pleasant at the Crawfords' this morning, but don't start down that road. This will be forgotten sooner than you think. With the war and the bombing, folk have got a darn sight more to talk about than the odd bit of scandal. And don't you go giving Tom Crawford the power to affect your life now he's gone, or it'll be your fault and no one else's. He's dead, lass. Dead. And burning in hell, if there's any justice. And you and Jacob and Daisy and me and the rest of us are alive. Overshadow us with his presence – my backside!'

Lucy had been so affronted that she hadn't said another word before leaving the house, but now, as she entered the confines of the hospital, a reluctant smile played across her lips. Oh, Ruby, she thought, don't ever change. And it came to her just how much of a rock Ruby had been over the years. She would tell her so when she got home, she promised herself. And apologize for being huffy.

Because her sister was right. She and Jacob were alive, and she wouldn't allow any spectres or ghosts from the past to spoil what little time they'd have together before he had to go away again.

When she reached the ward the Sister came hurrying over before she'd barely stepped foot in the door. 'Hello, Mrs Alridge.' Her face was kind. 'How are you and the rest of the family bearing up?'

For a moment Lucy had thought it was bad news about Jacob, as the curtains were still drawn around his bed, but no doubt they were just seeing to it that he was kept quiet. 'We're all right, thank you, Sister. How is Jacob?' she added, looking towards his bed again.

'A little better, but very sleepy. That's the way with concussion. But he's a young, strong lad and I wouldn't be surprised to see him on his feet in a day or so.' She hesitated. 'We're all very sorry about what's happened, but keep your chin up, my dear, and look to the future.'

Lucy smiled. There *were* nice people in the world. Kind people who weren't out to gossip and tear others to pieces with their tongues. That's what she had to remember in the next weeks and months when some of the old wives who came into the shops whispered behind their hands. And they would. And what they didn't know for sure, they would make up and would thoroughly enjoy themselves in the process. She had got on, that was the thing. Risen above her beginnings and, as such, would be termed an upstart behind her back. And upstarts were always suspect.

She stood for a moment outside the curtains, feeling suddenly shy. Jacob knew everything, and she was glad he did – so glad – but deep, deep inside there was still a feeling of shame, of degradation about what had happened that night so long ago. She knew in her head it was silly, that it hadn't been her fault – she and Ruby had talked about this often – but she didn't want him to see her differently. Or for it to colour the way he regarded Daisy. Yesterday he'd been barely conscious, but today he would have had time to think about things. What Tom had done to her, her running away when Jacob was still so ill in the hospital, marrying a man she didn't love, keeping the truth from him for so long . . . She truly didn't see, even now, what she could have done differently, but that wasn't to say that Jacob would understand. She had hurt him so badly, and not just once.

She glanced around the ward as if seeking help. The odd visitor or two was trickling in now and a low hum of conversation was beginning. She couldn't delay any more. Nerving herself, she moved the curtain and stepped into the little private bubble that the drapes provided. Jacob's eyes were open and he was half-sitting up, but it was the look on his face as he saw her that told her, without words, that her fears had been groundless. And then she was in his arms, and he was kissing her as she had never been kissed – kissing her until the breath seemed to leave her body and he was the only thing in the world that mattered.

'Oh, my darling, my darling.' His mouth had moved

from hers, but only to whisper endearments. 'I love you, my sweet girl. More than life itself.' And then he was kissing her again, until a chair scraping outside the curtains at the next bed to Jacob's, and a voice saying, 'What's the matter with him next door then? On his way out, is he?' brought them back to reality.

She drew away slightly, their faces still close, and as if it had reminded him, Jacob whispered, 'I'm sorry about Don, Lucy. He was a grand bloke. The police said Mam told them that after Tom had knocked me out, Donald went for him with a knife. He must have had it in his pocket and meant to do for Tom all along. He was going to leave me with you and find him, I'm sure of it, because he told me some cock-and-bull story about having to come to the hospital for some pills, but they knew nothing about it.'

She had been leaning across the bed, but now she sat down in the chair without letting go of his hand, nodding as she whispered back, 'He felt he had to make everything right, I think. I saw your mother this morning and she said that, before the police came, he asked her to keep my name out of things. Oh, Jacob, she's beside herself. I don't know what will become of her now.'

He didn't reply directly to this, shutting his eyes for a moment and then opening them as he squeezed her fingers. 'I can't think of anything but you and what you've gone through. A lifetime won't be long enough for me to make it up to you.'

'None of it matters now.'

'I hate him, lass. With every fibre of my being, I hate him. His death was too quick, he should have suffered more.'

'Stop it.' She put a gentle finger to his lips and repeated the words Ruby had spoken to her. 'Don't give him the power to affect your life now that he's dead. He's gone, and we're here. Please, if you love me, try and think of it like that.'

'I'll try.'

She could see that talking had tired him and he was struggling to keep his eyes open. 'Sleep a while, I'm not going anywhere.'

He smiled tiredly. 'I don't want to waste a minute of being together. I can't believe I'm stuck in here. This wasn't what I'd planned for my leave.'

She stroked his forehead as his eyes closed. 'What had you planned?' she whispered softly.

'I was going to wine and dine you, take you and Daisy out for tea, take you dancing . . .' His voice was slurring, becoming slow. 'I wanted you to know . . .' he sighed, 'to know that I . . . '

He slept. Lucy smiled, gazing down at his battered face as though it was the most beautiful sight in the world.

Visiting was over before Jacob awoke, but one of the nurses promised to tell him that Lucy had stayed until the bell had sounded. Visiting hours were from two to four o'clock in the afternoon on Tuesday and Thursday only during the week, and from two to five o'clock at weekends. Consequently Lucy spent the following day, a

Friday, in an agony of frustration at the rules that kept them apart.

She had a surprise visit in the afternoon, though. Abe and Dolly knocked on the door, Dolly full of self-recrimination and tears for the way she'd misjudged Lucy, and Abe repeating over and over again, 'We didn't know, lass. We just didn't know.' They had been to see Enid and Aaron, who had told them the full story whilst swearing them to secrecy about the true identity of Daisy's father, for the child's sake. By the time they left Lucy knew she had two staunch new friends.

On Saturday Daisy asked to come with her to the hospital and Lucy hadn't got the heart to say that she wanted time with Jacob alone. As it happened, the three of them only had a few minutes together before first Dolly and Abe and then Enid and Aaron turned up. There was a strict rule of four visitors to a bed, so Lucy and Daisy made their goodbyes and left. Lucy could have cried, but she comforted herself with the fact that Jacob was much better. Time was slipping away, though. He was due to return to his unit soon.

An air-raid alert that night meant a couple of hours in the dubious comfort of the shelter, although no bombs fell on Sunderland. Newcastle wasn't so fortunate – they were regularly getting pounded.

Lucy was deathly tired when she awoke on Sunday morning. The others were dressed for church when she came downstairs, but she declined to go with them. The events of the last few days had caught up with her and the thought of chatting with friends and acquaintances after the service, all of whom would be dying to know more about what had happened, was beyond her.

After waving the others off, she made herself a cup of tea and walked through to the sitting room, where the French doors were open to the glorious June sunshine. She had intended to sit in the garden, but finding the sight of Donald's empty deckchair too painful for the moment, she sat down in the sitting room and shut her eyes.

She must have dropped straight off because when she awoke from a deep sleep, to a knocking at the front door, her tea was cold and untouched. Feeling slightly woozy, she made herself get up and answer the door, hoping against hope that it wasn't another of the neighbours, or a friend with a bunch of flowers and condolences about Donald. The *Echo* had got hold of the story in the last couple of days, and since then people they barely knew had been popping up out of the woodwork.

She opened the door, a polite smile in place. Jacob stood there, his bruised face abeam and, without a word, he took her in his arms. He did not kiss her immediately. His lips brushed her forehead, her cheeks, her nose, before taking her mouth in a kiss that must have hurt his swollen jaw, such was its fierceness.

'Come inside.'

She managed to find the strength to come back to Earth long enough to pull him into the house, away from prying eyes, and shut the door, and then they were kissing again, hungrily and without restraint.

It was minutes later when she murmured, 'When did you leave the hospital?'

'A little while ago. I came straight here.'

'I'm so glad you did.'

'Where is everyone?' It only now dawned on him that the house was quiet.

'At church – they'll be back soon.'

'Then come into the sitting room. I've got something I want to say. I was going to ask you to come for a walk, but if we're alone?'

'We are.'

He pulled her into the sitting room, pushing her down in a chair and then kneeling down in front of her.

'Jacob?'

'Shush!' He touched her lips with one finger. 'Lucy, I have always loved you. Never for one moment have I stopped loving you, and I never will. You are my sun, moon and stars, my universe, my everything. Will you marry me, my love? Will you be my wife and let me take care of you and Daisy and any little ones we might have together? Will you wait for me, because I intend to come back to you and nothing will stop me, I promise.'

She knew he had no power to keep such a promise, but at that moment it didn't matter. Her eyes shining, she flung her arms round his neck and slid down onto the floor with him. 'Yes, yes, yes.'

And then they were laughing and rolling about like two children, before he became serious again, sitting up and reaching into his pocket. She looked at the small velvet box he was holding and, as he lifted the tiny catch and then the lid, she caught her breath. The ring was beautiful, a large sapphire surrounded by a bevy of small glittering diamonds. 'Will you wear it until I come back and can put a gold band beside it?' he asked softly.

She nodded, her heart so full she couldn't speak.

He slid the ring onto the third finger of her left hand and she knew a moment's deep thankfulness that she had moved Perce's wedding ring to her right hand a day or two ago. It had seemed time somehow, the end of an era, and she had felt that Perce would have understood. And it made this moment, which had been so long in coming, perfect.

'I bought it before I came home on leave,' he murmured, looking into her shining eyes. 'In faith.'

'It's beautiful.' She touched his face. 'I love you so much.'

The following day Lucy stood with Daisy on the platform of Central Station waving Jacob off. She was glad Daisy had asked to be there; but for her daughter's presence, she didn't know if she would have been able to stop herself running after the train screaming and crying for Jacob. He had survived Dunkirk, he'd done his bit; it didn't seem fair that the war machine expected more of him. But for his sake and for Daisy's, she made herself smile and wave until the train had disappeared and even the clouds of steam had evaporated in the warm sunny air. And then the reality that he was gone swept over her and she couldn't stop the tears.

'It's all right, Mam.' Far from being embarrassed by the heightened emotions and shows of affection she'd been witness to over the last twenty-four hours, Daisy had taken it in her stride. She'd recently discovered Jane Austen and the Brontë sisters and had been reading their books avidly; now she was captivated by her mother's real-life story of childhood sweethearts who had been separated through no fault of their own, only to find each other again. Lucy had told her only what she needed to know; there had been no mention of Tom Crawford, simply that they'd been thrown out of their home after the menfolk were killed, and her Uncle Donald had gone down south at a time when Jacob had been desperately ill and out of the picture. Daisy's father, Lucy had emphasized, had been a wonderful man, who had taken them in and married her to give her his name and protection, and they had been thrilled when she had come along to cement the marriage.

Now Daisy slipped her hand in her mother's, squeezing it tightly. 'You still have me,' she whispered.

'Oh, I know, my sweetheart, I know.' Lucy hugged her daughter to her. 'And I can't tell you how precious you are.' She took a deep breath and then wiped her eyes. The war would be over one day and Jacob would come home to her. She had to believe that, and keep believing it . . .

Chapter Twenty-Eight

August saw Sunderland's first air-raid casualties of the war when the Germans bombed the shipyards and docks, and within two days the Luftwaffe were back. It was the beginning of Sunderland's Blitz, and life was never to be the same again. Especially for Lucy's family. On the same day she received a letter from Jacob informing her that his unit had been ordered to Egypt immediately, but he would write when he could, Flora and Bess told her that, after much deliberation, they'd decided to go to Newcastle to work in a munitions factory and would take lodgings there.

'We want to get involved in proper war work,' Bess said over the family evening meal, 'and you can easily replace us at the shop with lads fresh out of school. They keep saying women are needed to free more men for active service, don't they?'

'And Bess and I are strong and healthy,' Flora put in. 'We want to do our bit.'

Lucy couldn't argue with that, although privately she

agreed with Ruby's summing up of the twins' decision: the girls might want to contribute to the war effort, but an added incentive was the big wages they'd earn in the factories, plus the excitement of the night life in Newcastle and the number of soldiers, sailors and airmen who'd be in and out of the city. But they would be eighteen years old on their next birthday, they were children no longer, and they were determined to go. So, with many misgivings, she and Ruby made the journey to Newcastle with the twins, found them lodgings in a good area with a motherly landlady who promised Lucy she'd keep an eye on the girls, and by the beginning of September they had gone.

Within the week, Matthew had joined the Navy. He had become increasingly unhappy about merely serving in the Home Guard – as Winston Churchill had renamed the Local Defence Volunteers – in spite of the provision of uniforms and real weapons, and having had his seventeenth birthday in the summer had decided to enlist.

Lucy came home from work to find Matthew and Charley waiting for her, Charley dressed in Matthew's Home Guard uniform and holding one of the First World War rifles that had recently been distributed to the volunteers. Before she could ask any questions, Matthew said, 'Charley's taking my place in the Home Guard. He's turned fifteen now and we've been to see the Sergeant Major and he says it's all right.'

Numbly, knowing the answer, Lucy said, 'And you?'

'I enlisted today.' His eyes on her stricken face, he said softly, 'I had to, Mam. Please try to understand.'

He had called her Mam from the day she had married his father, and indeed he felt as much her son as Daisy did her daughter. She loved Charley, and she never made any distinction between the two brothers, but Matthew held her heart as a son of her own flesh would.

He was already a head taller than she was, and now he took her into his arms and hugged her as he whispered, 'It'll be all right, Mam. Don't worry.' He was lean and gangly and his lanky frame, with hands and feet that seemed too big, was so painfully boyish she couldn't bear it. But he had looked so proud when he'd told her he'd enlisted, and Charley, standing in Matthew's uniform with the rifle over his shoulder, had been trying to stop himself from beaming. They were babies – her babies, both of them – and she couldn't protect them from this terrible war and a world gone mad.

With John and Matthew and the twins gone, the house seemed painfully empty. The Battle of Britain waged in the skies above, and everyone knew the mass raids by the Germans was Hitler's attempt to clear the way for invasion. London was being hammered, as one newscaster put it, but in spite of sleep made impossible by the sound of bombs, anti-aircraft guns and the shrill bells of fire engines and ambulances, Londoners continued to function with a quiet stoicism that impressed foreign observers.

'Here, listen to this,' Ruby said one night as she sat reading the paper after their evening meal while Lucy helped Daisy with her homework. 'It says Londoners haven't lost their traditional cockney humour, whatever old Hitler tries. A police station, its windows shattered and its door hanging off its hinges, bore a sign saying: "Be good, we're still open." I like that, don't you?' She grinned at Lucy. 'That's what the Nazis don't understand: that we'll never give in.'

Lucy smiled back but said nothing. She had read the paper earlier and it had been the report that the Italian Army had advanced into Egypt and was engaged in fighting British defences at Mersa Matruh that had caught her eye.

As September turned into October the battle for control of the Atlantic began. With the Luftwaffe having lost the Battle of Britain, it was generally thought that the long-promised invasion of Britain would be shelved by the Nazis until the spring, but now it seemed that Hitler had decided to try to beat his only fighting foe by starving her out. Although Sunderland wasn't having anything like the bad time London and Coventry were enduring, the bombing continued and the rationing bit harder. Lucy decided to convert Perce's original shop in the East End into a refuge and soup kitchen for folk who were bombed out and needed shelter and food for a while, until accommodation of a more permanent nature was found. The council agreed to fund the project, and although the man of the family she'd installed in the shop was away fighting, his wife and daughters were enthusiastic about it.

By the end of November, when food shortages were

commonplace, the refuge was up and running. Charley had left school in the summer and was delighted when Lucy involved him by letting him help manage the refuge. It stopped him brooding about being too young to fight. Lucy wasn't so easily distracted. She thought about Jacob and the others constantly. Jacob had written since arriving in Egypt to say he was safe and now she eagerly awaited his letters each week.

Flora and Bess came home for the Christmas holiday and they all went to church on Christmas Day. The building was full with people praying for loved ones in the thick of the war. The six of them exchanged gifts later, and Lucy cooked the Christmas dinner. She'd managed to obtain a turkey from Farmer Thornhill, a rare luxury, but carrots had taken the place of dried fruit in the Christmas pudding. The extra Christmas rations of four ounces of sugar and two ounces of tea didn't go far, either.

Nevertheless, it was lovely to have the twins home for a couple of days and they made the most of being together again, pulling the crackers that Daisy had made for everyone and singing along with the carols broadcast on the wireless. Each one of them was painfully aware of the empty places at the table, but no one said anything.

Within days everyone knew Christmas was well and truly over when the Luftwaffe turned the City of London into an inferno. The raid had been planned to coincide with the tidal lowpoint in the Thames, water mains being severed at the outset by parachute mines. For a time the blaze created by 10,000 German fire-bombs raged out of control, firemen being unable to use the mains supply or pump water from the river. It was only the weather unexpectedly deteriorating over the low-lying German airfields that caused the Luftwaffe to call off the raid before the whole of London and its inhabitants were annihilated.

To Lucy, it was another example of German thoroughness and the ruthlessness that had typified the enemy from the outset of the war. The thought of Jacob falling into their hands and being transported to one of the concentration camps they'd heard so much about was a constant worry. Each time she received a letter and knew he was all right her relief was immense, but then she immediately started worrying as to when she'd hear from him again.

And then, within a week of each other in January, she heard from John and Matthew that they were leaving England's shores. John's battalion was being sent to bolster the Allied troops in Malaya, and Matthew was sailing to reinforce the British Mediterranean Fleet, who were continuing to engage Mussolini's navy. She was distraught, and Charley, somewhat insensitively, made no effort to hide the fact that he was green with envy.

At the start of the winter it had been predicted that, after the extraordinarily clear and sunny summer, they'd be in for some severe weather. In February it arrived with a vengeance. Wearside was gripped by the worst blizzards in living memory. Power lines were brought down due to the weight of snow and ice, and Charley was shocked and distressed when two of his pals died, one treading on a power line and the other killed trying to pull his friend clear. Even Abe and Dolly's weekly visits in the horse and cart ceased, much to Daisy's distress. She had taken to the couple and they were unashamedly besotted with her – at long last Daisy had some grandparents, and Dolly the grandchild she'd often dreamt about.

Rationing, along with a lack of fuel, added to their trials and, as if life wasn't hard enough, on the last Sunday of the month, another sub-zero raw night, the sound of the sirens preceded an air-raid attack in which several streets were set on fire. The rescue services were hampered by the freezing conditions, many roads being impassable with snow, and just starting their vehicles had proved a battle. Leaving Ruby to take care of Daisy, Lucy and Charley made their way to the refuge in the East End to help Mrs Kirby and her daughters once the All-Clear sounded. By the end of the night some thirty people who had been made homeless had been fed and bedded down, and as Lucy and Charley tramped home in the stingingly cold but bright morning, Lucy reflected on some of the stories she'd heard and the tales of bravery.

The landscape of the town was changing, with more and more streets bearing witness to the devastation caused by Hitler's bombs; and ordinary men, women and children, babies too, were dying in the wreckage of their homes, although she hadn't heard one person in the refuge bemoan their lot last night. She looked up into the silvery, mother-of-pearl sky where a winter sun shone without warmth, ribbons of pink and opalescent dove-grey winding through the iridescent expanse. It was beautiful. The *world* was beautiful, the natural world, and most folk just wanted to live and work in peace and be happy with their families.

She glanced at Charley, trudging along beside her. 'You were brilliant last night,' she said quietly. She had intended to go to the shelter on her own, but he wouldn't hear of it.

He grinned at her, looking so like his father it was as though a young Perce was walking beside her. 'I like to help.'

'I know you do.' And it came to her, on a wave of revelation, that but for the circumstances which had driven her from Zetland Street, her two boys wouldn't be in her life and it would be so much the poorer for it. In spite of Tom Crawford's devilishness, his manipulation and mania where she was concerned, good had come out of bad. There was so much love in her life. 'Let's have a bacon sandwich when we get home,' she said, knowing it was Charley's favourite breakfast.

His grin widened. 'Farmer Thornhill?'

She laughed out loud. 'The very same, God bless him.'

The bombing continued through the spring and into the summer, but with the bad weather behind them, one problem was eased. In spite of the ever-present anxiety about their loved ones, life inevitably settled into something of a routine for Lucy's family. Clothes coupons were introduced in June and coal rationing began in July. Flora and Bess made the odd day-trip home; Lucy converted another of her shops off High Street West into a refuge-cum-soup-kitchen, which she ran herself; Charley did manoeuvres and now manned anti-aircraft batteries with the Home Guard most nights; and any letters from the 'boys' were read over and over again, although Lucy kept Jacob's letters for her own eyes. These were few and far between. Jacob's unit was part of the 22,000 men holding the garrison at Tobruk against Field Marshal Rommel's huge German army, and the garrison could only be supplied by sea, as Allied anti-aircraft gunners fought to keep the harbour open. The siege was in its fourth month and the Allies had fended off repeated attacks as they stood their ground. A German newspaper had dubbed the British defenders the 'Rats of Tobruk', a name they had happily embraced.

'Desert rats are cunning and tough and vicious,' Jacob had written in his last letter:

Good attributes in a war, don't you think? But this desert rat is missing you so much, my darling. But for the fact we are fighting an evil which, if left to its own devices, would swallow up everything good and noble in life, I would swim the Mediterranean tomorrow. But our time will come, I know it. God is on our side. One day I will kiss you and hold you and make you mine, in body as well as soul. I think of that in the dark moments, my sweet girl. My Lucy.

She slept with his letters under her pillow, taking them out of their envelopes at night when she couldn't sleep and touching and kissing the words his hand had written. They were a physical link, however tenuous, with him and, as such, infinitely precious.

By the time the summer was over and a wet and windy autumn had arrived, many areas of Sunderland had suffered considerable bomb damage and some famous landmarks had been blitzed. The Winter Gardens, Daisy's favourite place, had been badly damaged and Binns Store on the east side of Fawcett Street was reduced to a shell, along with others. Everywhere you looked, there was devastation. The newspaper and radio reports declared that a jubilant Hitler was nearing the gates of Moscow, and General de Gaulle, the leader of the Free French, called for a national five-minute strike in protest at the German occupation, which was carrying out scores of civilian executions daily. No one in England was unaware that what was happening in France could easily happen on British soil, should the Germans invade, and the Channel seemed a very narrow barrier.

At the end of October, with Lucy's blessing, Ruby answered the increasingly strident calls of the government for women to enter the hitherto male domains of industry, particularly the shipyards. At the outbreak of the war such a thing would have been deemed unthinkable, but now, with the supply of men to the front becoming desperately urgent, it was a necessity. Frank and Ralph had been called up at the end of the summer, much to

Enid's despair, and more men were leaving every day. Someone had to take their place and, in spite of old-timers like Aaron complaining that the shipyards weren't suitable places for the fairer sex, women were invading this sanctum of male labour.

Ruby took to the work with gusto. From sweeping up and generally making herself useful, she had progressed to trainee crane-driver within weeks. Furthermore, to Lucy's surprise and delight, her sister began walking out with a nice young man who'd been injured at Dunkirk and now worked in the yard office.

Lucy replaced Ruby in the shop with an elderly ex-fishmonger, who was more than seventy years old but as sprightly as a young lad and, as November passed, worked longer and longer hours to keep the business ticking over.

The garrison in Tobruk was reported to have been relieved in November, after a siege of 242 days, fifty-five days longer than the siege of Mafeking in the Boer War. Rommel had been forced to abandon his position and retreat, the radio broadcaster crowed, but when Jacob wrote to her, he wasn't as elated as Lucy had expected:

> They're telling us it's the first defeat of German land forces in the war, and our defence has kept Turkey from being used as a springboard by Hitler for his attack on Russia, delaying it enough so that the Russian winter can help beat the Nazis. And we're glad here the pressure's off, don't get me wrong, but the general opinion among the blokes is that the

Desert Fox won't give up so easily. He'll be back. I tell you, lass, I wish Rommel was on our side. He might be a German, but he and his panzers fight like the dickens.

But for now Jacob was safe. That was the main thing, Lucy thought, pressing his letter to her heart. He and his fellow soldiers must be exhausted. It seemed so strange that he was far away in a hot country and she was here in the midst of an icy winter, with the snow a foot deep and winds cold enough to cut you in two. But she would be thankful for what she had. A day at a time. It was the only way to get through the war. She had said the same to Enid, when she had visited Jacob's mother a few days ago. Enid was a shadow of her former self, beset by remorse and sorrow, but Frank's and Ralph's wives and their bairns were very good to her, calling round more or less every day and spending hours with her until Aaron got home from the shipyard. No one had put it into words, but in the early days after Tom's death they'd all been frightened of what she might do to herself, if she was left alone for any length of time. Lately, though, she was beginning to pull round, albeit slowly.

It was in the first week of December that several things happened in quick succession that rocked Lucy's world and caused her to remember what she'd said to Enid.

She and the family had just sat down to their evening meal when there was a knock at the front door. Lucy answered it, and for a moment she didn't recognize the woman standing on the doorstep. It was the twins' landlady. There had been a direct hit on the factory, she explained. A number of women had been killed, Flora and Bess among them. It was a terrible, terrible tragedy, but by all accounts they wouldn't have known a thing, which was a blessing, wasn't it? She'd wanted to come and tell them herself, the girls had been such dear souls. No, she wouldn't come in, thank you. Her Henry had brought her, he had his own taxi business, but time was money and he needed to get back to Newcastle to earn some proper fares. She'd brought the twins' things with her. Perhaps someone could help Henry bring them in?

Charley obliged. As the taxi drove off, the four of them stood numbly in the hall with the front door wide open and Flora and Bess's belongings at their feet. It was Daisy collapsing on the floor in a heap that brought Lucy to herself. She would have given anything to be able to give way to the hysteria of shock and grief that was just below the surface, but Daisy needed her to be strong, and so did Ruby and Charley.

The endless night passed in a haze of getting a distraught Daisy to sleep sometime after midnight, and then an hour or so later Charley, who was all for lying about his age and joining up immediately so that he could 'bomb them filthy Nazis to hell and back'. Once they were finally alone, Lucy and Ruby sat in the kitchen and gave vent to the storm of tears they'd been struggling to hold at bay. When they were cried out, they sat numbly holding hands over the kitchen table, hardly able to believe what had befallen their family.

'They had their whole lives in front of them,' Ruby whispered after a while. 'And they were so excited about being in Newcastle and at the hub of everything. It isn't fair, I can't bear it.'

Nor could she. Lucy gazed at her sister, but in her mind's eye she was seeing Flora and Bess when they were small. Their tiny hands, their little faces which were so ridiculously alike, and the way they'd hugged their raggy dolls before going to sleep. She had brought them up, she had been both sister and mother to them, with her own mam so poorly after their birth, and she'd been so very proud of the fine young women the twins had become.

It seemed impossible she would never see them again. Never feel their arms round her, in one of the quick hugs they always gave her upon walking in when they came home. And to die like that.

Please God, she prayed silently, let it be true they didn't suffer. She wanted to believe what the landlady had told them, but folk said such things at times like this to comfort the relatives of the ones who had gone. Please, please, let it be true that it all happened so quickly they knew nothing about it.

Dawn began to break and Lucy made a pot of tea, but neither she nor Ruby could eat anything. They sat watching the sky lighten as it brought forth a new day, but Lucy knew this day and the ones that followed would never be the same again. She would carry the ache in her heart until the day she died, the sense of loss and anger at the futility of the twins' passing, the regret that she hadn't stopped them going to Newcastle, that she hadn't done something – anything – to stop their lives being cut short so horribly.

A wan Daisy and a subdued Charley came down later that morning to find Lucy and Ruby on their umpteenth pot of tea. The panacea for all ills, her mother had used to call it, Lucy remembered. But not this ill.

The day was a Sunday, the first in December, and the four of them spent it quietly together, trying to come to terms with the enormity of what had happened. They all felt they wanted to go to the eventide service at the local church, although they knew they would cry, but when they arrived a little late to find the service under way, it soon became apparent from what the vicar was saying that something catastrophic had happened over the ocean in America. For once Lucy hadn't turned on the wireless and so the news had passed them by, but apparently Japanese war planes had made a massive surprise attack on the US Pacific Fleet in its home base at Pearl Harbor in Hawaii. Japanese planes had also attacked American bases in the Philippines and on Guam and Wake Islands in the middle of the Pacific. The US was at war.

After the service ended the congregation gathered together in hushed but excited groups talking about what a difference this might mean to Britain, but Lucy and the others made their way straight home. As she walked, Daisy's arm linked through hers, all Lucy could think of were the many grieving families over the ocean who had lost their loved ones as unexpectedly as they had lost Flora and Bess. She had tried to pray in church, but she'd been able to form no words other than 'My darling girls; God, my darling, darling girls.' But perhaps He understood when words were inadequate.

Three days later it was reported that Japanese divisions had invaded British-held Malaya and the northern Philippines. British forces were fighting hard to hold the offensive, but were being forced to retreat south. The British Army had no tanks, whereas the Japanese had more than 200, and the Japanese Air Force was also carrying out a series of air attacks on Allied positions.

Daisy summed up what everyone was thinking when she said, 'Not John, too. Isn't it enough that Flora and Bess have been killed in this horrible war?'

'John will be fine.' Lucy hugged her. 'I know he will.'

'No, Mam.' Daisy looked at her, a long look. 'You don't.'

It was true. She didn't. Lucy stared into the young face swollen with crying, and then glanced at Ruby and Charley. 'We can't give up hoping for John, for them all,' she said gently. 'If we do that, the enemy has won. John and Matthew and Jacob, and us here in our own way, we're all fighting for what is right. We didn't start this war and I can't bear it that Flora and Bess have gone, but I'll fight the Nazis to my last breath.'

'Your mam's right.' Ruby put her hand over that of Daisy, who was now sobbing, curled up in a corner of the sofa. 'My Ron says that Hitler might have crushed one of his legs so it's no good, but the Nazi scum'll never crush his spirit. He says you have a choice about that.'

Even in the midst of her sorrow and worry, Lucy liked the sound of 'My Ron'. It sounded permanent. Ruby had never walked out with a fellow before; she'd had offers, but had always declared she hadn't got time for 'all that', but from the minute she'd laid eyes on Ron Stratton she'd been smitten. Not that Ron was particularly handsome or charismatic, but he did have a quiet strength about him, which was immensely attractive. Certainly to Ruby.

Daisy sat up and then flung herself at her mother's feet, putting her head in Lucy's lap. 'I'm frightened,' she whispered. 'I'm sorry, but I am. I know I shouldn't be, but I can't help it.'

Charley, Daisy's hero, spoke before Lucy could. 'There's nowt to be sorry about,' he said gruffly. 'Everyone's scared, Daisy. Manning them anti-aircraft guns regularly gives me the skitters – me bowels have never worked so well before – but it don't mean I'm a coward. A coward is someone who runs away from what they're frightened of and you'd never do that, same as the rest of us. Matthew told me on the day he joined up he felt sick, but it didn't stop him doing it.'

Daisy raised her head, sniffing and rubbing her nose. 'I wish there was something I could do. You all *do* something.'

Lucy stared at her daughter. She hadn't known Daisy

was feeling like this. She was so busy trying to cope with the refuge and the soup kitchen, and running the other two shops whilst keeping an eye on how Charley was managing the East End premises, that she hadn't talked to Daisy – *properly* talked – for months. She still thought of her as a little bairn, for she was small for her twelve years and slender, but at her age Lucy had been running a home, with her mother so ill. Quietly she said, 'I need help, Daisy, I really do. After school you could come to the refuge and help me. I'd have said something before, but there's your homework and, war or no war, your schoolwork is important.'

'I'll fit my homework in.' Daisy knelt on the floor, looking up at her. 'I want to help.'

She had none of her father's innate selfishness and lack of compassion, Daisy was all hers. Lucy bent forward and hugged her daughter, feeling the slim arms come round her with a deep thankfulness. Thank God. Oh, thank God!

Flora and Bess's funeral was harrowing, but somehow they got through the day. Nine other women and one man, a foreman, had also died, but the fact that the whole factory hadn't exploded, which would have devastated the surrounding streets, was a miracle, according to the vicar who took the service. Lucy and the other mourners couldn't quite see a miracle in the loss of their loved ones.

Christmas that year was a subdued affair, the only light on the horizon being that Britain no longer stood alone against her enemy. Backed now by powerful allies – Russia and the United States – the odds were, perhaps slowly, being stacked against the Axis forces, the government assured the people in every radio broadcast and all the newspapers; 1942 would be a year in which the tide turned. It didn't seem that way to Lucy, who missed Flora and Bess more with each day that passed, especially when January saw the Allies failing to halt the Japanese invasion of Malaya.

'You can get shot at from six sides at once,' John had written in his last letter, which they had received just after Christmas. 'The Japanese buzz round you like bees and, like bees, there are so many of them you don't know which one to swat first; and even when you get one, another ten take their place.'

At the end of January it was reported that the Allies were in retreat across the Johore Strait to the island of Singapore, blowing up the causeway behind them as they went. Then, in the middle of February, came the news they were dreading: Singapore, the great naval base and a fortress considered to be impregnable, had fallen to the enemy. General Arthur Percival, the leading British commander, had surrendered his remaining 138,000 men to the Japanese.

It was a week later when the telegram came, very early, at six o'clock on a bitterly cold, snowy morning. Lucy got to the door first in her dressing gown, taking the telegram with trembling fingers. She read it as Ruby and the others came pounding down the stairs. When she had finished, she couldn't speak, handing the telegram to Ruby.

'He's a prisoner of war?' said Charley hopefully. It was the best they could hope for.

Lucy shook her head. All her brothers gone, and two of her sisters. There was only her and Ruby left now, of the seven of them. It seemed impossible, but it was true.

Chapter Twenty-Nine

The next months were hard, but in a strange way the horror stories they were hearing regarding the Nazis' 'Final Solution' to what they described as the 'Jewish problem' hardened British resolve. Whatever they were going through, it wasn't so bad as those poor devils – that was the general opinion. Hitler needed to be stopped before he wiped out an entire race. Belzec, Treblinka, Ravensbrück and Auschwitz, along with many more camps, became household names, and freedom had never been so worth fighting for.

For Lucy and the family, struggling to come to terms with the loss of Flora and Bess and then John so soon afterwards, daily life was coloured by deep grief and sadness. It was a dark, dark time.

The cold months passed, spring came and then summer. The seasons continued whatever the madness of man. And then, in June, Jacob was proved right.

Rommel returned to Tobruk, and this time there was no air support from the beleaguered Allies. The Luftwaffe pounded the fortress and, besieged on every side, the garrison surrendered; 35,000 British troops were captured by the Germans.

Lucy heard the news when she was alone, having returned home in the middle of the day feeling unwell. The newscaster called the defeat a national disaster. For Lucy, it was something much worse. She walked out into the garden and sat down on the small stone wall that separated the concreted area near the house from Daisy's vegetable patch. Daisy had taken to gardening like a duck to water and now kept the family supplied in seasonal vegetables as another of her contributions to the war effort.

But Lucy wasn't thinking about Daisy as she sat in the hot June sunshine, utterly bereft. She cried for more than an hour until she was sick, whether from sitting in the blazing sun with no hat when she'd already been feeling ill, or from heartbreak, she didn't know. And cared even less.

She had lost Jacob. She felt it deep inside, and without him the future had no meaning. Her fight to survive the chain of events that had been set in motion the day her father and Ernie died so horribly would have been for nothing.

It was her blackest hour.

After a while she dragged herself to her feet and went into the house. She ran a shallow bath, after which she dressed in fresh clothes and took a pill for the grinding headache that had developed. Then she cleared up the mess in the garden and made a pot of weak tea.

The nausea had passed, but she felt sick to the heart of her. Sick, lonely and frightened. Jacob had loved her as she would never be loved again. He had loved her all his life and he had waited for her as long. They were connected in a way that bypassed time and circumstances and she would never love anyone else.

She drank two cups of tea, black and scalding hot, and by the time Daisy came in she had composed herself, but it was a fragile composure. Knowing it wouldn't survive telling her daughter the news, she said nothing. Nor did she speak of it to Charley when he came home. It was only when Ruby walked in at gone six o'clock that she took her sister into the kitchen, shut the door so that the two of them were alone and couldn't be overheard, and said, 'Tobruk's fallen, it was on the wireless. Lots of casualties and thirty-five thousand of our soldiers taken prisoner.'

Ruby's eyes widened for a moment. 'Oh, lass, lass.'

'I've got a feeling on me, Ruby.' When her sister would have taken her in her arms, Lucy gently pushed her away. 'I'll never see Jacob again. It's like I know he's already dead. I can't explain it, except I feel it's over and that Tom Crawford has won. If I hadn't been so scared and stupid, if I'd gone to Enid the day after it happened instead of running away from him, Jacob and I could have had years together. Instead he's dead, and wherever his brother is, he's laughing at us—'

'Enough!' Ruby's voice was sharp, and when Lucy stared at her, she said, 'You don't know that Jacob is dead. No, you don't, lass, so don't look at me like that. You don't *know*, all right? And as for the other, if you'd gone to Enid Crawford, she'd never have believed her precious Tom had forced you. It would have been his word against yours. He wanted to marry you, don't forget, so he'd have been the one with the halo, and he'd have managed it somehow, by hook or by crook. Jacob wouldn't have survived long after leaving hospital, either. I don't know how Tom would have managed it, but he'd have made sure Jacob was out of the picture for good the next time. You know that, Lucy. Your life would have been a misery – all our lives would – and Daisy would have grown up with an evil, murdering swine of a father. So no regrets. You did what you had to do.'

'Oh, Ruby.' Lucy's voice was husky. 'What would I do without you? You're so good.'

'Aye, that's me. Saint Ruby of Sunderland. Now I'm going to make us a nice cup of tea and I'm putting a tot of something in yours, for the shock. And we're not crossing any bridges till we come to them. I know it's hard, lass, but all we can do is wait to hear.'

Lucy nodded, taking a deep breath and smiling shakily. 'I'm supposed to be the big sister who talks sense. Not you.'

'A change is as good as a rest.' Ruby hugged her. 'And with everything that's happened in the last months, you're bound to think the worst. Wait till you know. Meself, I think he's all right. Like Mam used to say, I've got a feeling in me water.'

Lucy was always to remember the long, hot July of 1942 for the rest of her life. There was a respite in the air raids and the blue skies overhead seemed harmless. The American GIs were beginning to arrive, their snazzy uniforms, endless supplies of forgotten luxuries and Yankee chit-chat making them a big hit with young British girls, who were all too willing to be swept off their feet. British servicemen thought differently, deeply resenting their American cousins' success with the women, but most of all it was the outrageous difference in pay that made them spitting mad. An American private received three pounds, eight shillings and ninepence a week, while his British counterpart earned just fourteen shillings. With beer costing one shilling and thrupence a pint, most British servicemen couldn't afford to give a girl a good time. The Americans had brought a splash of colour and glamour to a grey and tired Britain, however, and in Sunderland as well as other towns and cities a buzz was in the air. 'Boogie Woogie Bugle Boy' could be heard in the dance halls, and nylon stockings replaced gravy and painted-on seams on some girls' legs.

Everyone seemed to be enjoying themselves that July, or at least Lucy felt they were, whereas for her each day was endless and the nights were worse. She barely ate and she couldn't sleep. It didn't help that Charley had bought Daisy a second-hand record player for her birthday in February, which had sent her into raptures and which she kept in her bedroom, and every so often he treated her to a new record for her small collection. The hot weather meant that Daisy's windows were permanently open and the strains of 'Kiss Me Goodnight' or 'That Lovely Weekend' or 'When They Sound the Last All-Clear' floating on the air did nothing for Lucy's emotional wellbeing as she waited for news about Jacob.

She was constantly worried about Matthew, too. The British Fleet in the Mediterranean was ranged against a substantially larger enemy navy and had sustained serious losses since the beginning of the war in a number of battles. Somehow, and she thanked God for it, Matthew had come through unscathed and at present was in Alexandria. He wrote rarely, but when he did he sounded cheerful, even happy, which was amazing in the circumstances, although Lucy suspected much of that was for her benefit. Nevertheless, for the moment he was alive and he was free.

On the first day of August, a Saturday, Lucy and Daisy got home late after going to the cinema. The Havelock on the corner of Fawcett Street and High Street West had been showing *Casablanca* and Daisy had desperately wanted to go, after two of her school friends had told her about it. For Lucy it had been something of a penance. She knew she'd been short-tempered lately, nearly biting Daisy's head off once or twice, especially when she'd played 'We'll Meet Again' three times on the trot that morning.

They walked home in the mellow summer night, taking

their time and chatting and eating the last of their sweet ration as they went.

'It's funny, isn't it, but Matthew, Charley and I don't look remotely like each other,' said Daisy, out of the blue. 'You can see they're brothers, just, but neither of them looks like me.'

'Maybe that's because you're their half-sister,' said Lucy carefully, 'and you look so much like me, there's no room for anyone else.' She dug Daisy in the ribs and she giggled. 'Matthew looks like his own mother, by all accounts, although I never met her of course.'

'And Charley looks like our da.'

'Yes, he does.'

'Was he pleased to have a girl, my da?'

'Very pleased.'

'I wish he hadn't died.' Because of the furore at the time and the resulting publicity, she and Ruby had decided early on that it would be wrong to keep the truth from the children in case they heard it from someone else, so they had explained to each of them, when they were old enough to understand, that Perce had been attacked in the street and had died from his injuries. 'Especially like he did.'

'So do I.'

'But if he hadn't, you wouldn't be able to marry Jacob when he comes home.'

Lucy looked at her daughter. Stopping, she took Daisy's hands in hers. 'Your father was a very special man and will always have a very special place in my heart,' she said softly. 'Do you understand? No one can take that place, because it's his.'

'Did you love him as much as you love Jacob?'

Daisy had clearly been thinking about this for a while. 'I cared for your father in a different way from Jacob, because each person is different, but he was a wonderful man and I know we would have been happy together all our lives if he had lived. But he didn't, and I was heartbroken. Then I met Jacob again.'

Daisy nodded, her big eyes gleaming in the moonlight, which thankfully was bright that night. There were still a number of accidents in the blackout on moonless nights. 'I like Jacob, but I don't think it's right to call him Da. He won't mind that, will he?'

'No, he won't mind.'

'Perhaps Uncle Jacob. Does that sound right?'

Oh, the irony of it! Lucy wanted to press her hand to the ache in her chest, but she didn't. Instead she said lightly, 'I think that'd be fine.'

'He *will* come back, Mam.' Daisy's face was very serious. 'I know he will. God wouldn't take my da and then Jacob as well. He wouldn't do that to you.'

The childlike faith was a sword-thrust through her heart, and now she was praying for Jacob's return as much for Daisy as herself. 'I hope he'll come home, hinny, but God doesn't always stop bad people doing things to good people. If He did, we'd all be nothing more than puppets, wouldn't we? And life doesn't work like that.'

She bent and kissed her daughter's brow. 'I love you so much. Let's go home.'

Ruby met them in the hall when they entered the house. She had clearly been waiting for the sound of the key in the front door. Lucy didn't ask why, for she had seen the telegram lying on the hall table. 'When did it come?'

'You hadn't been gone above half an hour. I didn't know whether to come to the cinema and find you, but I thought . . .' Ruby's voice faltered.

'No, you did the right thing.'

'Ron's still here. He's in the sitting room. He wanted to wait till . . . He wanted to know . . .' Ruby seemed incapable of finishing a sentence.

'I'm sorry we're so late. It's such a lovely night we walked home.' She had to pick it up. She had to open it. But she couldn't. Such an insignificant little thing, but it held the rest of her life inside it. She looked at Ruby, who was equally transfixed.

In the end it was Daisy who picked the envelope up and handed it to her mother. Lucy took it, trembling, and like the day she had looked through the stained glass in the front door and seen Jacob sitting on the wall outside, all she could hear was the ticking of the grandfather clock in the dining room.

She opened the envelope and read the few words it contained. Then she looked into the two faces in front of her, which were rent with concern and love. 'He's a prisoner of war,' she said softly. 'He's alive.'

Chapter Thirty

October 1942, when General Montgomery battered down Rommel's defences with a massive artillery bombardment and a thousand tanks, many of them lent by the Americans, and defeated the Afrika Korps at El Alamein, marked the turn of the tide of the war. As Churchill claimed, 'Up to Alamein we survived. After Alamein, we conquered.'

Tobruk was in the hands of the Allies again, Rommel retreated back into Libya and in the middle of November the church bells – bells of victory – were ringing out through the length and breadth of Britain. From the towers of great cathedrals to the smallest parish church, the bells sounded the nation's joy at the news from Egypt, and the whole world heard the sound of Britain's rejoicing through the BBC's overseas services.

After a peal rang out from the bomb-shattered Coventry Cathedral – where the spire and bell-tower were still standing – an announcer asked: 'Did you hear them in Occupied Europe? Did you hear them in Germany?'

Had he heard? Lucy was with the others in the sitting

room listening to the wireless while their Sunday roast – or, thanks to rationing, their meat loaf – cooked in the oven. She wished she could believe so, but she knew it wasn't possible. Jacob was being held in Flossenbürg concentration camp in Germany and he was not allowed to write more than two letters a month by his captors. She knew that his letters to her were scrutinized by the guards, as were hers to him. Her letters could only be two sides of notepaper and no photographs or even drawings could be enclosed. She couldn't write about anything to do with the armed forces or the war effort, not even about rationing or food, and certainly nothing connected with politics. Any infringement of these rules, she had been warned, would mean that all communication was stopped. Consequently, terrified she'd inadvertently say something she shouldn't, her letters tended to be almost carbon copies of the ones before.

His letters to her were similarly constrained. He couldn't complain about his treatment, the conditions, what went on in the camp or his German guards. Even writing about his fellow prisoners wasn't encouraged. She had no real idea of the day-to-day nightmare he was enduring, although terrible stories about the German death camps, like Auschwitz and Ravensbrück, were filtering through. It was known that massive gas chambers and crematoria capable of burning as many as 2,000 bodies at a time and reducing living and breathing human beings to ashes with insane speed were present in some of the camps, and these were called death camps and were different from the concentration camps. But in the concentration camps POWs were dying too. No one was exempt.

She was allowed to send him a 'next-of-kin' parcel four times a year, but again these were opened and inspected by the guards. She had despatched her first parcel as soon as his whereabouts had been confirmed and intended to send another in time for Christmas.

Ruby, who always seemed to know what she was thinking, leaned across and said quietly, 'The news will filter through to him in time, lass. The Germans won't be able to keep it quiet, however much they'd like to. And it'll give him heart. It'll give them all heart. And I tell you something else: we're going to win this war, and they know it.'

Whether they did or not, the balance of power had changed. At the end of January 1943 the Germans surrended in Stalingrad and in February Japan abandoned the Solomon Islands. Bombing raids by the Allies began to smash the heart out of German industry, and new techniques by the Allies in the Atlantic war had the U-boats on the run. In July the Russians whipped the Germans in the greatest tank battle in history on the flat cornfields south of Moscow, and the Americans took Palermo, the Sicilian capital, setting the scene for Italy to surrender to the Allies unconditionally in September.

And in November all communication from Jacob ceased. The last time Lucy had received a letter had been at the beginning of October and for two or three weeks she didn't panic. The Allies had made great gains in the last twelve months, and it seemed – whether by coincidence or not – that every time there was a victory Jacob's letters were held up. It was as though the camp guards needed to assert their authority.

By the end of November she had written umpteen times and sent a parcel, but had heard nothing. December was the same. By Christmas she was frantic. She tried not to let her despair colour the festivities, but it was hard.

On Christmas Eve, a Friday, she was sitting on a sofa set at an angle to the fire and thinking of Jacob. A border of snow festooned the French windows. It had been snowing for days and the outside world was white. Ruby was with Ron at his parents' house, and Charley and Daisy had met friends to go ice-skating on a field near Springwell Farm, which had flooded earlier in the month and then frozen hard. The afternoon sky had been clear but icy cold, and now a rosy sunset was bathing the snow in a pink haze.

Lucy turned her head and looked to the windows, the beauty outside a subtle mockery of her dark fears. Everyone had kept assuring her that Jacob was alive and well, to the point where she hadn't wanted to talk about it any more. It didn't do any good, not really.

She rose to her feet, walking restlessly to the windows. A bright-eyed blackbird was busy pecking at a few morsels that she had put out earlier after she'd cleared a small space on the concrete. She wondered how he fared on a day-to-day basis now that rationing had caused everyone to tighten their belts. He caught sight of her, pausing with a chunk of the coarse-grained bread they now ate, since the baking of bread with white flour had been banned the year before, hanging out of his yellow beak. He tilted his little head to one side for a moment, summing her up, and then, deciding she was no threat, made short work of his meal.

She smiled. The blackbird was one of the few that had no objection to the change of diet. 'Happy Christmas,' she said softly. And then wondered if she'd finally lost her reason, talking to a bird.

When the doorbell rang, she thought it was Charley and Daisy, having forgotten their keys again. Stitching a seasonal smile on her face, she opened the front door.

'Hello, Mam.' Matthew stood there, balancing on crutches. No mean feat in the weather conditions. 'Any room at the inn for a wounded sailor?'

Christmas was transformed, the more so when it transpired that Matthew's leg had been smashed so badly that he had been told by the Navy doctor there was no chance he'd be going to sea again.

'But why didn't you write and *tell* me you'd been injured?' They were sitting together on the sofa that Lucy had recently vacated, a pot of tea in front of them and a slice of Daisy's Christmas cake, made without eggs and with a great deal of grated carrot, raw potato and a cup or two of breadcrumbs, besides other ingredients. Matthew had taken a bite of his piece and declared it 'interesting'.

'Once I knew how bad it was, and that they were going to boot me out, I wanted to get home for Christmas and surprise you.' Matthew grinned at her. 'And I did surprise you, didn't I?'

'You did.' Lucy sat, her eyes drinking him in. Amazingly, he was still the same Matthew. Tanned, taller, but still her boy. 'Now, tell me what happened, and don't leave anything out, mind.'

They talked for a couple of hours until it was pitch-dark outside. Matthew had been injured during a skirmish at sea with a German U-boat at the end of November, and Lucy was so glad to see him that she didn't have the heart to reprimand him for keeping her in the dark. She told him their news in a way she could never have done in letters, finishing with the fact that she hadn't heard from Jacob for nearly eleven weeks.

'Don't worry about it, Mam. He's likely got up some guard's nose and they're not letting him write,' said Matthew, as though he was an authority on life in the concentration camps. 'Jacob's a survivor, he's proven that, hasn't he? First when he was a young lad, and then when Tobruk was taken. If anything had happened to him they'd have let you know. They have to do that, same as we do with theirs.'

They both knew that, with the death camps and the concentration camps, normal treatment of POWs had broken down in this war, but neither of them voiced it. It was Christmas Eve. Matthew was home and done fighting. With that she would be content. And tomorrow, and all the tomorrows following, she would believe Jacob was coming home, she told herself, watching Matthew eating his cake as though he was enjoying it. A miracle had happened: her boy was home. Not quite in one piece, perhaps, but although he would always have a gammy leg, he'd be able to lead a good life. She would believe for another miracle. It was Christmas.

That resolve was tested over the next months when there was no word from Germany.

The year of 1944 was a struggle for many Sunderland folk. Large areas of the town had been flattened, but people got on with their lives as best they could and without grumbling.

Charley tried to enlist in January, but was turned down when the doctors discovered a hitherto-undetected heart murmur. Matthew took on both of the fish shops, proving himself to be an astute businessman and a very good fishmonger, which left Lucy and Charley to run the other side of the business. Ruby married her Ron in the autumn, and Lucy's wedding present to the happy couple was the deeds of a small terraced house close to the shipyard where they worked. She had bought it outright for them.

And then it was Christmas again. Lucy no longer looked immediately to the hall table when she came home from work, and her heart no longer raced if the doorbell rang. If she had been going to get a telegram, it would have come by now. Jacob seemed to have simply disappeared, and the frightening thing – the terrible thing – was that so many other POWs had met the same fate. But she still believed and hoped. She had to. It was that which kept her going, along with the fact that everyone knew the end of the war was in sight.

As 1945 began to unfurl, a glimpse into hell – as the Nazi death camps fell – shocked even the most seasoned veteran of war. In March, Allied prisoners who had begun to be liberated were reporting horrific stories of life in German POW camps, with frequent beatings, starvation rations and no contact with the outside world. Only about thirty of the seventy known camps of Allied prisoners had been liberated by the first week of May when, strangely suddenly, peace came to a battered Europe on the seventh of the month in a small red schoolhouse in Rheims, where General Eisenhower, the Allied Supreme Commander, had his HQ, and where the German Army Chief of Staff signed the document of unconditional surrender.

The next day, VE Day, the whole of Britain took to the streets to celebrate the victory.

For Matthew and Charley and Daisy's sake, Lucy went with them to the Town Hall in Fawcett Street, where a fanfare of trumpets and a speech by the Mayor, with the police brass band playing before and after the announcement and the National Anthem being sung with great fervour by the 10,000-strong crowd, heralded the celebrations.

Unlike London, where the whole population went crazy with joy, Sunderland's celebrations were more subdued. Many local servicemen were POWs of the Japanese, some still fighting, and others like Jacob had been interned in German concentration camps and still had to return home.

Matthew, Charley and Daisy were disappointed by the lack of fervour, although some streets were decked out for parties and their houses had flags flying. Some sailors tried to liven up the day a little by firing off a gun on a ship berthed in the Wear. Around a dozen 20mm anti-aircraft shells fell in the Roker and Fulwell areas, damaging houses, but no one was hurt.

Lucy didn't say so to the youngsters, but the sober mood suited hers perfectly. It was awful, and she knew it was, she told herself, but she didn't want to celebrate, not without Jacob. And not knowing if he was alive or dead was a hundred times worse now, with the war over and people happy and expecting you to be the same.

After they had listened to the band in the pouring rain and people were beginning to disperse, one of Daisy's old school friends joined them and invited them to the party that her street was holding. 'Everyone's welcome,' she insisted. 'The more, the merrier. And my da and some of the other men have put tarpaulins up and whatnot, so you won't get wet. Well, not much anyway.' She smiled at Matthew and Charley, fluttering her eyelashes. 'It'll be a bit of fun.'

Lucy was reminded again, by the girl's forwardness, that her own daughter was no longer a child. Daisy had turned sixteen at the end of February and although she was small and slight, she was turning into a beautiful young woman. She had insisted on leaving school the year before, the minute she could, working in a day-nursery with children whose mothers were occupied in jobs for the war effort, but it had only been a stopgap until she could fulfil her main ambition and start to train to become a nurse. As always, she knew exactly what she wanted.

Sixteen years old. Lucy's breath caught in her throat. Sixteen years that she and Jacob had lived without each other. She smiled at the others. 'Go and have fun then,' she said, 'and I'll see you later.'

They began to protest, but she waved their objections aside, knowing they were worried that she would be alone on VE Day. But she wanted to be alone. Away from all the smiling faces and laughing and gaiety. And if it meant she was turning into a cranky old woman at the ripe age of thirty-two, so be it.

She walked home rather than getting a taxi, her tears mingling with the rain. Matthew and Charley were grown-up, young men, and soon they would be courting, and her Daisy had determined her own road already. And that was good. All of it was good and right and how it should be. She had fulfilled her promise to Perce: she had brought his boys up and they were fine young men and would make good husbands and fathers. But they would leave her. And, again, she wouldn't have it any other way; it was the natural order, but suddenly, today, it was also unbearable. She felt so alone, so lost. She wanted Jacob, more than life itself. To share everything with him, the ups and downs, to know that there was one person in this world she would always come first with, always be adored by.

Was that selfish? She blinked the raindrops from her eyelashes. Maybe. But she didn't care. She wasn't old, she didn't want her life to be over, and it would be if he didn't come back. She wanted to have more babies, Jacob's babies, while she was still young enough to enjoy them. She wanted . . . Oh, she wanted it all. She wanted her miracle.

Two weeks later, on a fine May evening tinged with wood-smoke and the sound of children playing in the park opposite, a lone figure stopped outside Lucy's house. After the hell he had been through, the evening was so quintessentially English that it was painful. He wanted to breathe it in, to absorb it, to roll in it and take it in through the pores of his skin. This was what had made him determined to survive the cruelties of the new camp commandant who had replaced Walther Von Brauchitsch when he'd been taken ill. Because this meant Lucy. And it hadn't been the physical afflictions or the starvation rations that had nearly done for him – oh no. It had been the mental starvation he'd endured, that they had all endured, of having no contact with home. No letters, not even a postcard. The commandant had known how to break a man's spirit all right, and he had broken a few. But not his. Because she was waiting for him. Heaven and hell might pass away, but Lucy would still be waiting for him. Of that he was sure. He hadn't been sure of anything else in that hell-hole, but he had been sure of Lucy.

It was dusk, and it was beginning to get dark. As he stood there, he heard a mother calling her children in the park and then after a minute or two all was quiet. He had been travelling for more than twenty-four hours and he was tired, so tired, but he knew he wouldn't rest until he saw her. Until he knew she was safe and well. Until she was in his arms.

He walked up the garden path and knocked on the front door, the nervous excitement that had sustained him over the last days not apparent in his exhausted face, where deep lines had been carved by pain and the terrible things he had seen done to his friends.

When she opened the door she was even more beautiful than he remembered. And then she fell into his arms, as he had imagined she would, and they were kissing, kissing, kissing until the breath had left their bodies and they had to take great gasping pulls at it.

'Lucy, Lucy . . .' He had been going to say so much, but he could only murmur her name, and his heart-cry was answered as she whispered his name in such a way it touched the soul of him. 'I came as soon as I could, the very second . . .'

'I know, I know you would have, my darling.'

'You're so beautiful, I can't believe how beautiful.'

He was aware of her drawing him into the house, her voice thick with tears when she whispered, 'They're all out. There's no one here. I thought one of them had forgotten their key . . .' And then they were half-laughing and half-crying and kissing some more.

A long time later they sat in the sitting room, trying to begin to fill in the last two years, but unable to stop touching each other and kissing and caressing.

Lucy was shocked at how ill and thin Jacob looked, but at the same time he had never appeared more handsome to her. He was here. It wasn't a dream. The war was over and Jacob was here. Between kisses she murmured, 'You must be hungry. I'll get you something to eat.'

'You still wear it.' He didn't seem to have heard her, his eyes on the tiny silver heart at her throat. He reached out, touching the necklace almost reverently.

'All the time.' Her blue eyes were misty.

'Dance with me, Lucy.'

'What?'

'Now, in the moonlight. Before anyone comes home. Dance with me again.' He pulled her to her feet, his arm going round her slim waist. 'Remember? Remember how it was?'

'You told me about the stars,' she whispered tremulously. 'And the frost sparkled like diamonds.'

Jacob led her into the garden and the soft May night embraced them in scented warmth. 'There's no frost,' he murmured into the soft silk of her hair as he took her into his arms and held her close, 'but the moonlight is the same, and we're together.'

They began to dance, wrapped in each other's arms and flowing as one, as they'd done so long ago in that other life. Lucy shut her eyes, heady with love. The long years melted away and she was a young girl again, on the brink of womanhood, dancing in the moonlight with the boy she loved.

Their lives were about to begin . . .

www.panmacmillan.com